James Burks

Bird & Squirrel

On the Run!

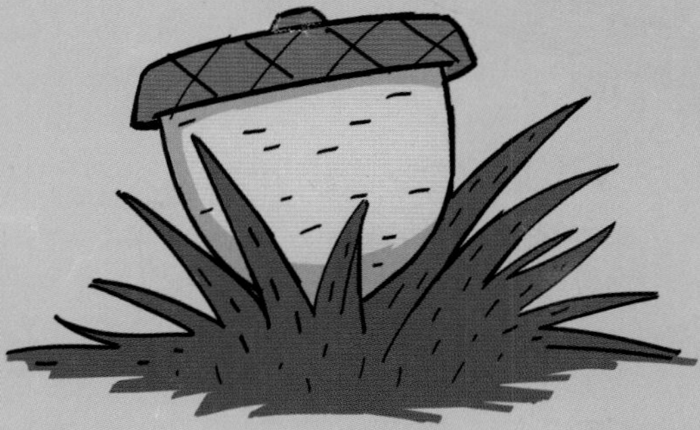

graphix

An Imprint of

SCHOLASTIC

New York Toronto London Auckland Sydney Mexico City New Delhi Hong Kong

For Bob and Teri,
Thanks for your friendship and support.

Library of Congress control number: 2011934532

ISBN 978-0-545-31283-7

12 11 10 9 8 7 6 5 4 3 2 1   12 13 14
Printed in China   38

First edition, August 2012

Edited by Adam Rau
Creative Director: David Saylor
Book design by Phil Falco

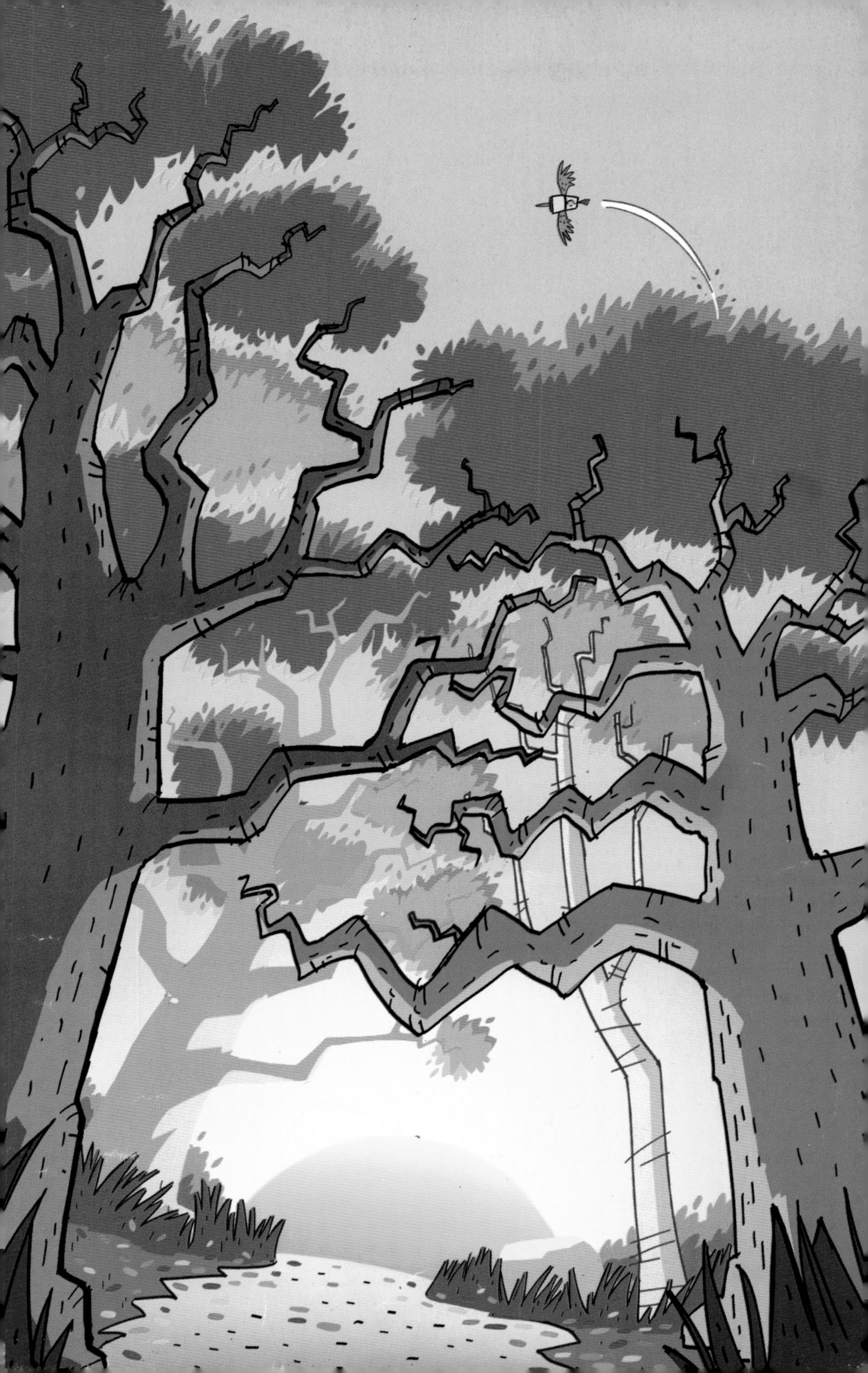

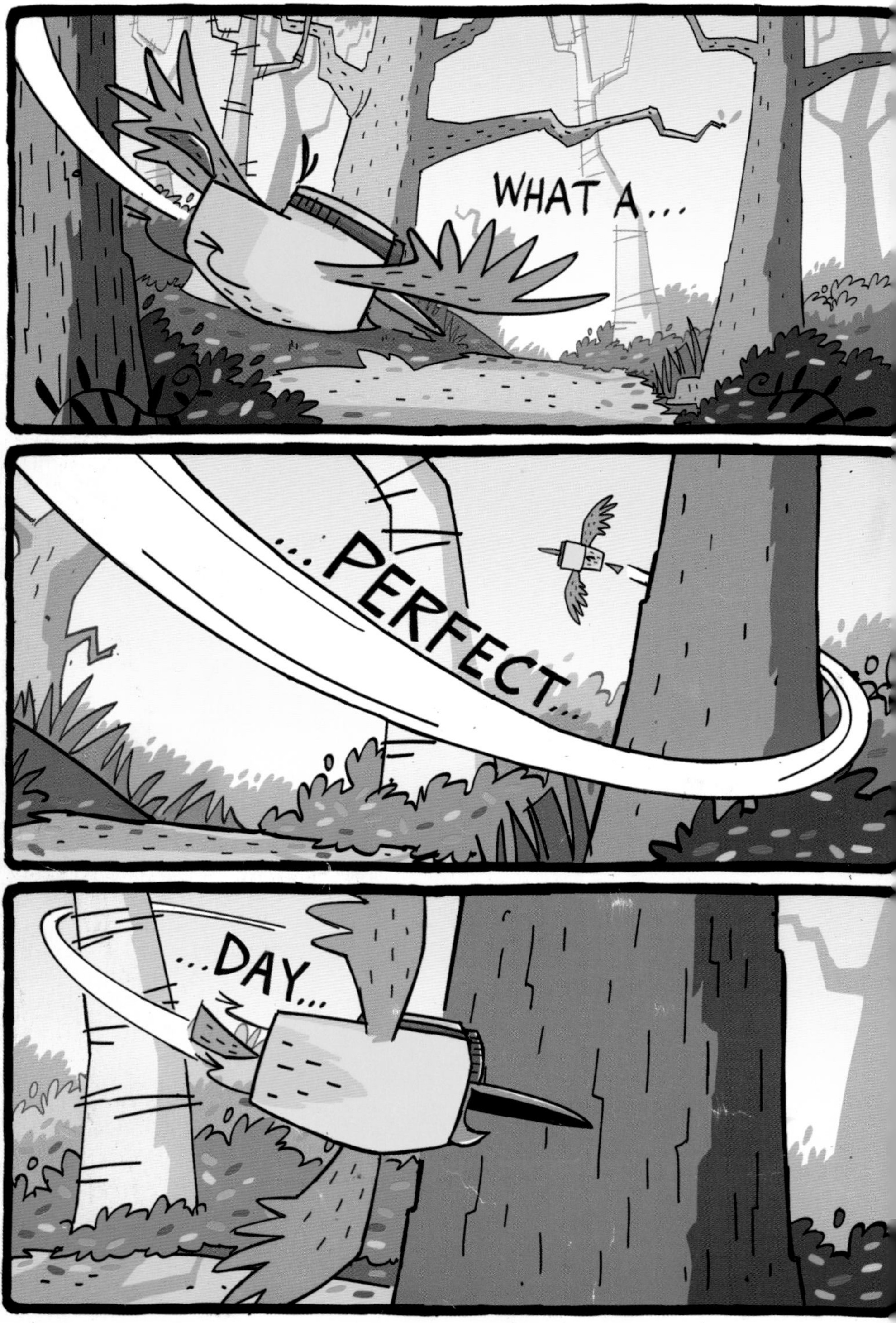
WHAT A...
...PERFECT...
...DAY...

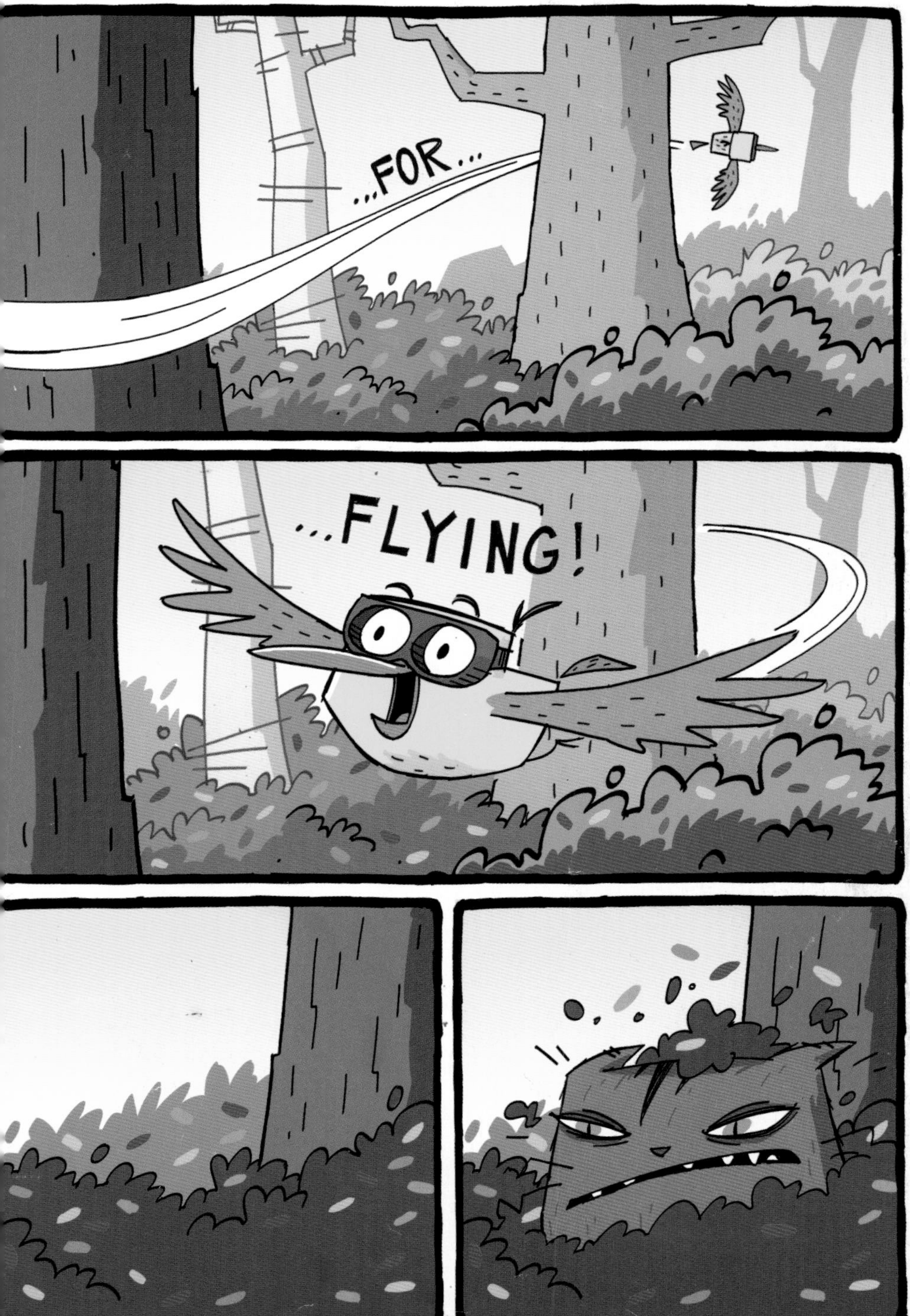

...FOR...
...FLYING!

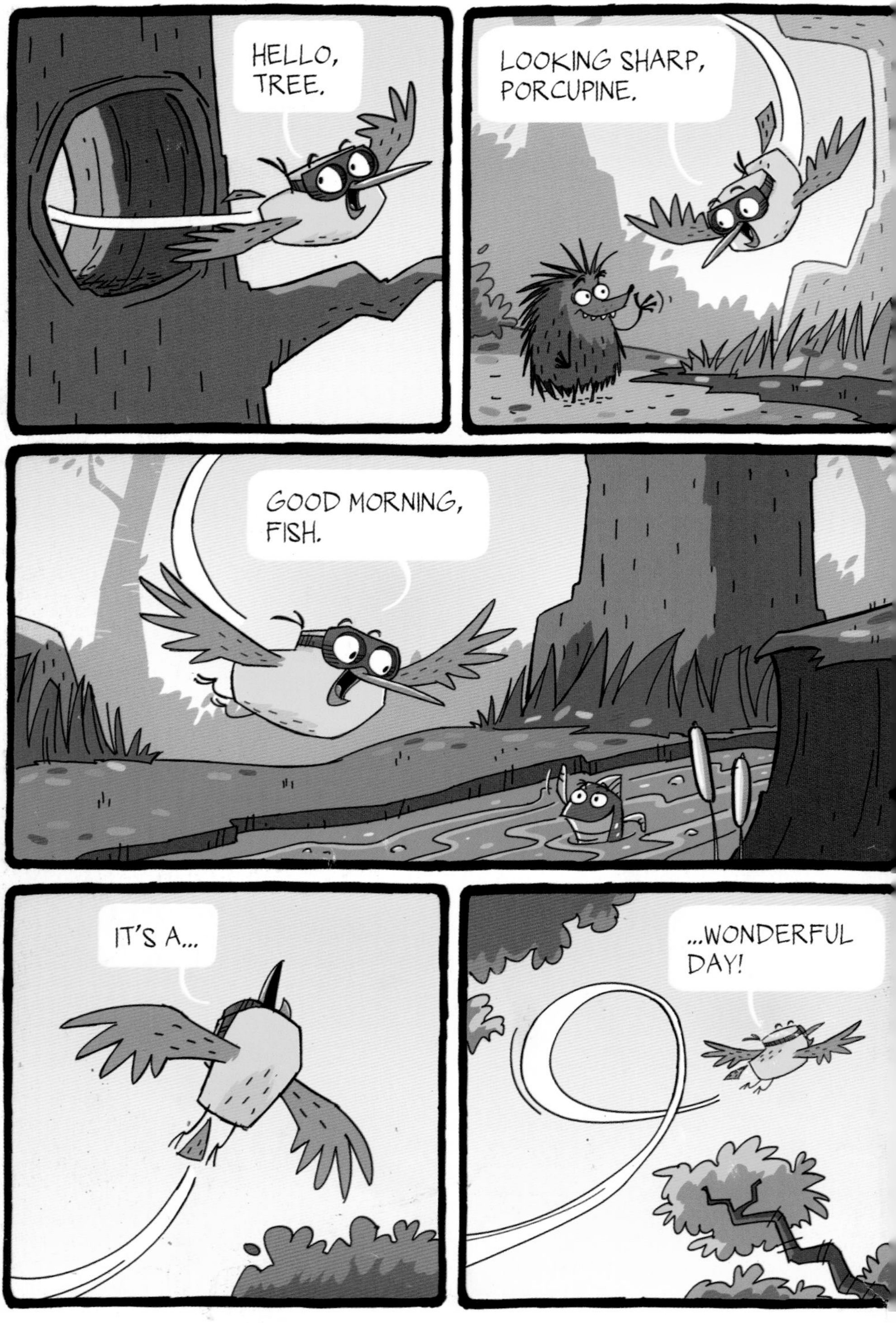
HELLO, TREE.
LOOKING SHARP, PORCUPINE.
GOOD MORNING, FISH.
IT'S A...
...WONDERFUL DAY!

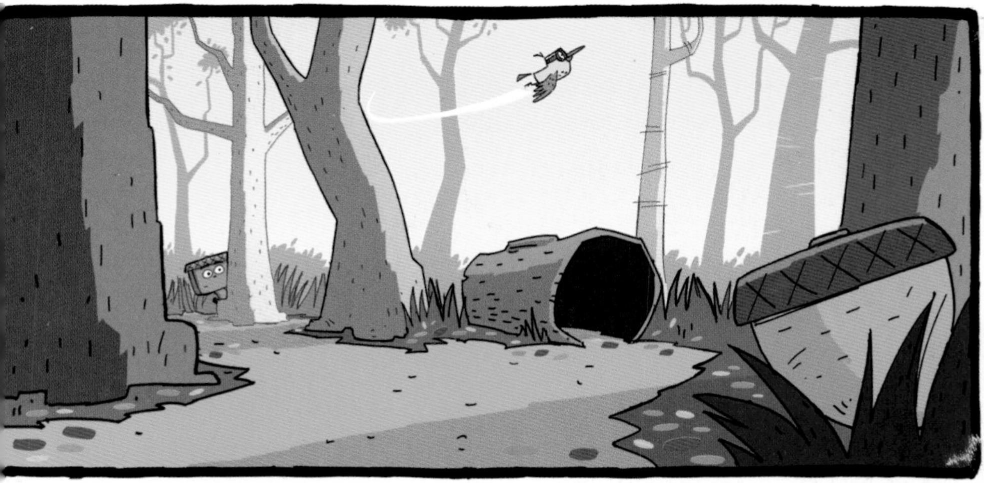

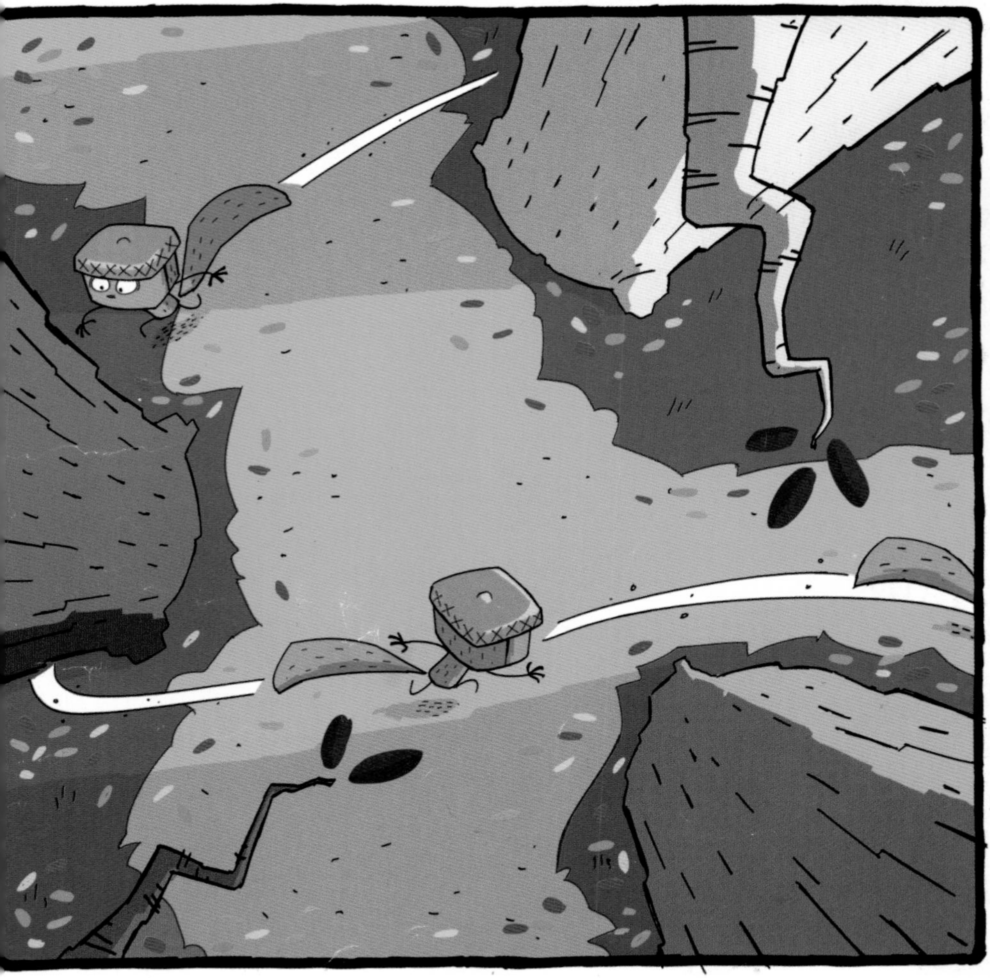

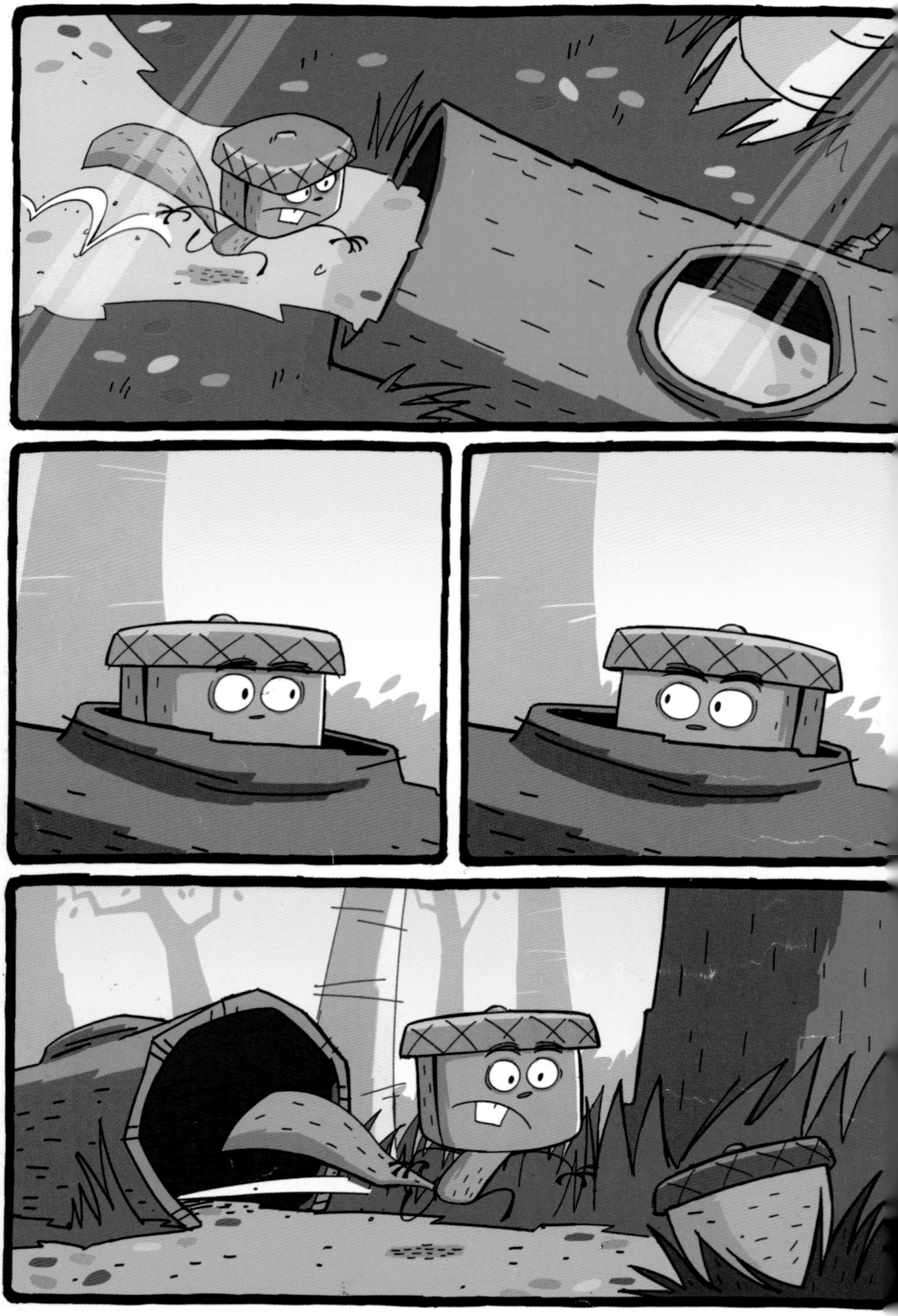

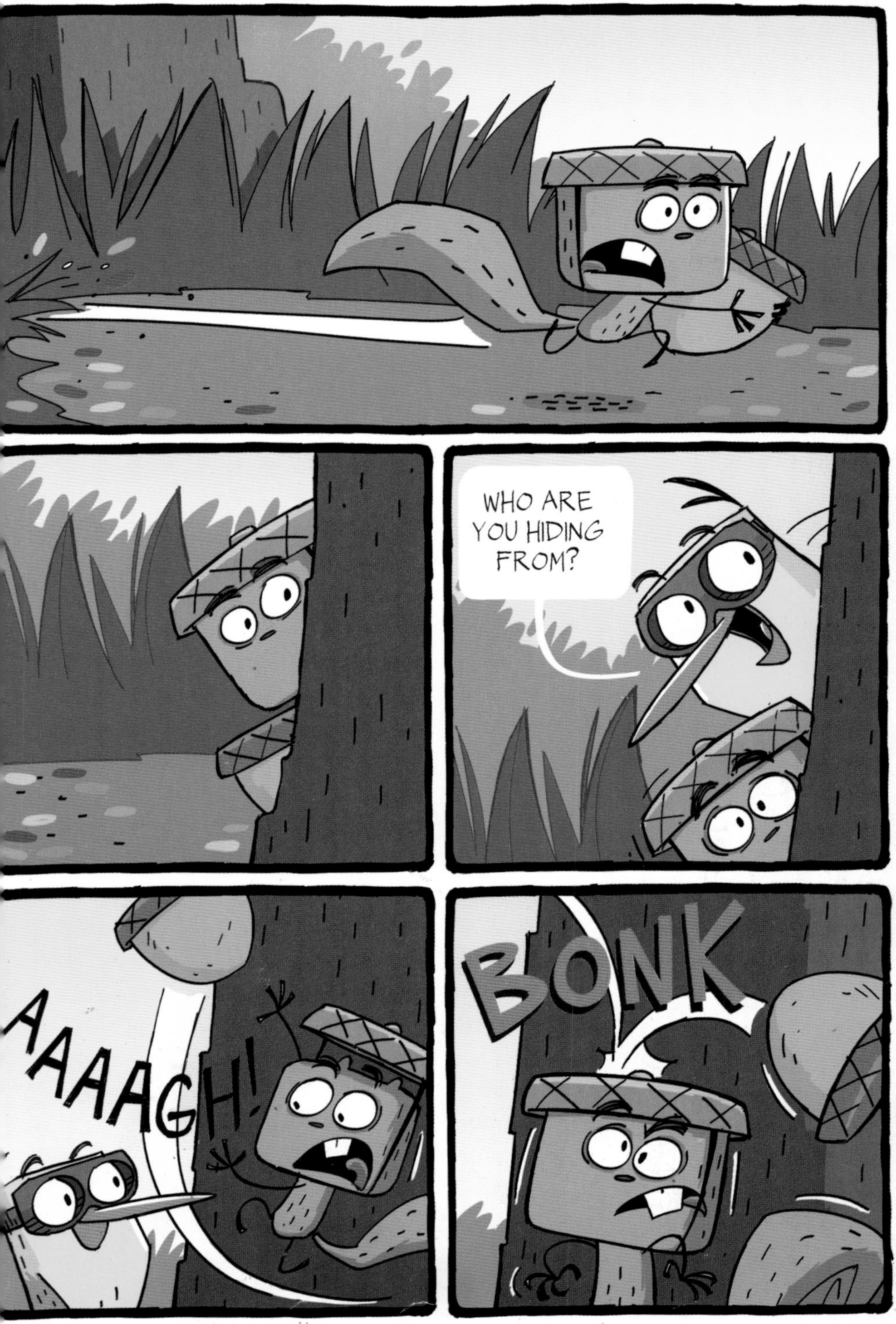
WHO ARE YOU HIDING FROM?
AAAAGH!
BONK

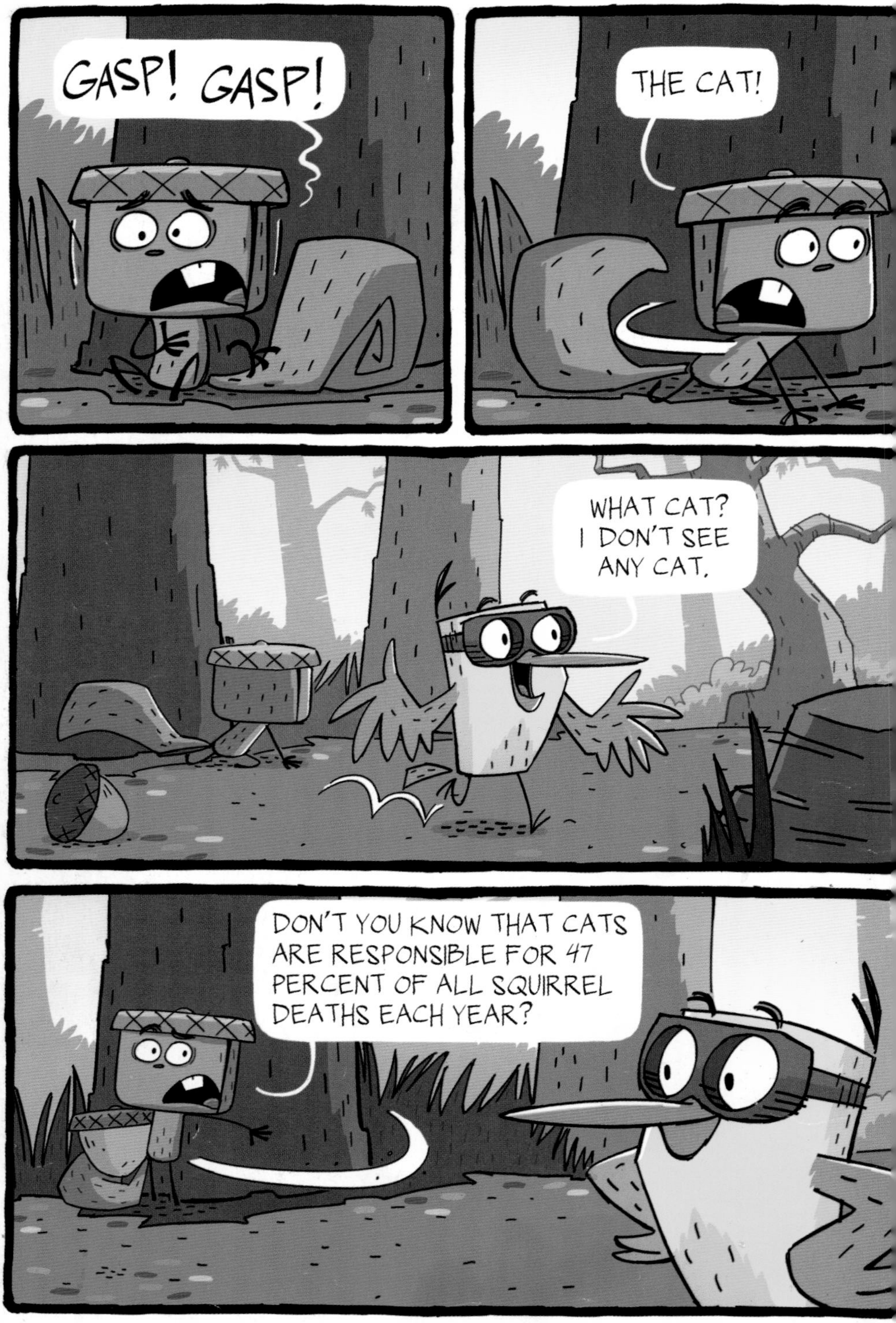
GASP! GASP!
THE CAT!
WHAT CAT? I DON'T SEE ANY CAT.
DON'T YOU KNOW THAT CATS ARE RESPONSIBLE FOR 47 PERCENT OF ALL SQUIRREL DEATHS EACH YEAR?

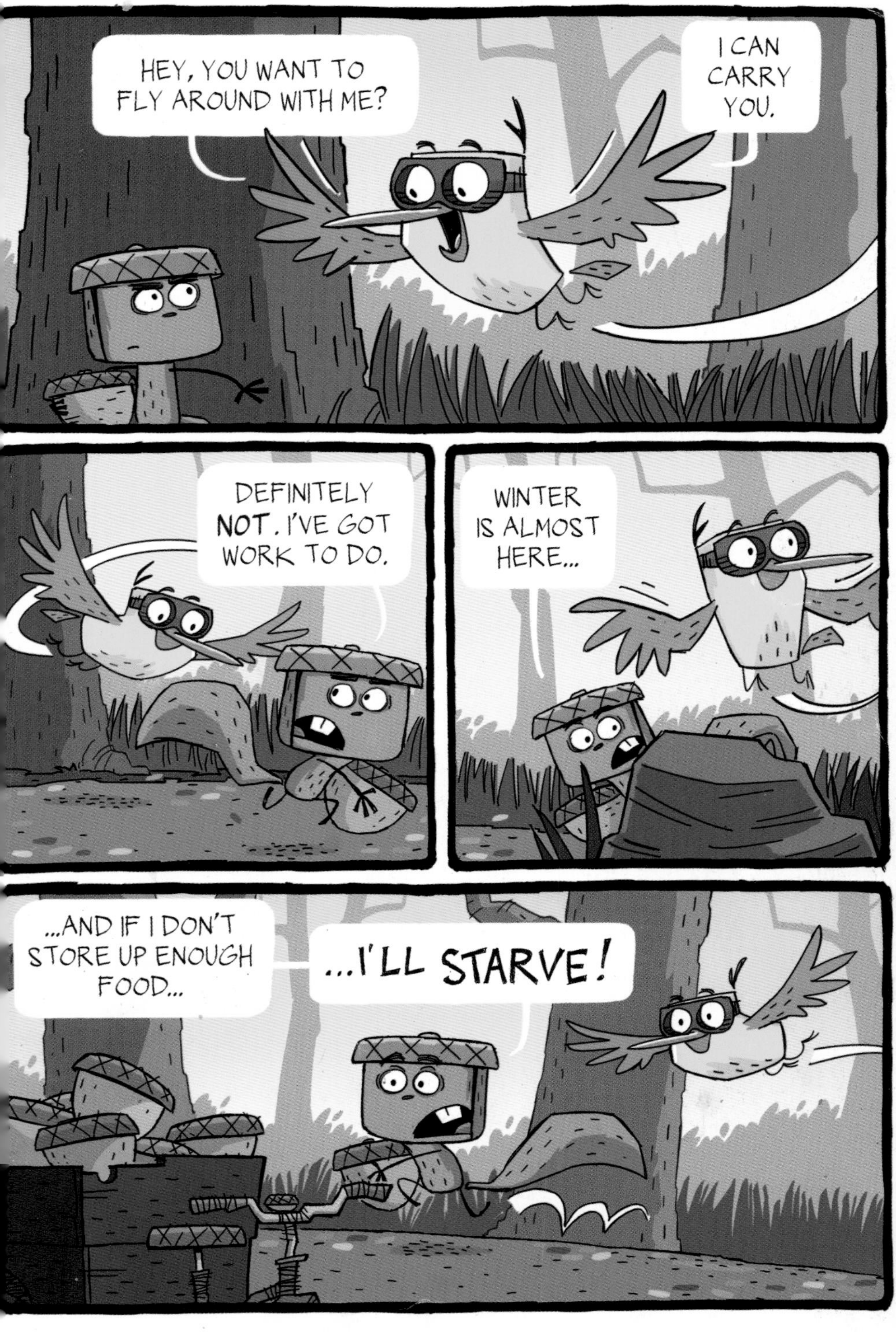
HEY, YOU WANT TO FLY AROUND WITH ME?
I CAN CARRY YOU.
DEFINITELY **NOT**. I'VE GOT WORK TO DO.
WINTER IS ALMOST HERE...
...AND IF I DON'T STORE UP ENOUGH FOOD...
...I'LL **STARVE**!

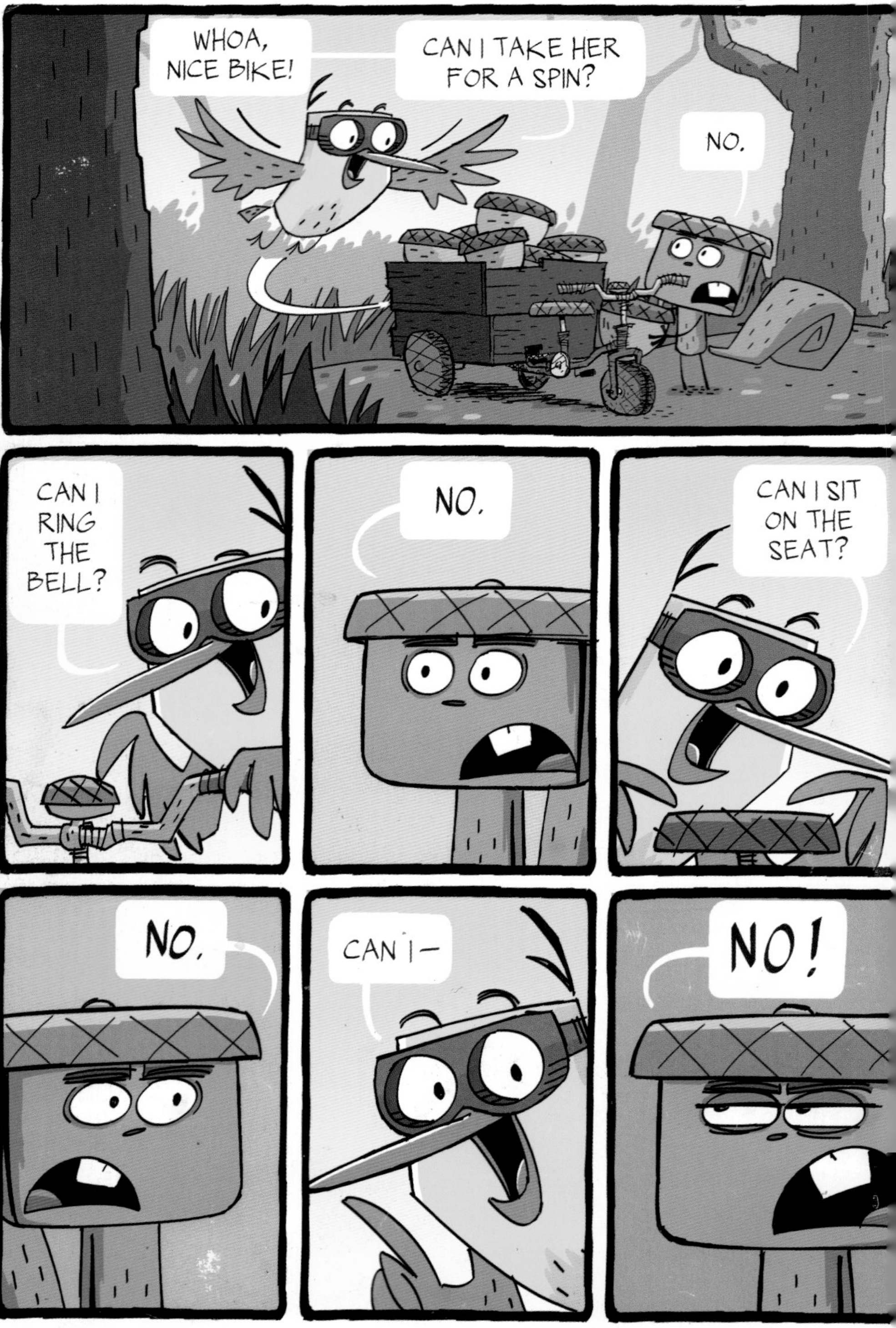
WHOA, NICE BIKE!
CAN I TAKE HER FOR A SPIN?
NO.
CAN I RING THE BELL?
NO.
CAN I SIT ON THE SEAT?
NO.
CAN I—
NO!

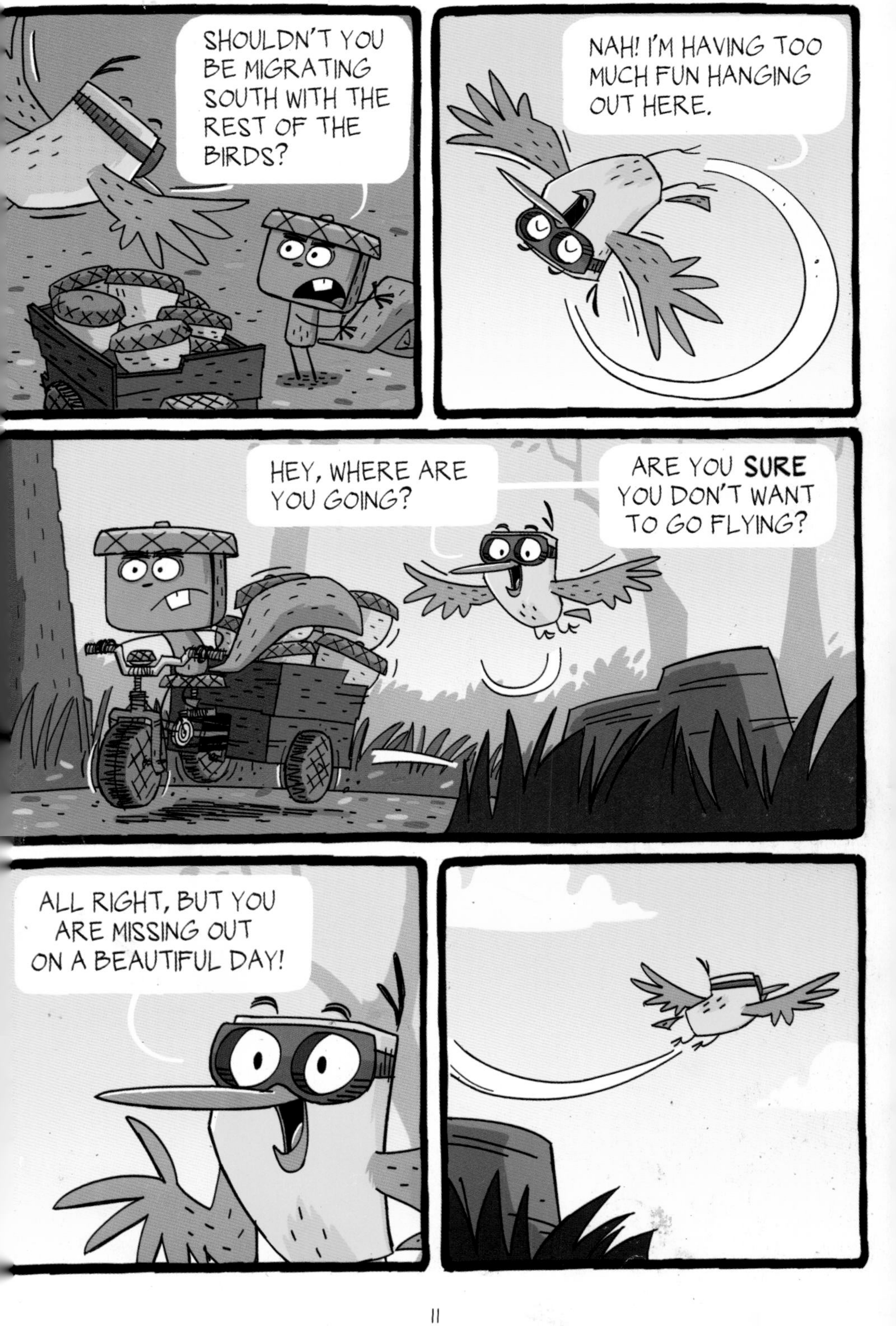
SHOULDN'T YOU BE MIGRATING SOUTH WITH THE REST OF THE BIRDS?
NAH! I'M HAVING TOO MUCH FUN HANGING OUT HERE.
HEY, WHERE ARE YOU GOING?
ARE YOU **SURE** YOU DON'T WANT TO GO FLYING?
ALL RIGHT, BUT YOU ARE MISSING OUT ON A BEAUTIFUL DAY!

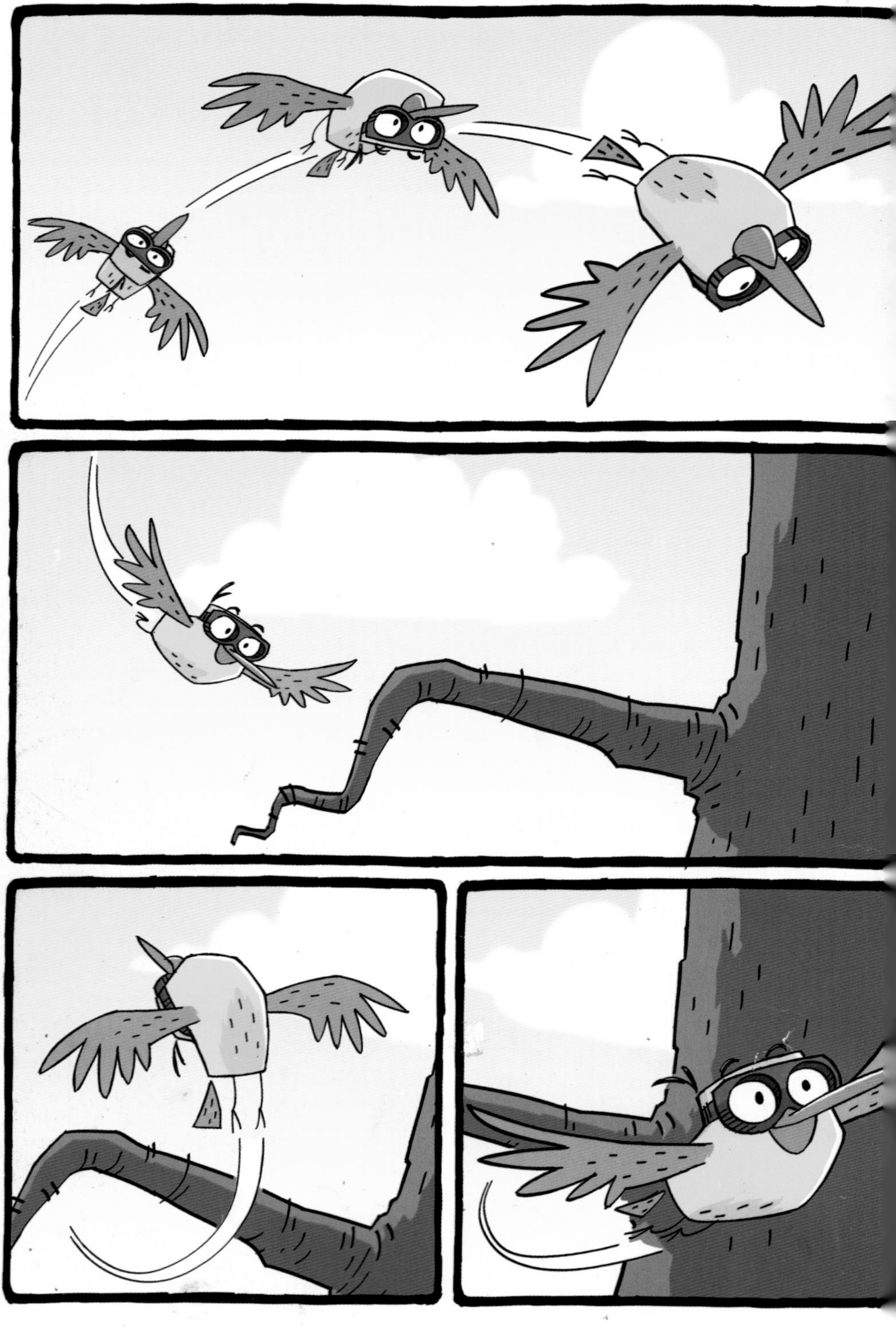

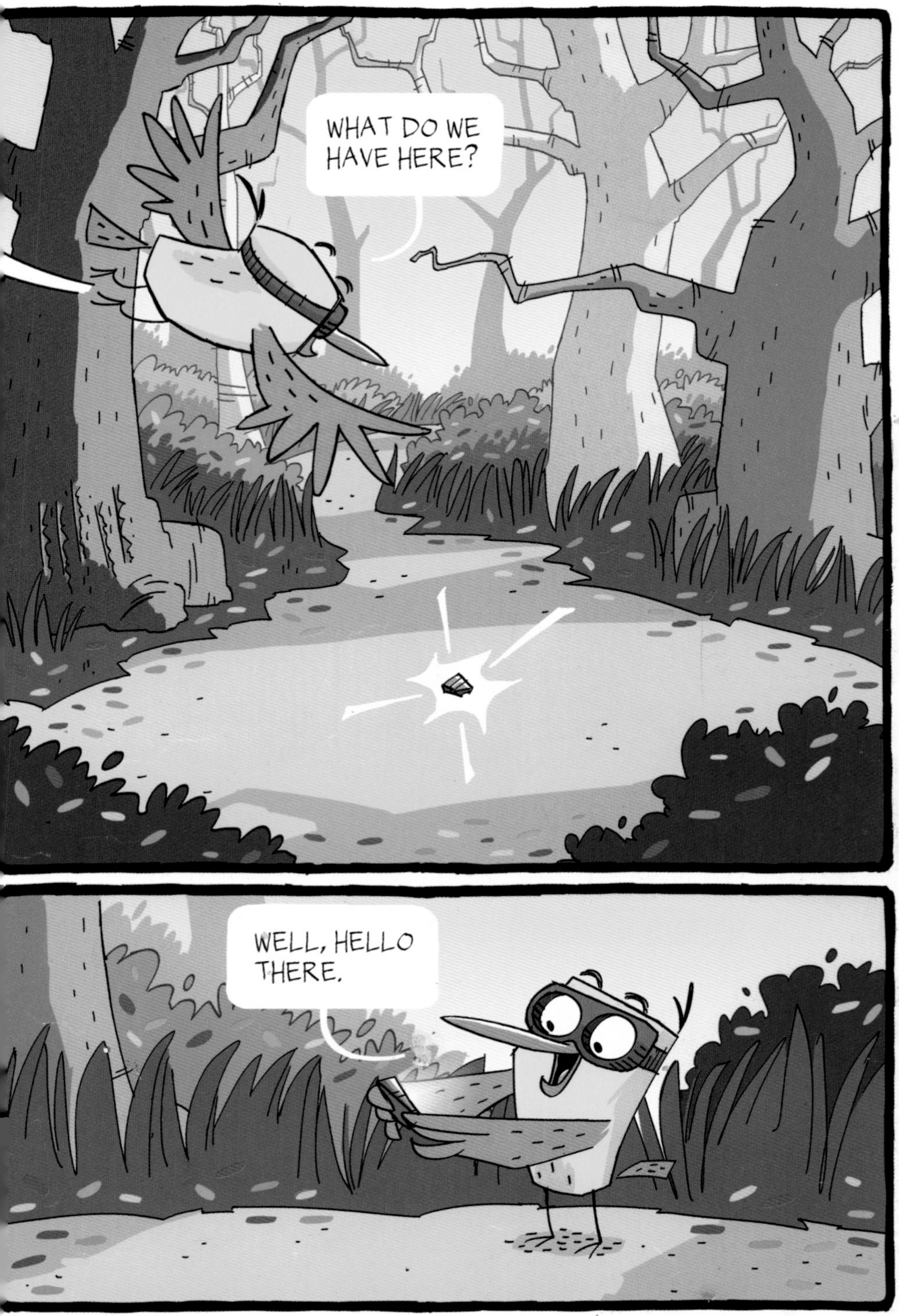
WHAT DO WE HAVE HERE?
WELL, HELLO THERE.

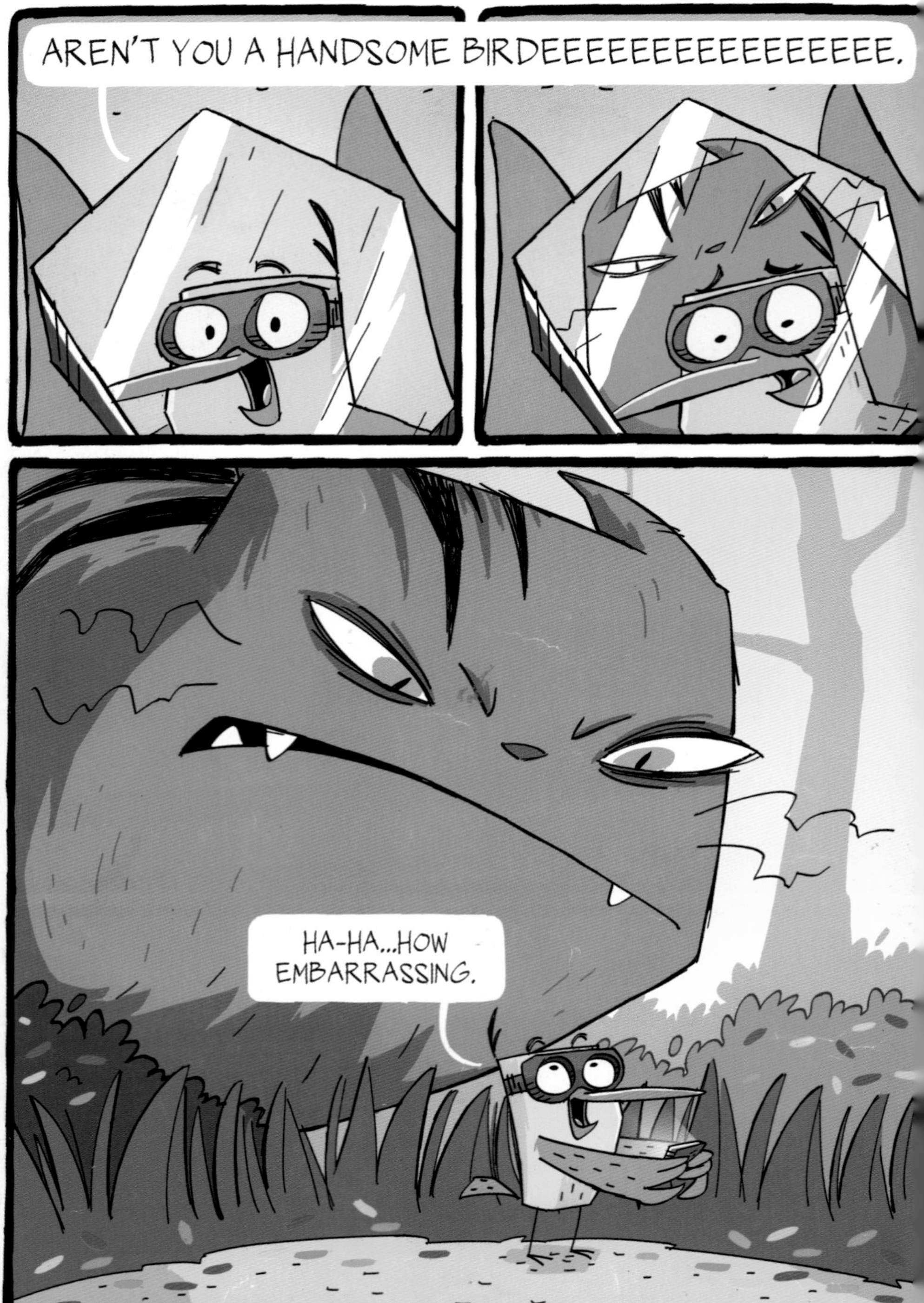
AREN'T YOU A HANDSOME BIRDEEEEEEEEEEEEEEEEEE.
HA-HA...HOW EMBARRASSING.

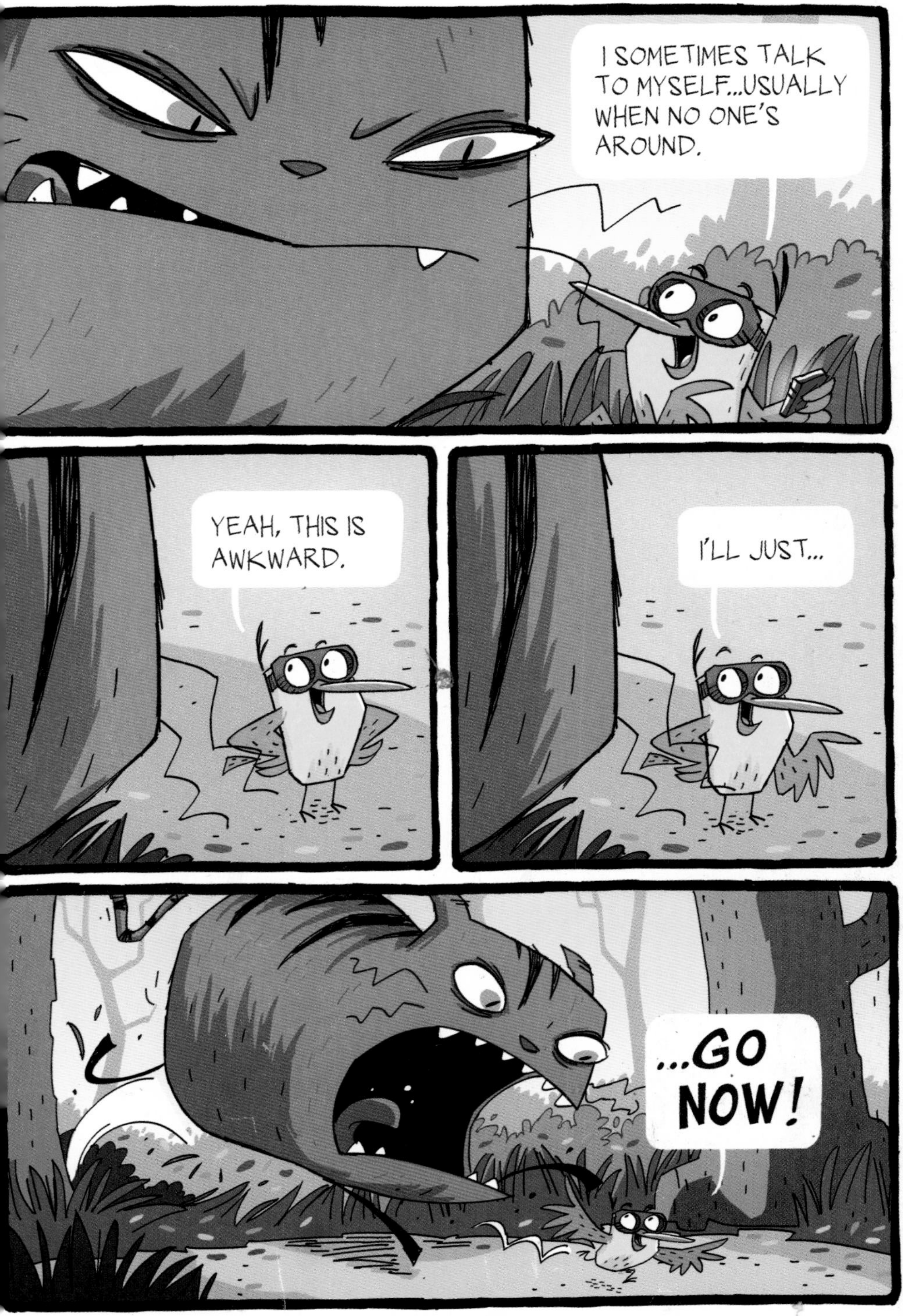
I SOMETIMES TALK TO MYSELF...USUALLY WHEN NO ONE'S AROUND.
YEAH, THIS IS AWKWARD.
I'LL JUST...
...GO NOW!

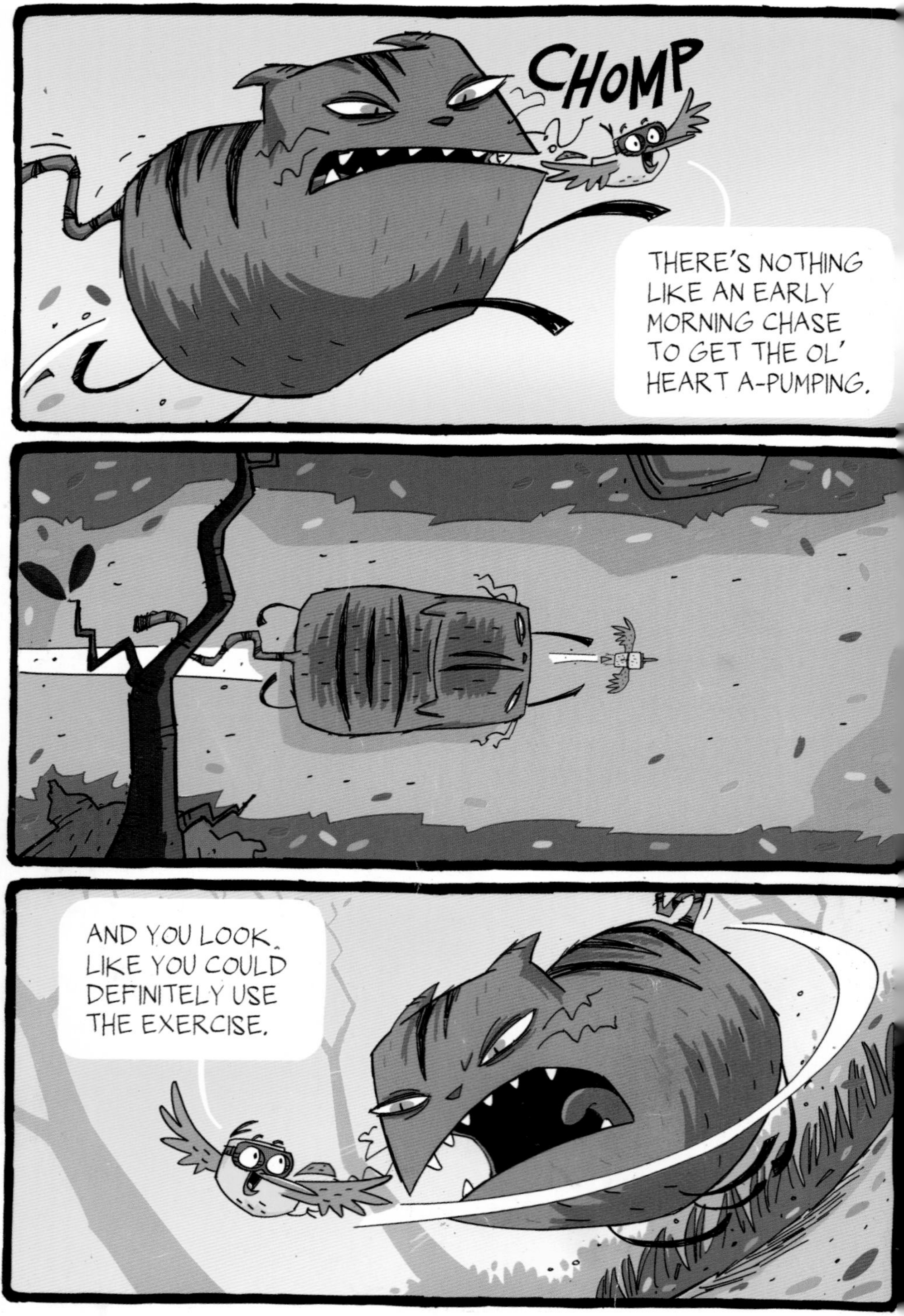
CHOMP
THERE'S NOTHING LIKE AN EARLY MORNING CHASE TO GET THE OL' HEART A-PUMPING.
AND YOU LOOK LIKE YOU COULD DEFINITELY USE THE EXERCISE.

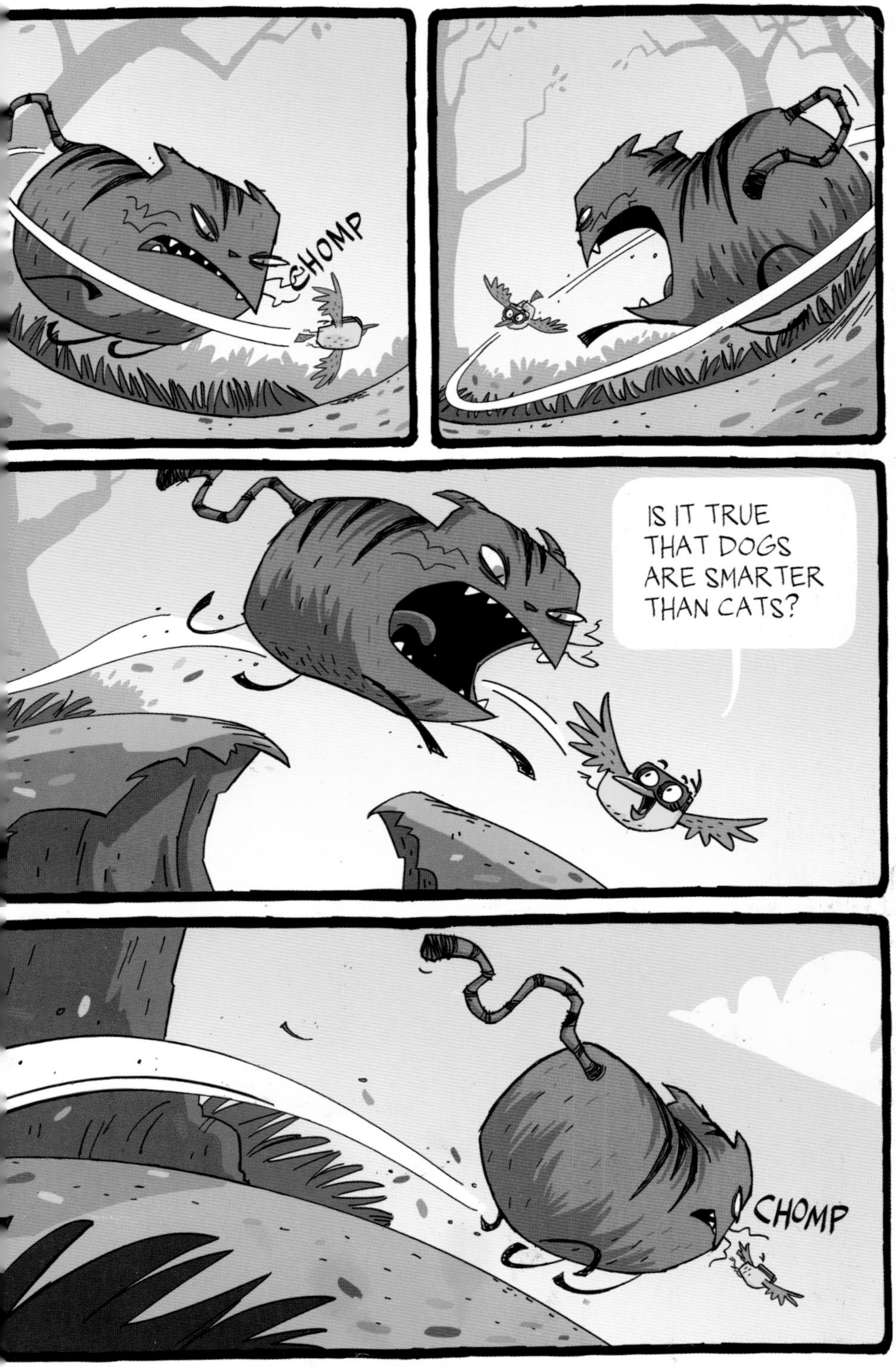
CHOMP
IS IT TRUE THAT DOGS ARE SMARTER THAN CATS?
CHOMP

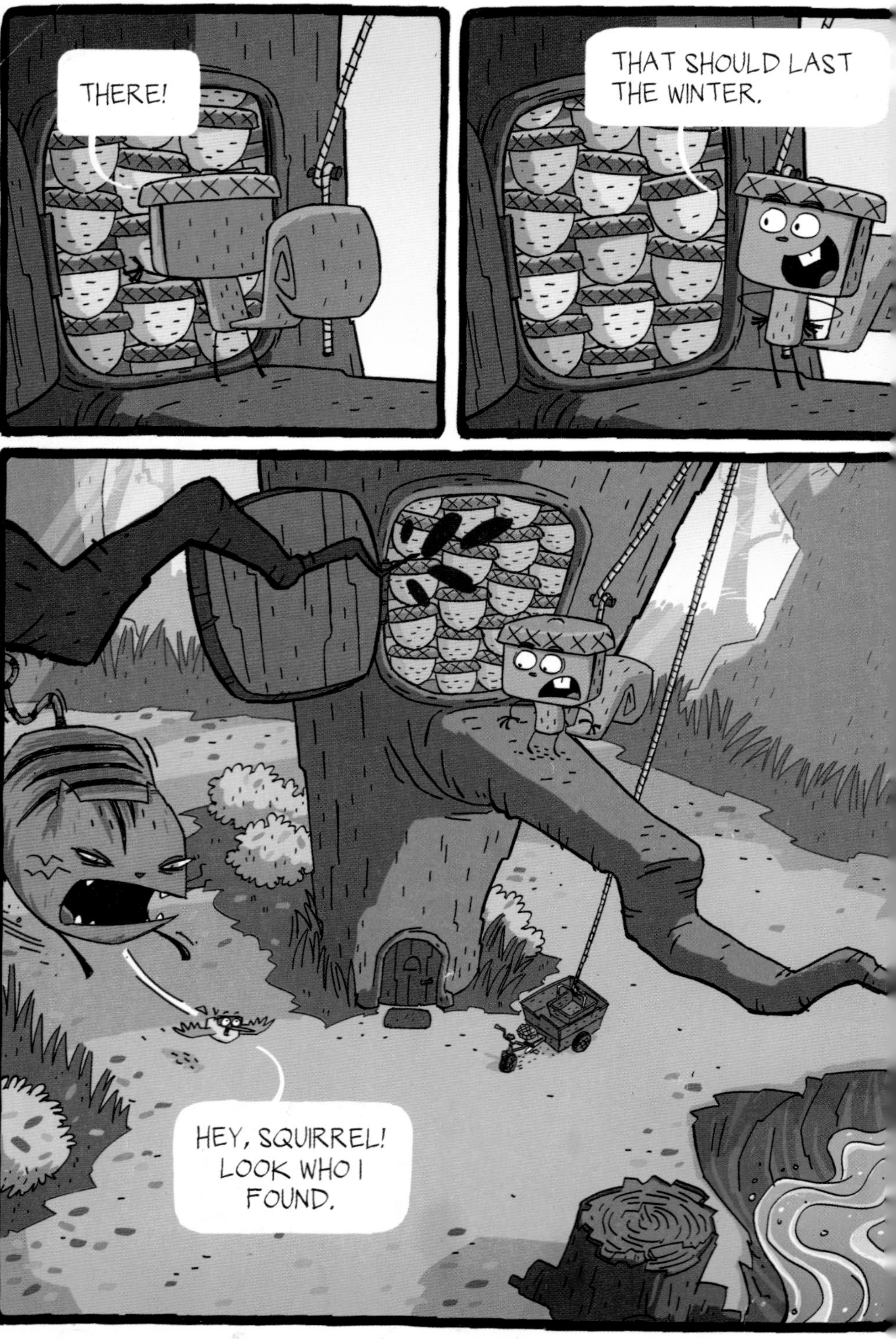
THERE!
THAT SHOULD LAST THE WINTER.
HEY, SQUIRREL! LOOK WHO I FOUND.

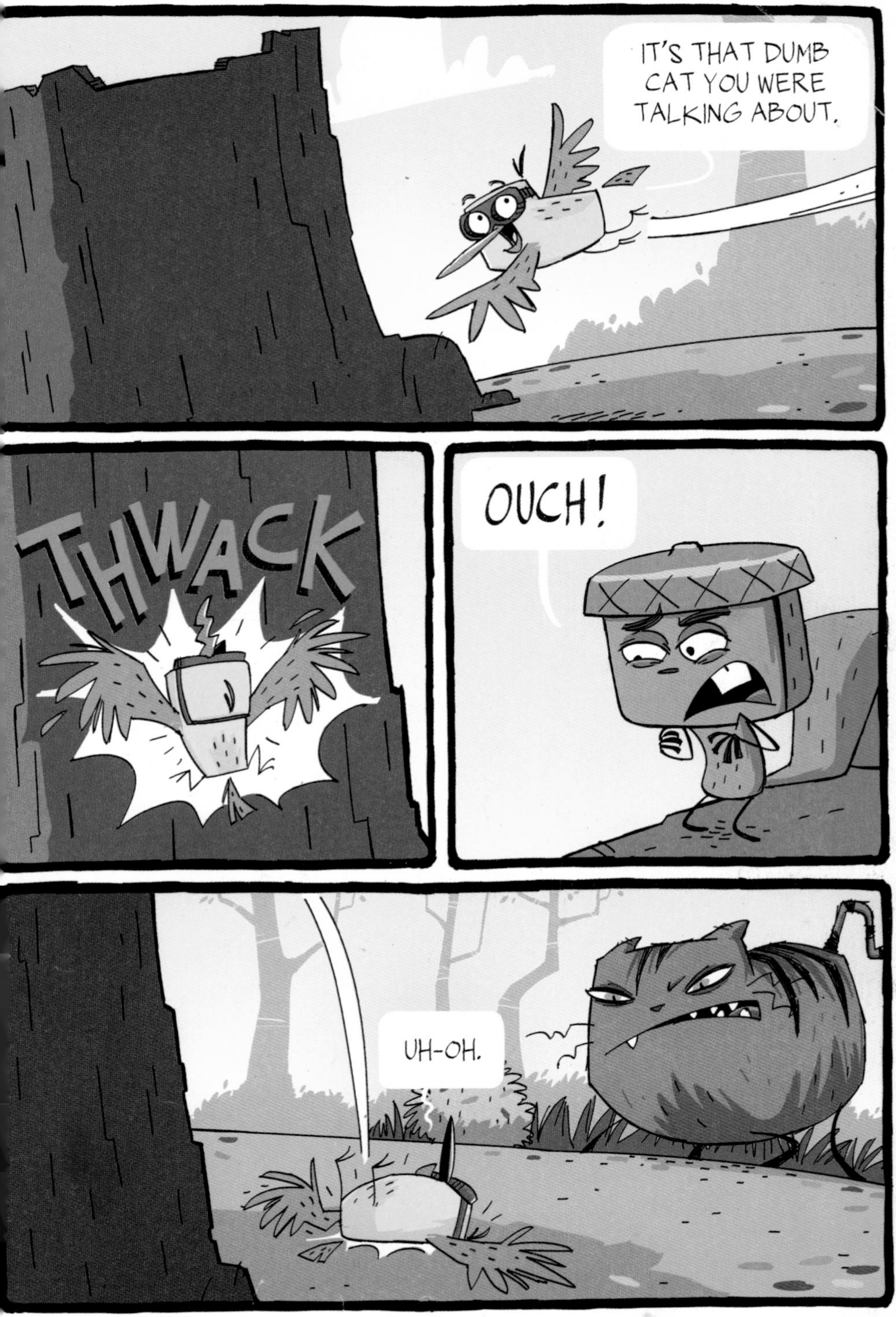
IT'S THAT DUMB CAT YOU WERE TALKING ABOUT.
THWACK
OUCH!
UH-OH.

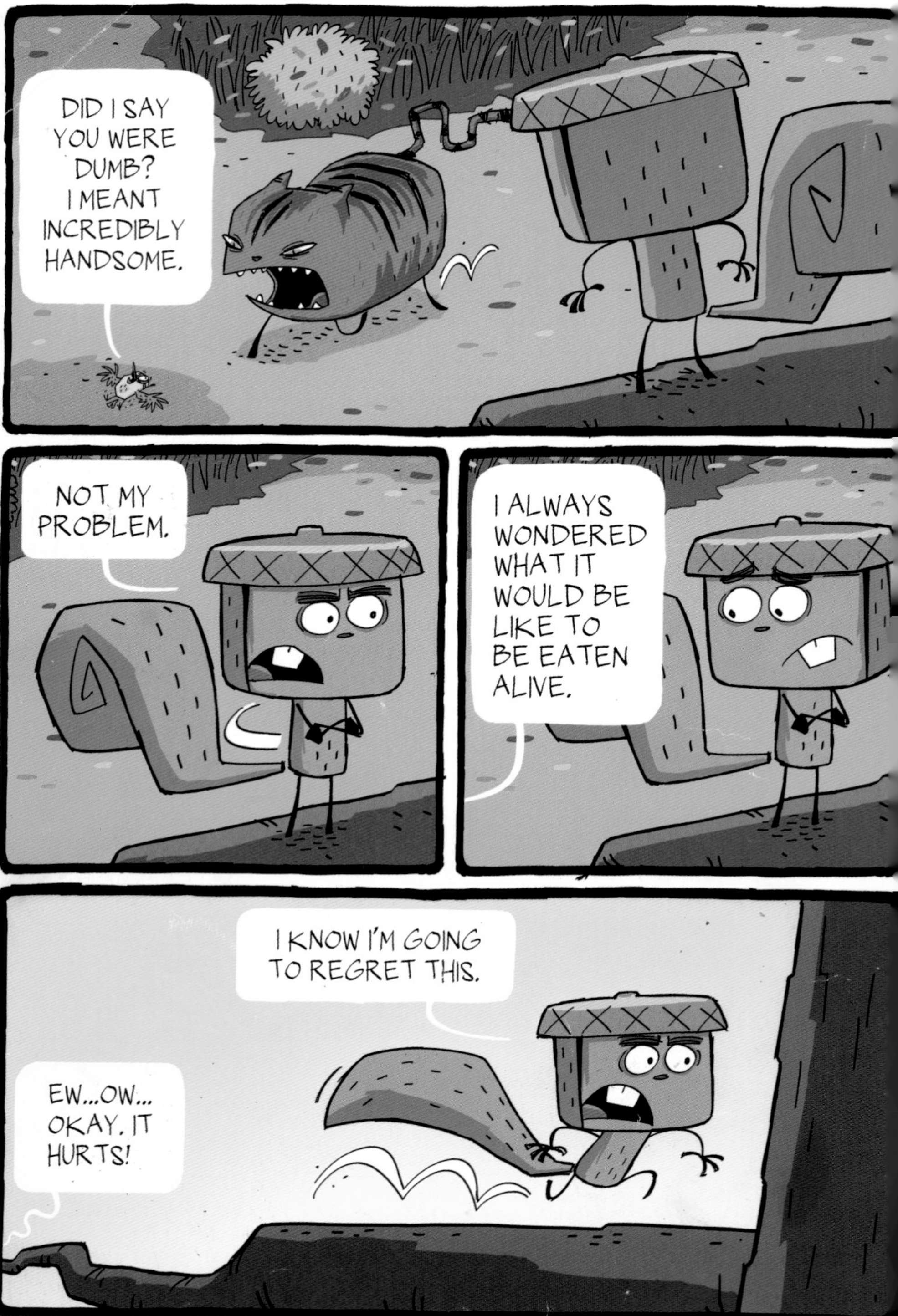
DID I SAY YOU WERE DUMB? I MEANT INCREDIBLY HANDSOME.
NOT MY PROBLEM.
I ALWAYS WONDERED WHAT IT WOULD BE LIKE TO BE EATEN ALIVE.
I KNOW I'M GOING TO REGRET THIS.
EW...OW... OKAY. IT HURTS!

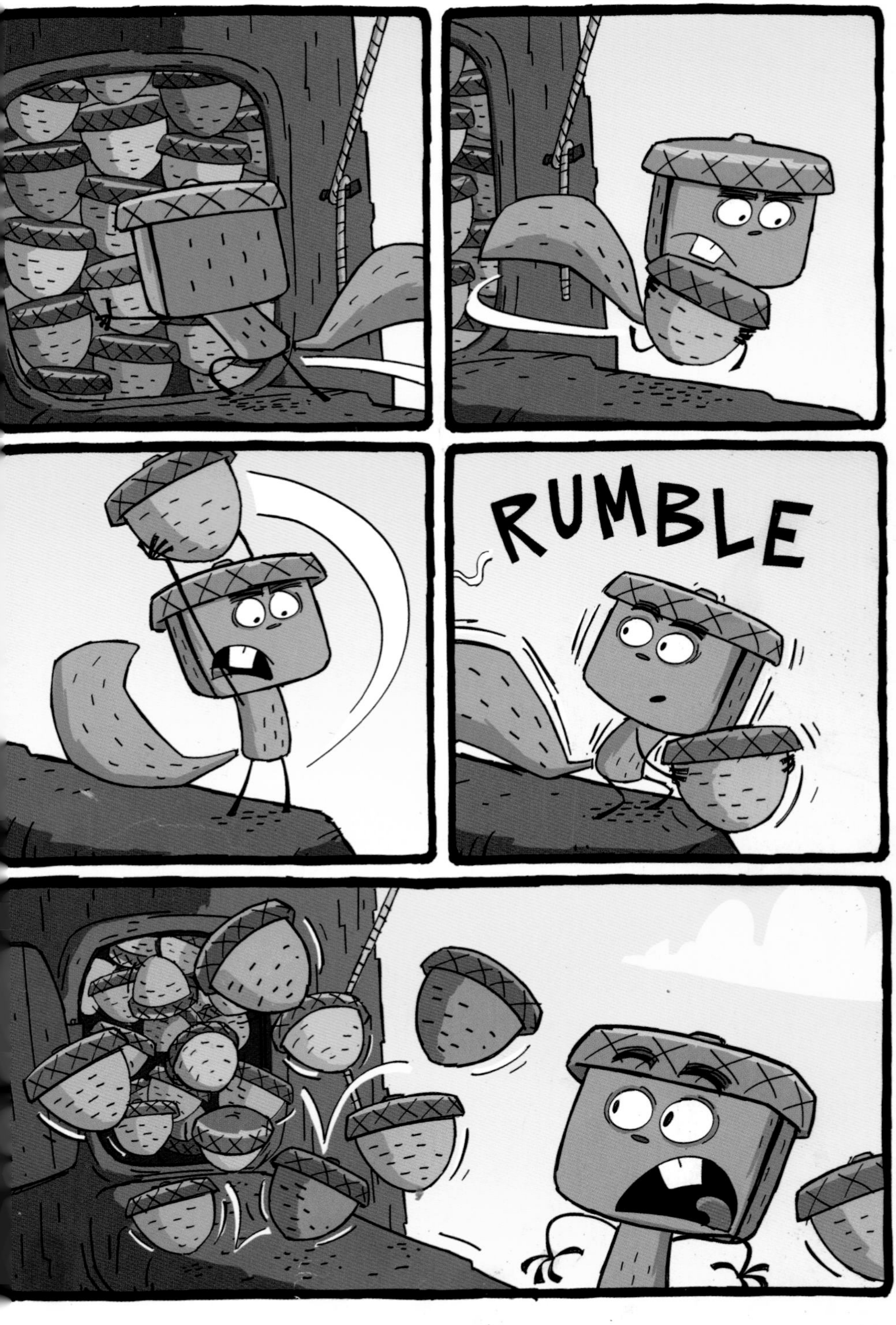
RUMBLE

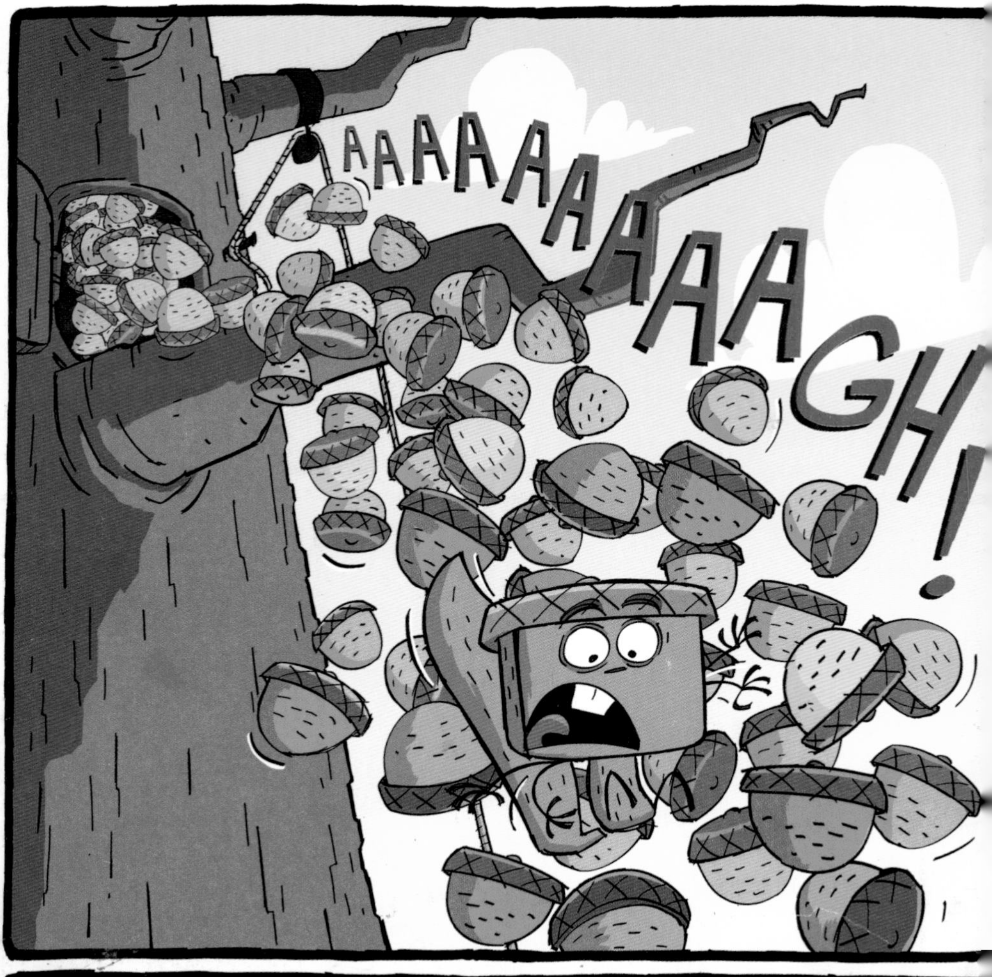
AAAAAAAAAAAAAAGH!

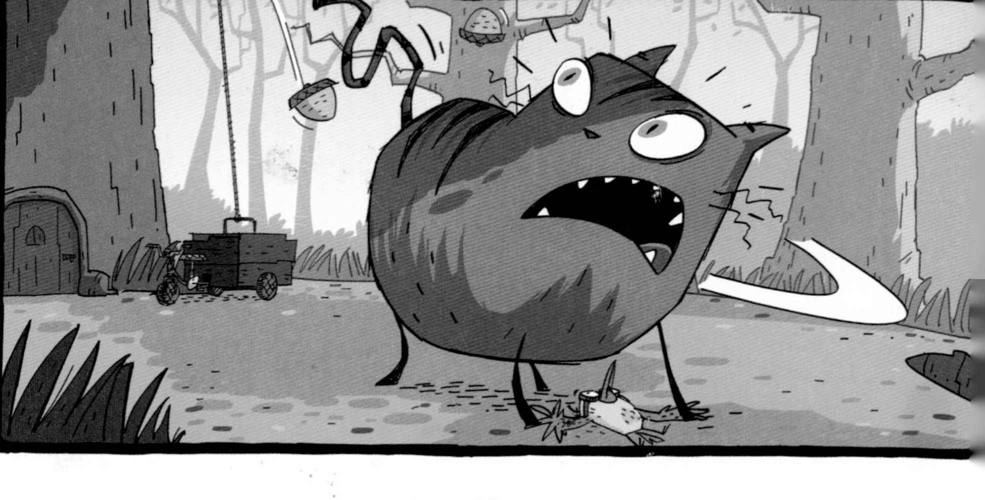

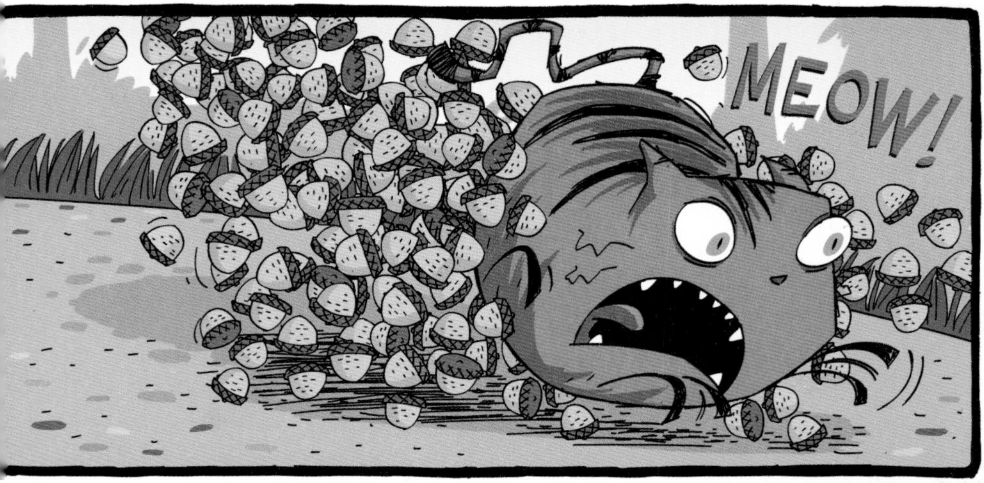
MEOW!

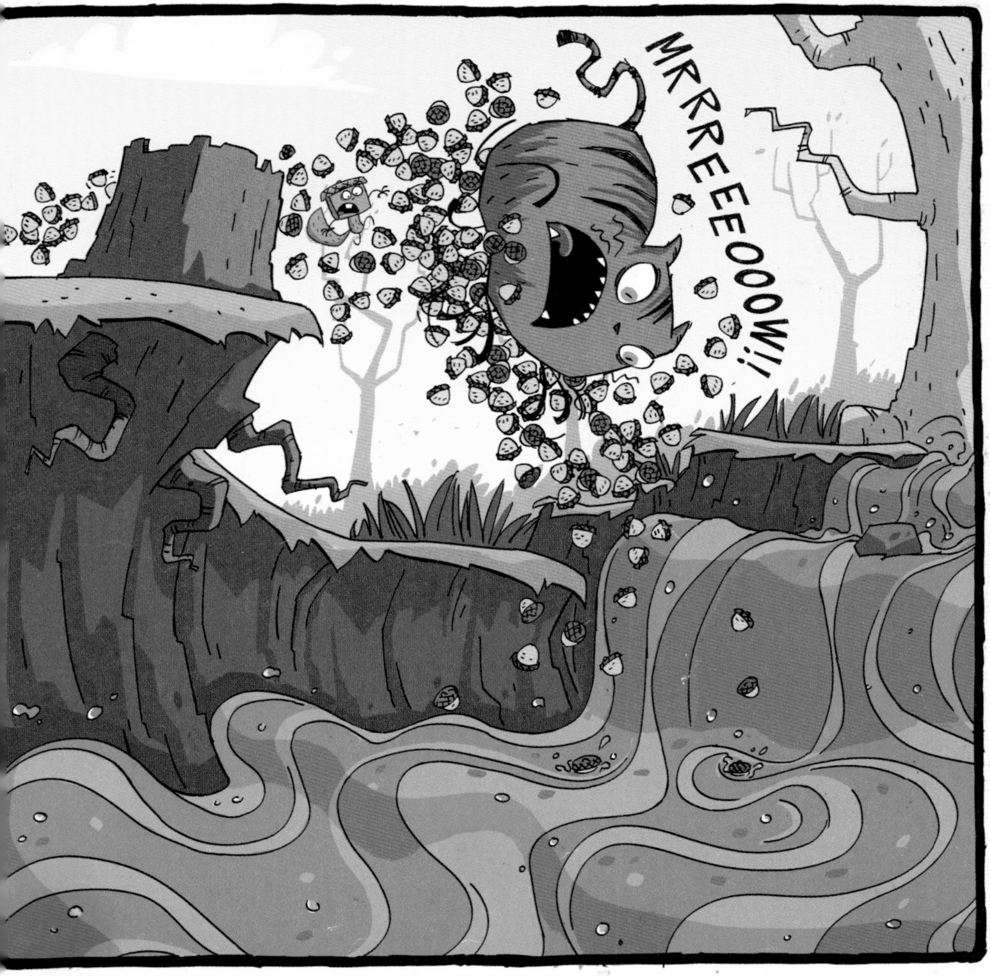
MRRREEEOOOW!!

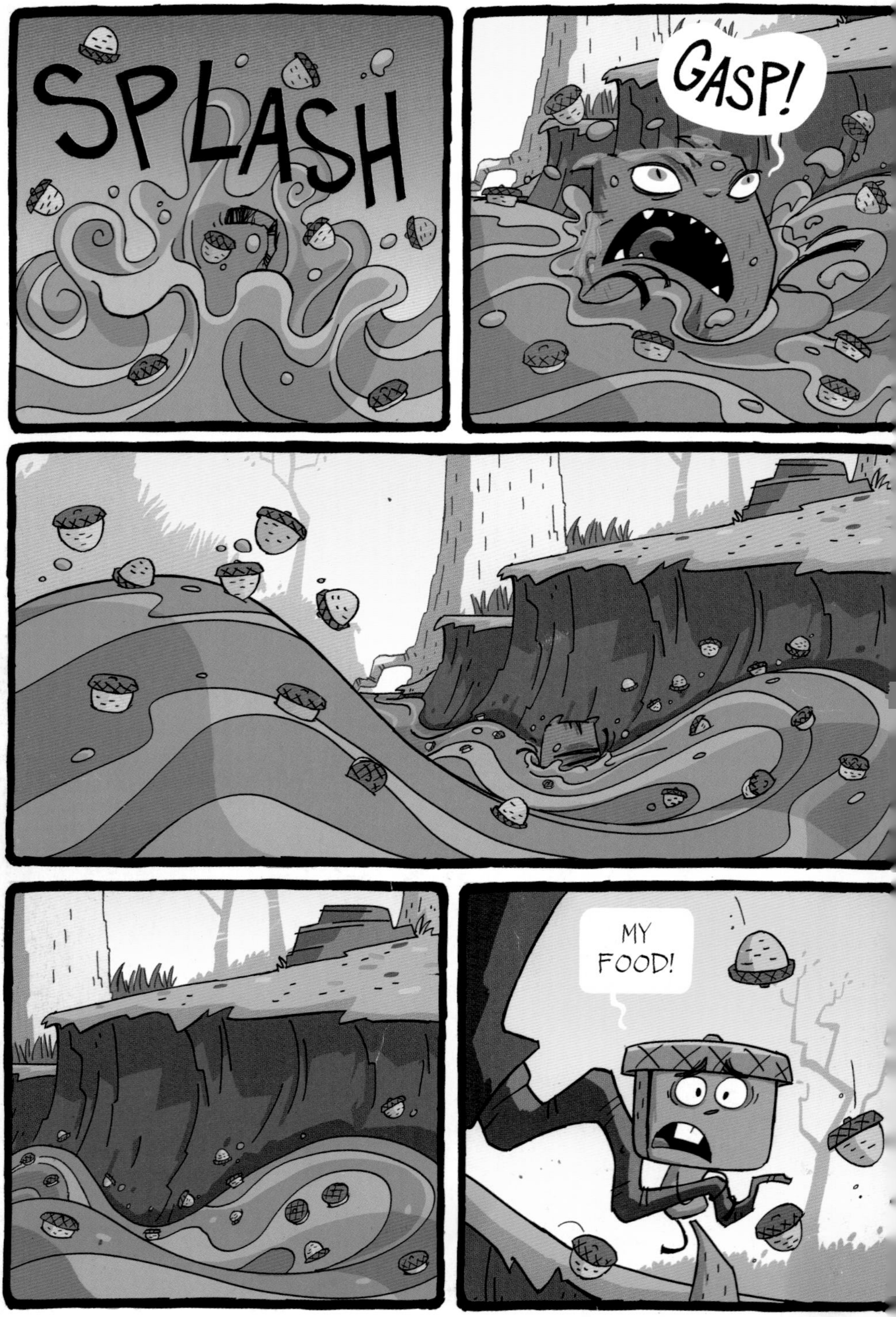
SPLASH
GASP!
MY FOOD!

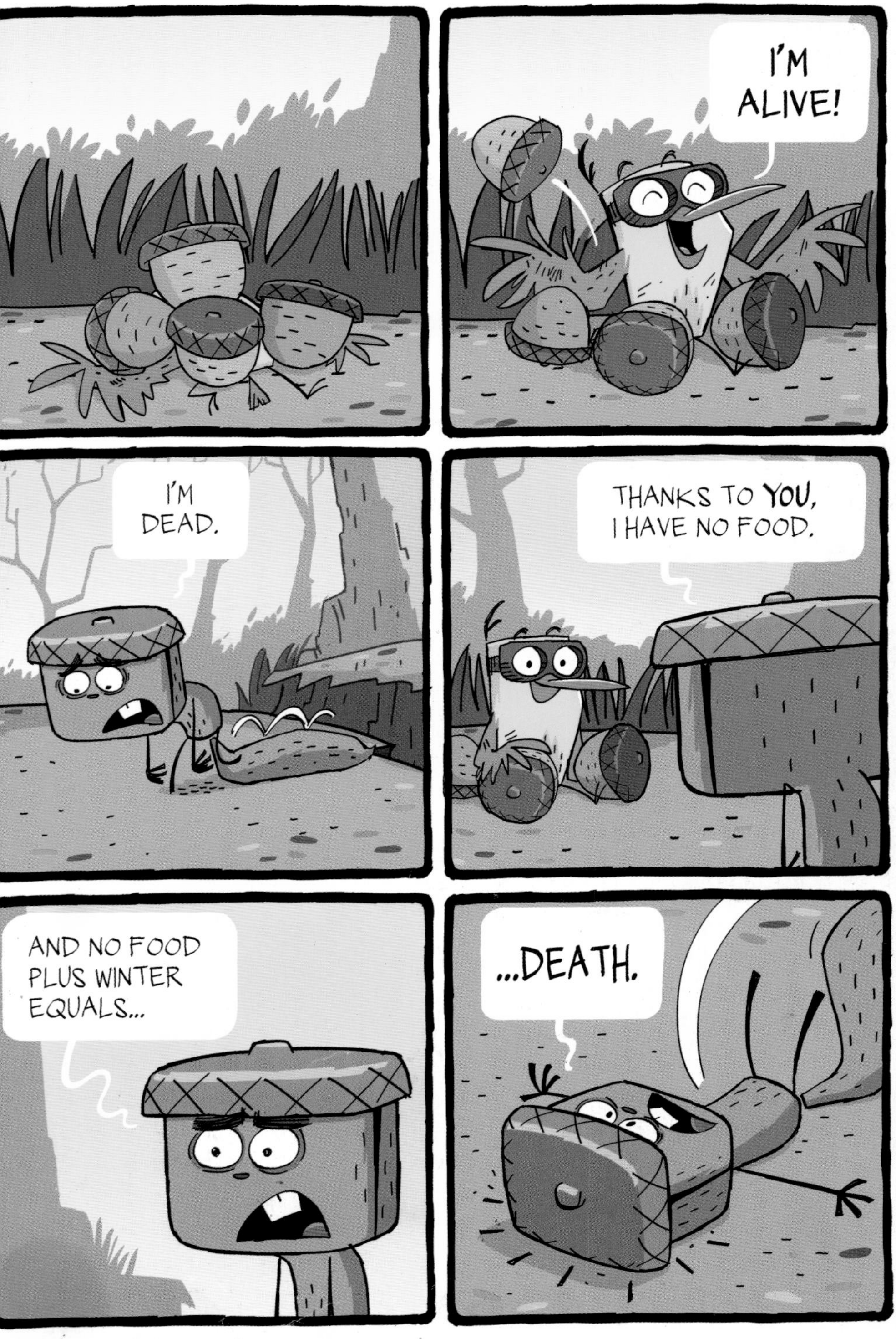
I'M ALIVE!
I'M DEAD.
THANKS TO YOU, I HAVE NO FOOD.
AND NO FOOD PLUS WINTER EQUALS...
...DEATH.

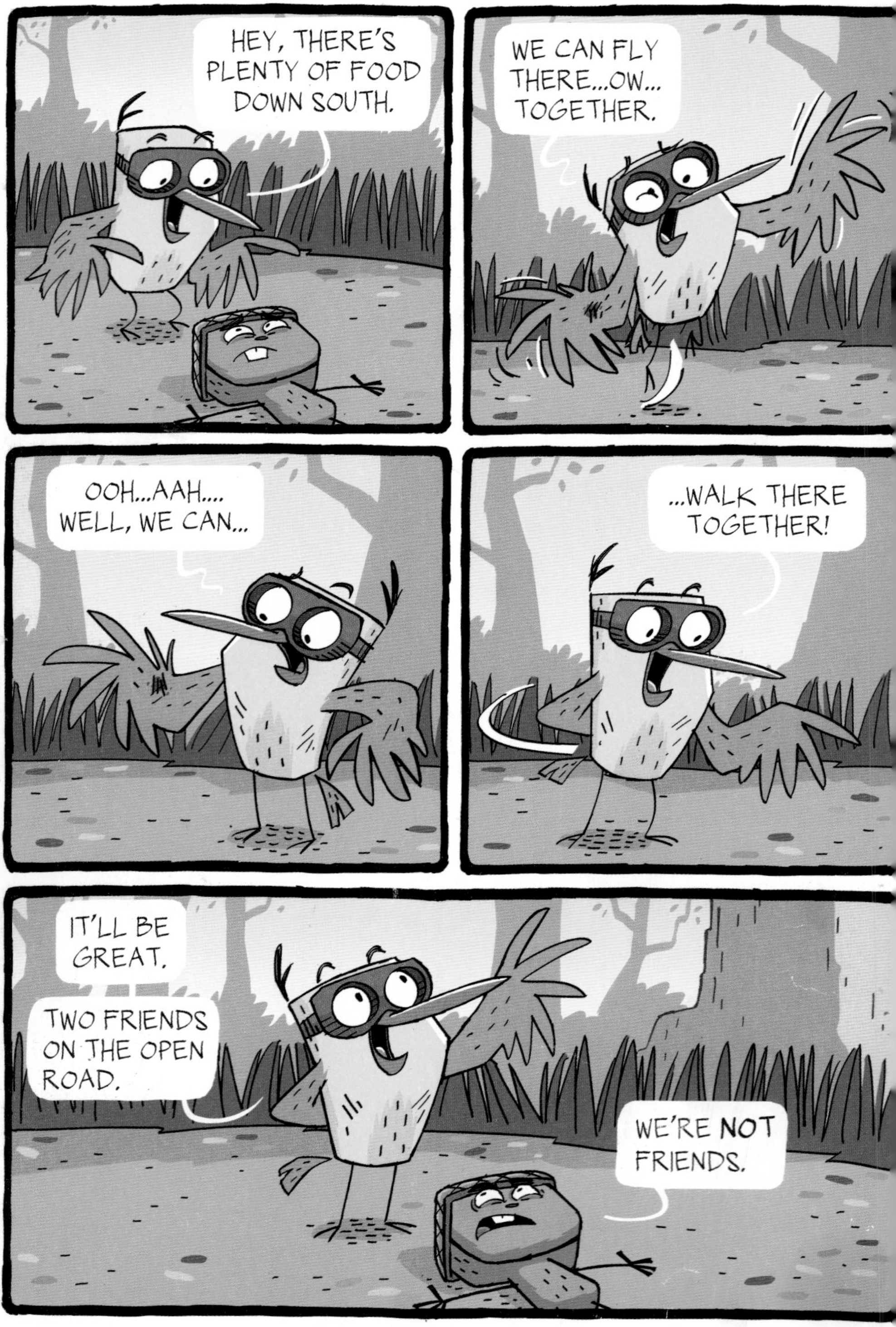
HEY, THERE'S PLENTY OF FOOD DOWN SOUTH.
WE CAN FLY THERE...OW... TOGETHER.
OOH...AAH.... WELL, WE CAN...
...WALK THERE TOGETHER!
IT'LL BE GREAT.
TWO FRIENDS ON THE OPEN ROAD.
WE'RE **NOT** FRIENDS.

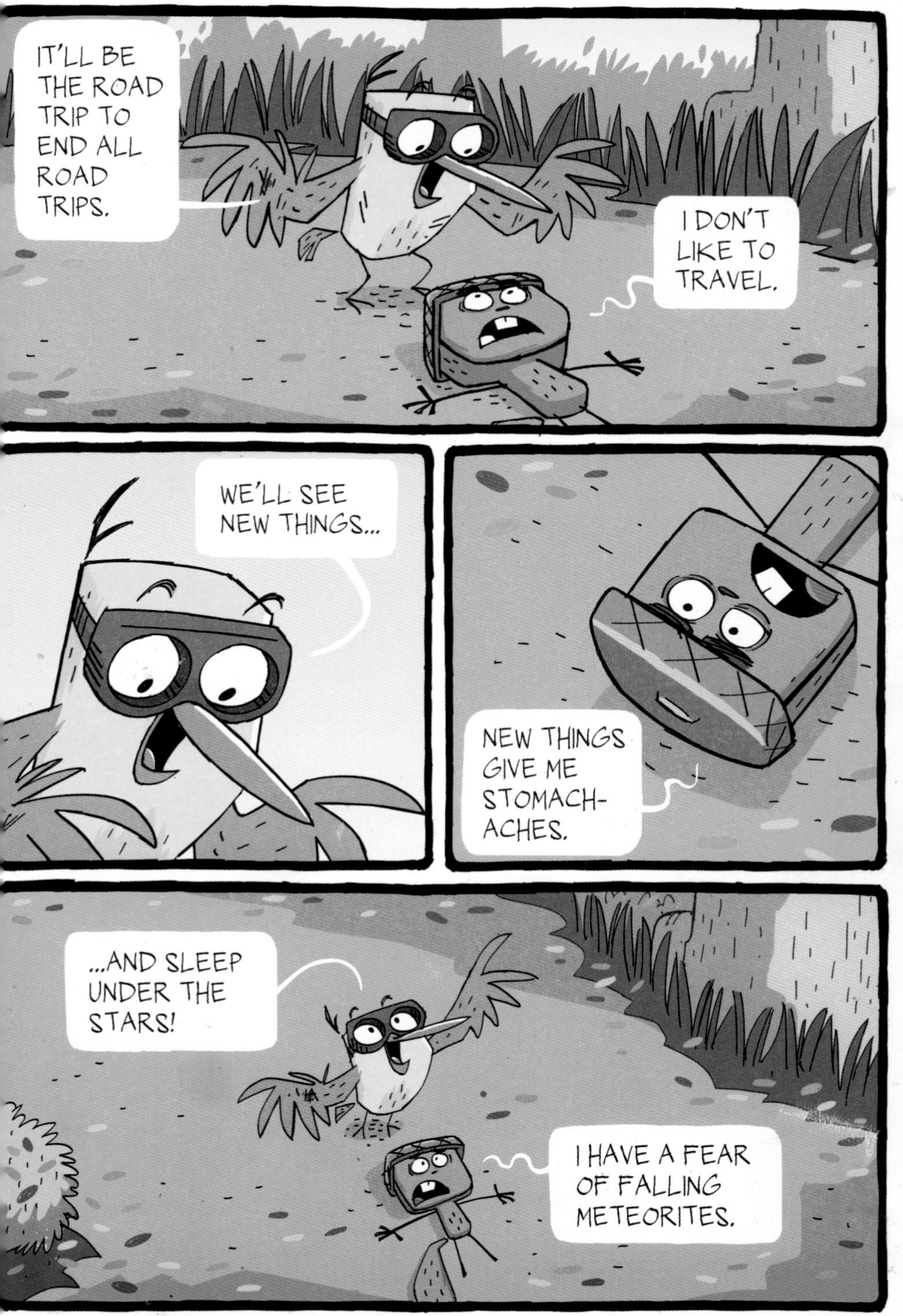
IT'LL BE THE ROAD TRIP TO END ALL ROAD TRIPS.
I DON'T LIKE TO TRAVEL.
WE'LL SEE NEW THINGS...
NEW THINGS GIVE ME STOMACH-ACHES.
...AND SLEEP UNDER THE STARS!
I HAVE A FEAR OF FALLING METEORITES.

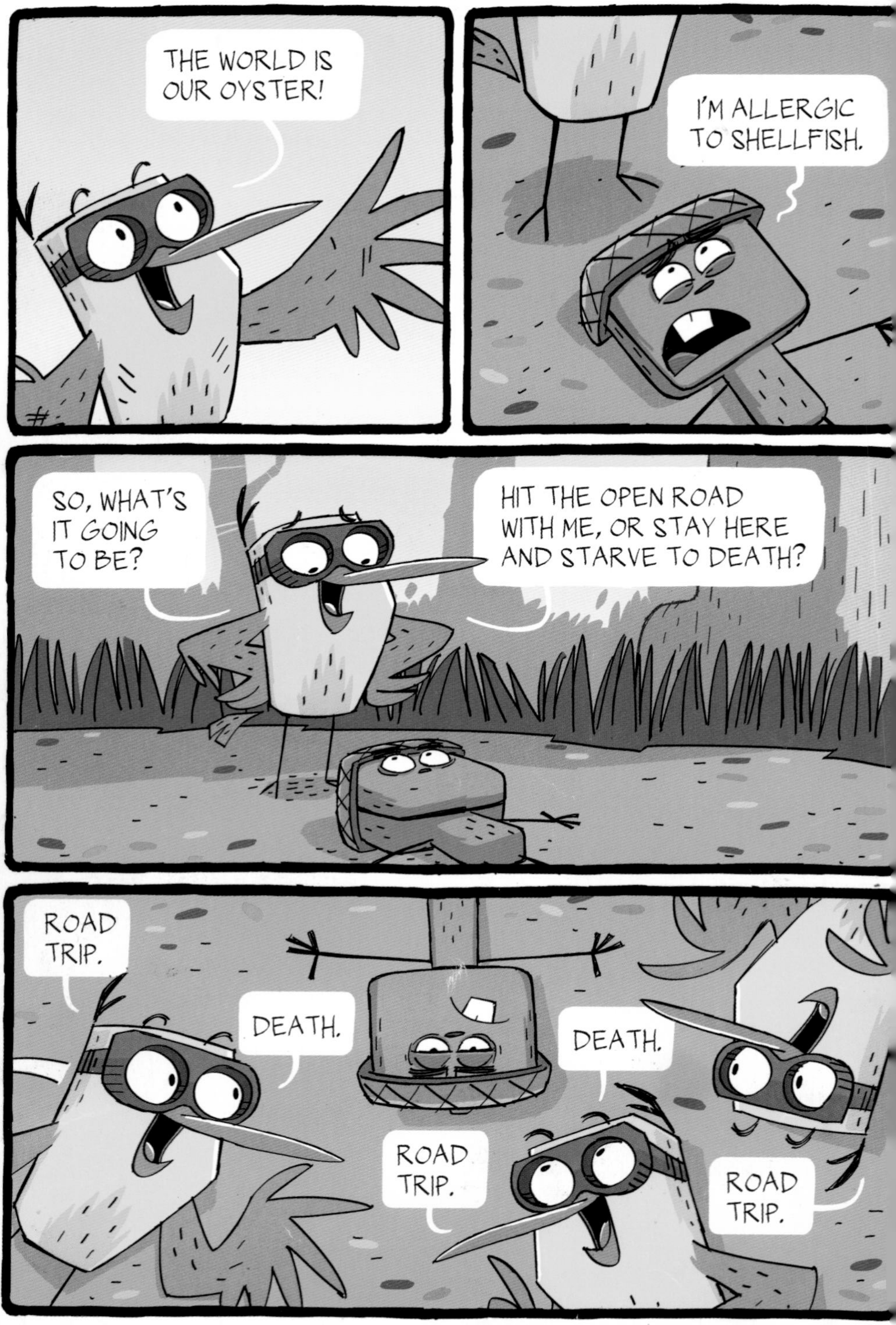
THE WORLD IS OUR OYSTER!
I'M ALLERGIC TO SHELLFISH.
SO, WHAT'S IT GOING TO BE?
HIT THE OPEN ROAD WITH ME, OR STAY HERE AND STARVE TO DEATH?
ROAD TRIP.
DEATH.
DEATH.
ROAD TRIP.
ROAD TRIP.

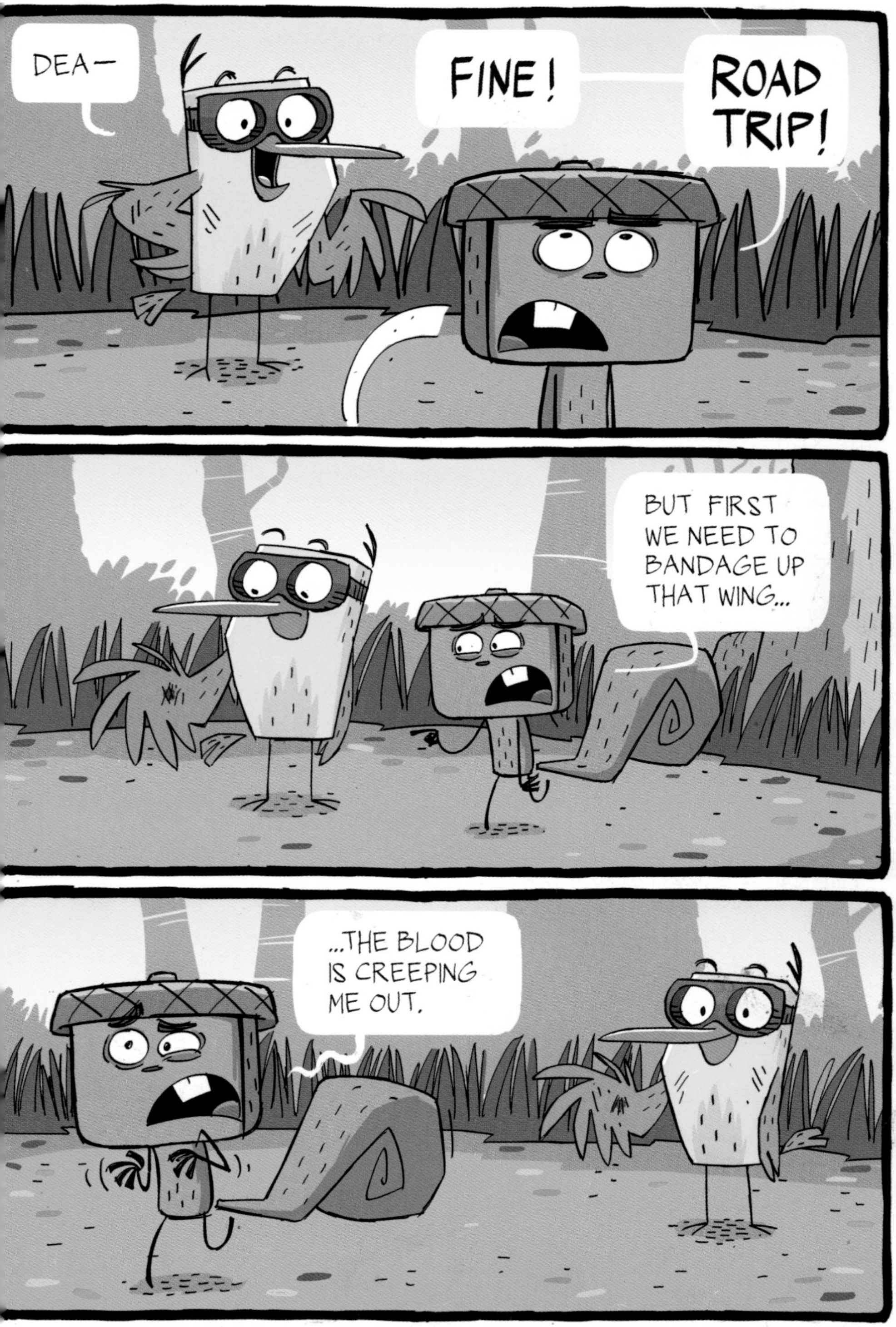
DEA—
FINE!
ROAD TRIP!
BUT FIRST WE NEED TO BANDAGE UP THAT WING...
...THE BLOOD IS CREEPING ME OUT.

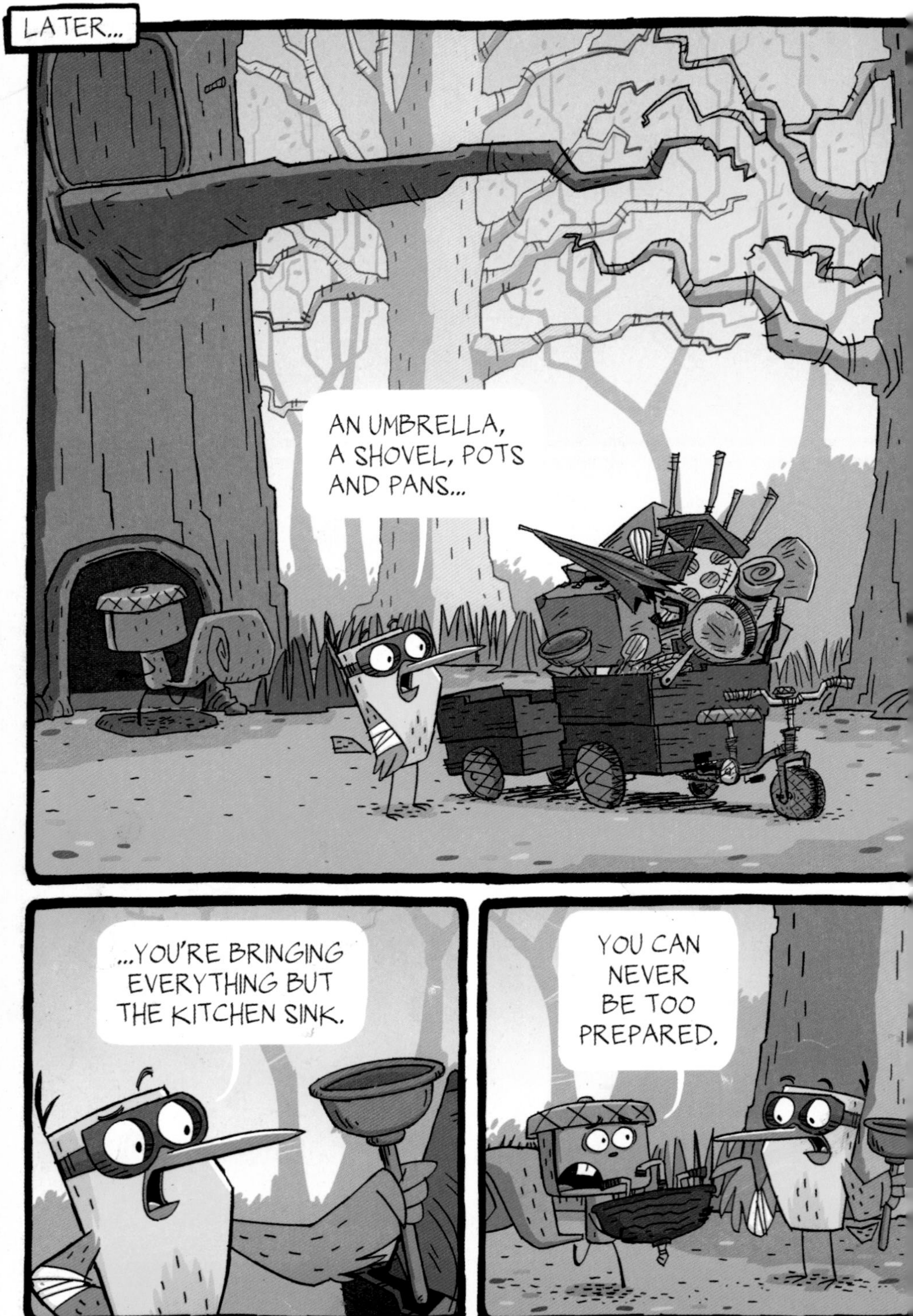
LATER...
AN UMBRELLA, A SHOVEL, POTS AND PANS...
...YOU'RE BRINGING EVERYTHING BUT THE KITCHEN SINK.
YOU CAN NEVER BE TOO PREPARED.

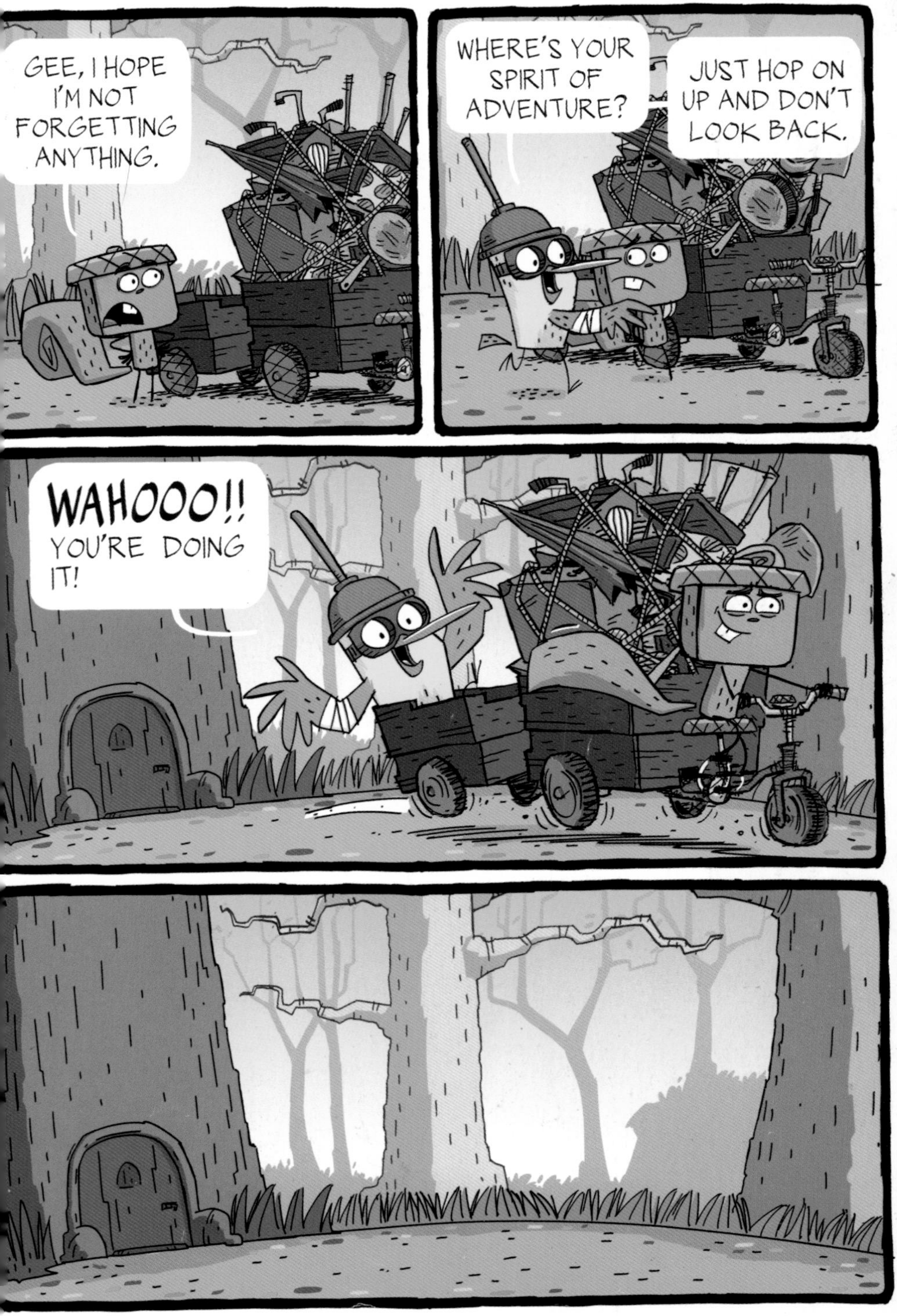
GEE, I HOPE I'M NOT FORGETTING ANYTHING.
WHERE'S YOUR SPIRIT OF ADVENTURE?
JUST HOP ON UP AND DON'T LOOK BACK.
WAHOOO!! YOU'RE DOING IT!

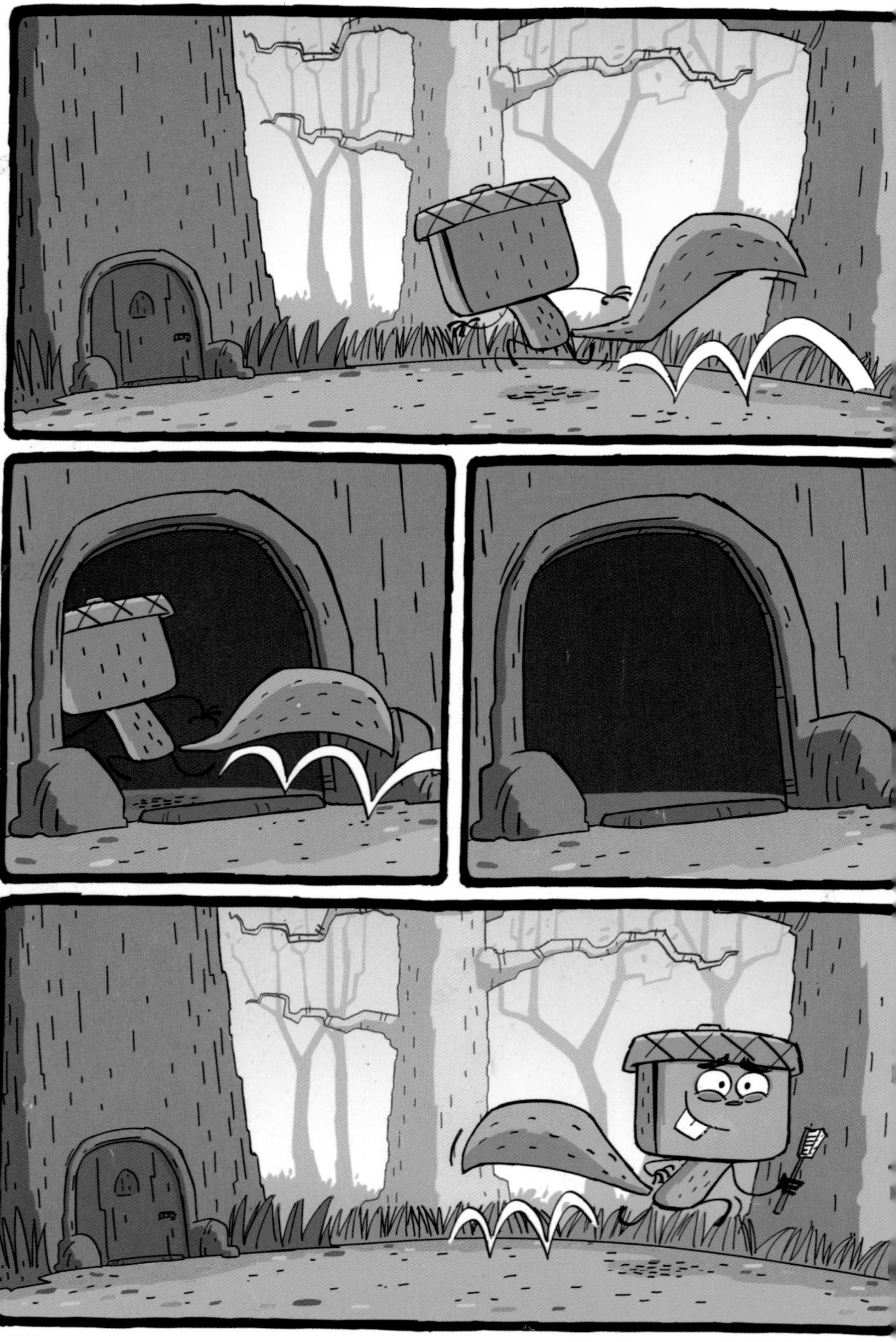

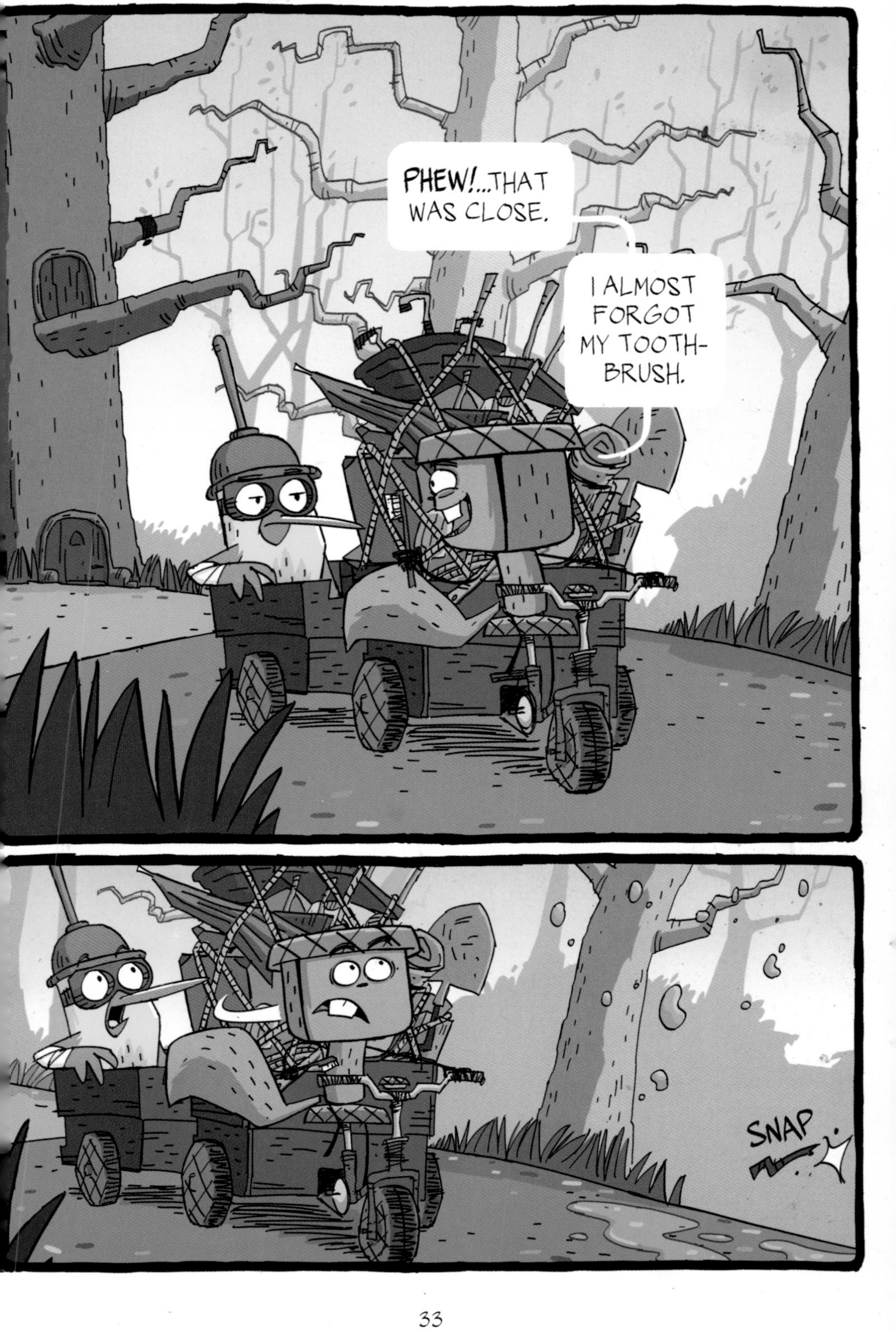
PHEW!...THAT WAS CLOSE.
I ALMOST FORGOT MY TOOTH-BRUSH.
SNAP

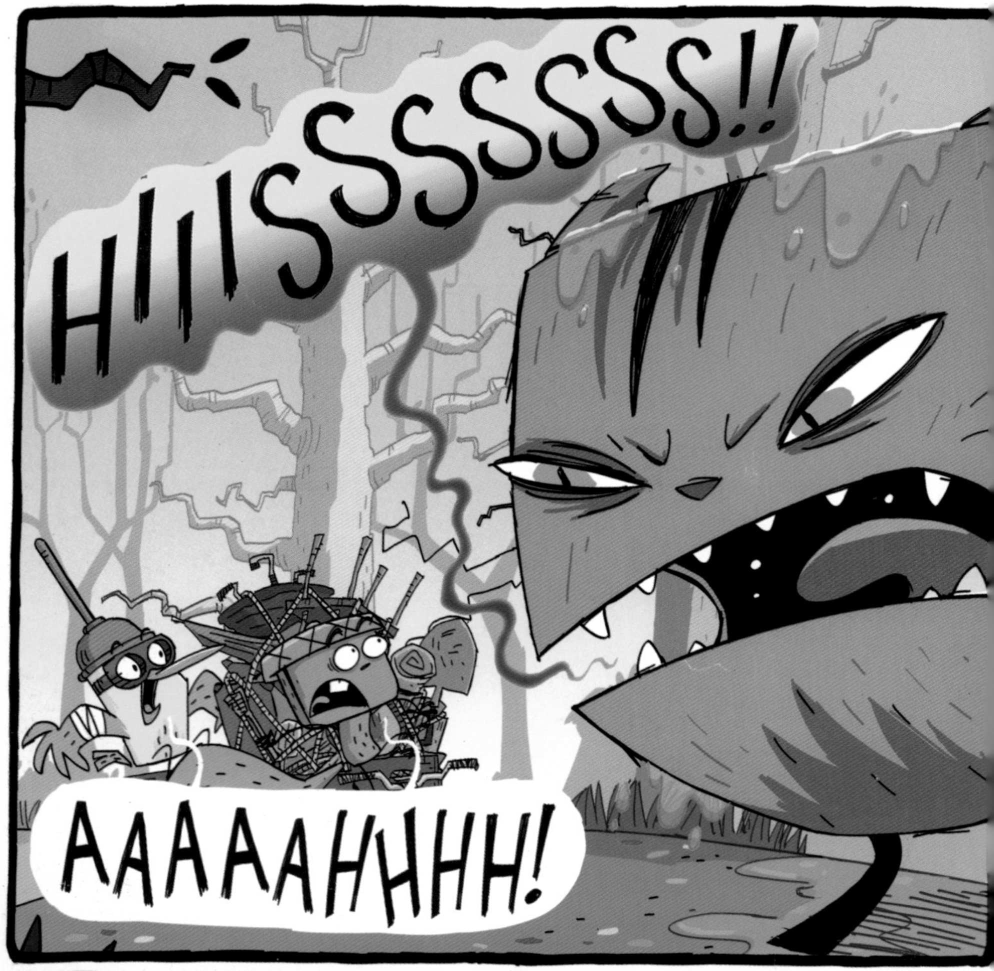
HIISSSSSSS!!
AAAAAHHHH!

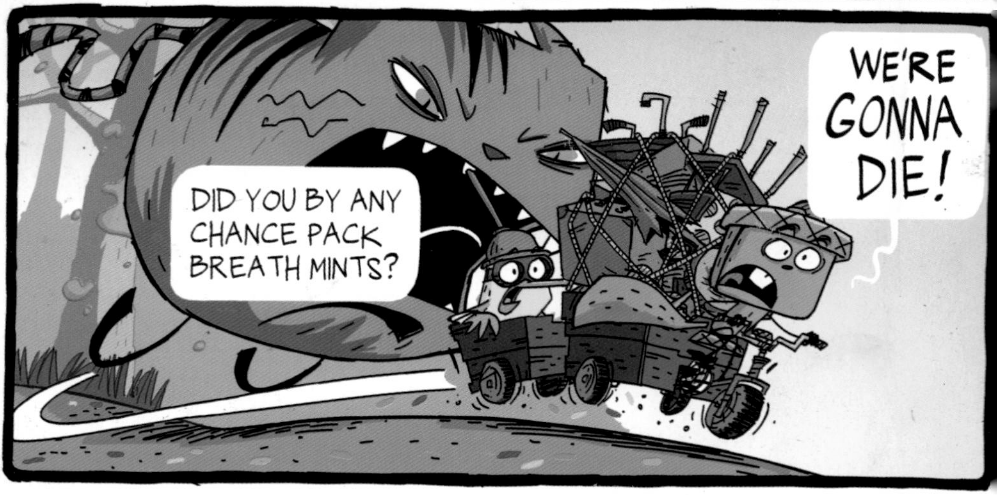
DID YOU BY ANY CHANCE PACK BREATH MINTS?
WE'RE GONNA DIE!

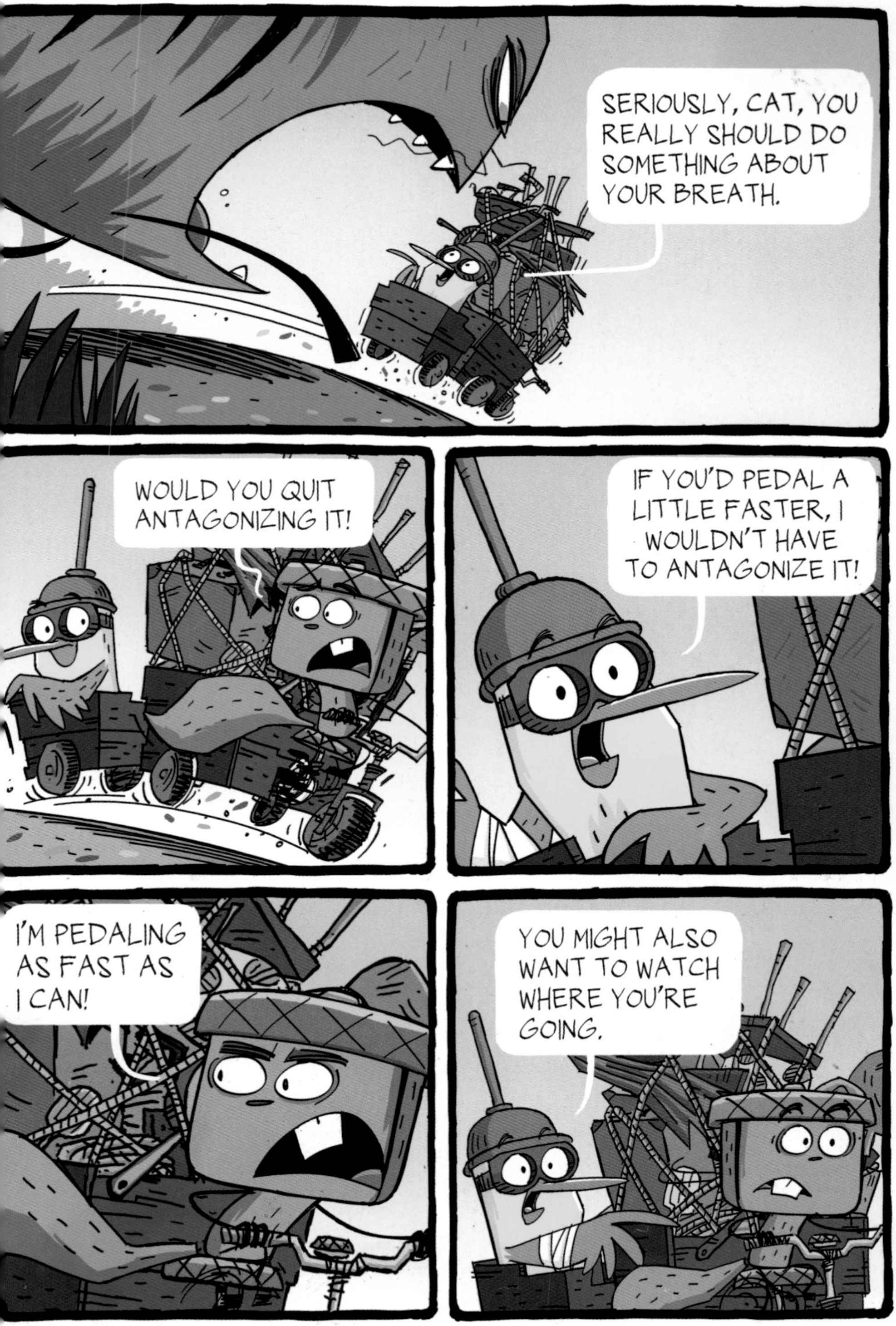
SERIOUSLY, CAT, YOU REALLY SHOULD DO SOMETHING ABOUT YOUR BREATH.
WOULD YOU QUIT ANTAGONIZING IT!
IF YOU'D PEDAL A LITTLE FASTER, I WOULDN'T HAVE TO ANTAGONIZE IT!
I'M PEDALING AS FAST AS I CAN!
YOU MIGHT ALSO WANT TO WATCH WHERE YOU'RE GOING.

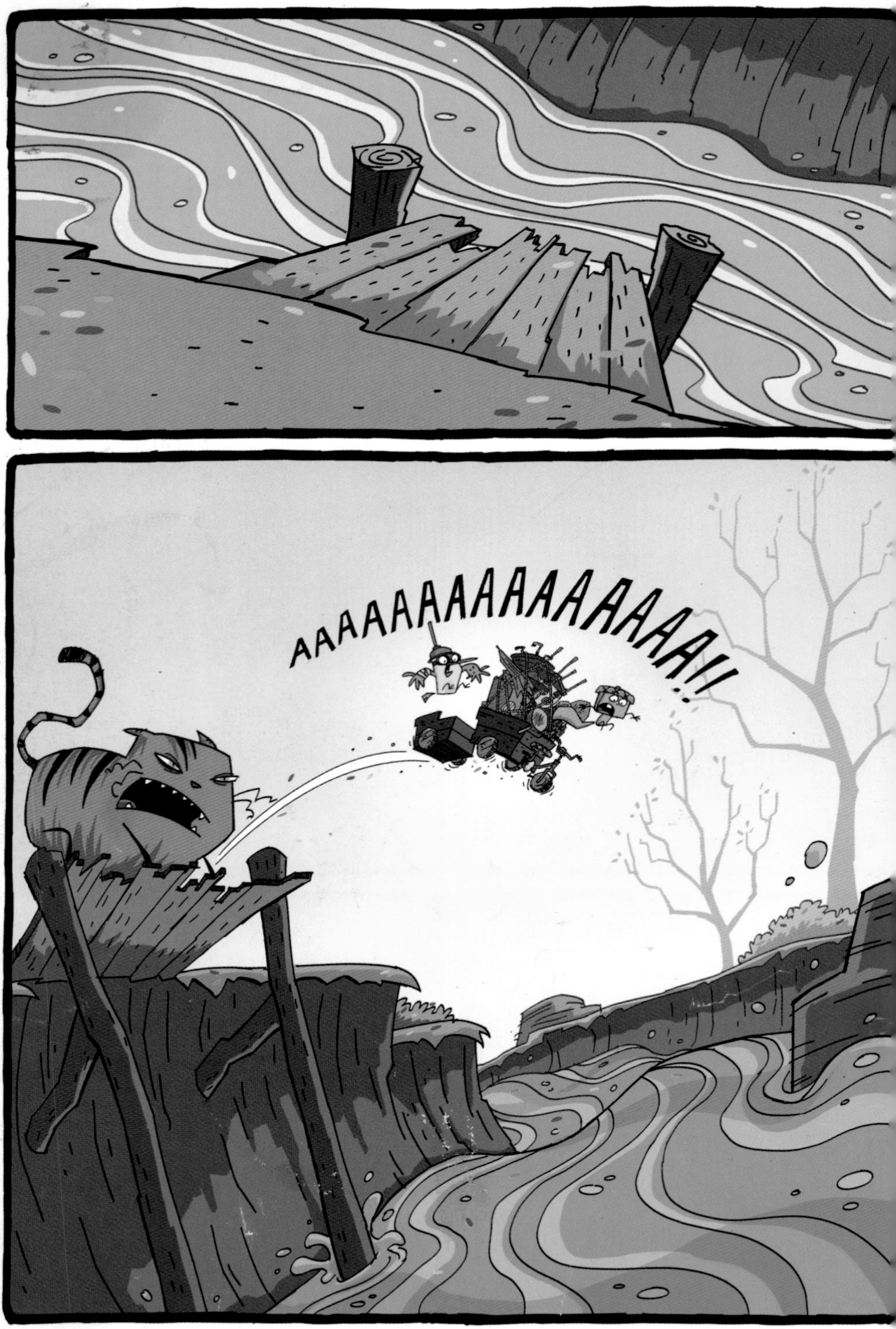
AAAAAAAAAAAAAAAAAAA!!

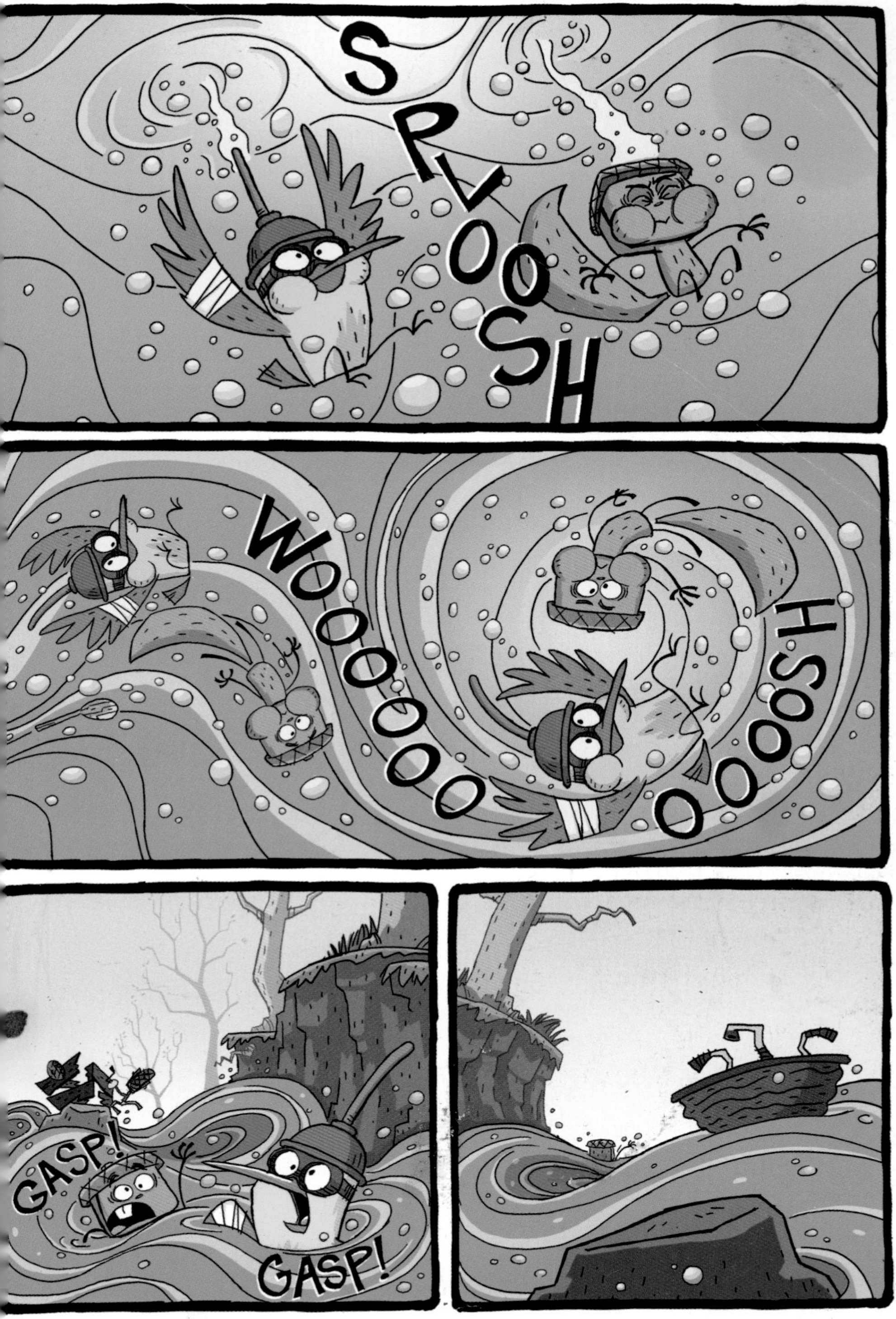
SPLOOSH
WOOOOOOOOOOOSH
GASP!
GASP!

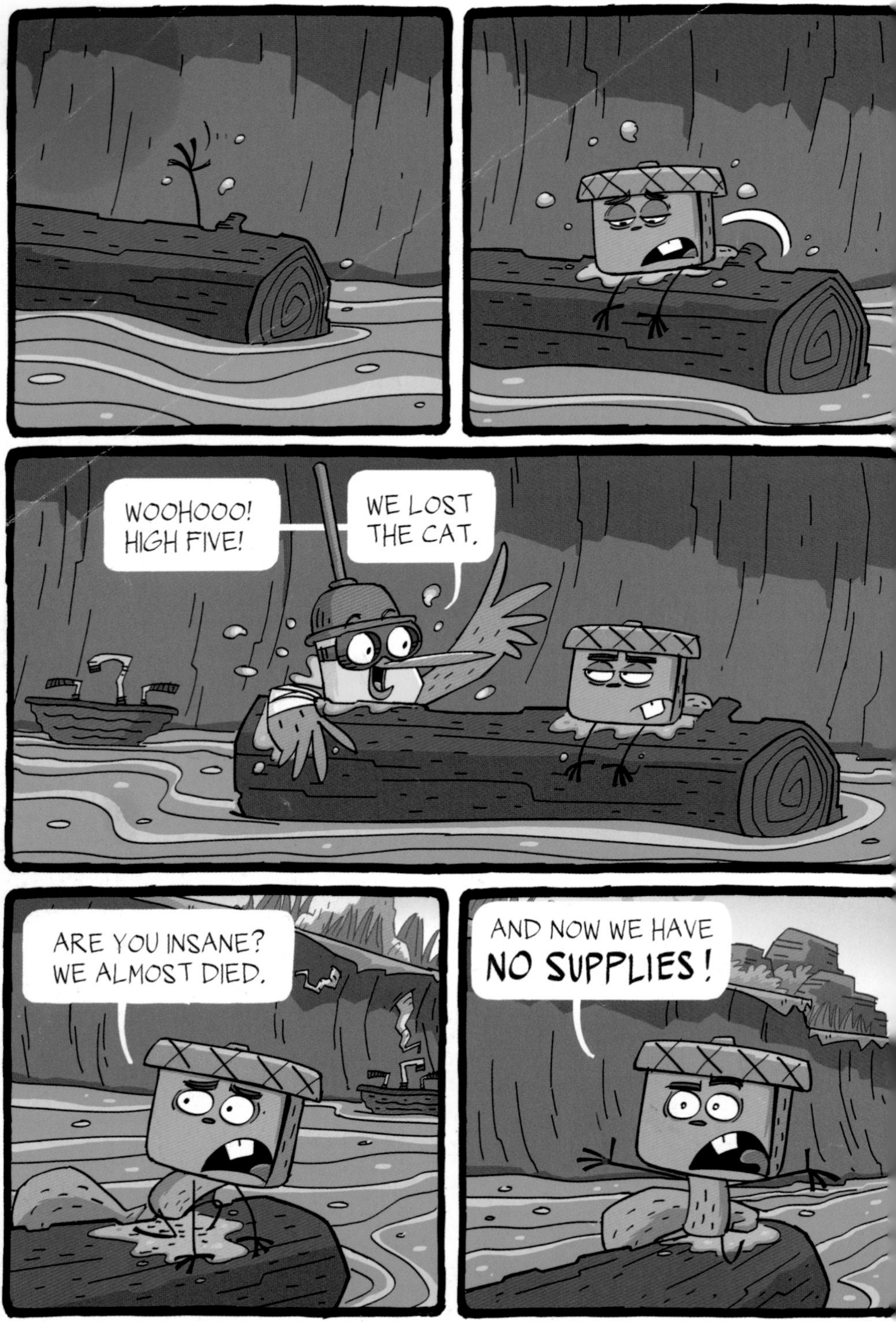
WOOHOOO! HIGH FIVE!
WE LOST THE CAT.
ARE YOU INSANE? WE ALMOST DIED.
AND NOW WE HAVE NO SUPPLIES!

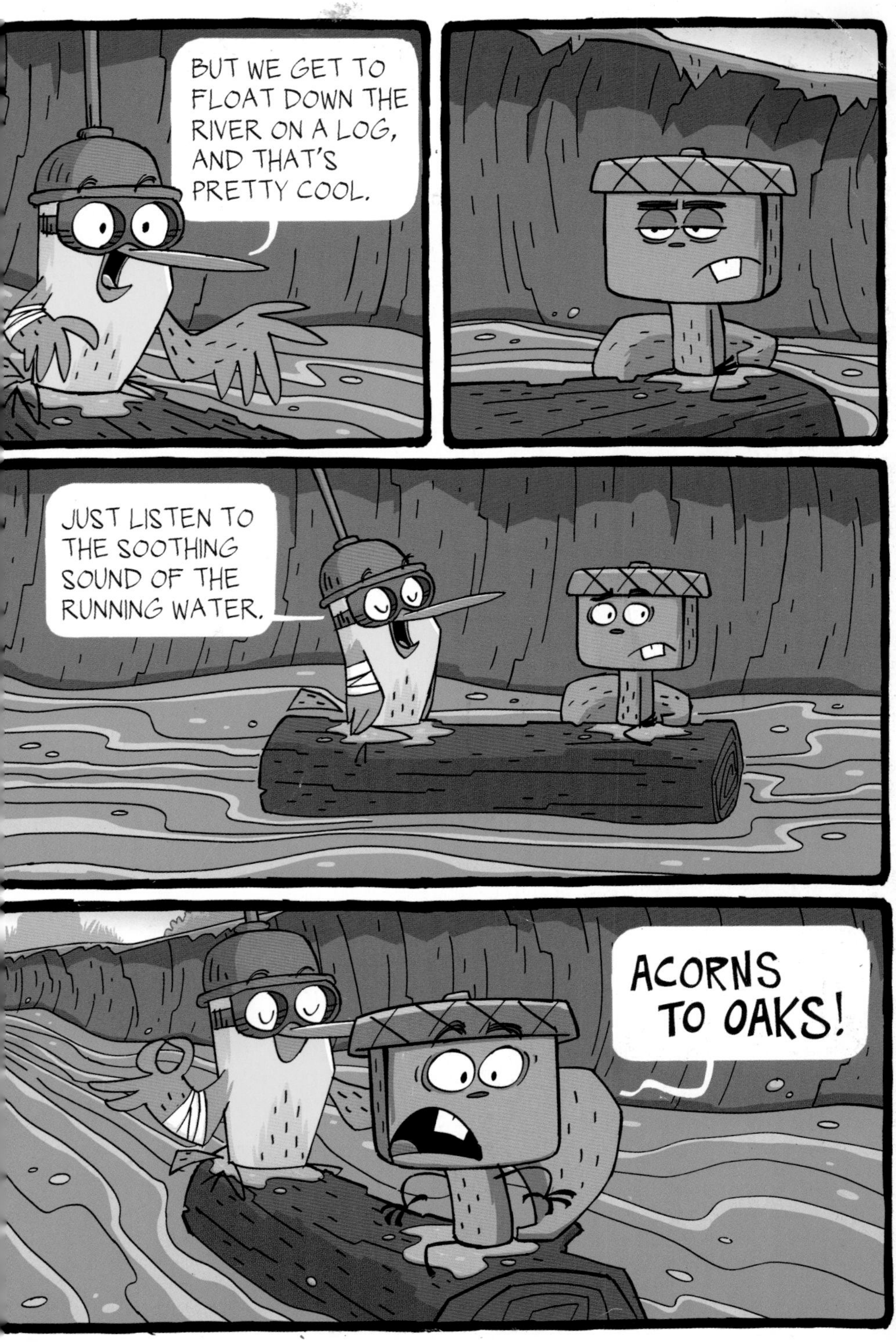
BUT WE GET TO FLOAT DOWN THE RIVER ON A LOG, AND THAT'S PRETTY COOL.
JUST LISTEN TO THE SOOTHING SOUND OF THE RUNNING WATER.
ACORNS TO OAKS!

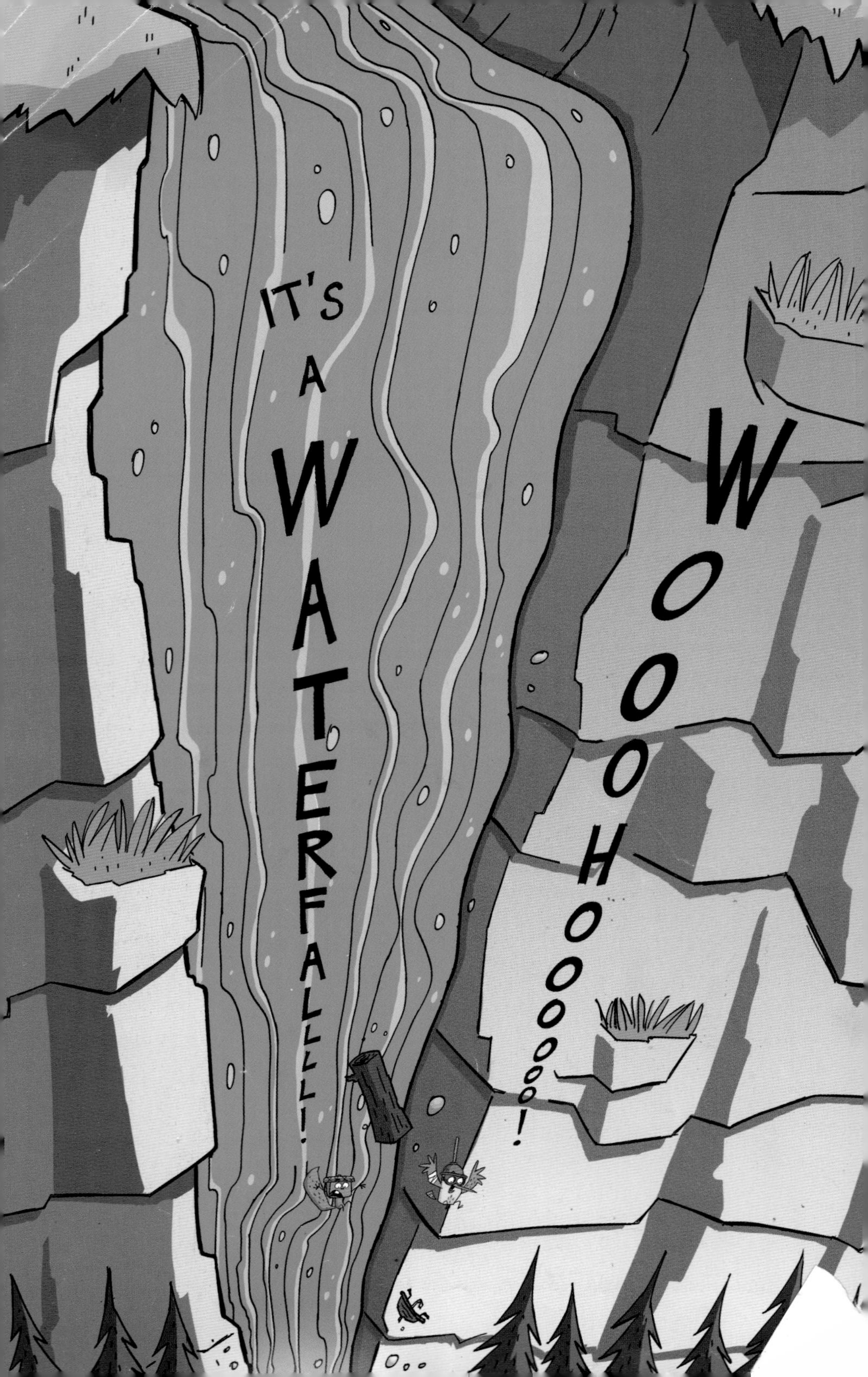
IT'S A WATERFALLLL!
WOOOHOOOOOOOO!

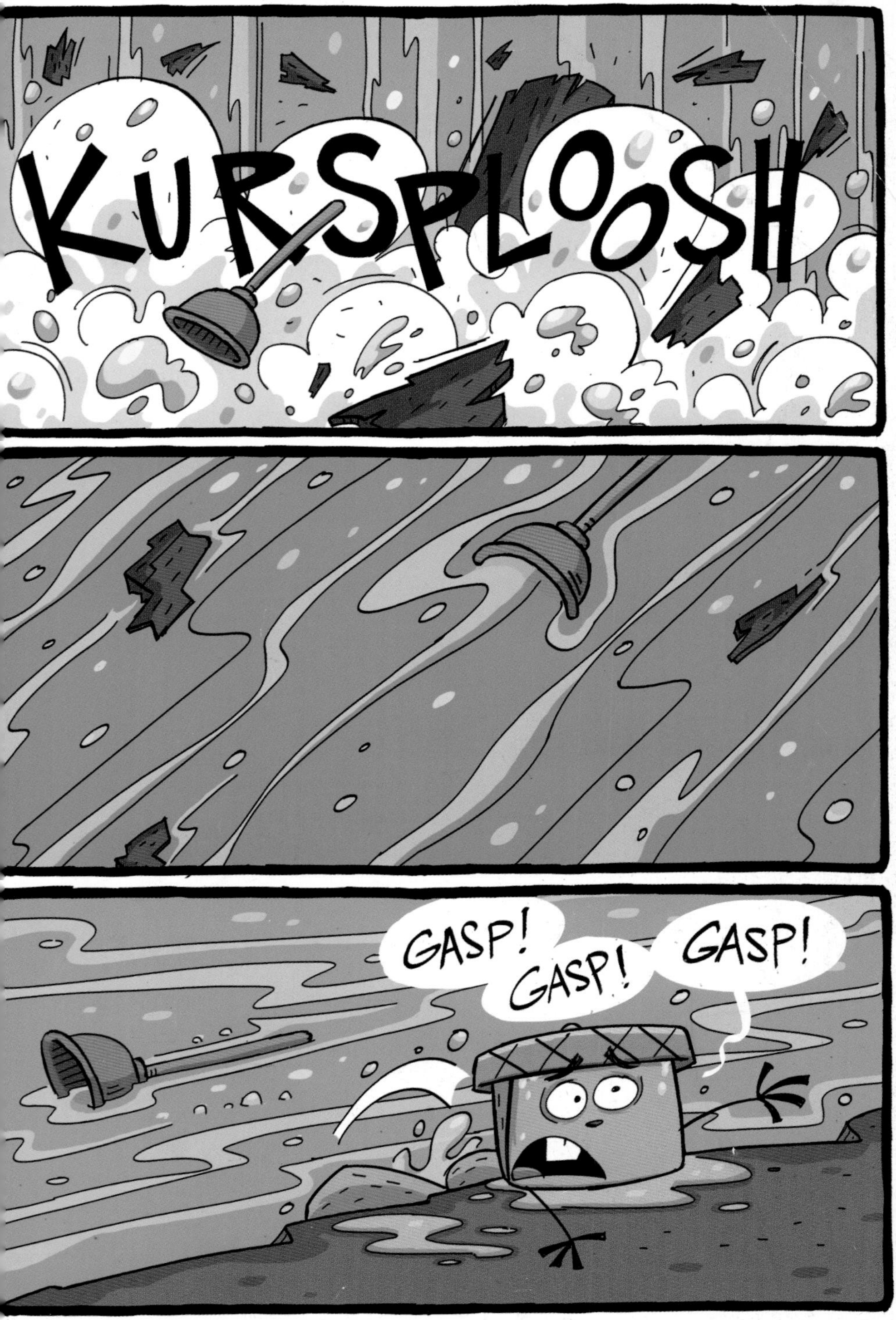
KURSPLOOSH
GASP!
GASP!
GASP!

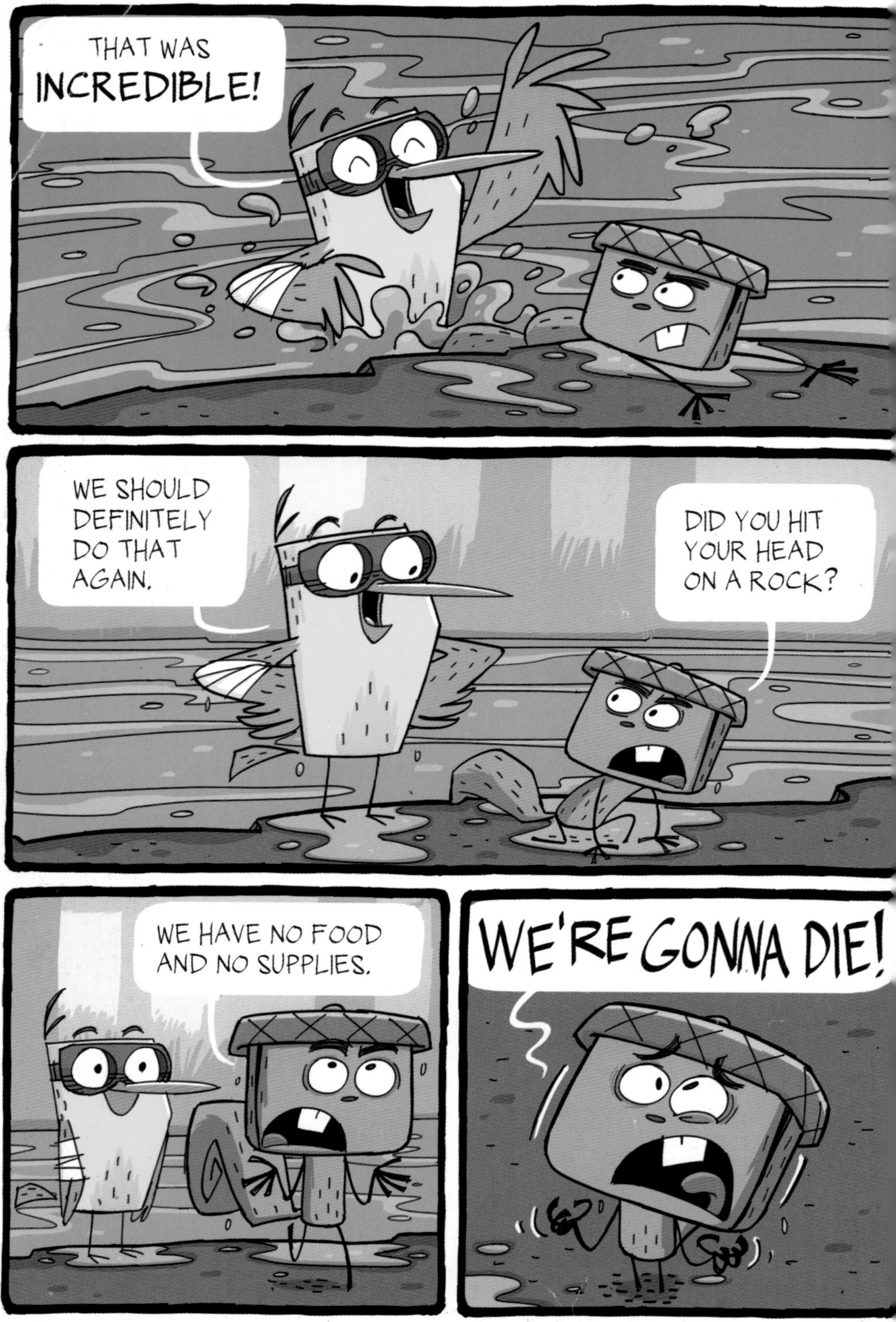
THAT WAS INCREDIBLE!
WE SHOULD DEFINITELY DO THAT AGAIN.
DID YOU HIT YOUR HEAD ON A ROCK?
WE HAVE NO FOOD AND NO SUPPLIES.
WE'RE GONNA DIE!

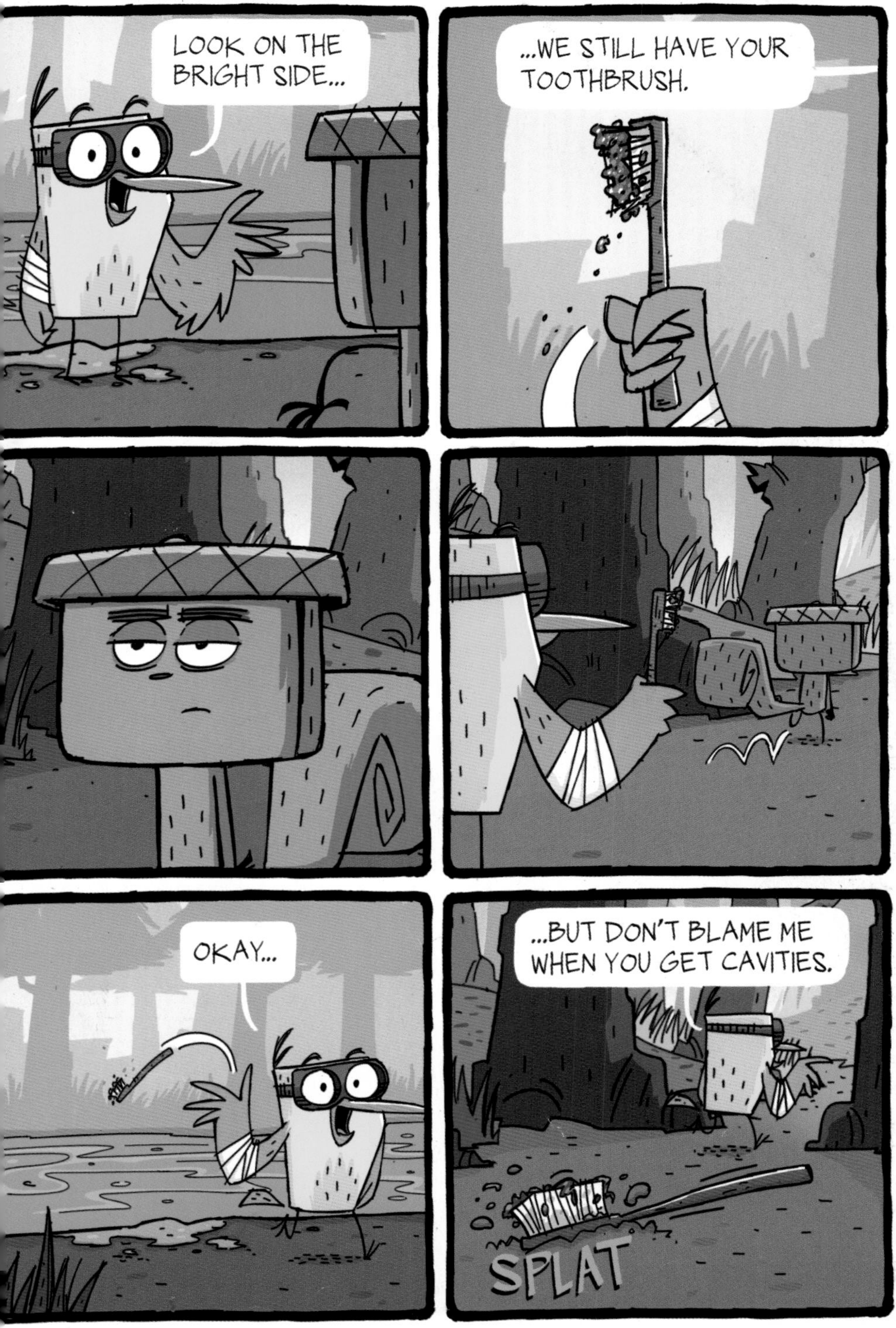
LOOK ON THE BRIGHT SIDE...
...WE STILL HAVE YOUR TOOTHBRUSH.
OKAY...
...BUT DON'T BLAME ME WHEN YOU GET CAVITIES.
SPLAT

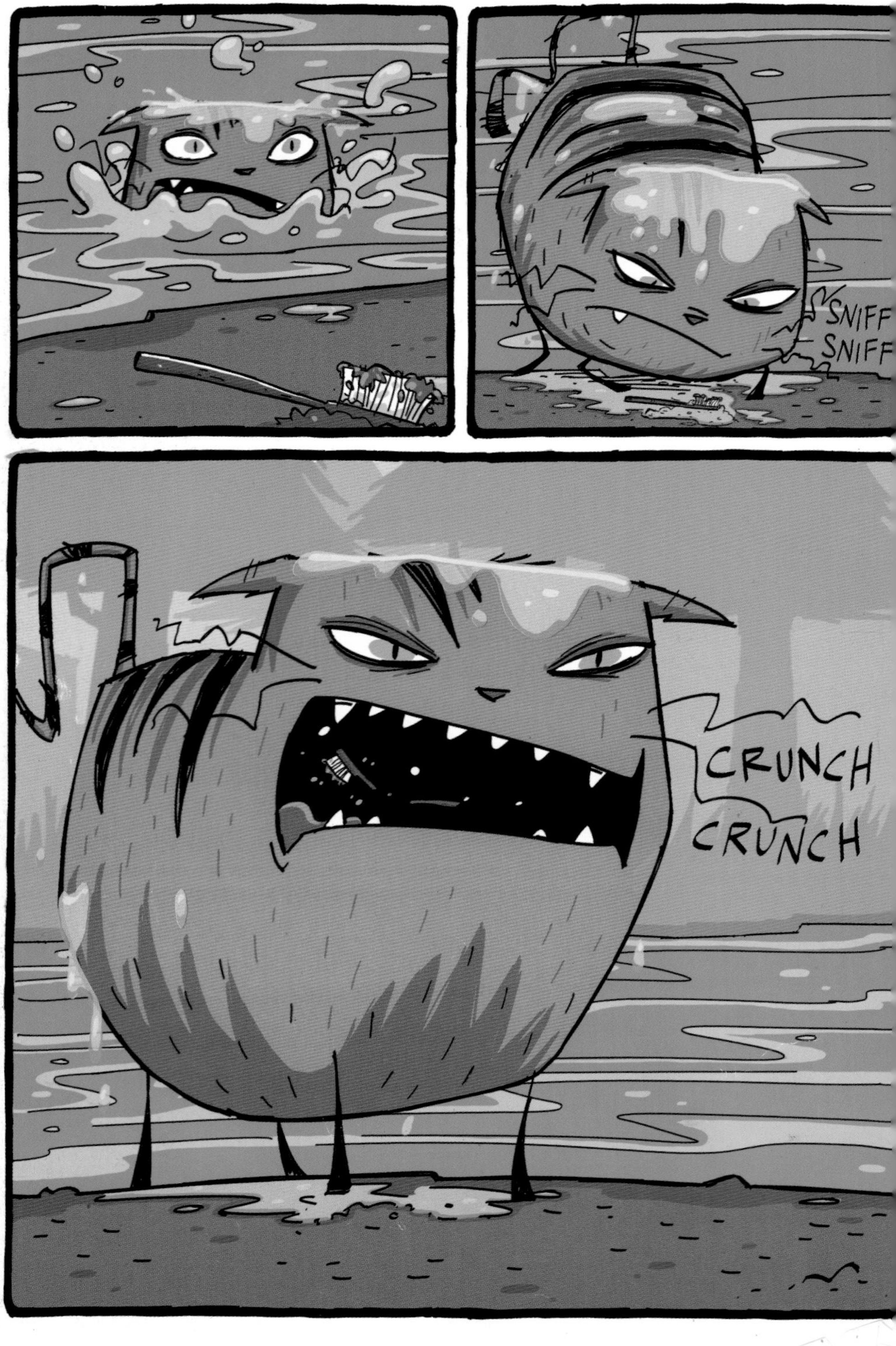
SNIFF
SNIFF
CRUNCH
CRUNCH

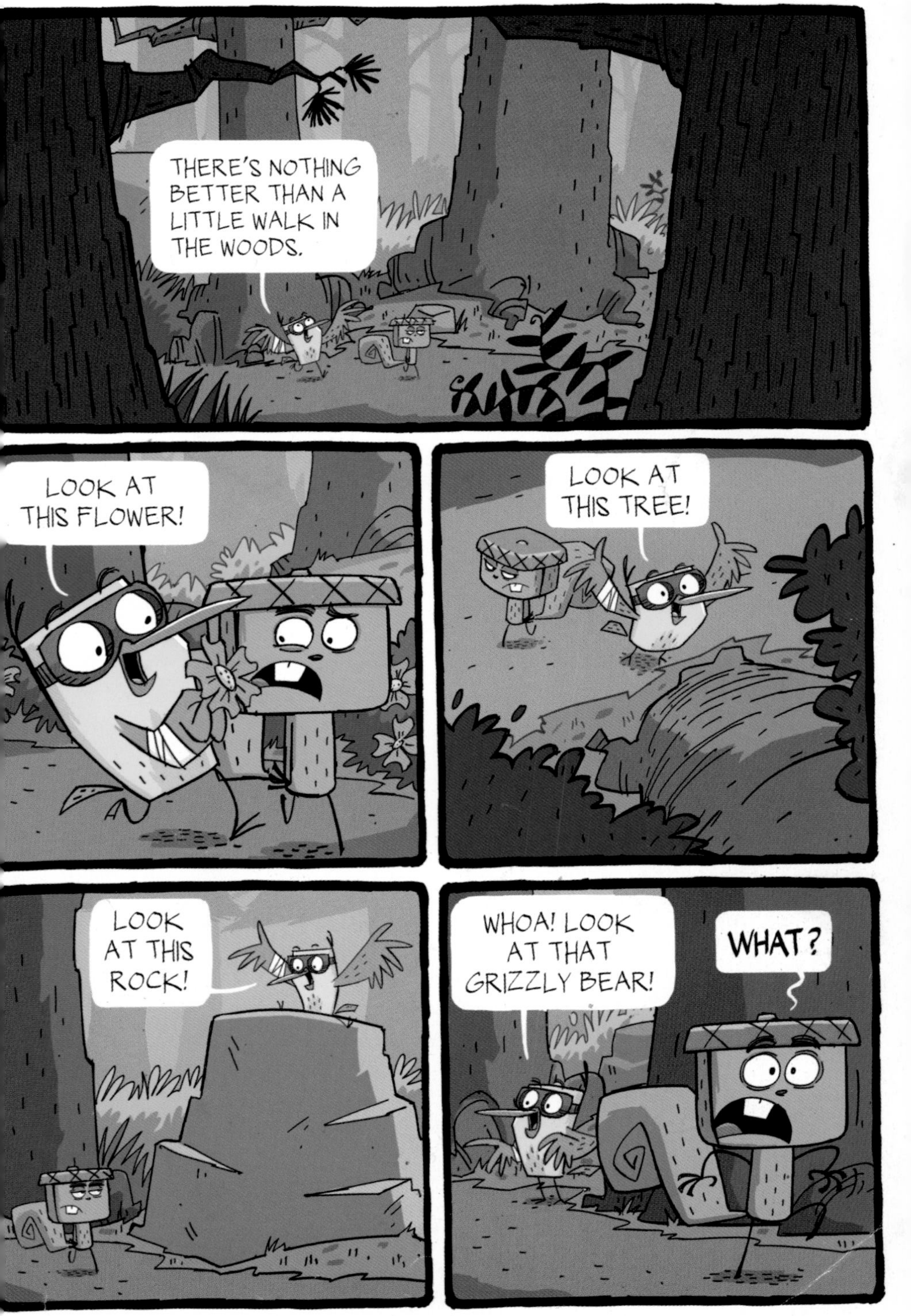
THERE'S NOTHING BETTER THAN A LITTLE WALK IN THE WOODS.
LOOK AT THIS FLOWER!
LOOK AT THIS TREE!
LOOK AT THIS ROCK!
WHOA! LOOK AT THAT GRIZZLY BEAR!
WHAT?

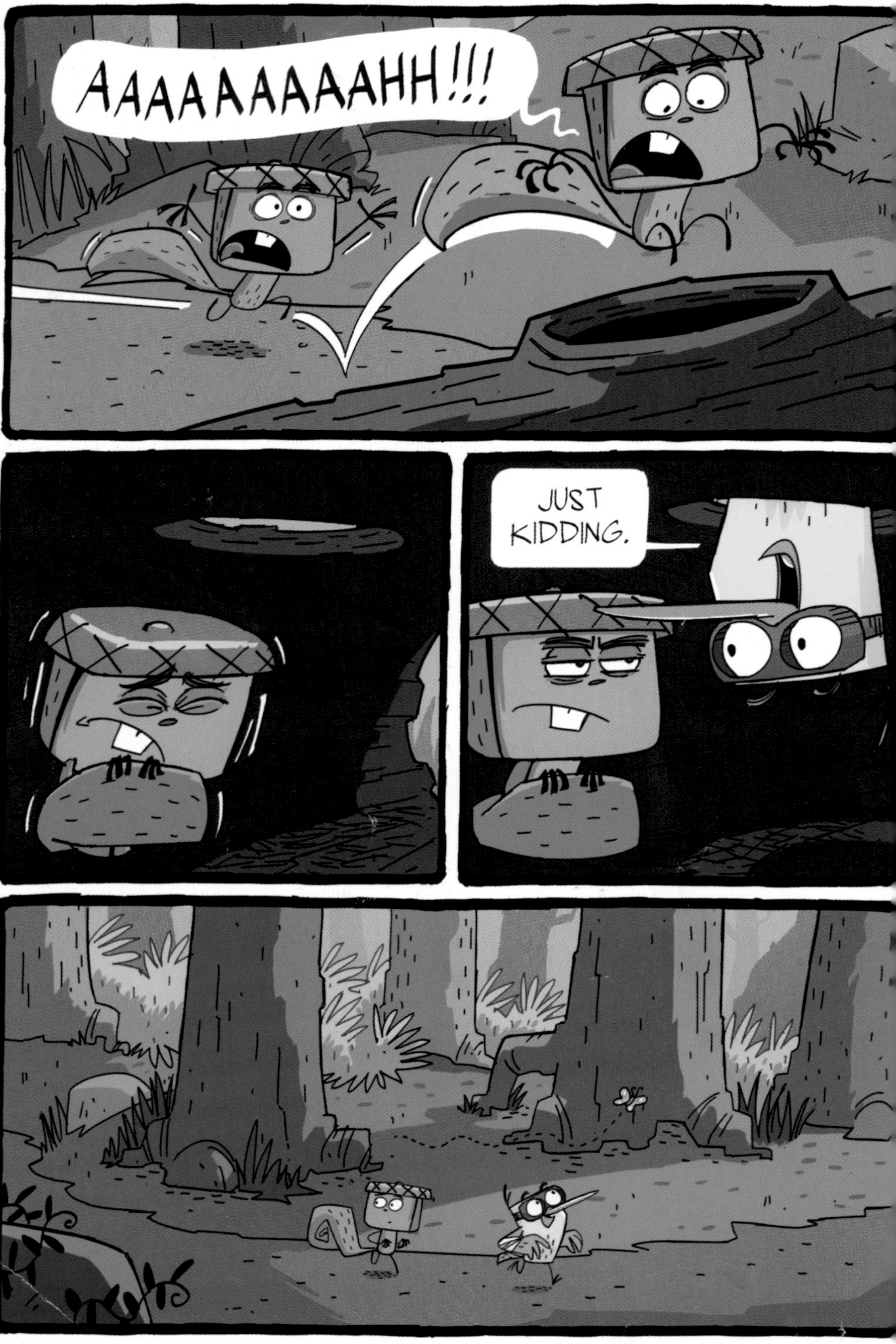
AAAAAAAAAHH!!!
JUST KIDDING.

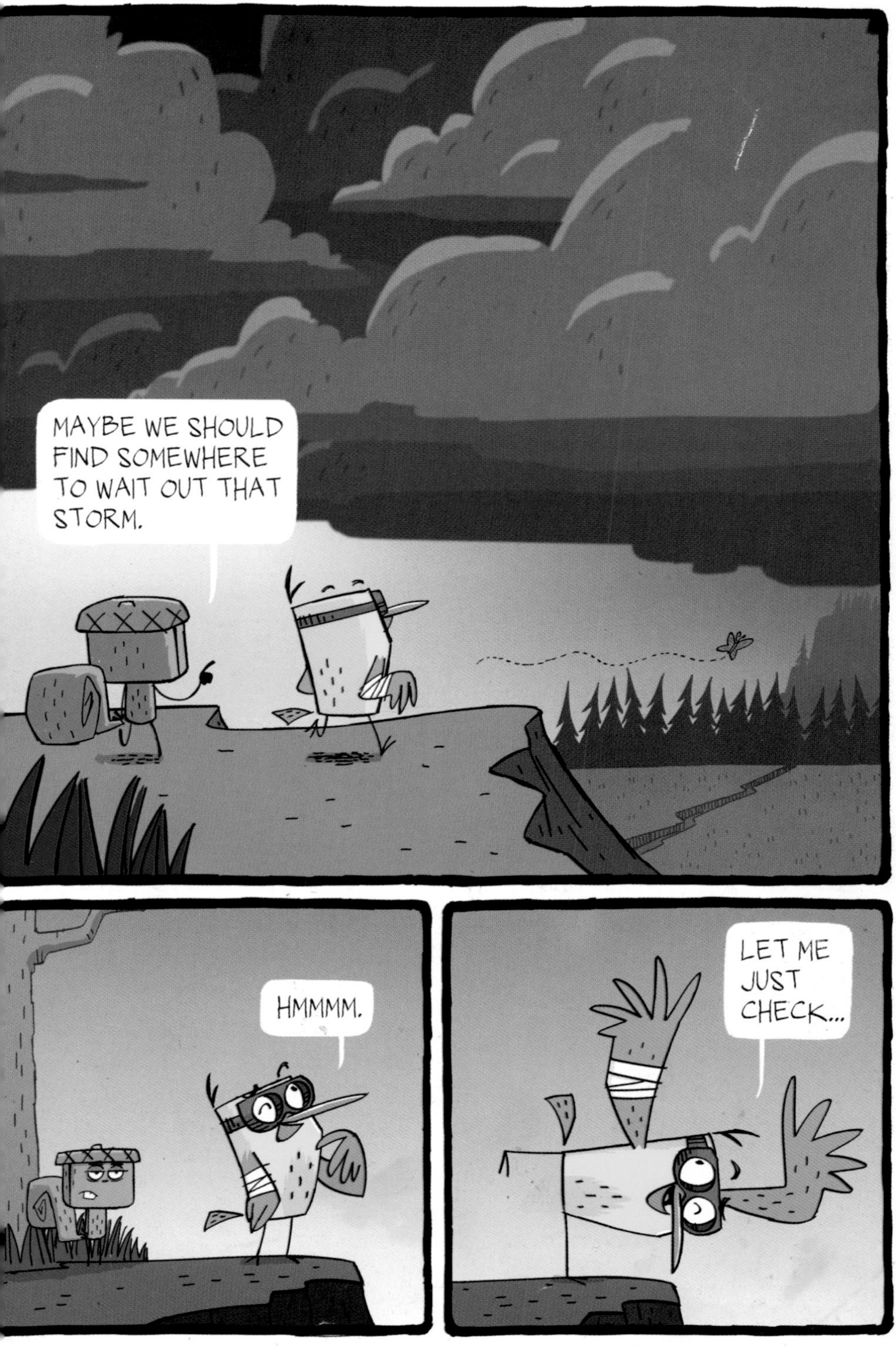
MAYBE WE SHOULD FIND SOMEWHERE TO WAIT OUT THAT STORM.
HMMMM.
LET ME JUST CHECK...

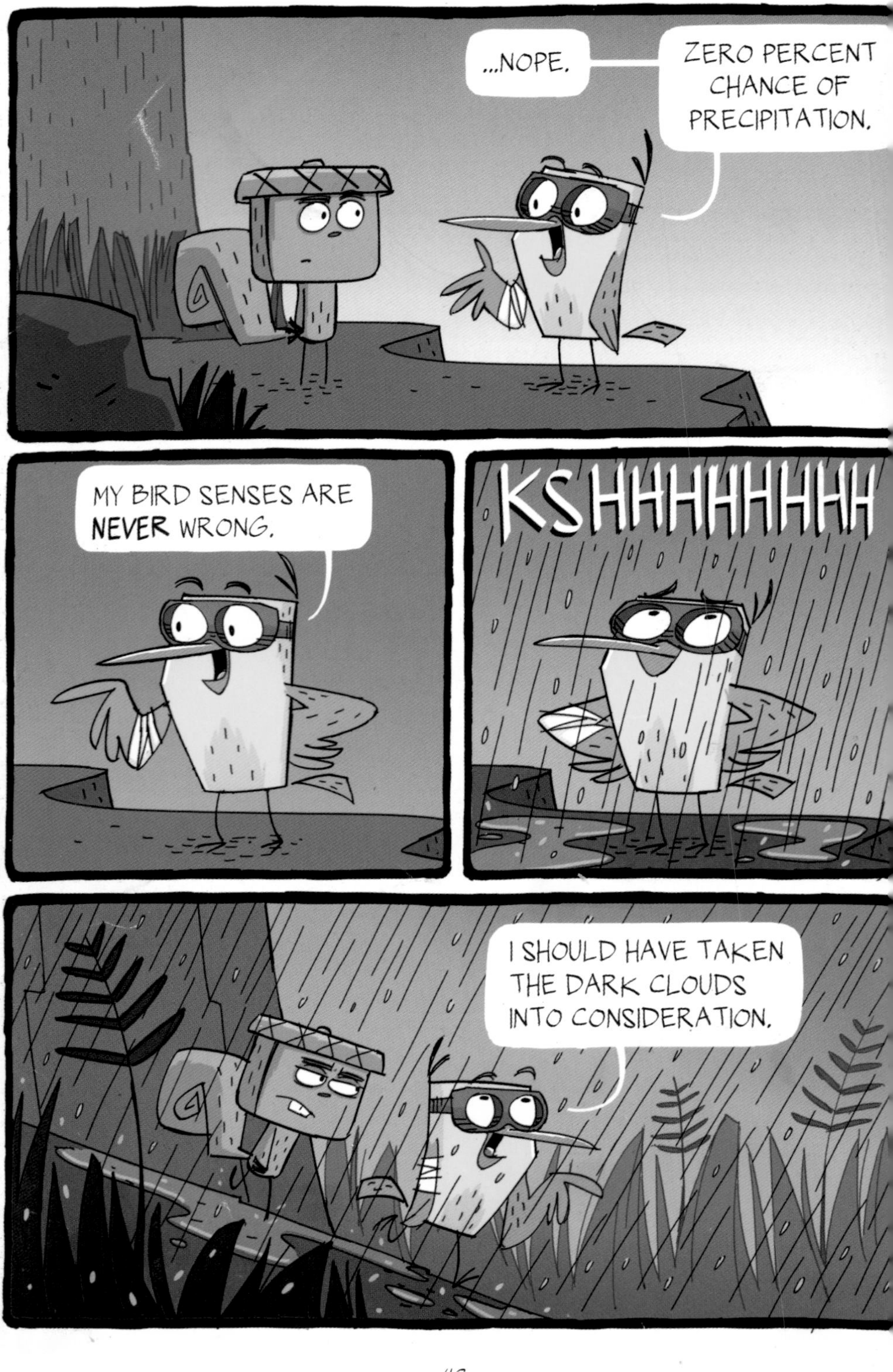
...NOPE.
ZERO PERCENT CHANCE OF PRECIPITATION.
MY BIRD SENSES ARE **NEVER** WRONG.
KSHHHHHHHH
I SHOULD HAVE TAKEN THE DARK CLOUDS INTO CONSIDERATION.

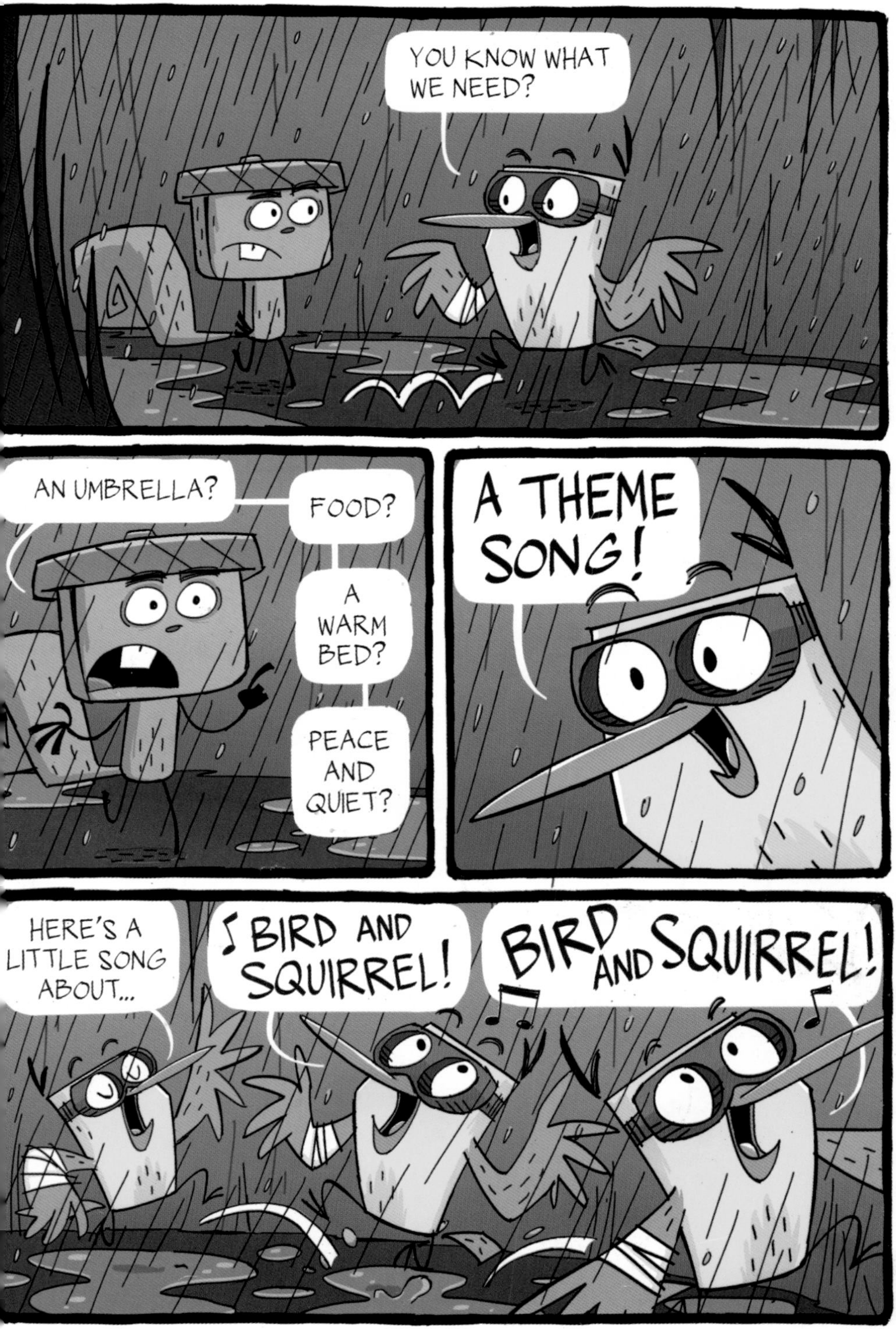
YOU KNOW WHAT WE NEED?
AN UMBRELLA?
FOOD?
A WARM BED?
PEACE AND QUIET?
A THEME SONG!
HERE'S A LITTLE SONG ABOUT...
BIRD AND SQUIRREL!
BIRD AND SQUIRREL!

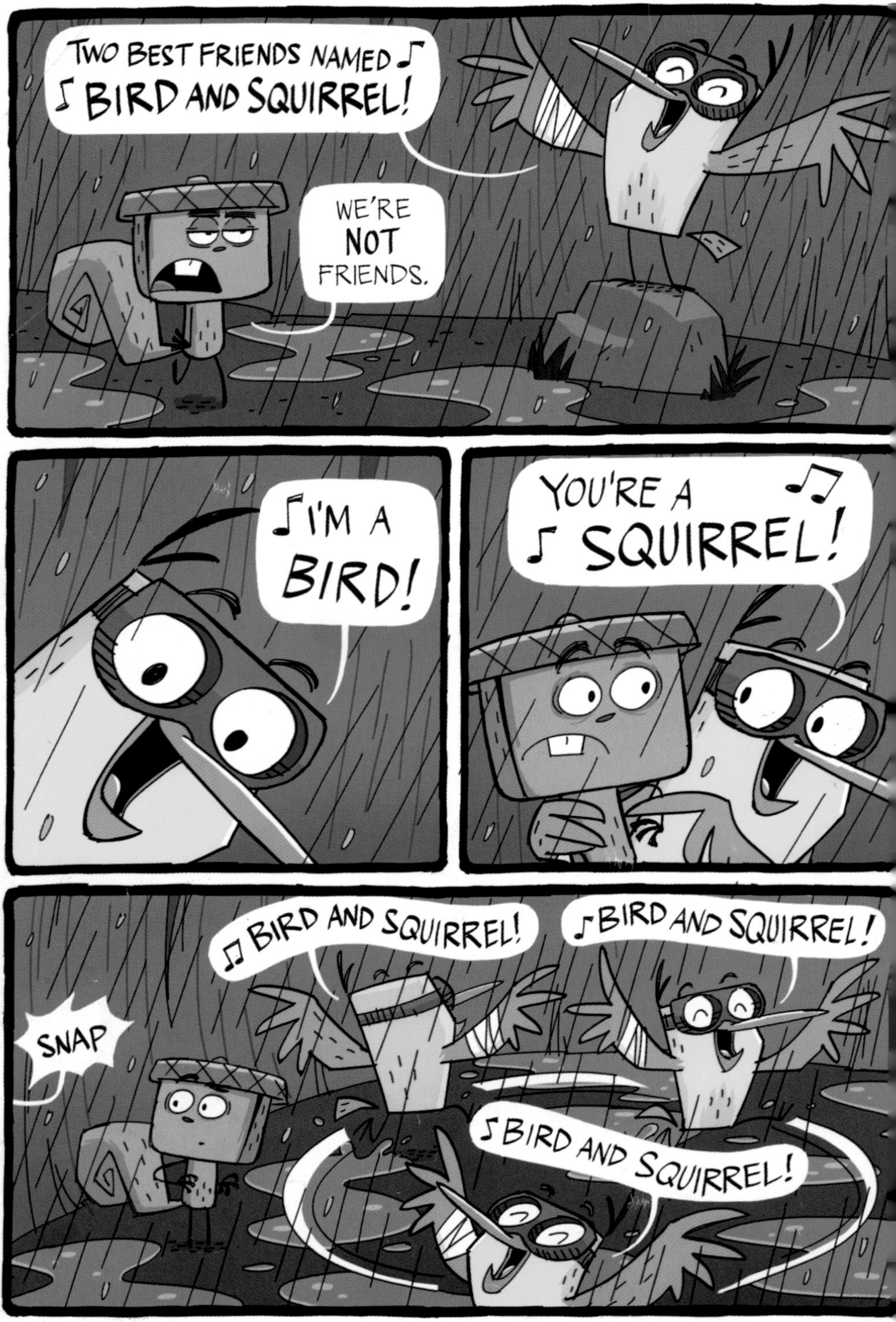
TWO BEST FRIENDS NAMED BIRD AND SQUIRREL!
WE'RE NOT FRIENDS.
I'M A BIRD!
YOU'RE A SQUIRREL!
SNAP
BIRD AND SQUIRREL!
BIRD AND SQUIRREL!
BIRD AND SQUIRREL!

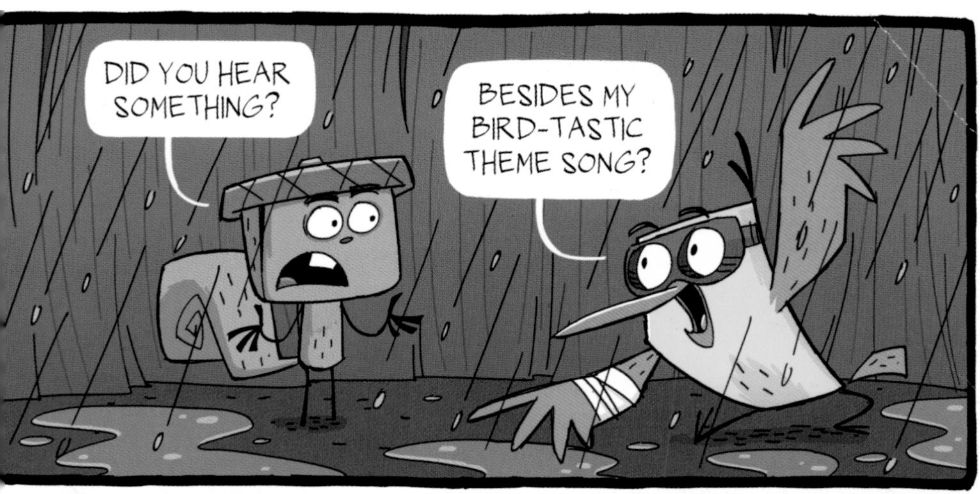
DID YOU HEAR SOMETHING?
BESIDES MY BIRD-TASTIC THEME SONG?

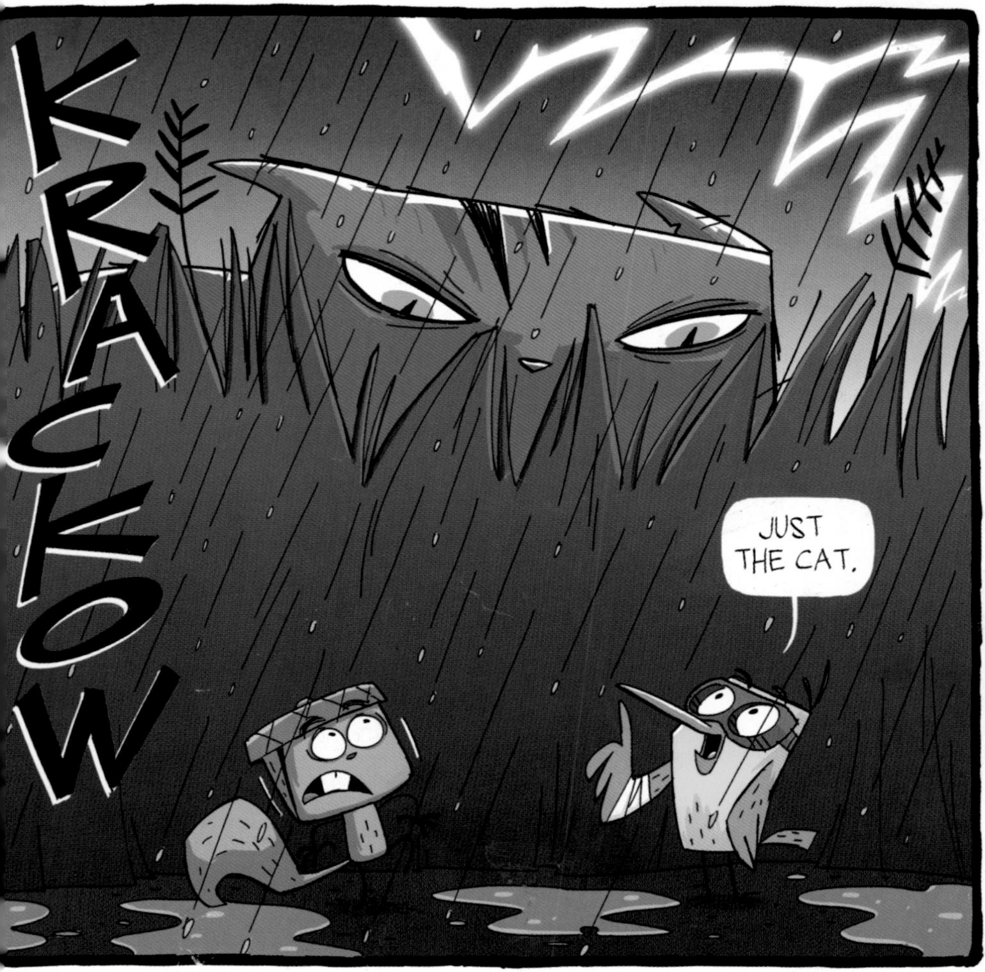
KRACKOW
JUST THE CAT.

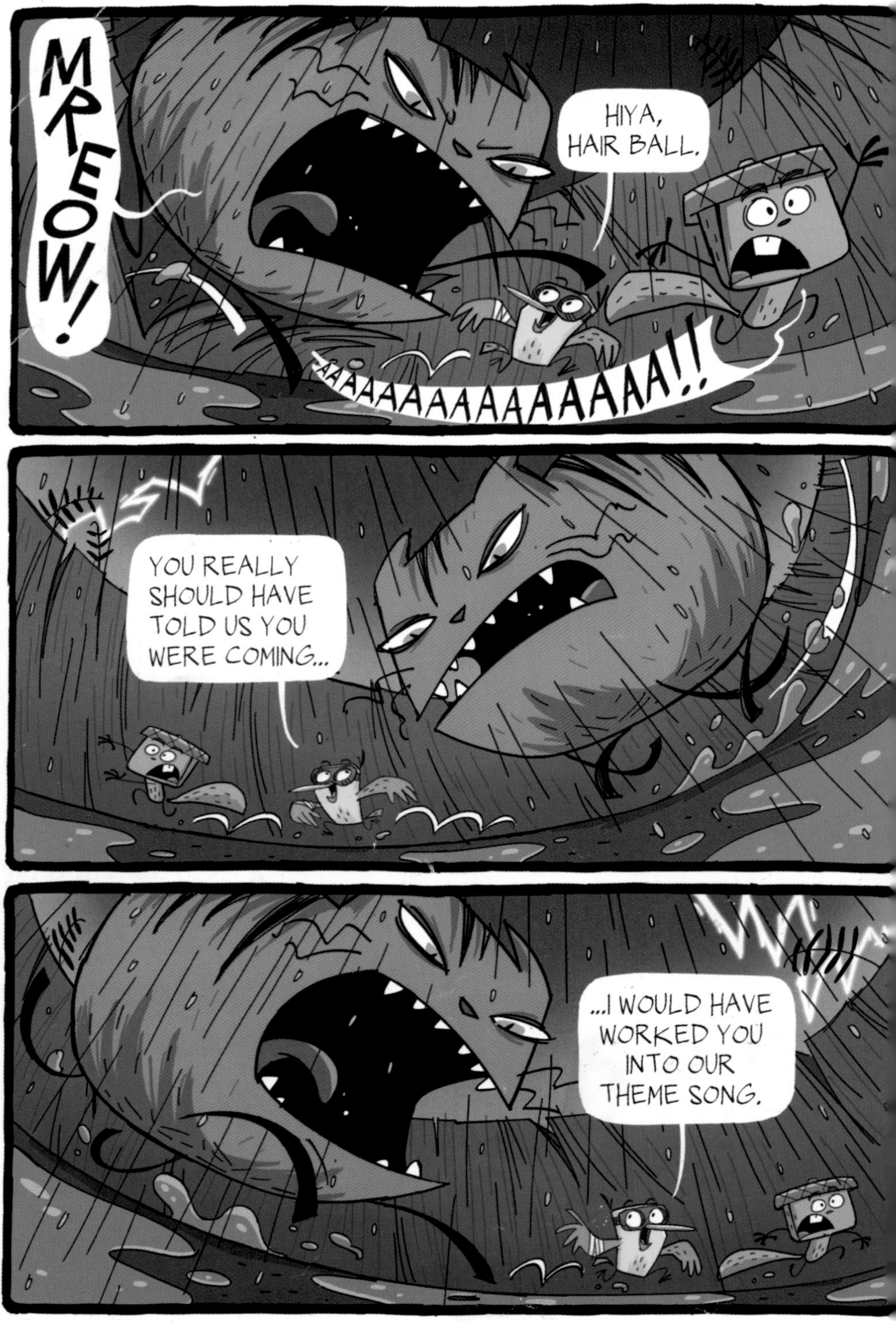
MREOW!
HIYA, HAIR BALL.
AAAAAAAAAAAAAAAAA!!
YOU REALLY SHOULD HAVE TOLD US YOU WERE COMING...
...I WOULD HAVE WORKED YOU INTO OUR THEME SONG.

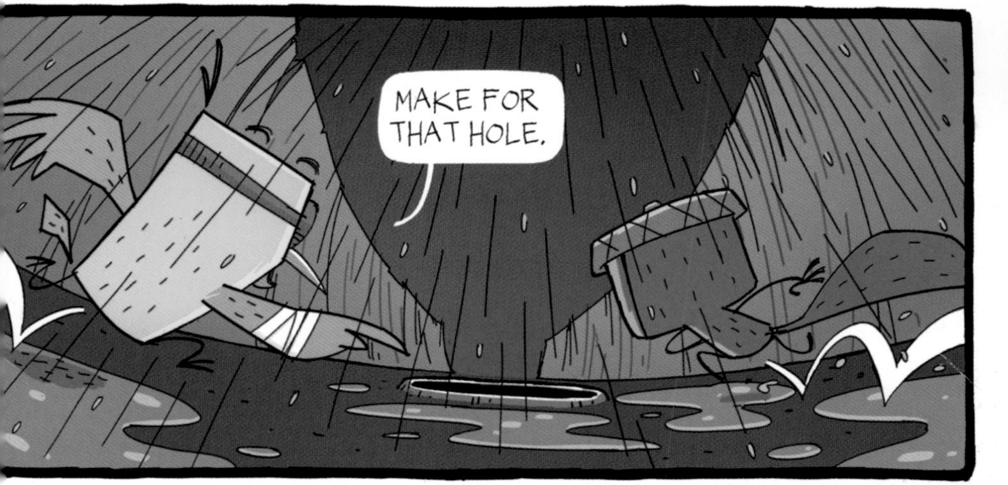
MAKE FOR THAT HOLE.

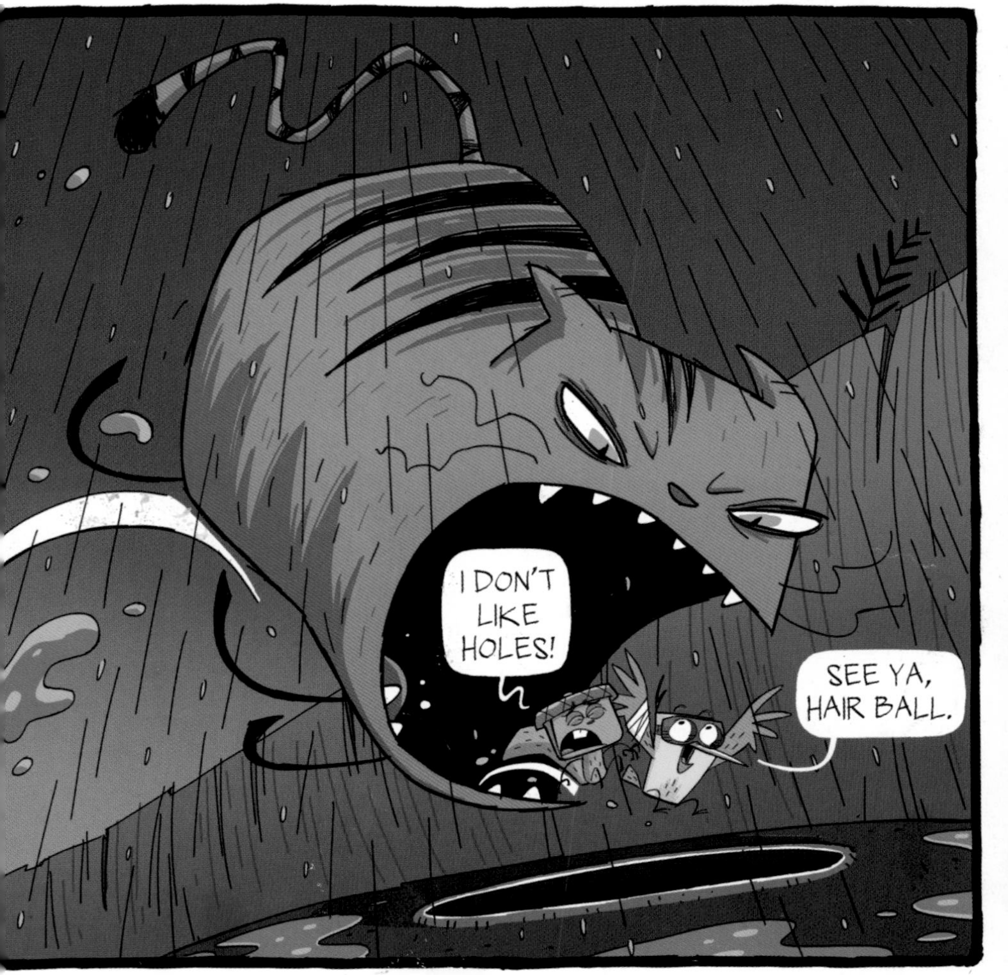
I DON'T LIKE HOLES!
SEE YA, HAIR BALL.

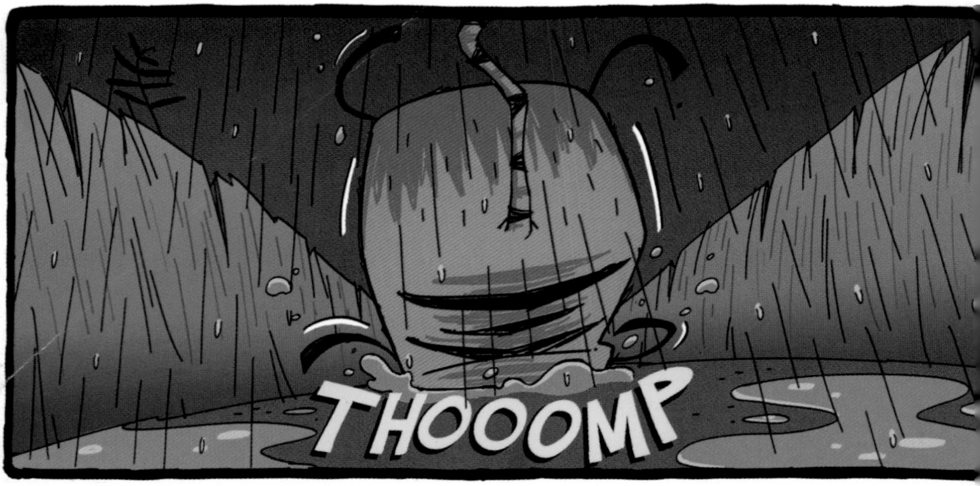
THOOOMP

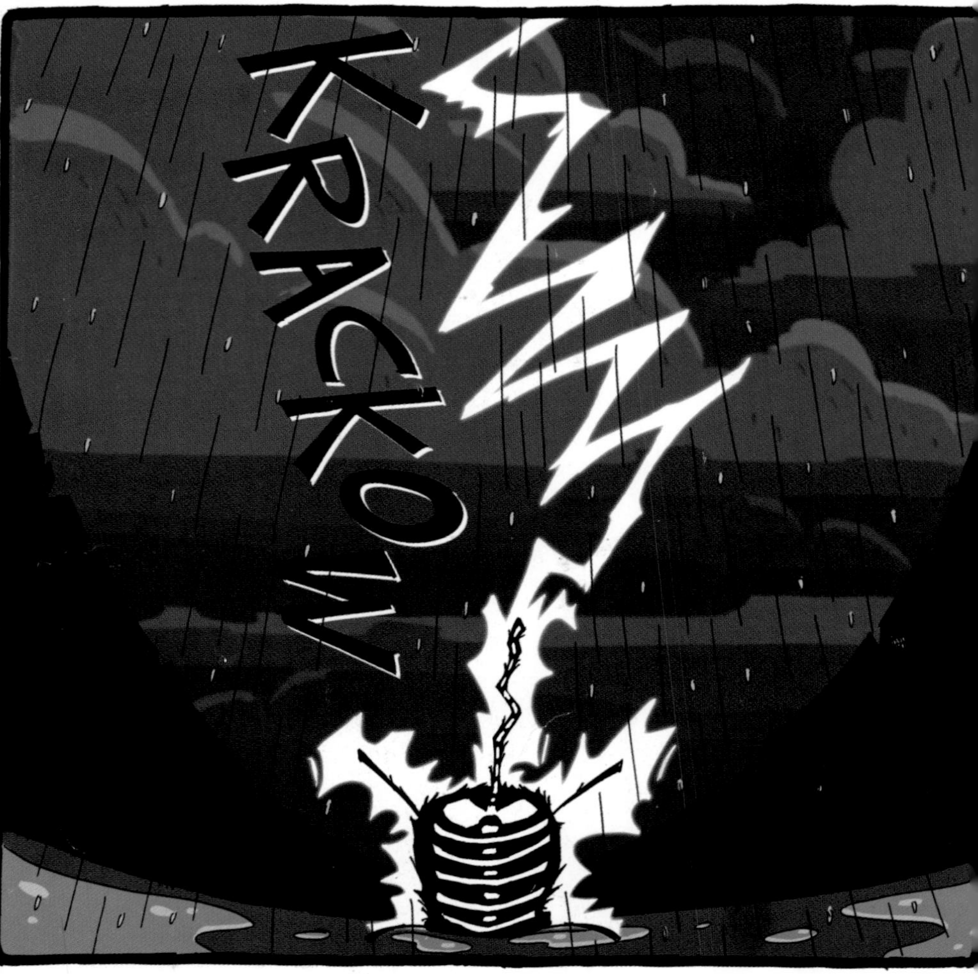
KRACKOW

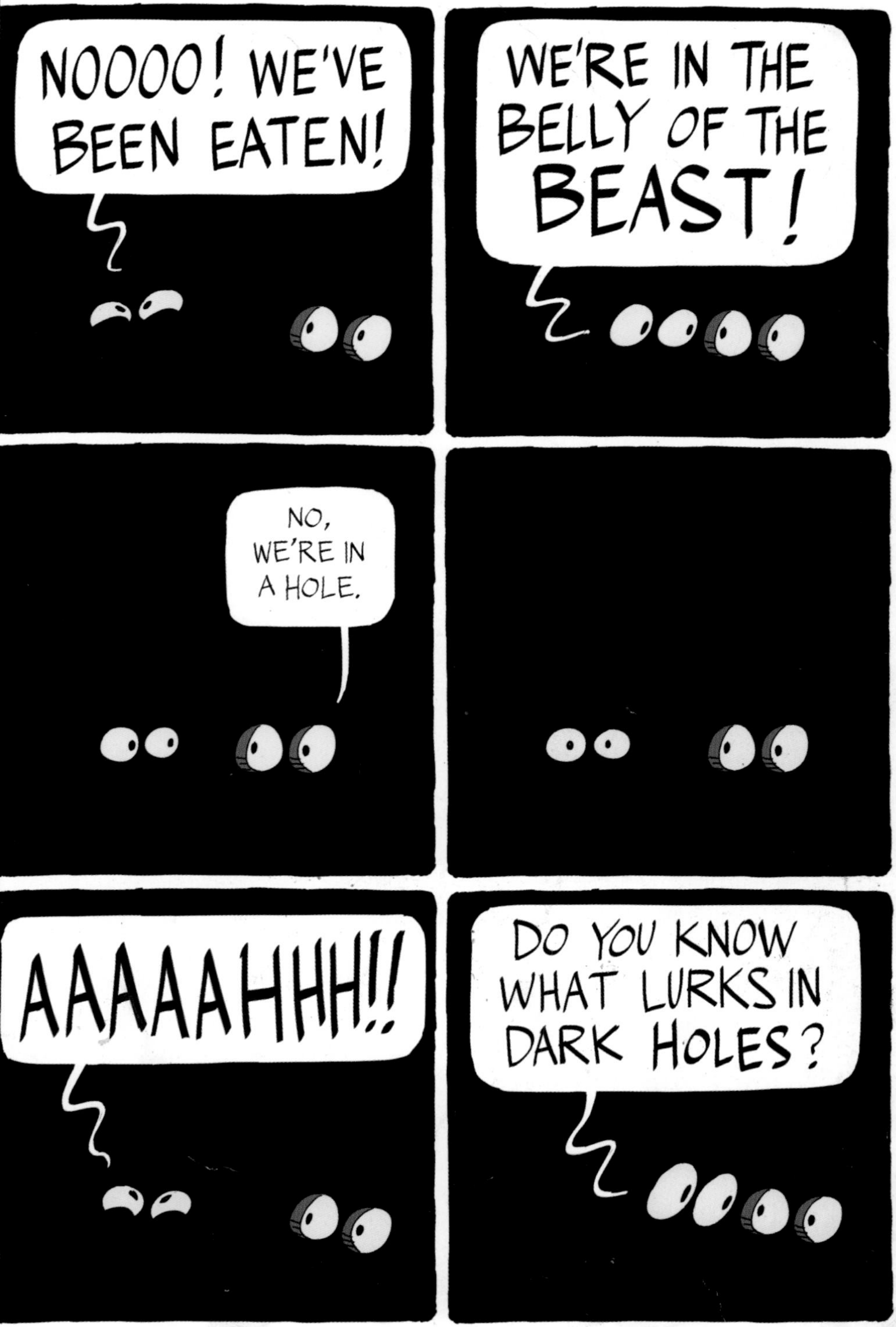
NOOOO! WE'VE BEEN EATEN!
WE'RE IN THE BELLY OF THE BEAST!
NO, WE'RE IN A HOLE.
AAAAAHHH!!
DO YOU KNOW WHAT LURKS IN DARK HOLES?

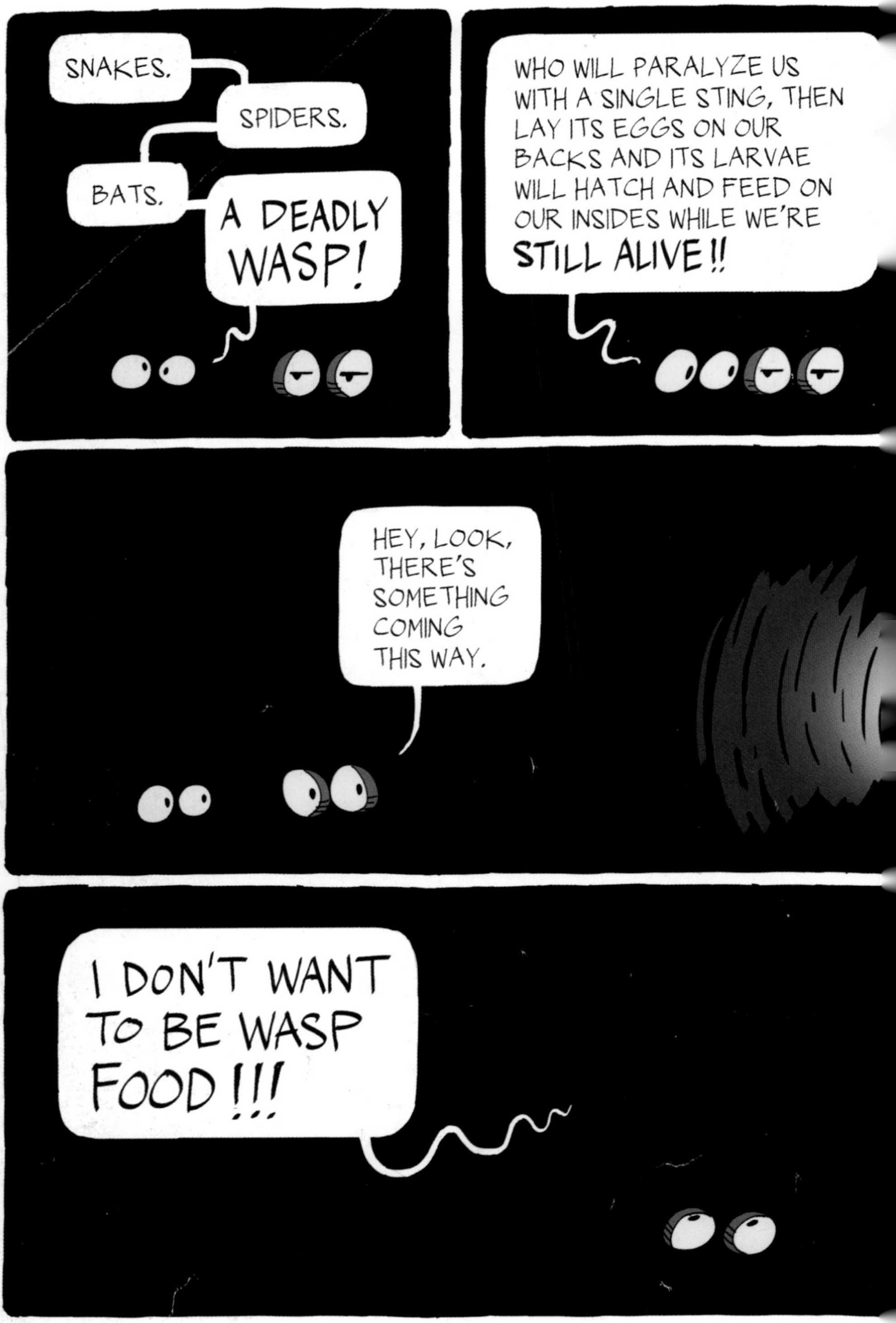
SNAKES.
SPIDERS.
BATS.
A DEADLY WASP!
WHO WILL PARALYZE US WITH A SINGLE STING, THEN LAY ITS EGGS ON OUR BACKS AND ITS LARVAE WILL HATCH AND FEED ON OUR INSIDES WHILE WE'RE STILL ALIVE!!
HEY, LOOK, THERE'S SOMETHING COMING THIS WAY.
I DON'T WANT TO BE WASP FOOD!!!

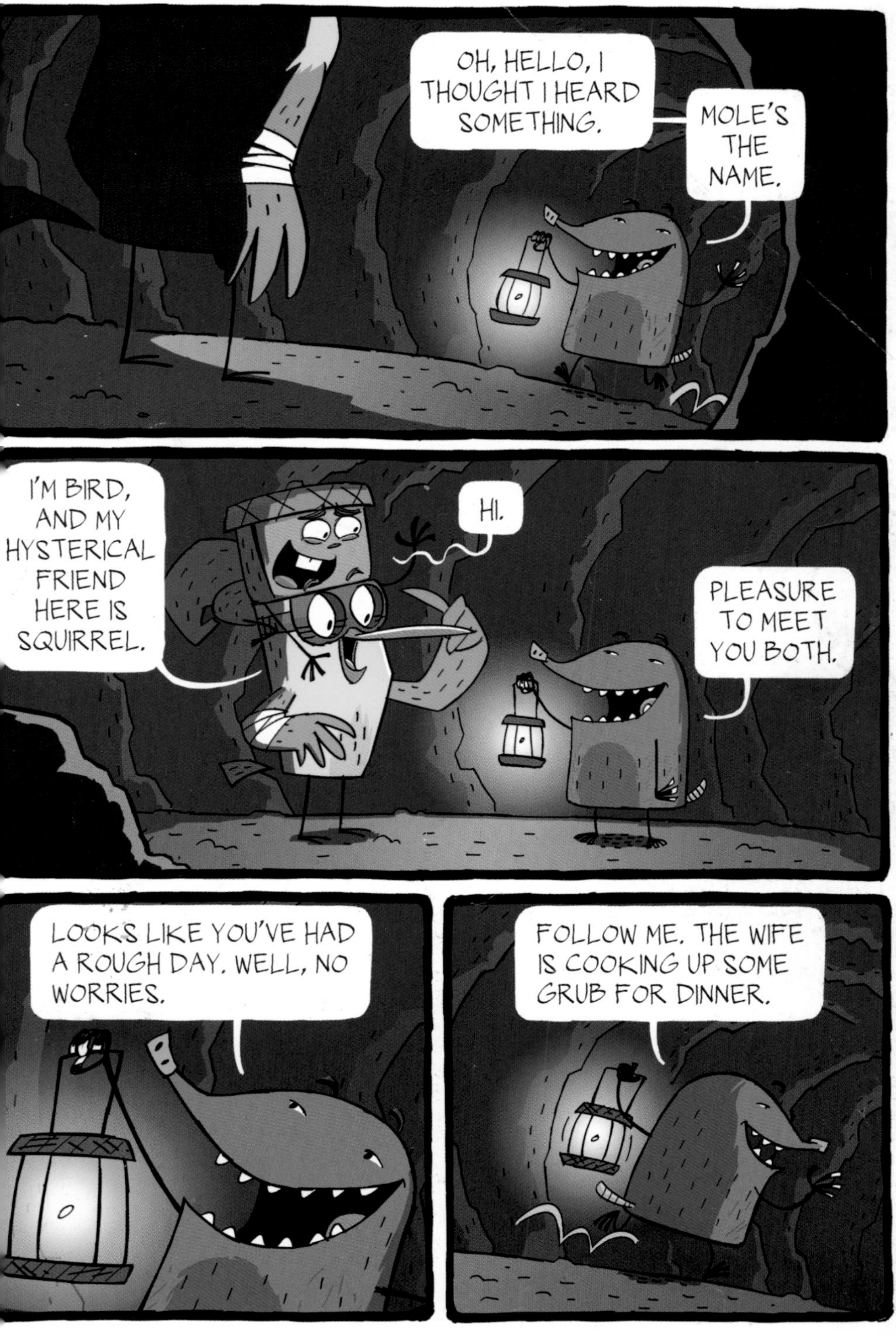
OH, HELLO, I THOUGHT I HEARD SOMETHING.
MOLE'S THE NAME.
I'M BIRD, AND MY HYSTERICAL FRIEND HERE IS SQUIRREL.
HI.
PLEASURE TO MEET YOU BOTH.
LOOKS LIKE YOU'VE HAD A ROUGH DAY. WELL, NO WORRIES.
FOLLOW ME. THE WIFE IS COOKING UP SOME GRUB FOR DINNER.

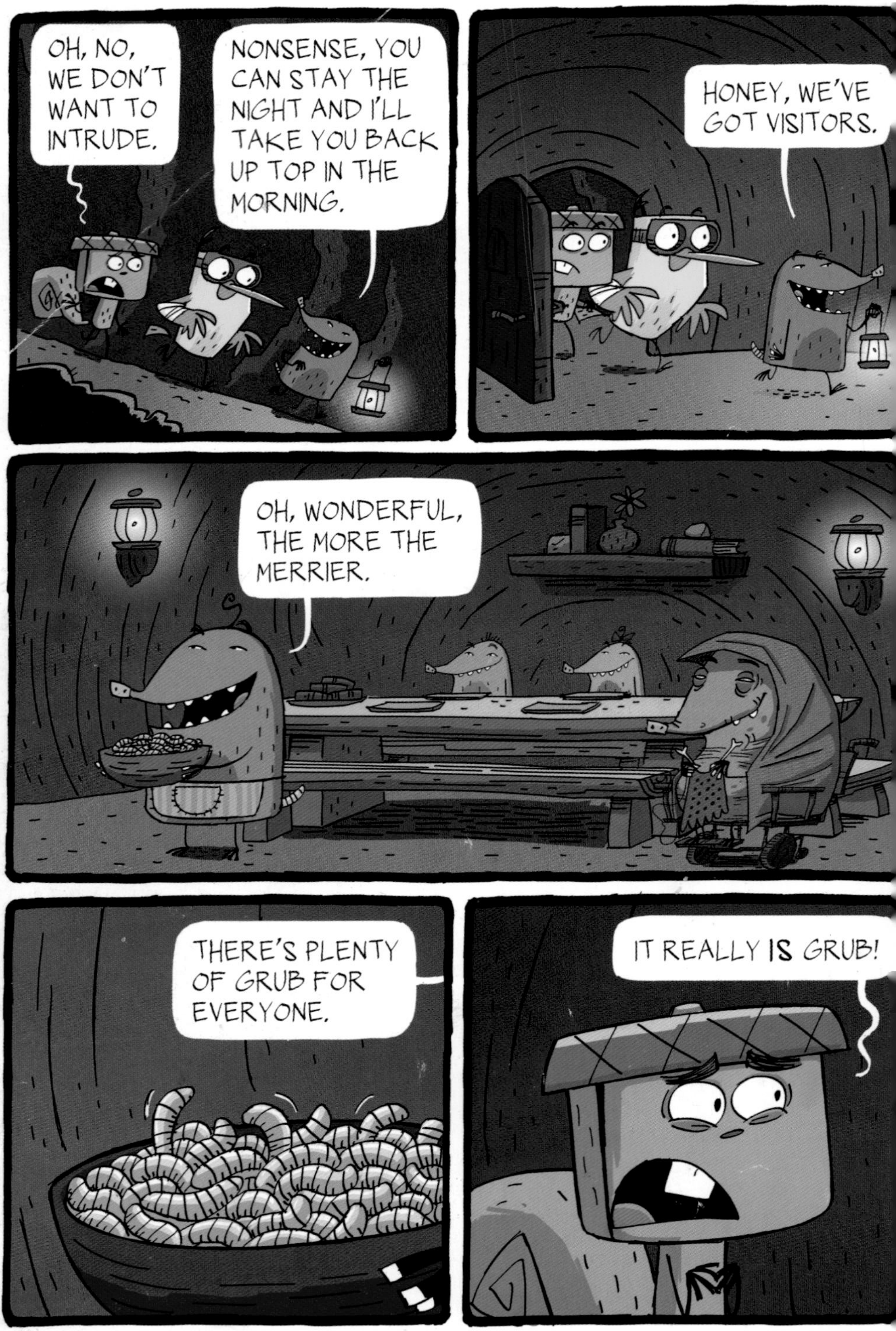
OH, NO, WE DON'T WANT TO INTRUDE.
NONSENSE, YOU CAN STAY THE NIGHT AND I'LL TAKE YOU BACK UP TOP IN THE MORNING.
HONEY, WE'VE GOT VISITORS.
OH, WONDERFUL, THE MORE THE MERRIER.
THERE'S PLENTY OF GRUB FOR EVERYONE.
IT REALLY IS GRUB!

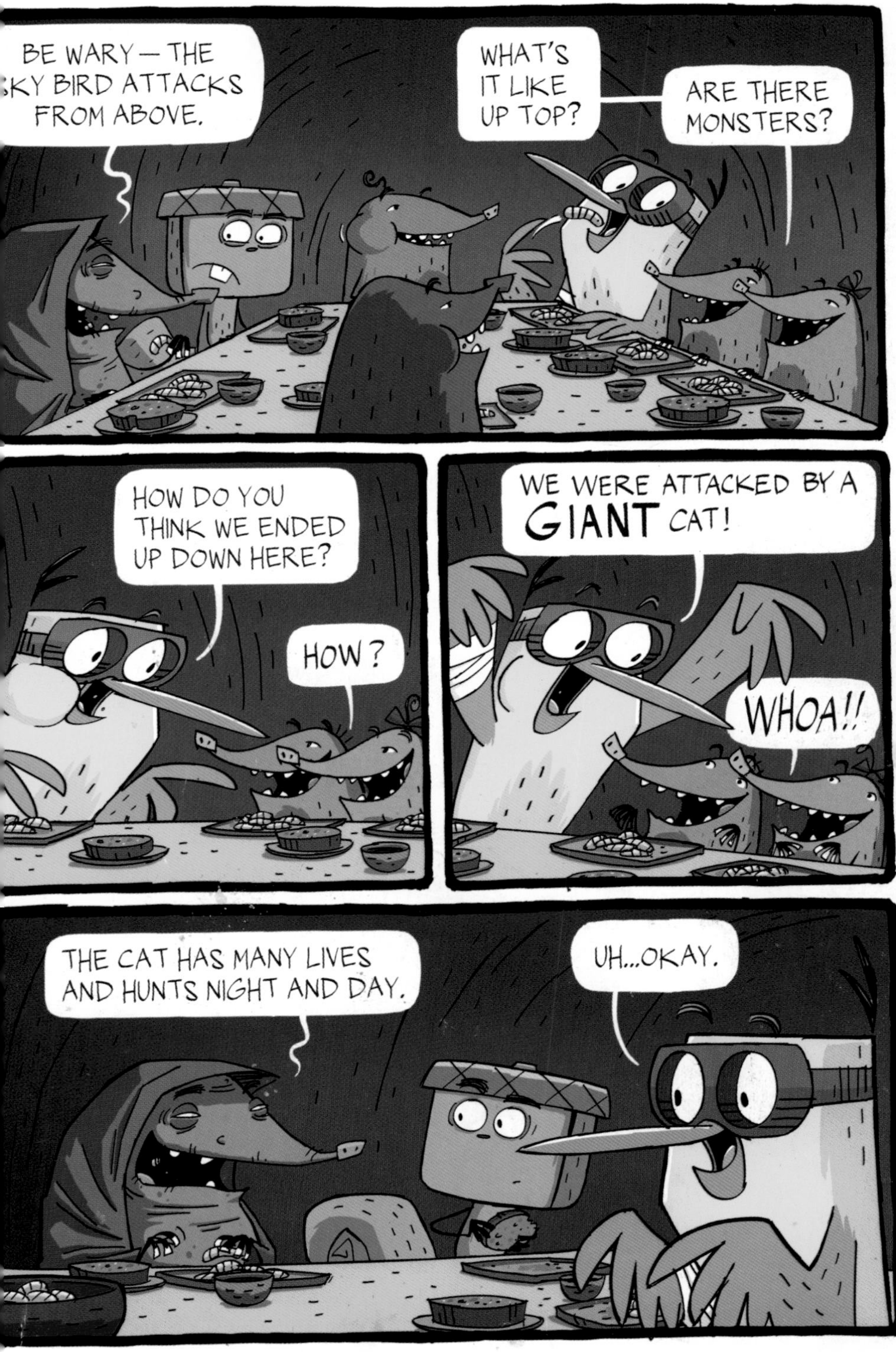
BE WARY — THE SKY BIRD ATTACKS FROM ABOVE.
WHAT'S IT LIKE UP TOP?
ARE THERE MONSTERS?
HOW DO YOU THINK WE ENDED UP DOWN HERE?
HOW?
WE WERE ATTACKED BY A GIANT CAT!
WHOA!!
THE CAT HAS MANY LIVES AND HUNTS NIGHT AND DAY.
UH...OKAY.

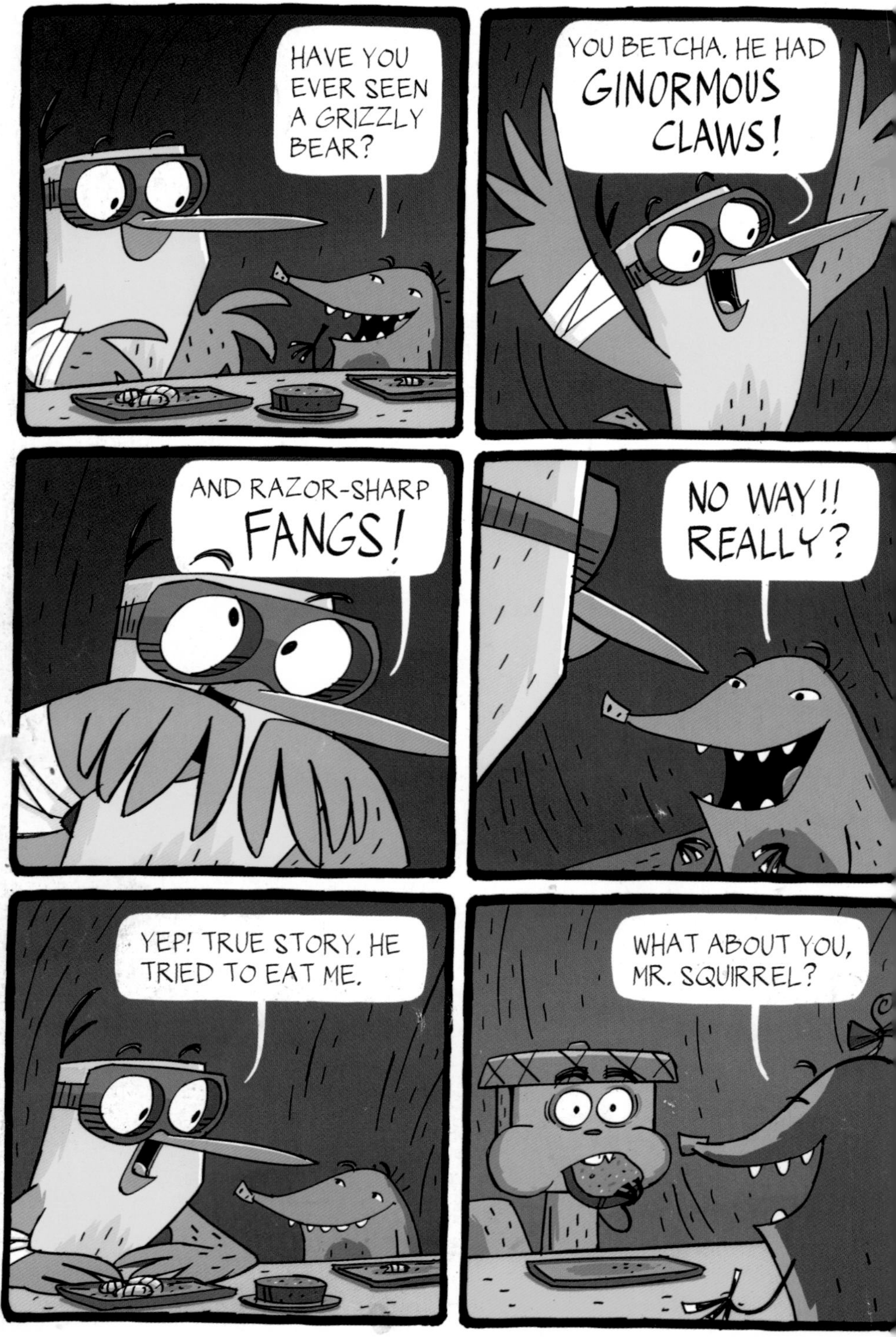
HAVE YOU EVER SEEN A GRIZZLY BEAR?
YOU BETCHA. HE HAD GINORMOUS CLAWS!
AND RAZOR-SHARP FANGS!
NO WAY!! REALLY?
YEP! TRUE STORY. HE TRIED TO EAT ME.
WHAT ABOUT YOU, MR. SQUIRREL?

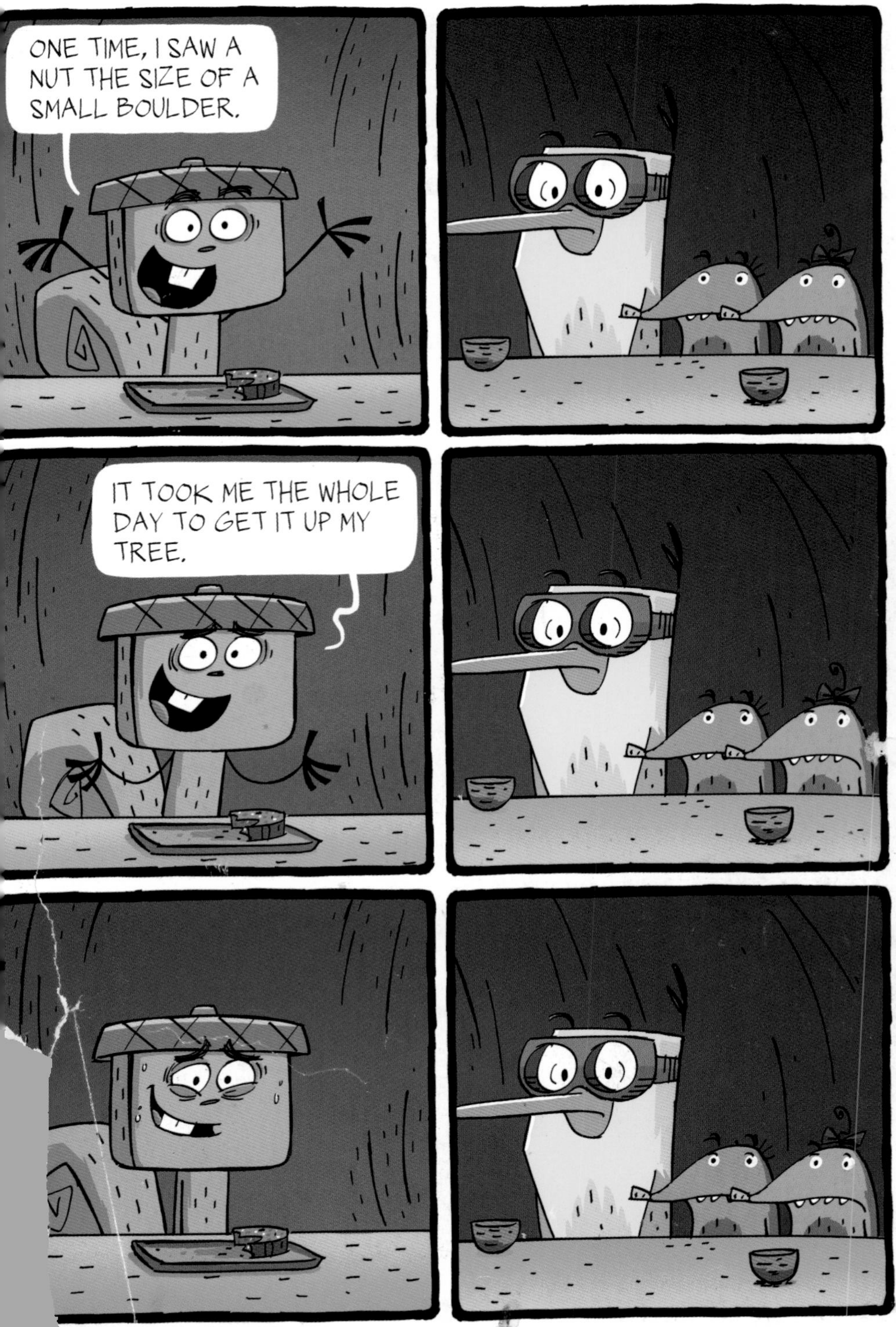
ONE TIME, I SAW A NUT THE SIZE OF A SMALL BOULDER.
IT TOOK ME THE WHOLE DAY TO GET IT UP MY TREE.

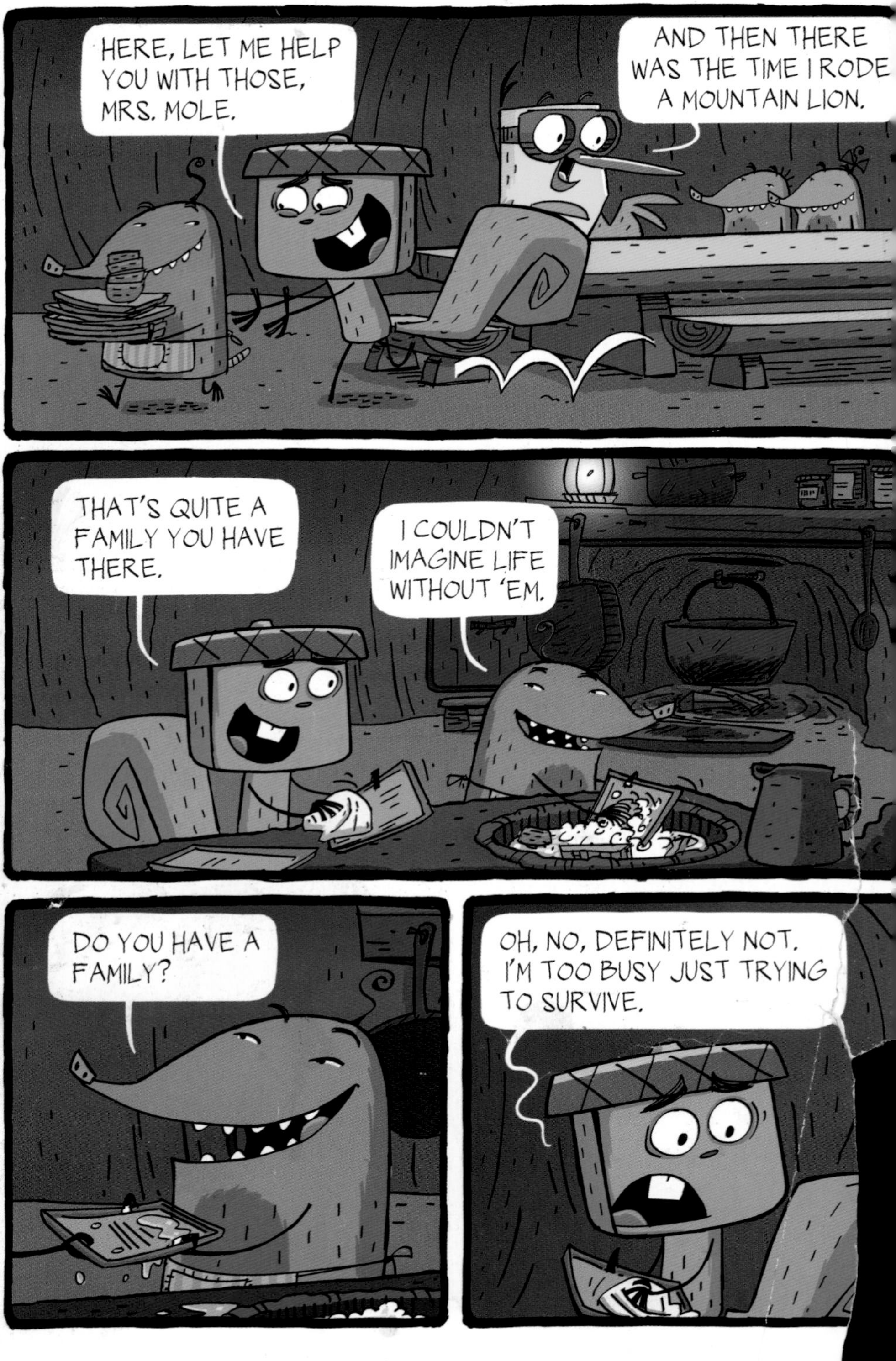
HERE, LET ME HELP YOU WITH THOSE, MRS. MOLE.
AND THEN THERE WAS THE TIME I RODE A MOUNTAIN LION.
THAT'S QUITE A FAMILY YOU HAVE THERE.
I COULDN'T IMAGINE LIFE WITHOUT 'EM.
DO YOU HAVE A FAMILY?
OH, NO, DEFINITELY NOT. I'M TOO BUSY JUST TRYING TO SURVIVE.

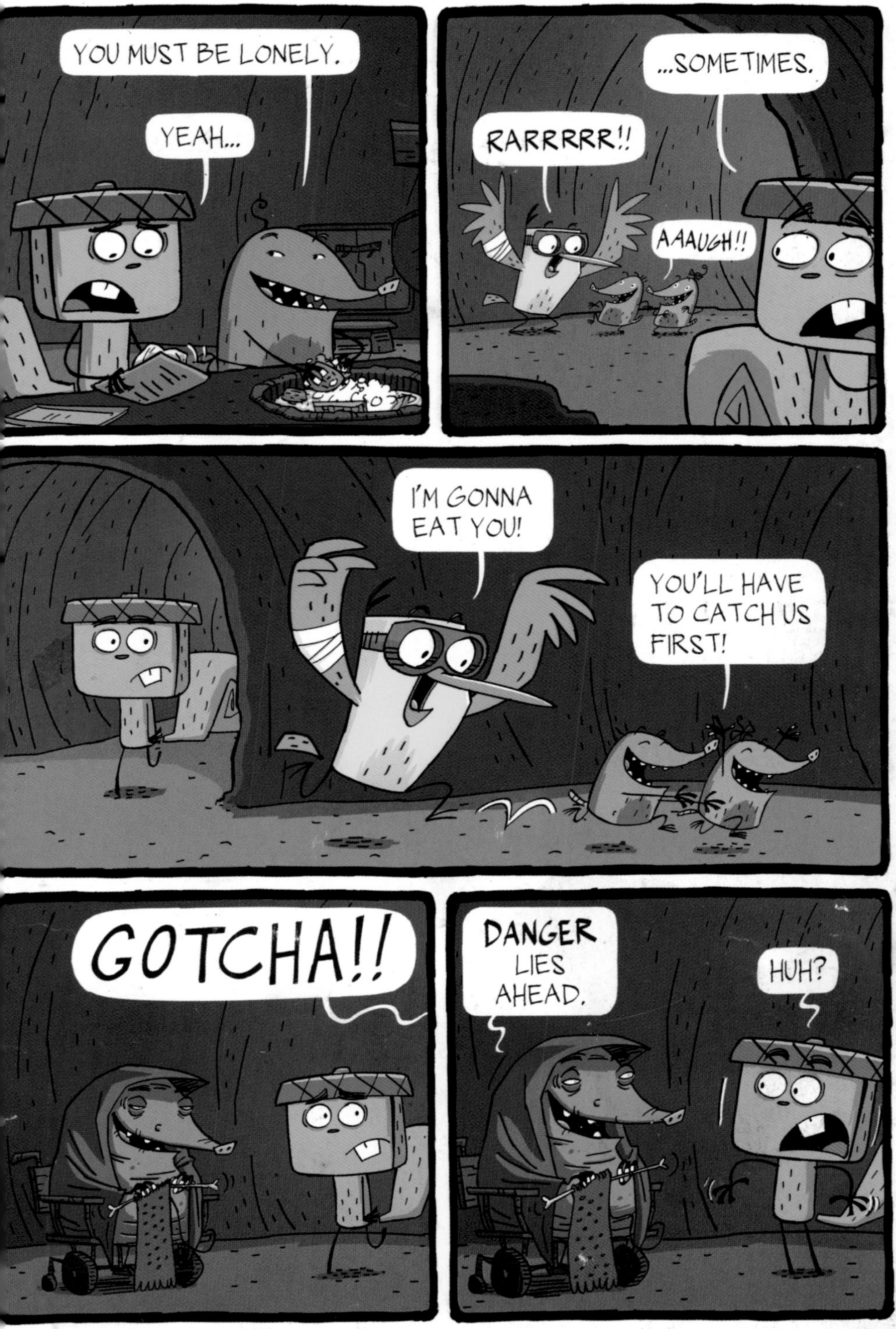
YOU MUST BE LONELY.
YEAH...
...SOMETIMES.
RARRRRR!!
AAAUGH!!
I'M GONNA EAT YOU!
YOU'LL HAVE TO CATCH US FIRST!
GOTCHA!!
DANGER LIES AHEAD.
HUH?

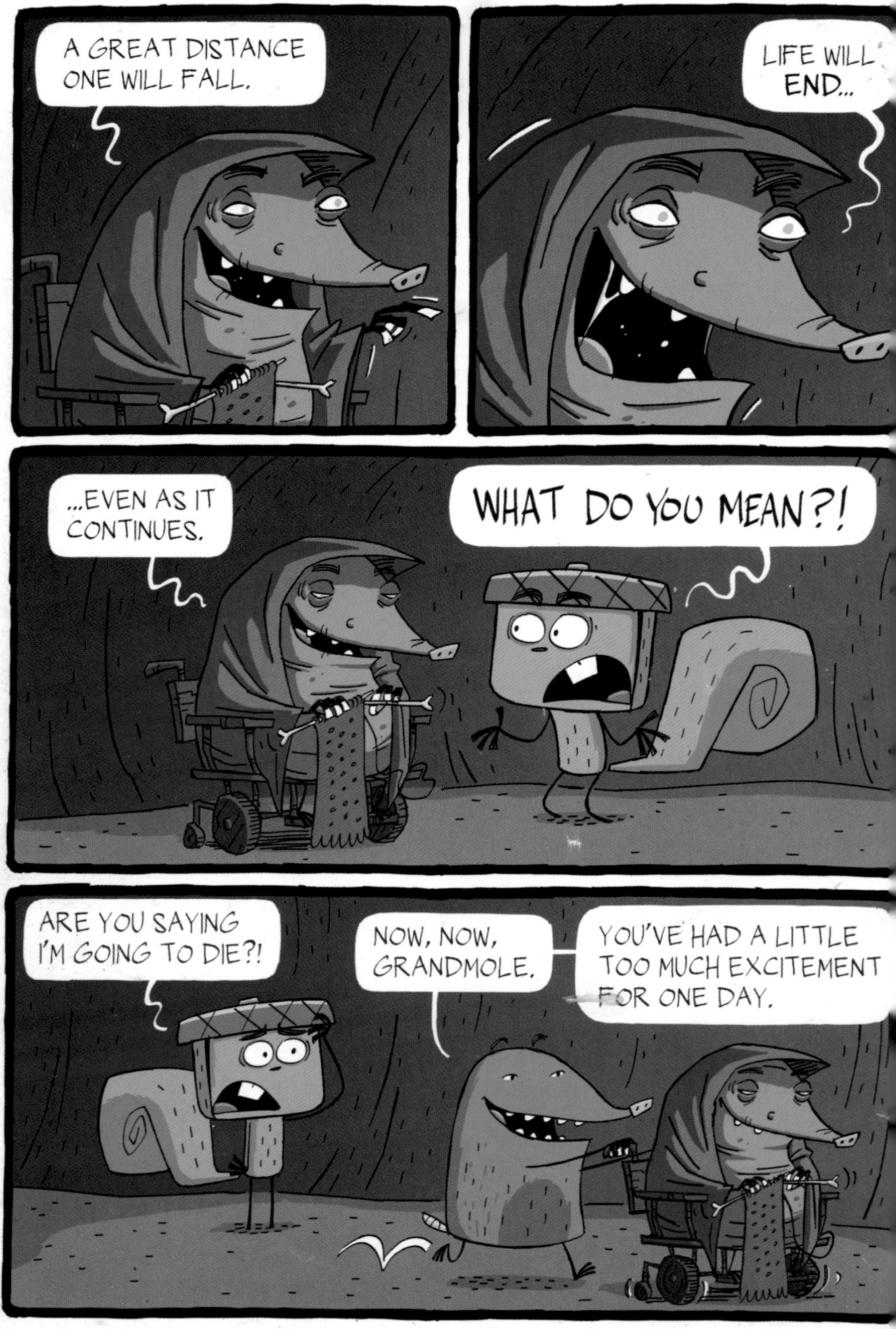
A GREAT DISTANCE ONE WILL FALL.
LIFE WILL END...
...EVEN AS IT CONTINUES.
WHAT DO YOU MEAN?!
ARE YOU SAYING I'M GOING TO DIE?!
NOW, NOW, GRANDMOLE.
YOU'VE HAD A LITTLE TOO MUCH EXCITEMENT FOR ONE DAY.

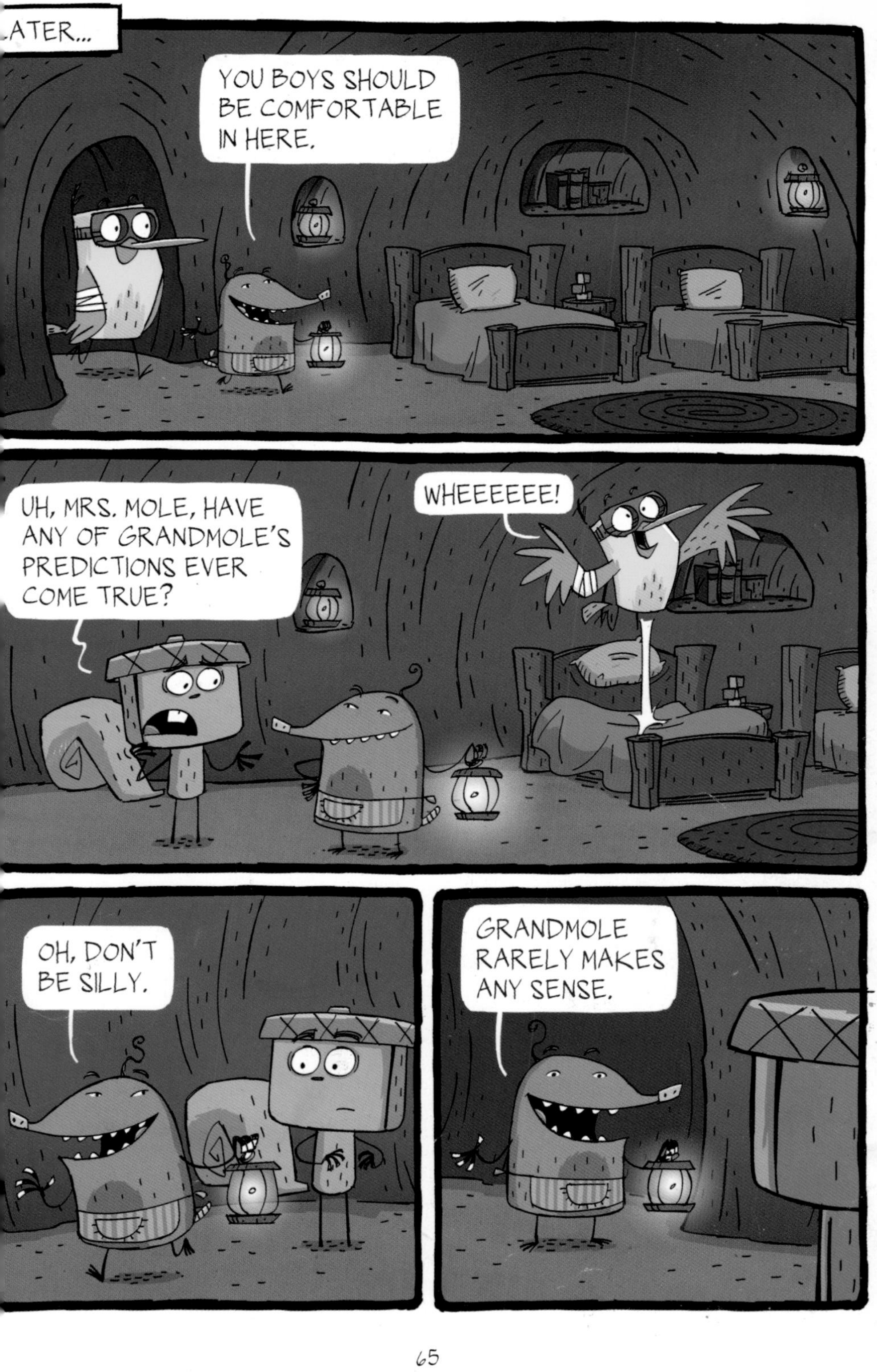
LATER...
YOU BOYS SHOULD BE COMFORTABLE IN HERE.
UH, MRS. MOLE, HAVE ANY OF GRANDMOLE'S PREDICTIONS EVER COME TRUE?
WHEEEEEEE!
OH, DON'T BE SILLY.
GRANDMOLE RARELY MAKES ANY SENSE.

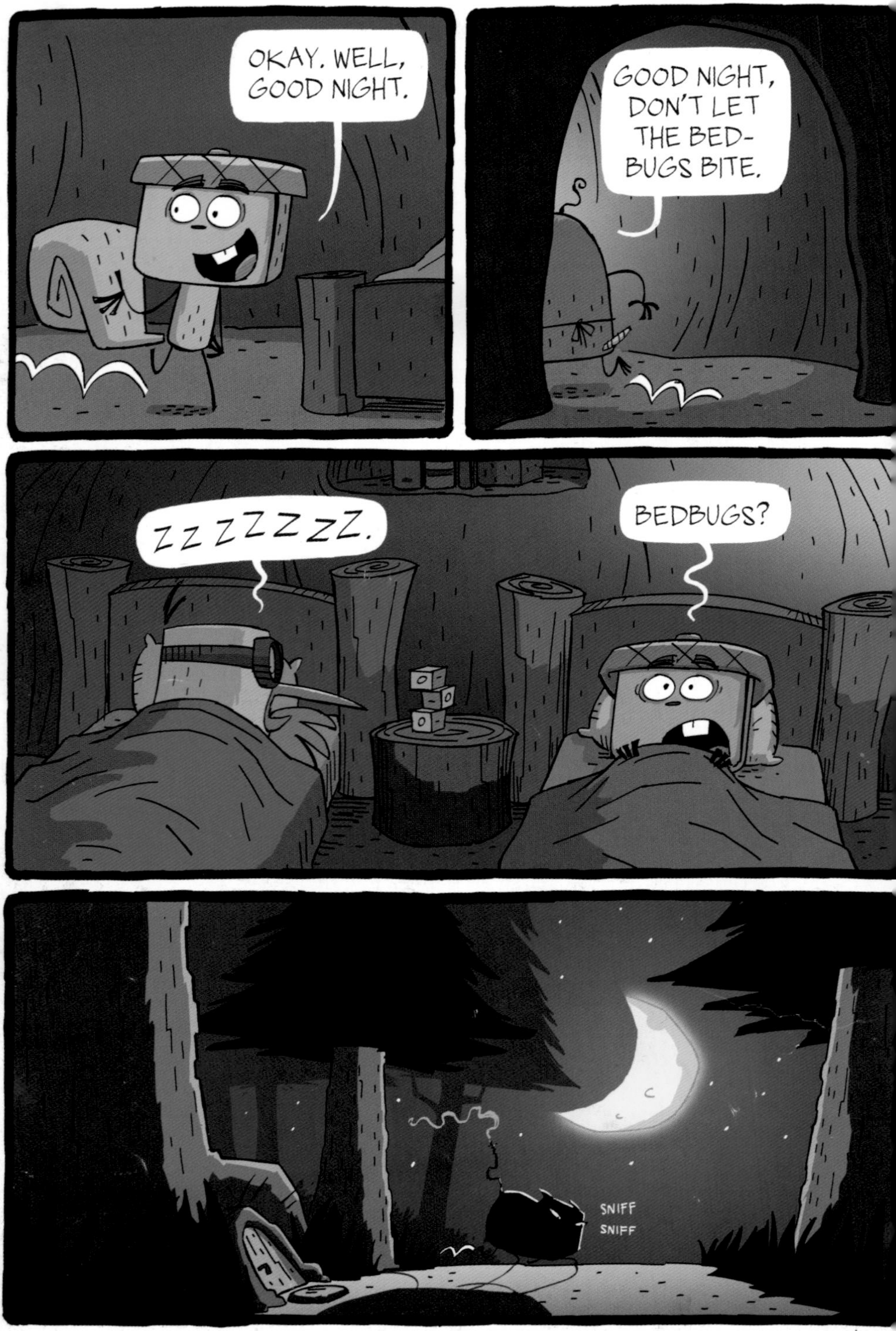
OKAY. WELL, GOOD NIGHT.
GOOD NIGHT, DON'T LET THE BED-BUGS BITE.
ZZZZZZZ.
BEDBUGS?
SNIFF SNIFF

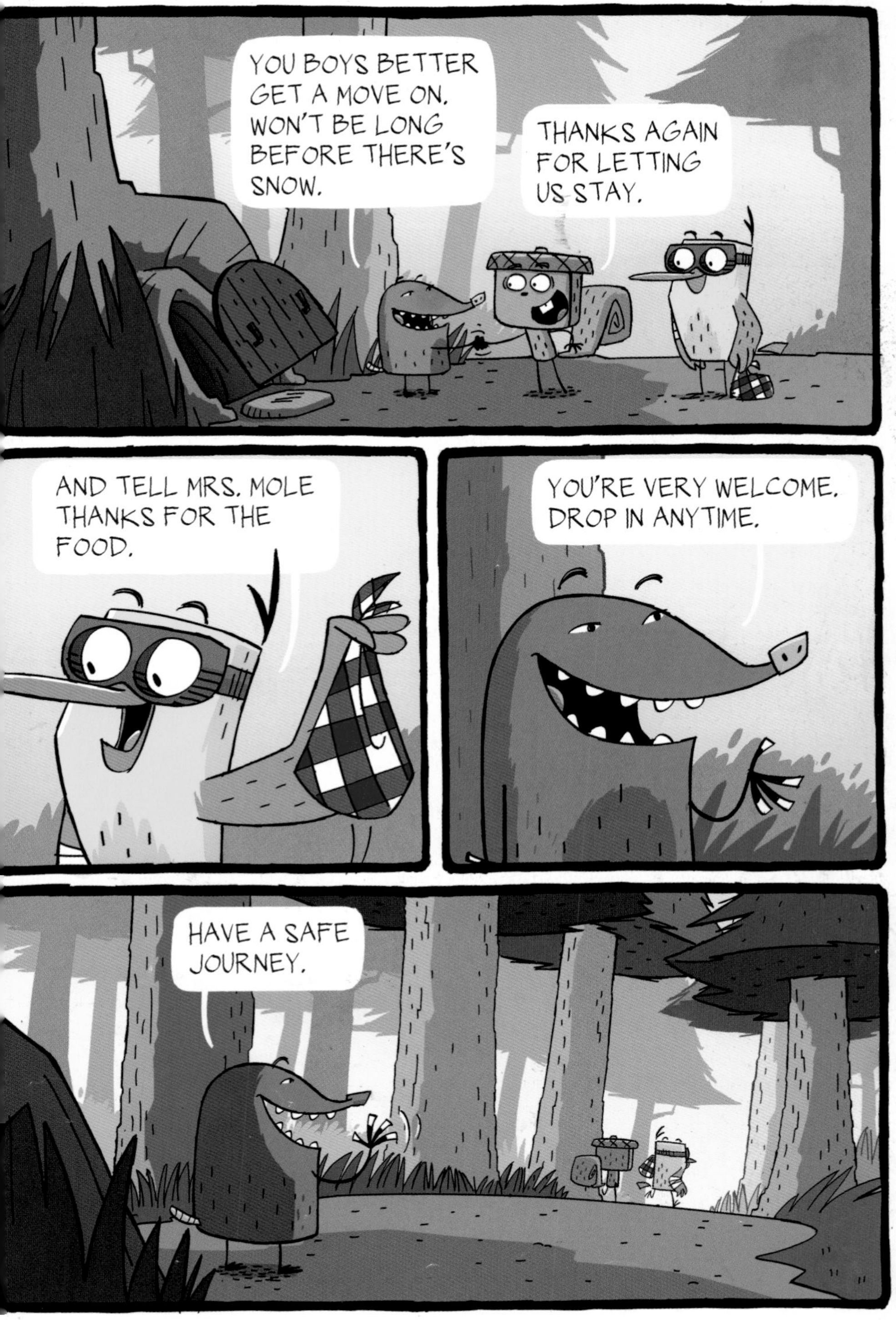
YOU BOYS BETTER GET A MOVE ON. WON'T BE LONG BEFORE THERE'S SNOW.
THANKS AGAIN FOR LETTING US STAY.
AND TELL MRS. MOLE THANKS FOR THE FOOD.
YOU'RE VERY WELCOME. DROP IN ANYTIME.
HAVE A SAFE JOURNEY.

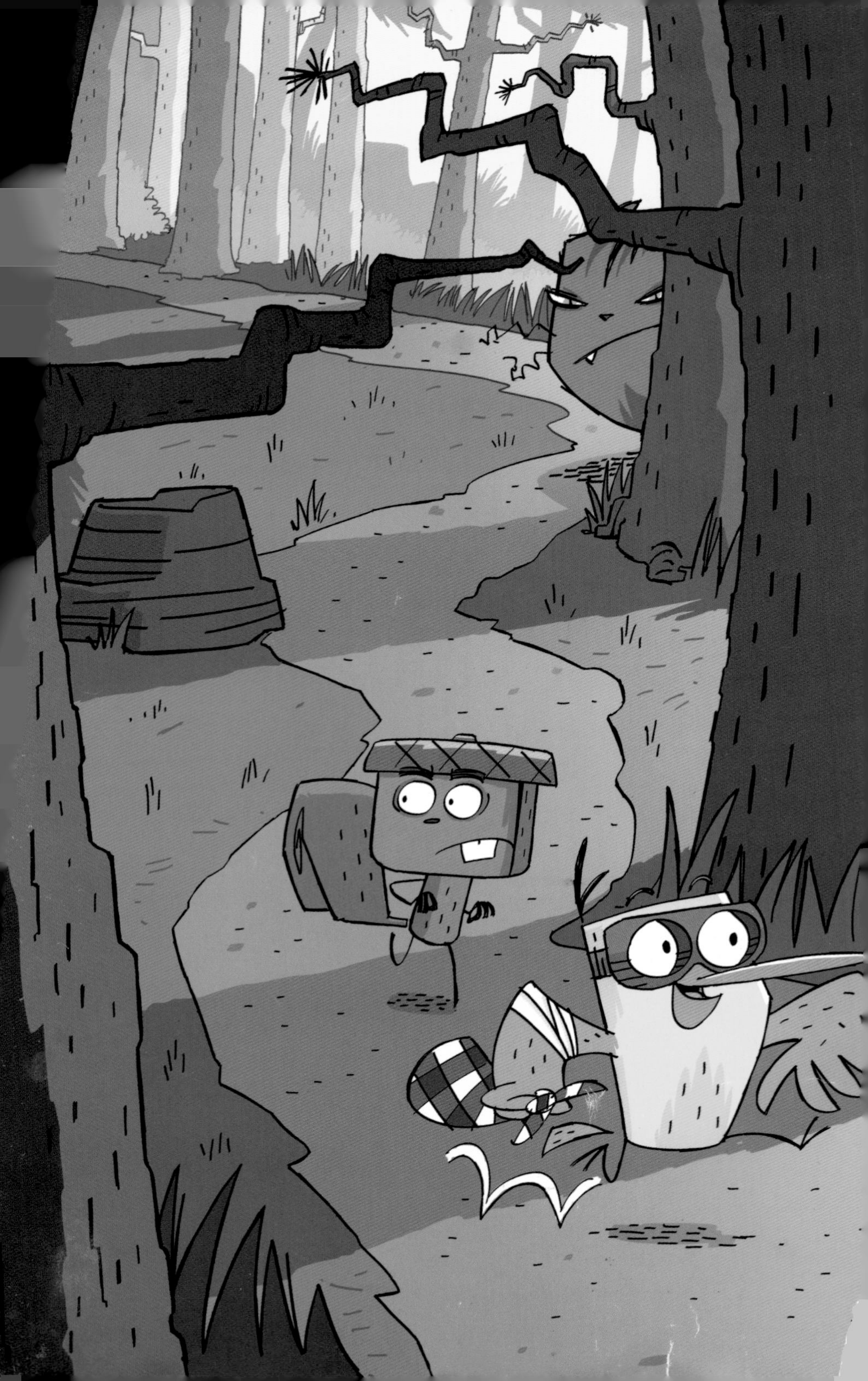

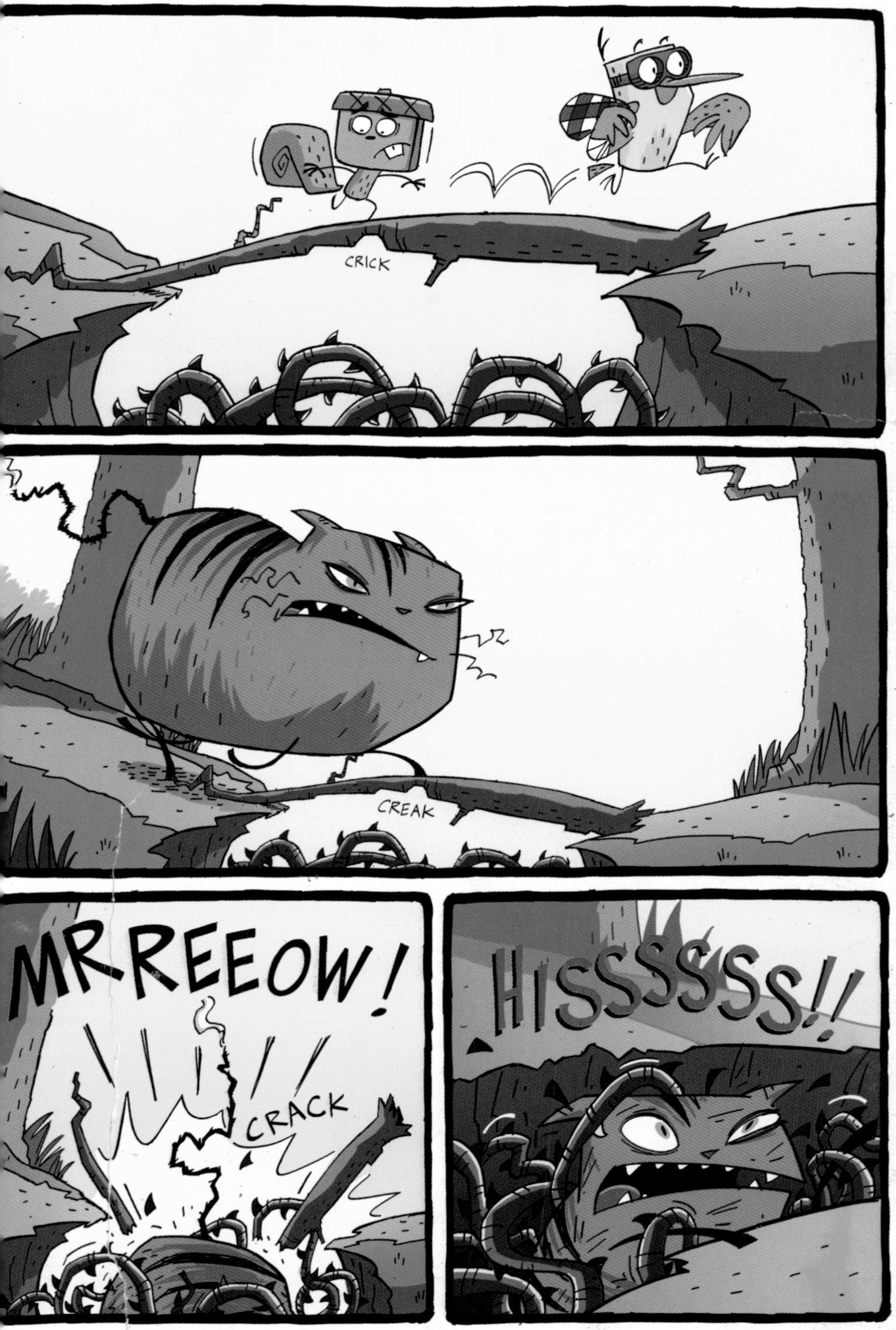
CRICK
CREAK
MRREEOW!
CRACK
HISSSSSS!!

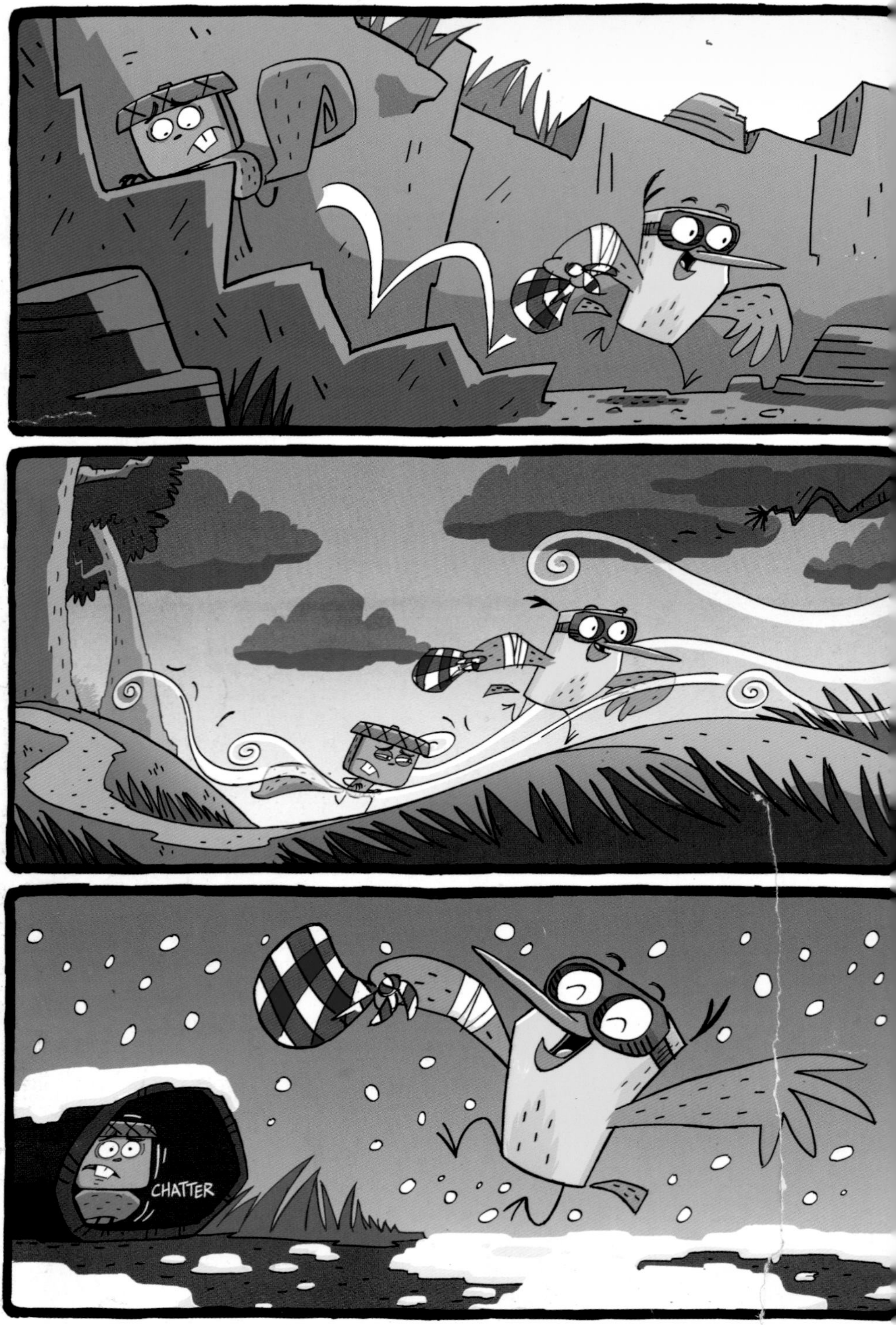
CHATTER

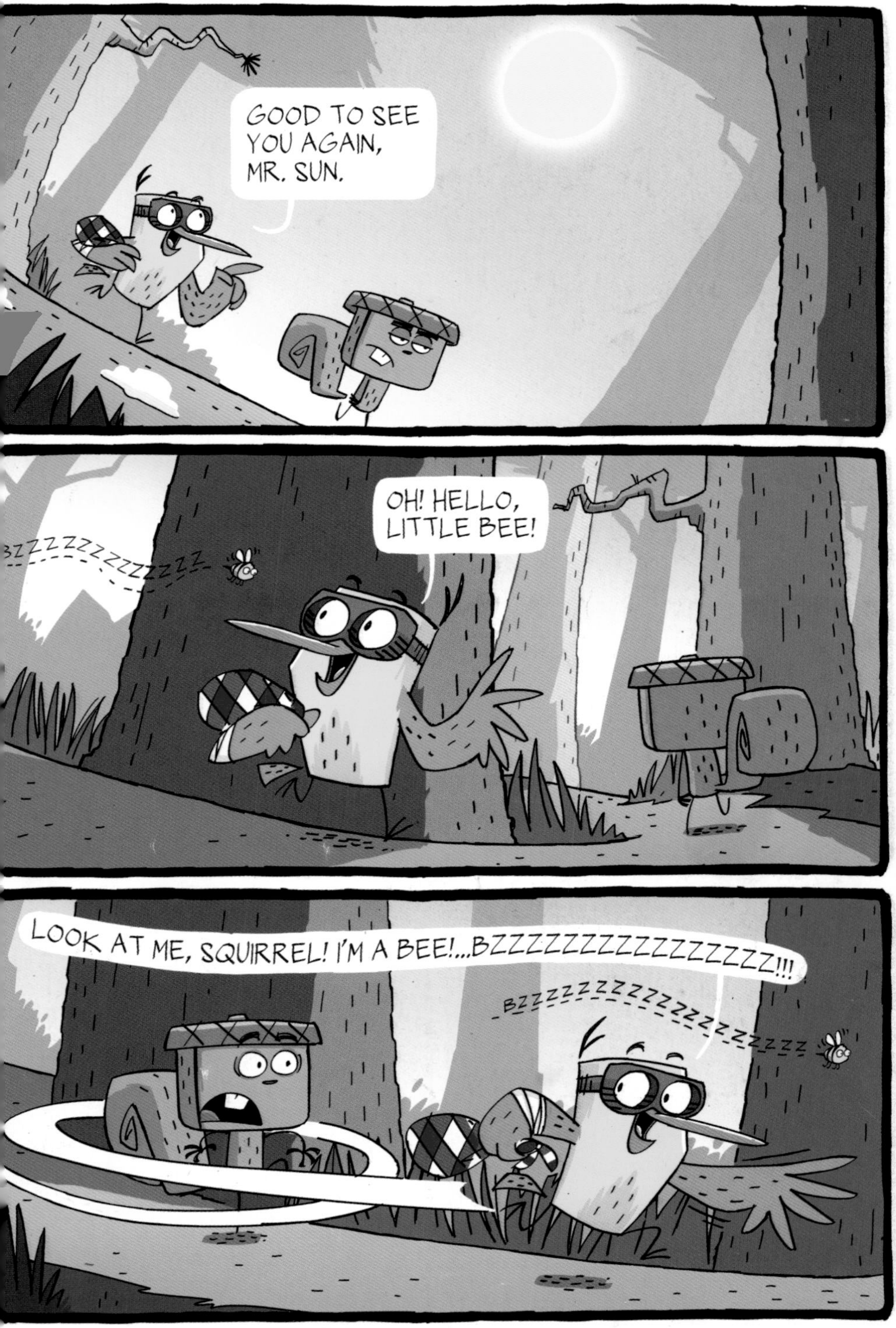
GOOD TO SEE YOU AGAIN, MR. SUN.
BZZZZZZZZZZZZZZZ
OH! HELLO, LITTLE BEE!
LOOK AT ME, SQUIRREL! I'M A BEE!...BZZZZZZZZZZZZZZZZZZ!!!
BZZZZZZZZZZZZZZZZZZZ

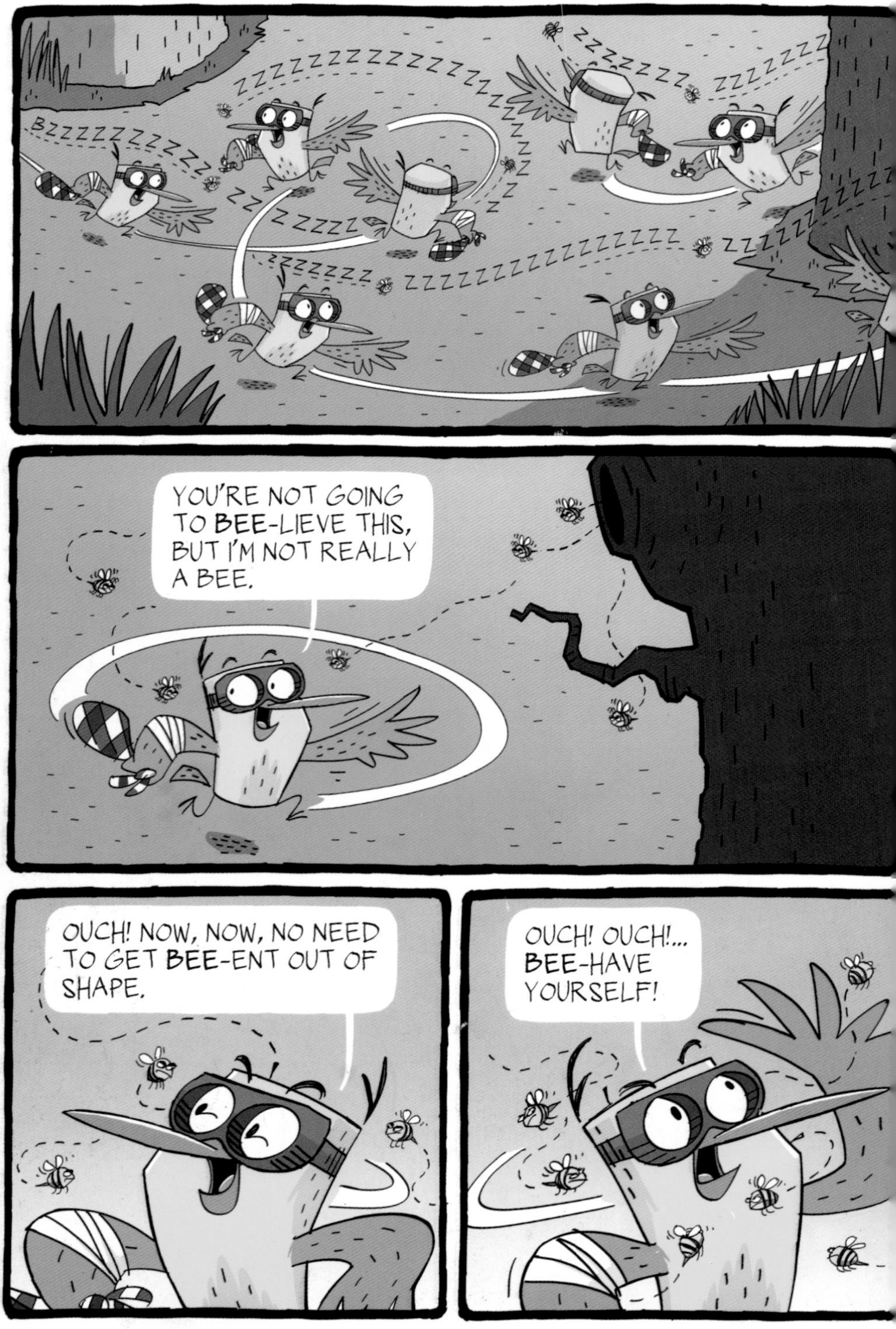
BZZZZZZZZZZZ
ZZZZZZZZZZZZZZZZ
ZZZZZZZ
YOU'RE NOT GOING TO BEE-LIEVE THIS, BUT I'M NOT REALLY A BEE.
OUCH! NOW, NOW, NO NEED TO GET BEE-ENT OUT OF SHAPE.
OUCH! OUCH!... BEE-HAVE YOURSELF!

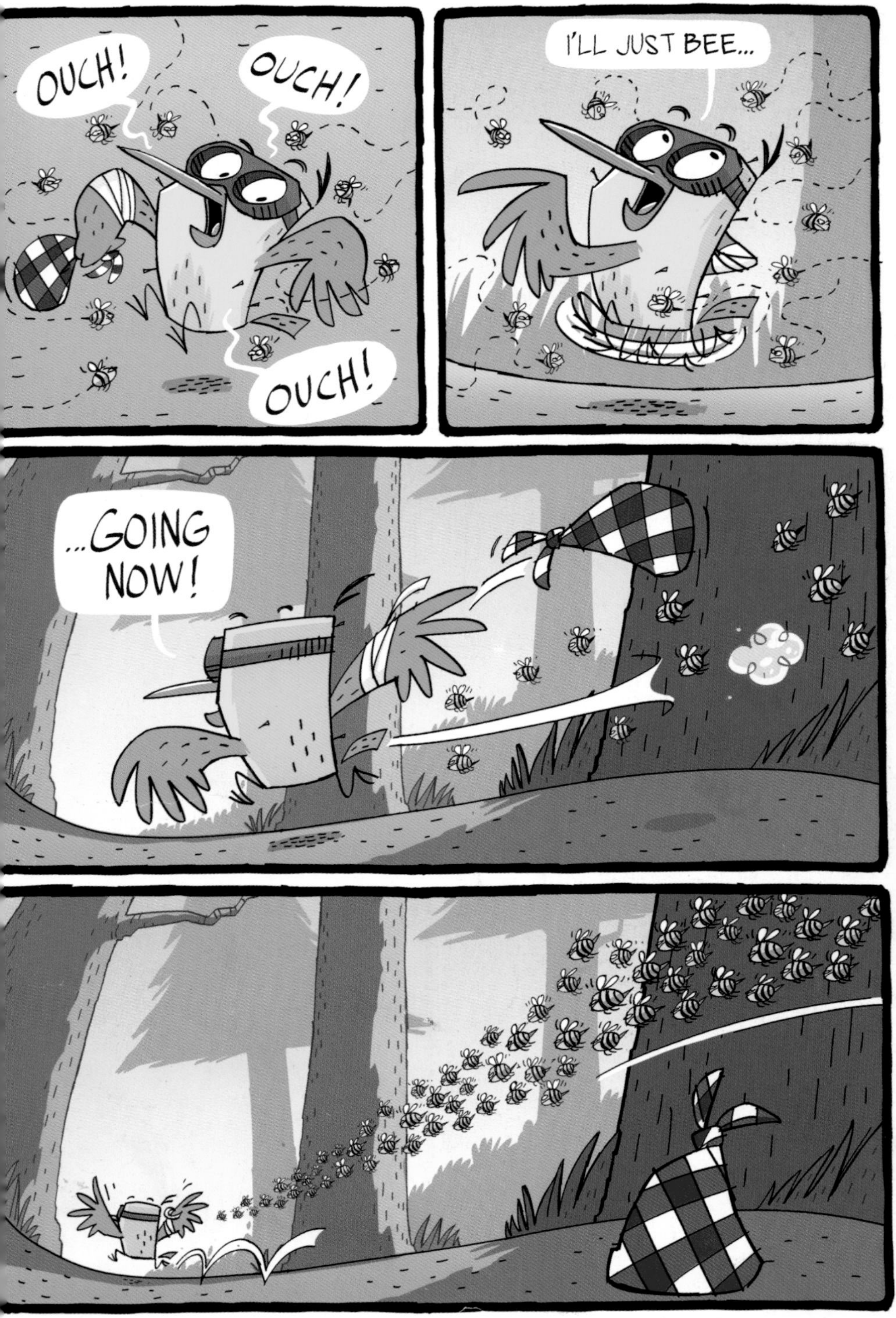
OUCH!
OUCH!
OUCH!
I'LL JUST BEE...
...GOING NOW!

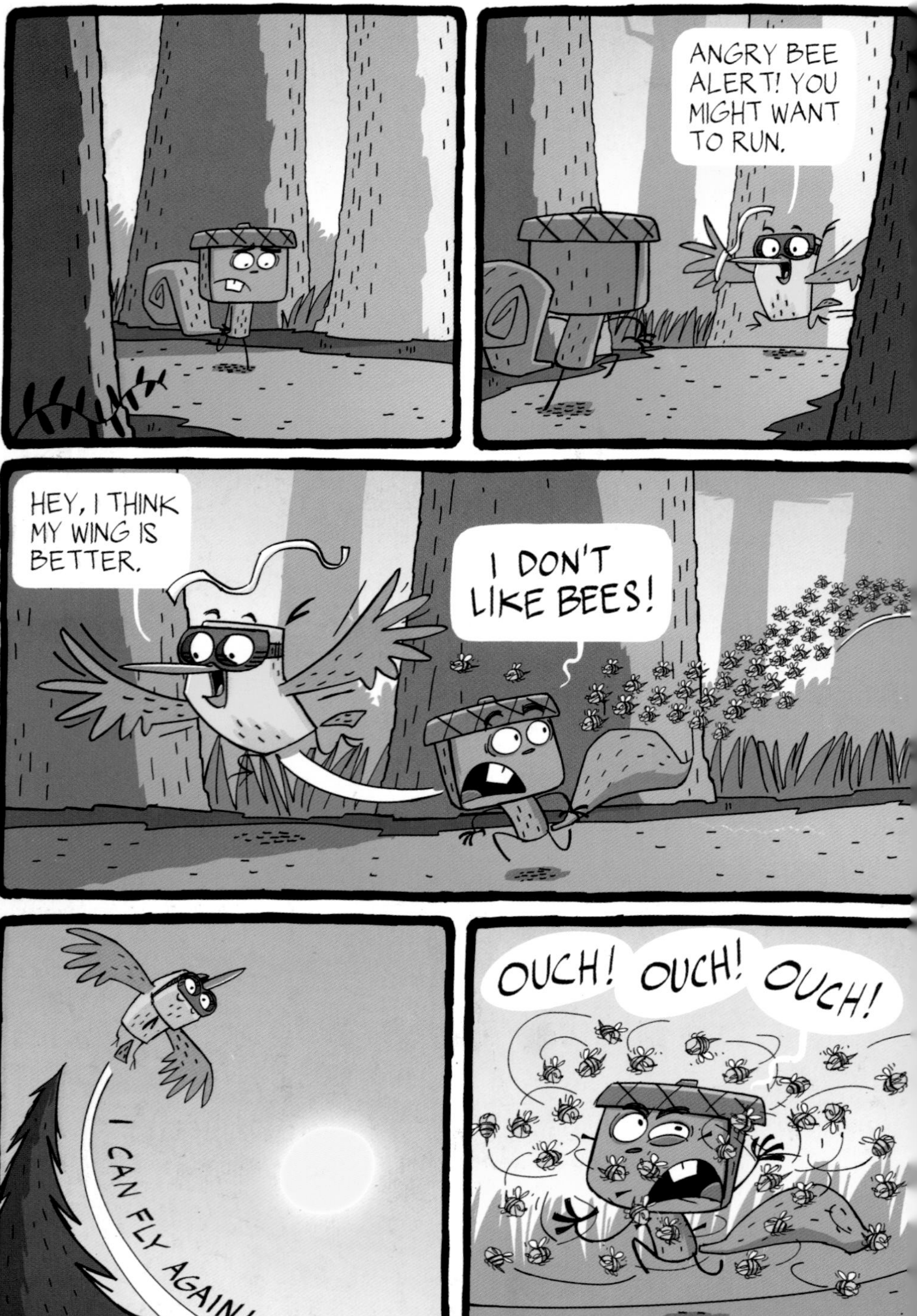
ANGRY BEE ALERT! YOU MIGHT WANT TO RUN.
HEY, I THINK MY WING IS BETTER.
I DON'T LIKE BEES!
I CAN FLY AGAIN!
OUCH! OUCH! OUCH!

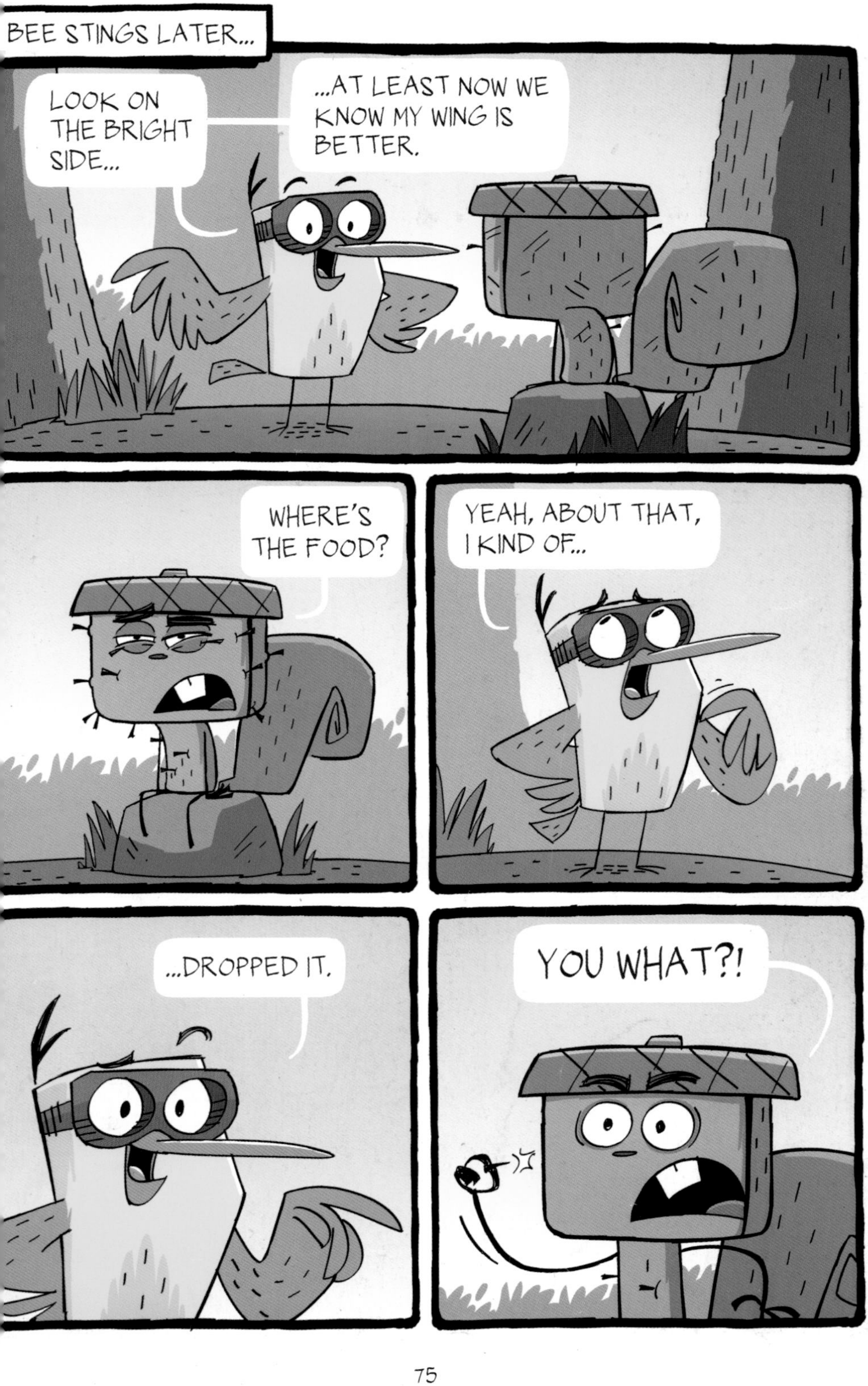
BEE STINGS LATER...
LOOK ON THE BRIGHT SIDE...
...AT LEAST NOW WE KNOW MY WING IS BETTER.
WHERE'S THE FOOD?
YEAH, ABOUT THAT, I KIND OF...
...DROPPED IT.
YOU WHAT?!

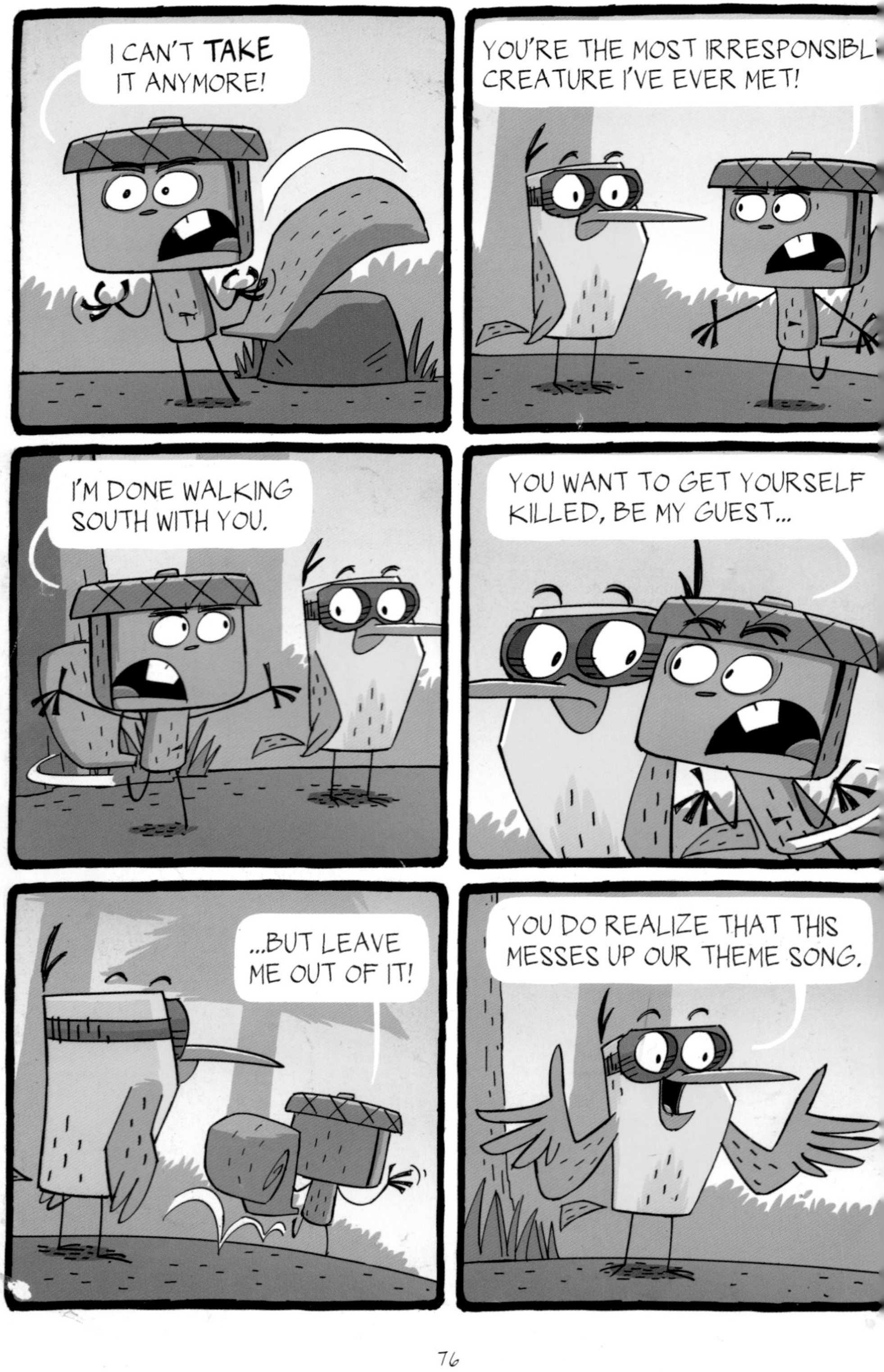
I CAN'T TAKE IT ANYMORE!
YOU'RE THE MOST IRRESPONSIBL CREATURE I'VE EVER MET!
I'M DONE WALKING SOUTH WITH YOU.
YOU WANT TO GET YOURSELF KILLED, BE MY GUEST...
...BUT LEAVE ME OUT OF IT!
YOU DO REALIZE THAT THIS MESSES UP OUR THEME SONG.

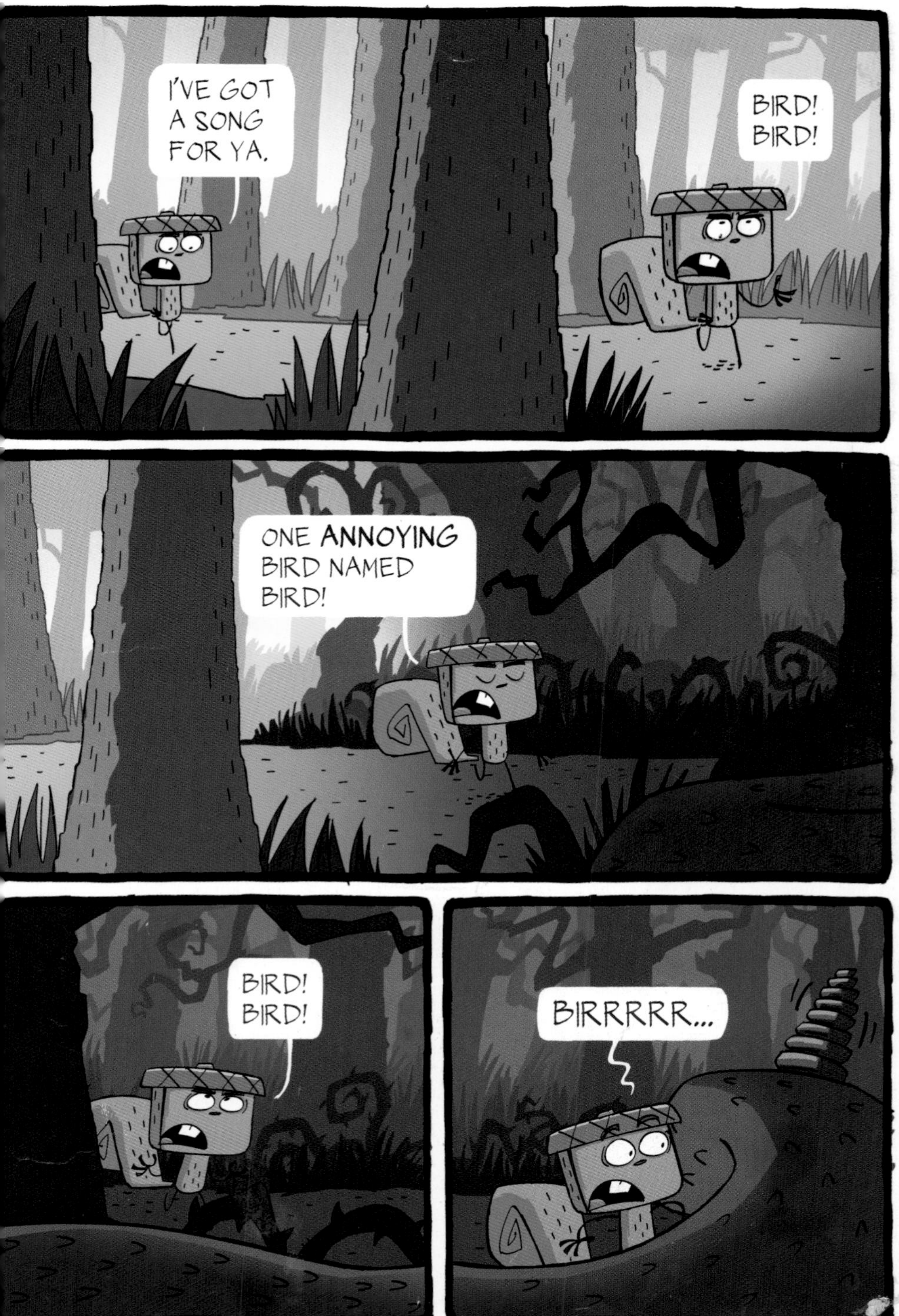
I'VE GOT A SONG FOR YA.
BIRD! BIRD!
ONE ANNOYING BIRD NAMED BIRD!
BIRD! BIRD!
BIRRRRR...

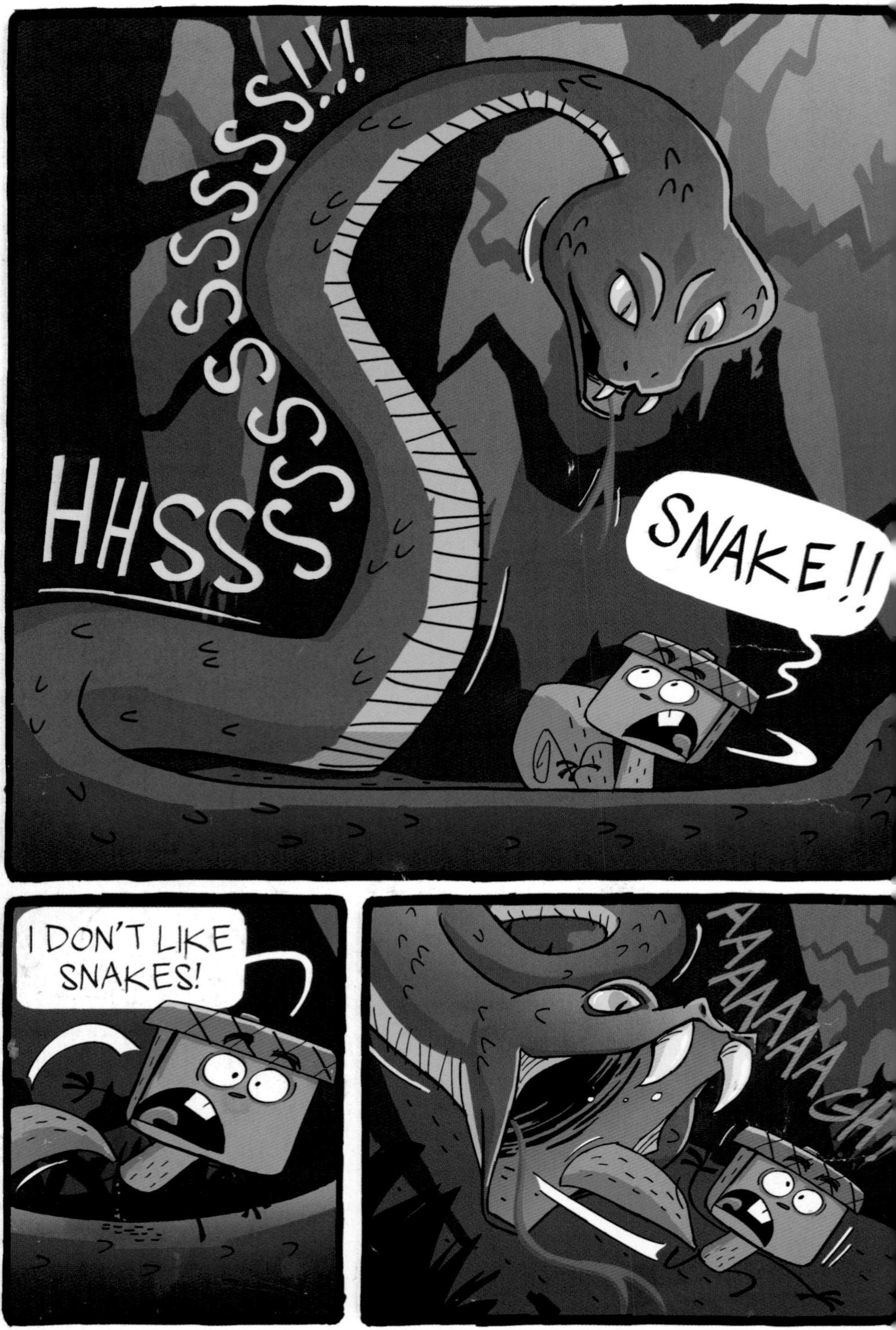
HHSSSSSSSSSSS!!!
SNAKE!!
I DON'T LIKE SNAKES!
AAAAAAAAGH!

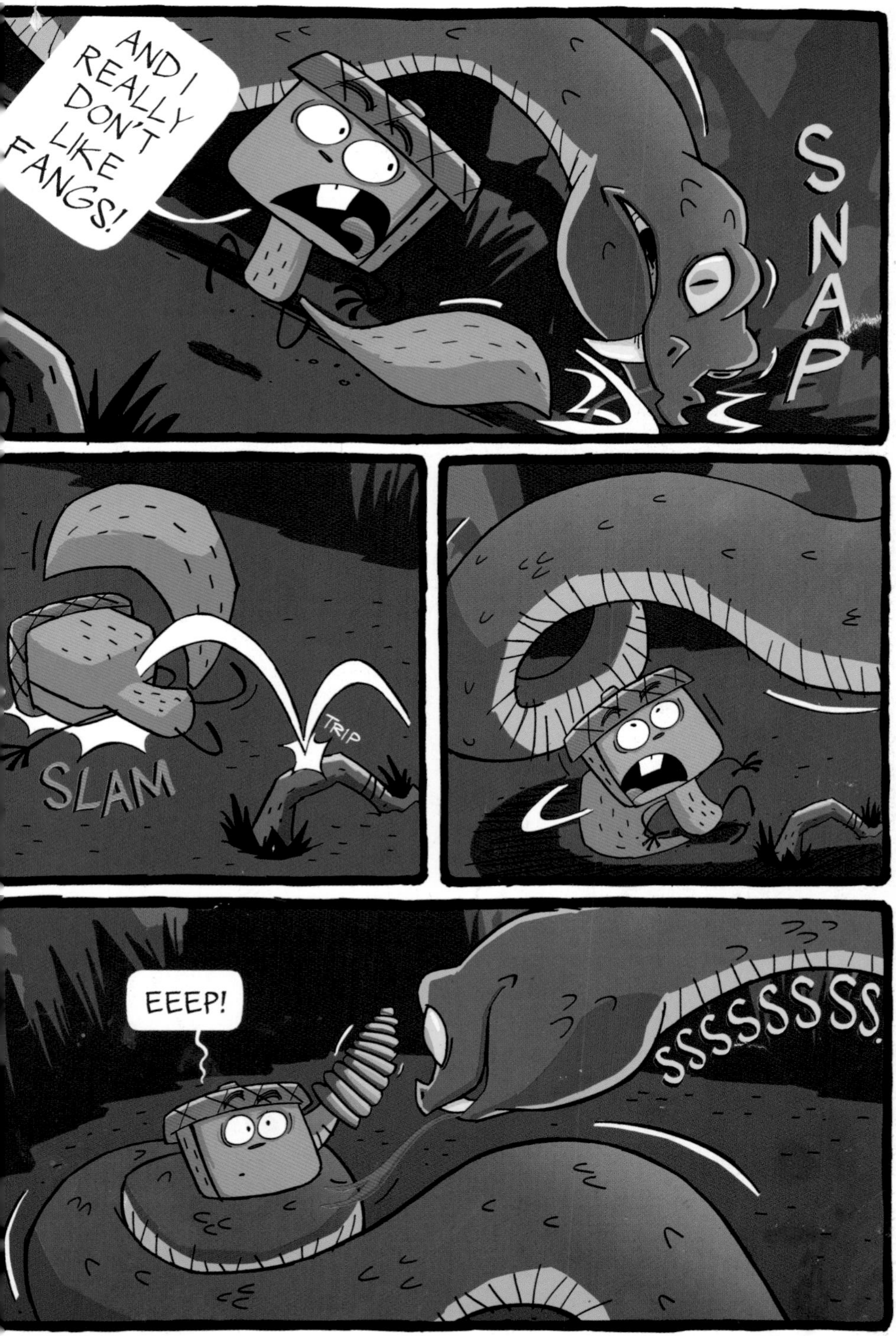
AND I REALLY DON'T LIKE FANGS!
SNAP
SLAM
TRIP
EEEP!
SSSSSSSSS

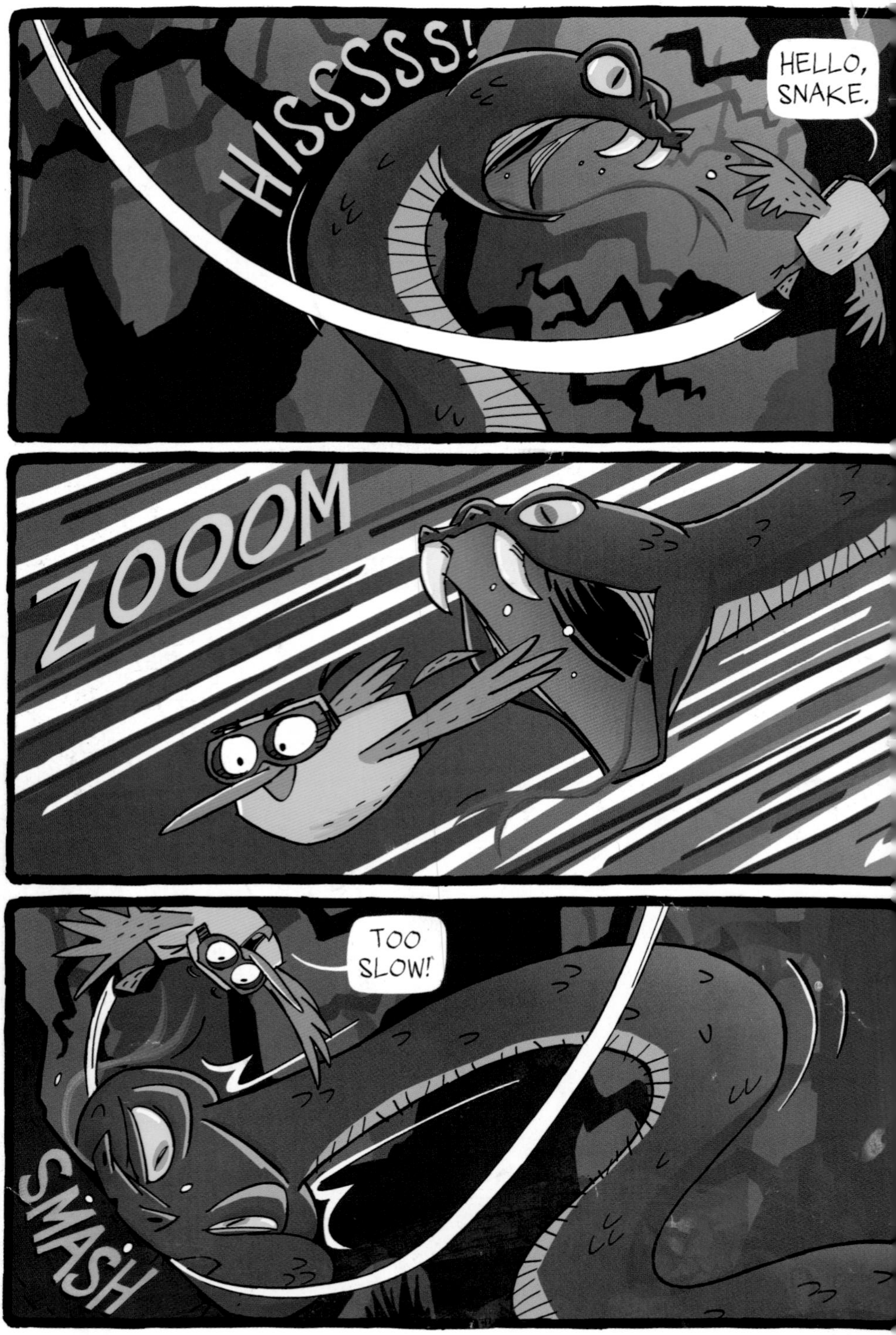
HISSSSS!
HELLO, SNAKE.
ZOOOM
TOO SLOW!
SMASH

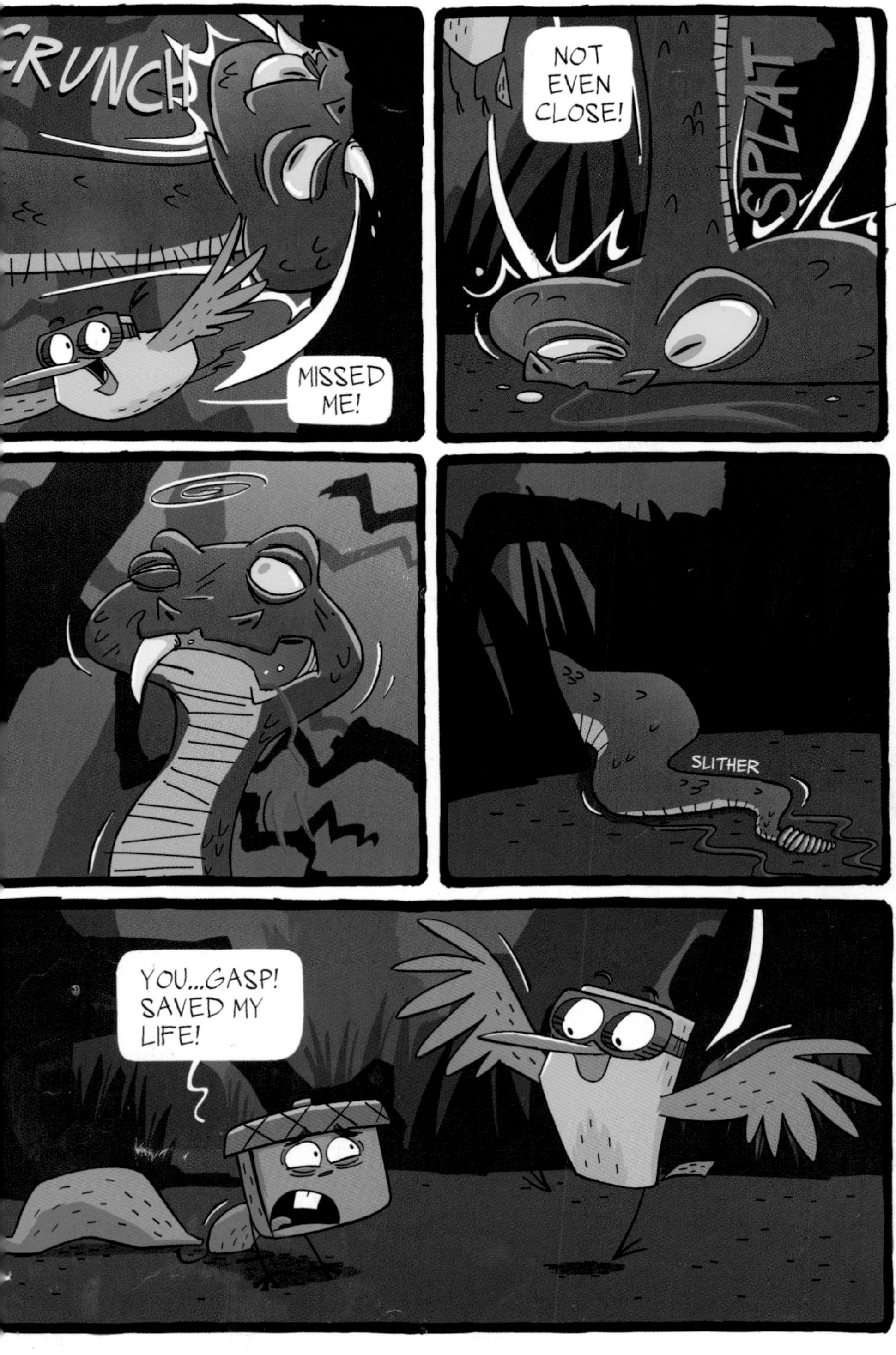
CRUNCH
MISSED ME!
NOT EVEN CLOSE!
SPLAT
SLITHER
YOU...GASP! SAVED MY LIFE!

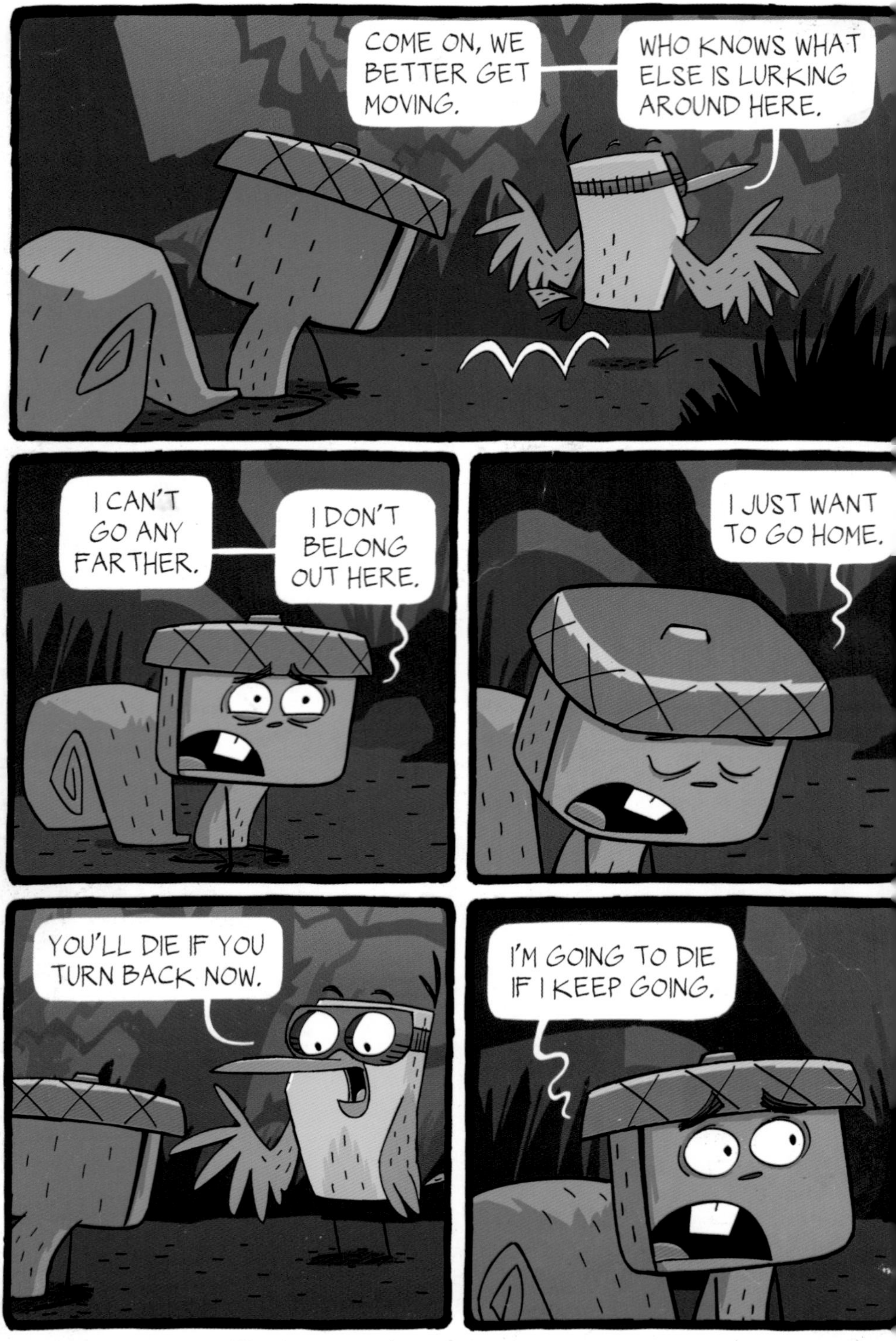
COME ON, WE BETTER GET MOVING.
WHO KNOWS WHAT ELSE IS LURKING AROUND HERE.
I CAN'T GO ANY FARTHER.
I DON'T BELONG OUT HERE.
I JUST WANT TO GO HOME.
YOU'LL DIE IF YOU TURN BACK NOW.
I'M GOING TO DIE IF I KEEP GOING.

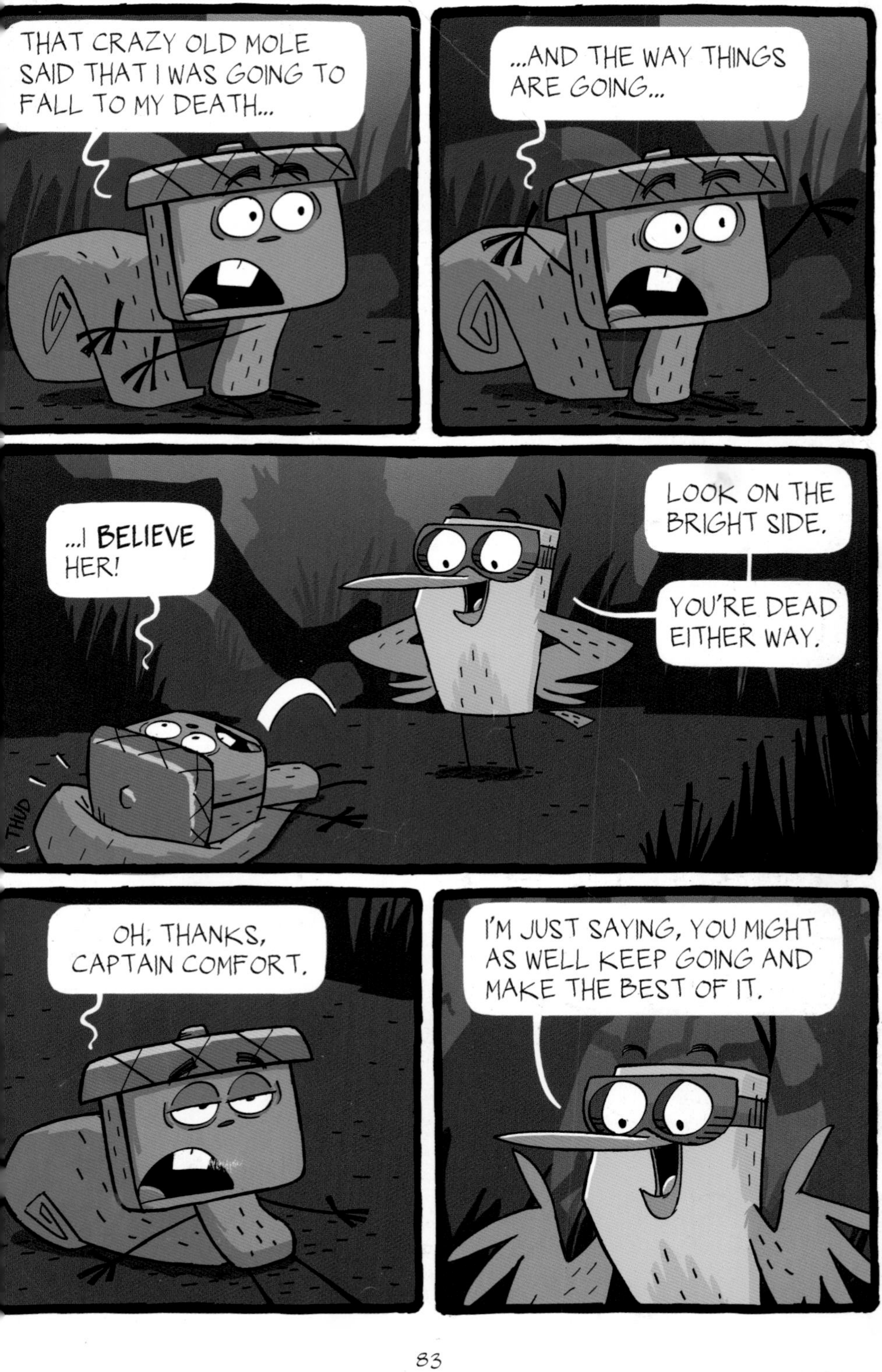
THAT CRAZY OLD MOLE SAID THAT I WAS GOING TO FALL TO MY DEATH...
...AND THE WAY THINGS ARE GOING...
...I BELIEVE HER!
THUD
LOOK ON THE BRIGHT SIDE.
YOU'RE DEAD EITHER WAY.
OH, THANKS, CAPTAIN COMFORT.
I'M JUST SAYING, YOU MIGHT AS WELL KEEP GOING AND MAKE THE BEST OF IT.

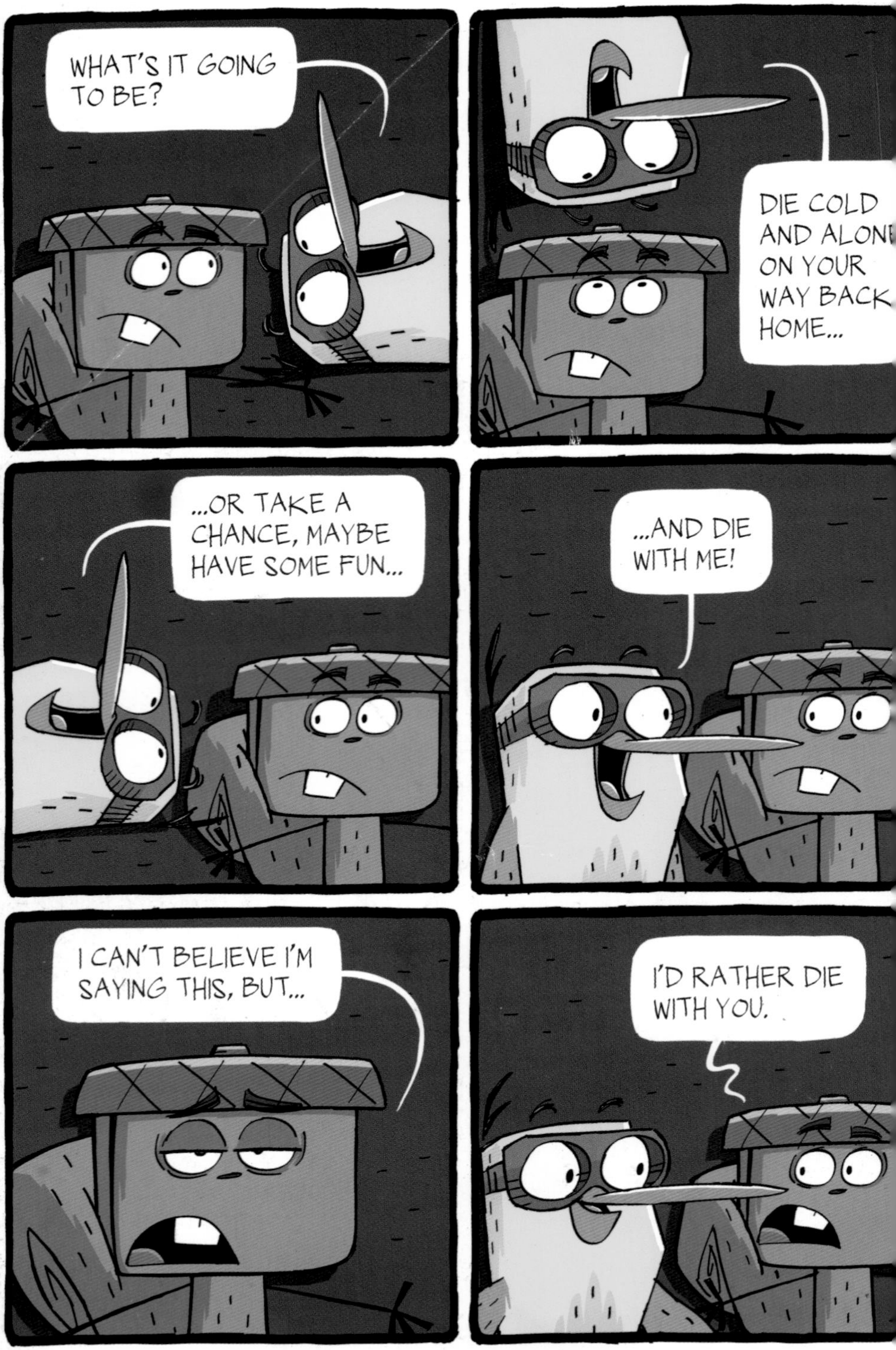
WHAT'S IT GOING TO BE?
DIE COLD AND ALONE ON YOUR WAY BACK HOME...
...OR TAKE A CHANCE, MAYBE HAVE SOME FUN...
...AND DIE WITH ME!
I CAN'T BELIEVE I'M SAYING THIS, BUT...
I'D RATHER DIE WITH YOU.

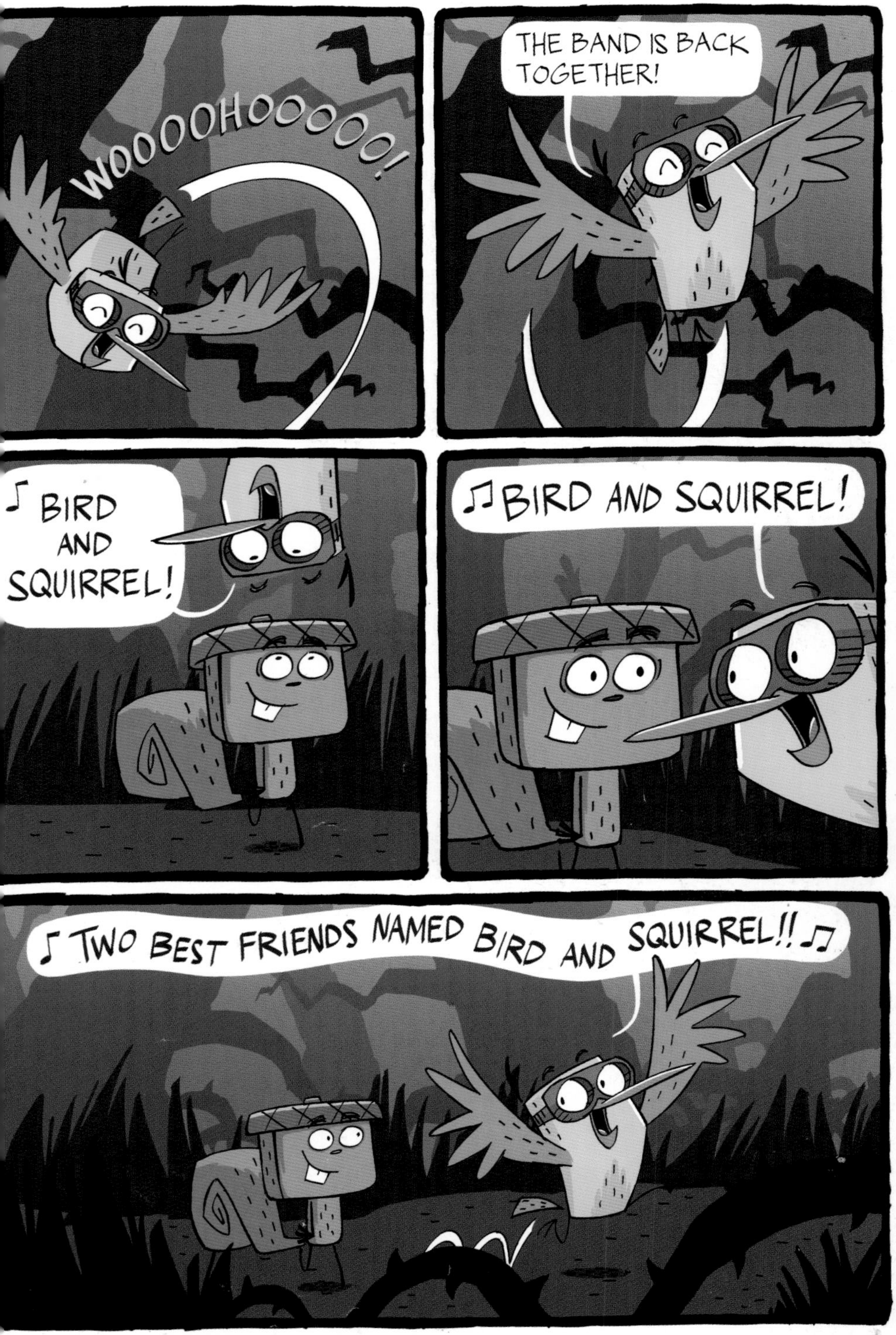
WOOOOHOOOOOO!
THE BAND IS BACK TOGETHER!
♩ BIRD AND SQUIRREL!
♫ BIRD AND SQUIRREL!
♩ TWO BEST FRIENDS NAMED BIRD AND SQUIRREL!! ♫

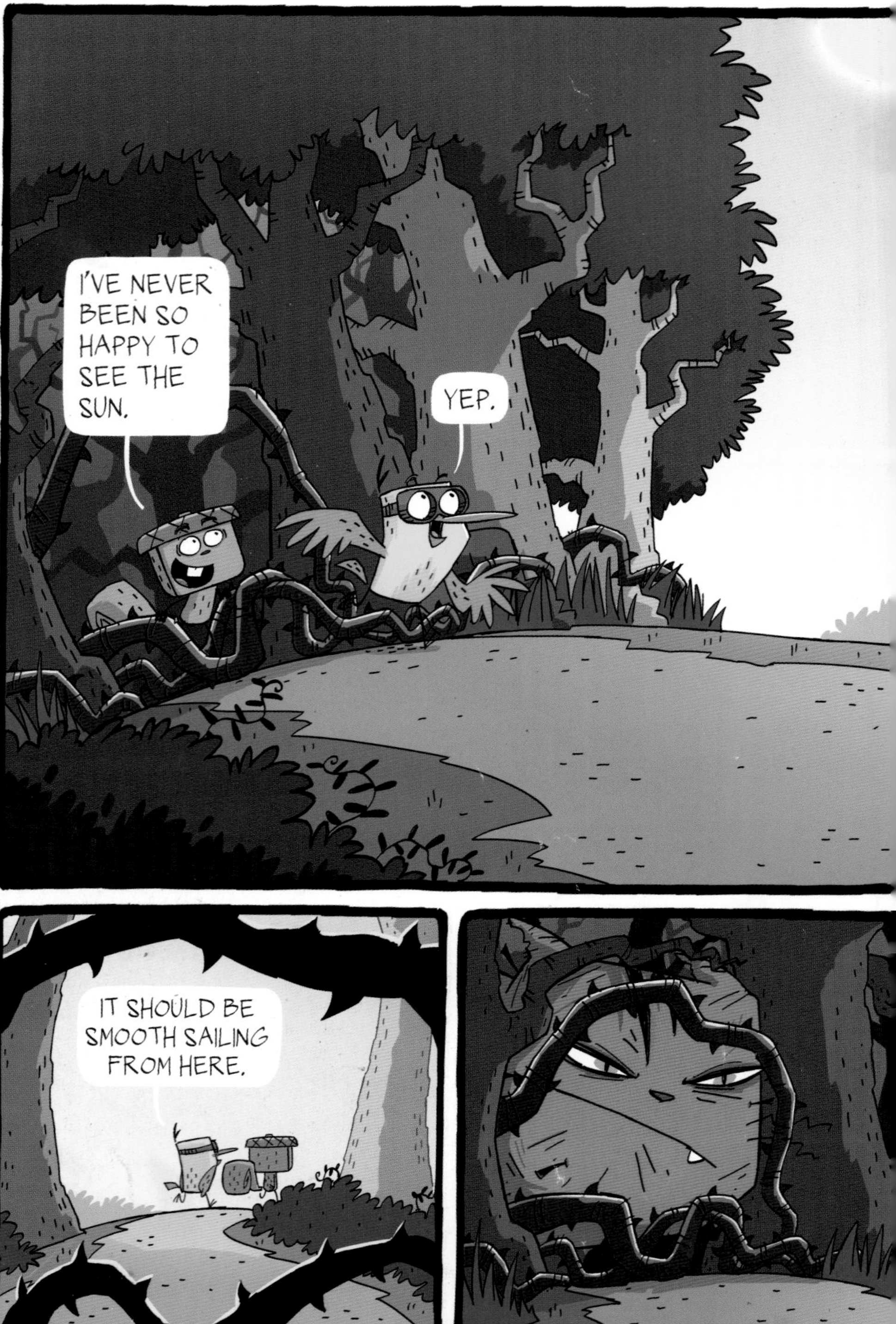
I'VE NEVER BEEN SO HAPPY TO SEE THE SUN.
YEP.
IT SHOULD BE SMOOTH SAILING FROM HERE.

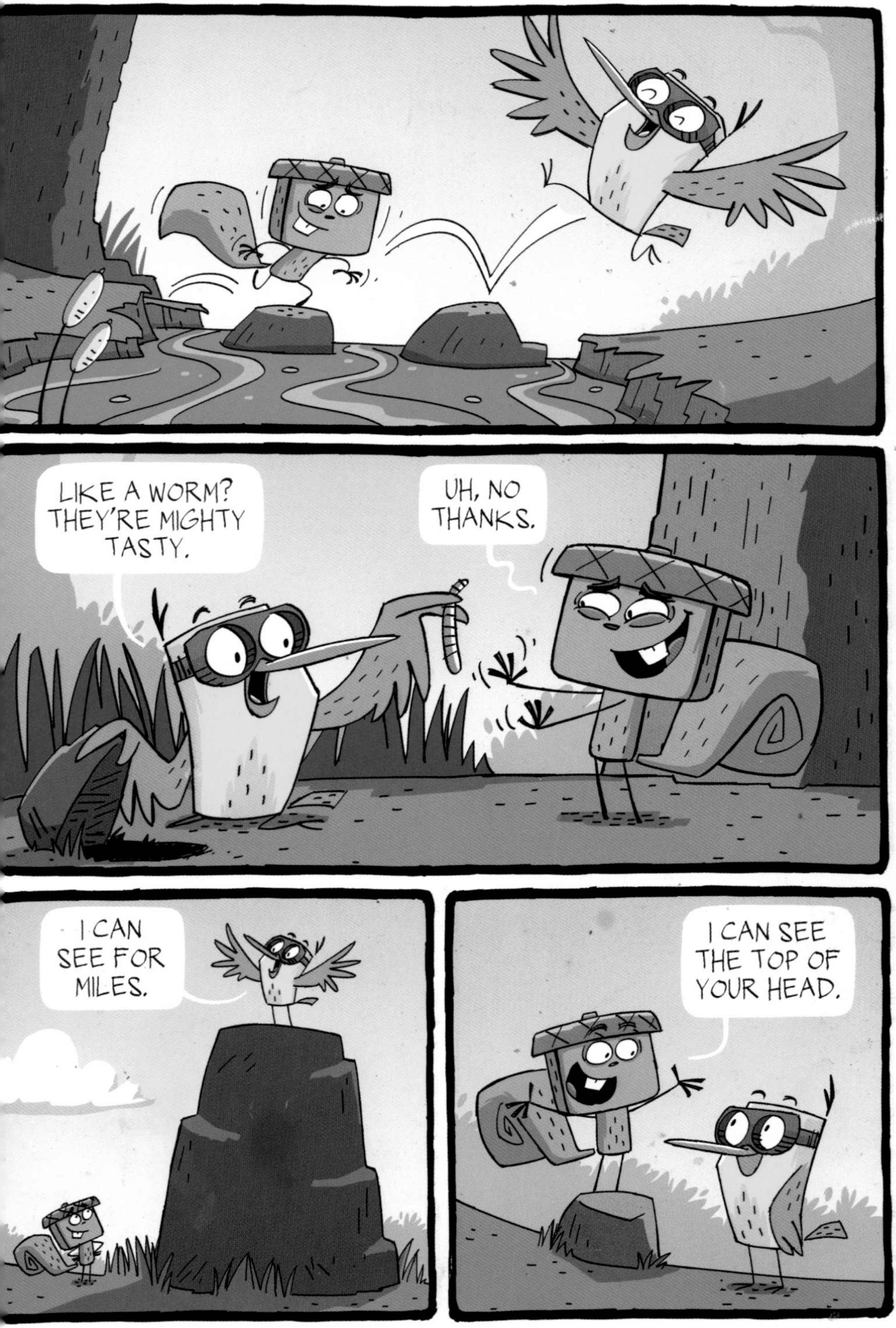
LIKE A WORM? THEY'RE MIGHTY TASTY.
UH, NO THANKS.
I CAN SEE FOR MILES.
I CAN SEE THE TOP OF YOUR HEAD.

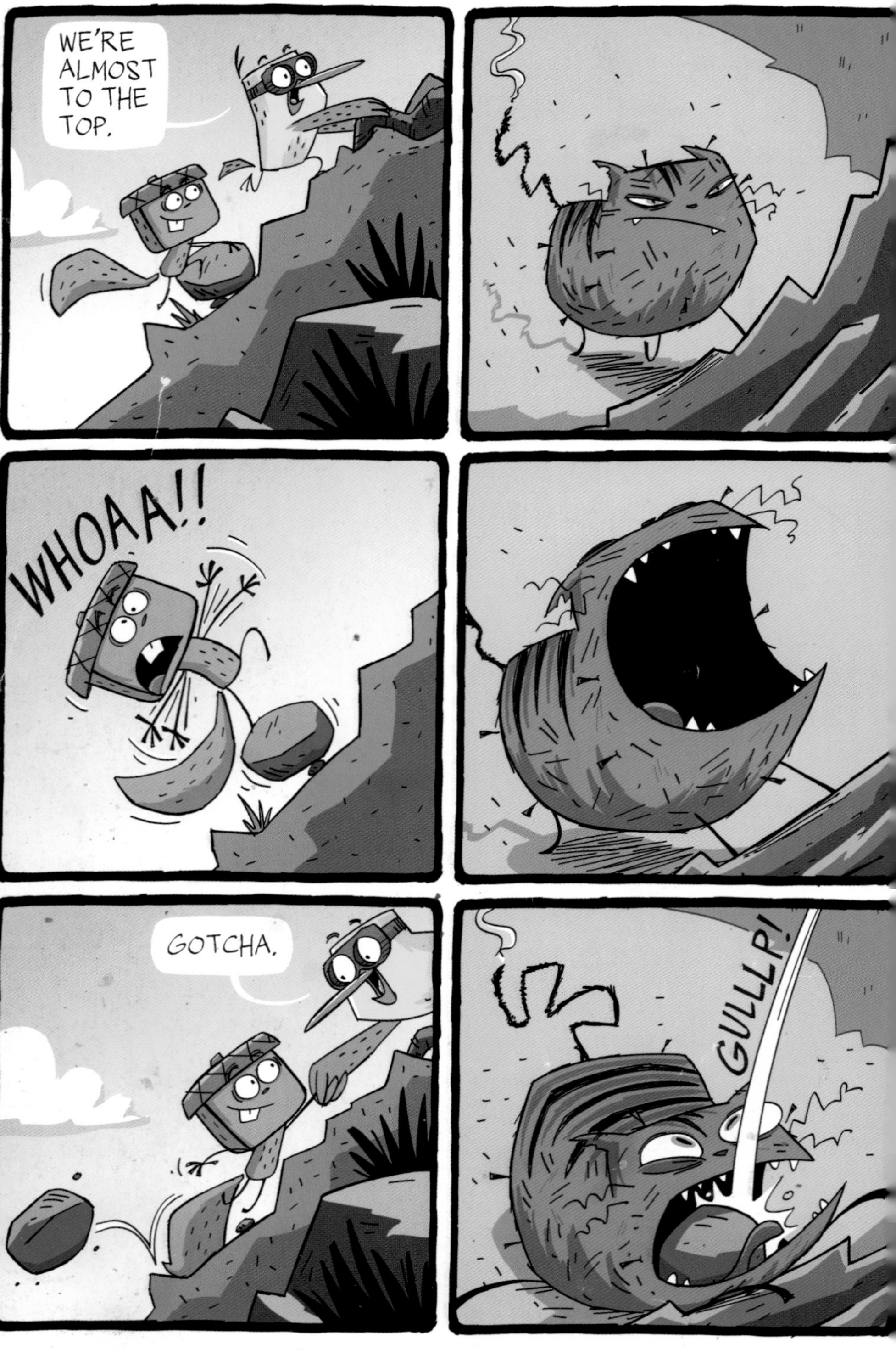
WE'RE ALMOST TO THE TOP.
WHOAA!!
GOTCHA.
GULLLP!

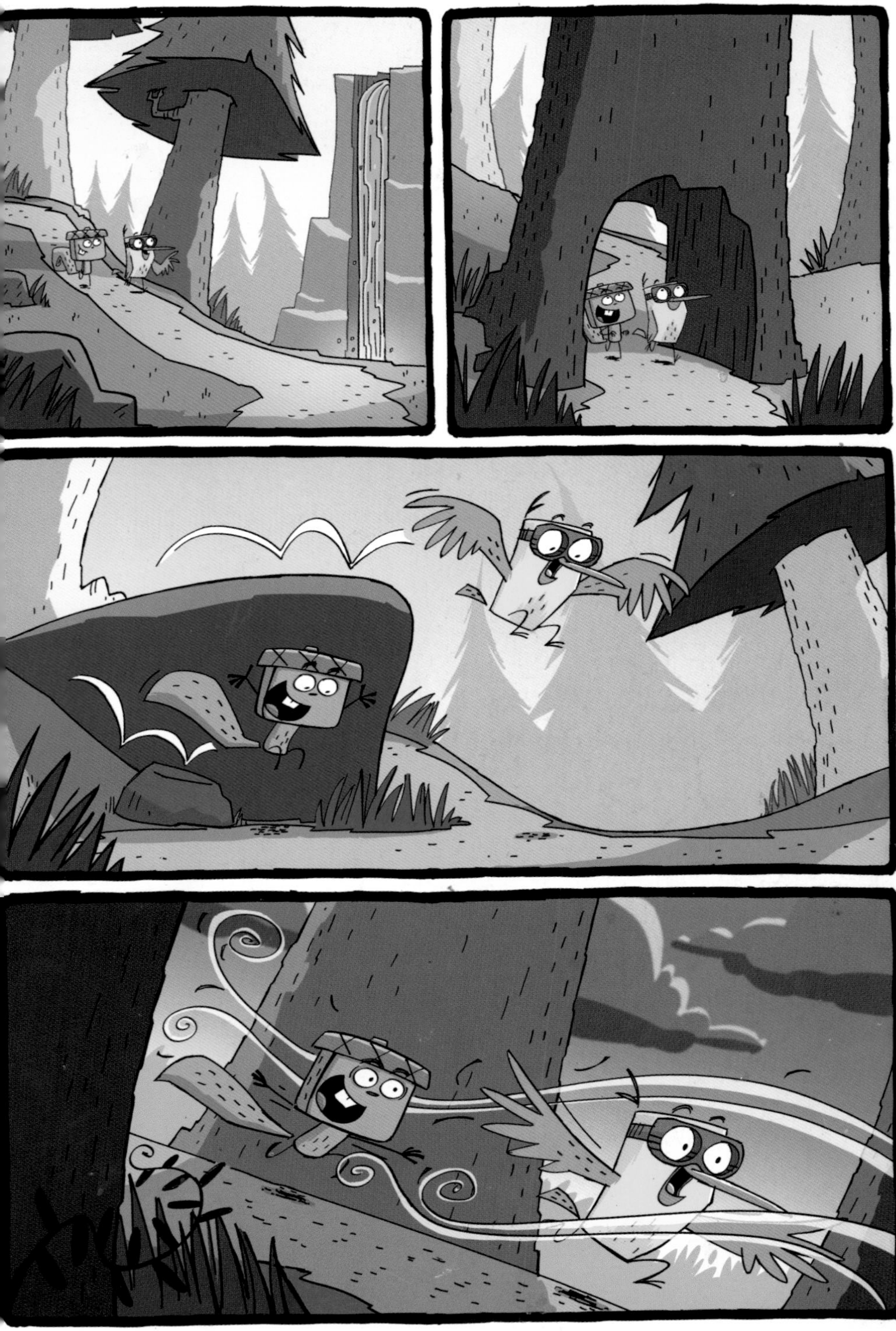

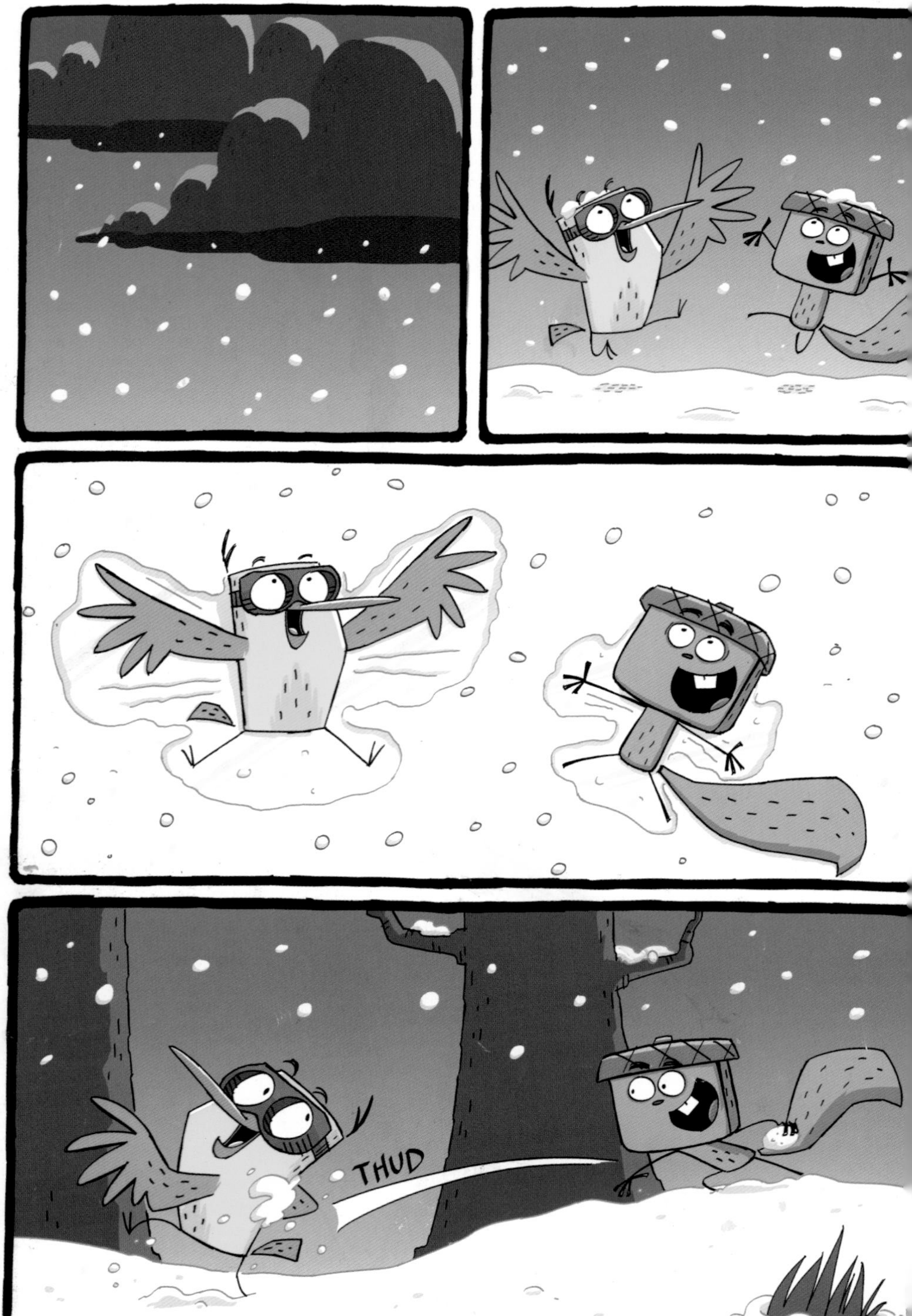
THUD

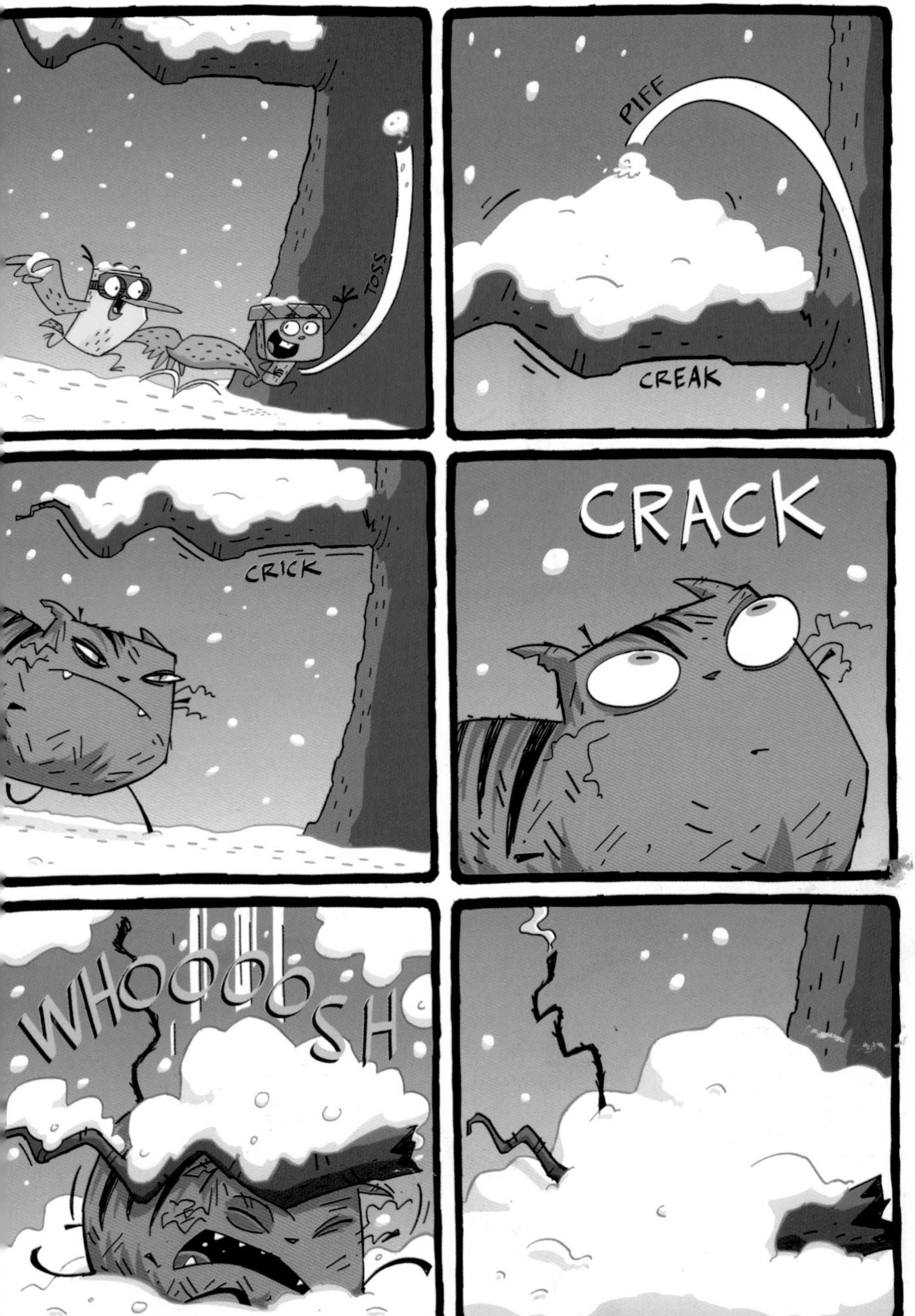
TOSS
PIFF
CREAK
CRICK
CRACK
WHOOOOOSH

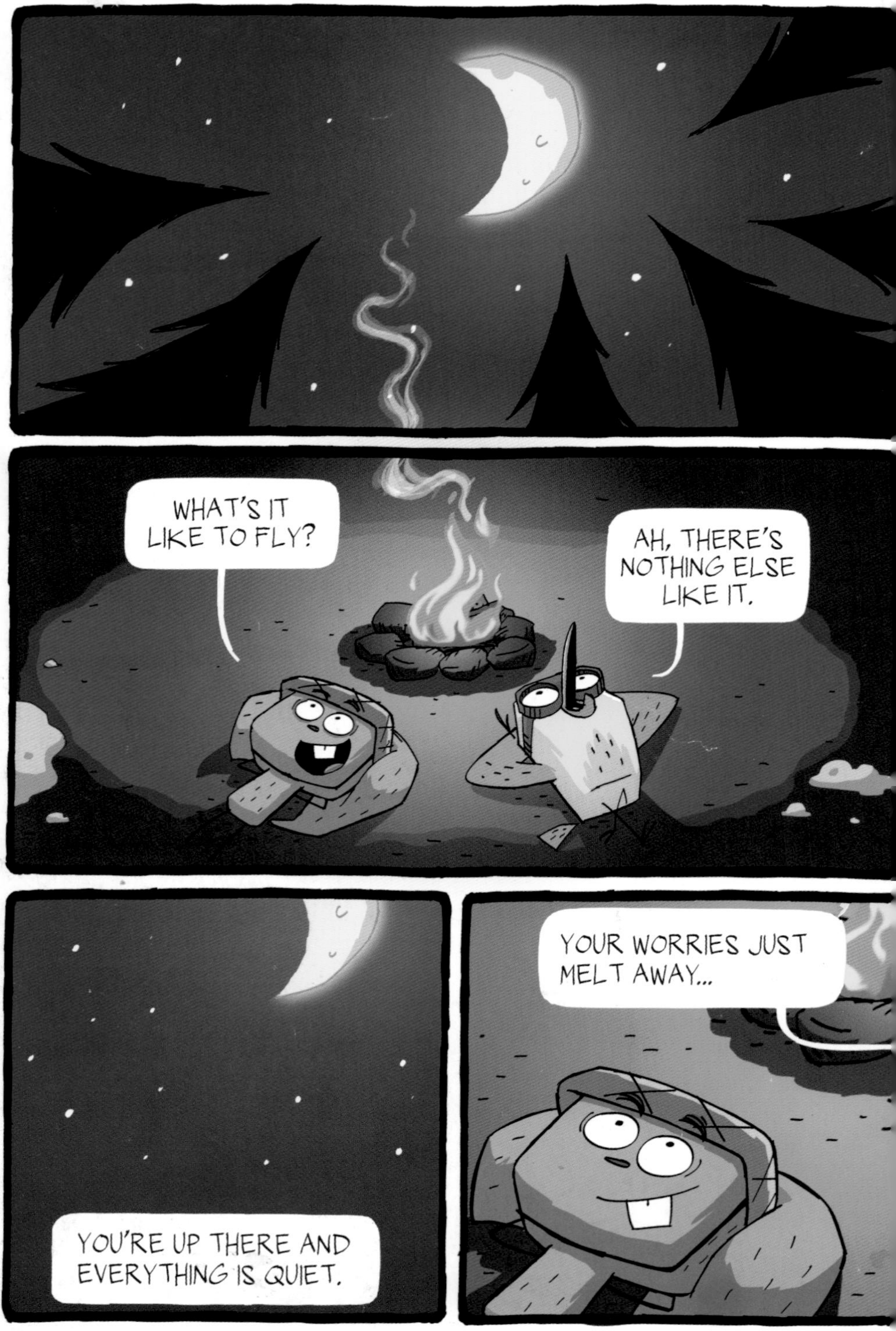
WHAT'S IT LIKE TO FLY?
AH, THERE'S NOTHING ELSE LIKE IT.
YOU'RE UP THERE AND EVERYTHING IS QUIET.
YOUR WORRIES JUST MELT AWAY...

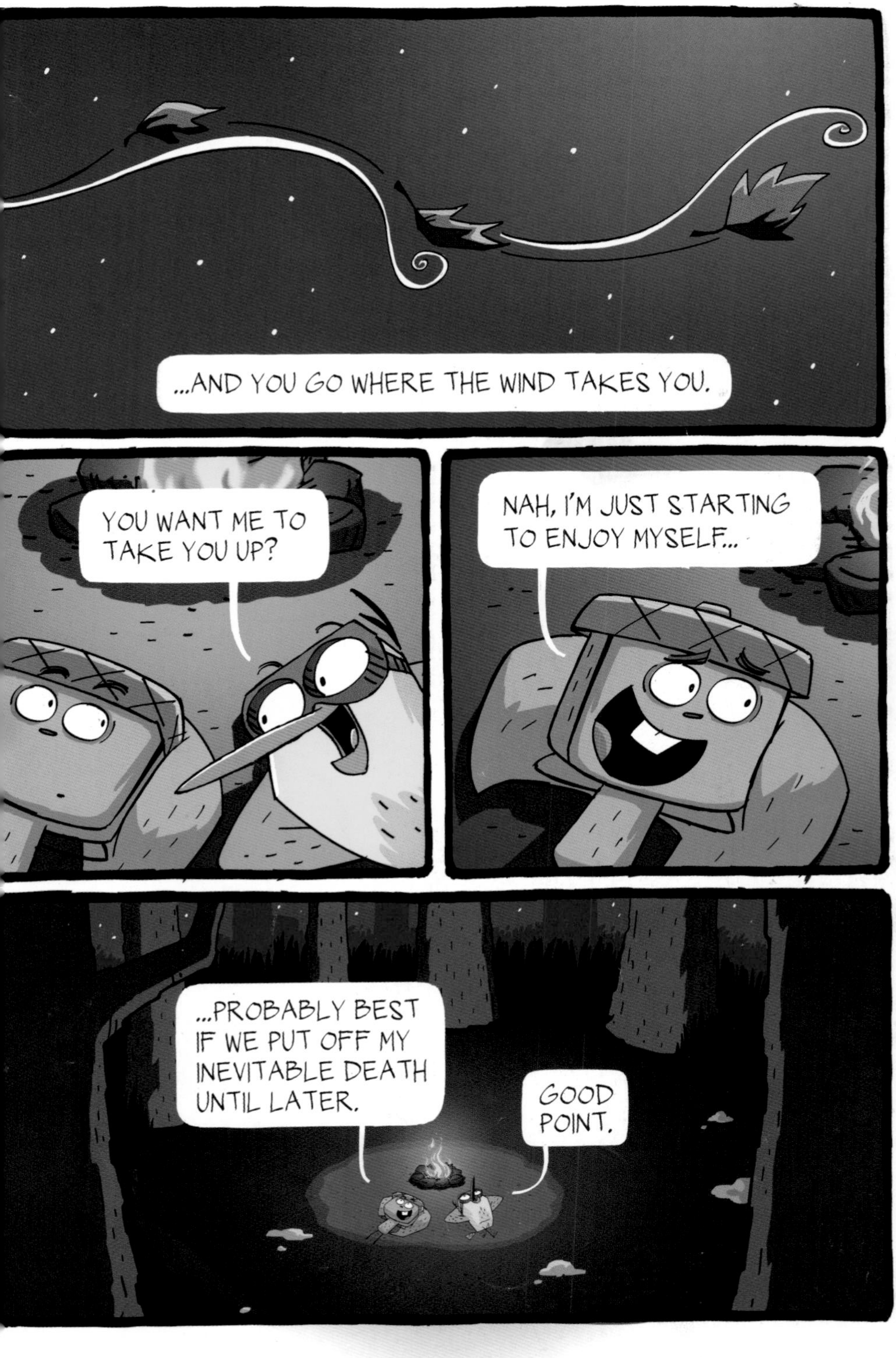
...AND YOU GO WHERE THE WIND TAKES YOU.
YOU WANT ME TO TAKE YOU UP?
NAH, I'M JUST STARTING TO ENJOY MYSELF...
...PROBABLY BEST IF WE PUT OFF MY INEVITABLE DEATH UNTIL LATER.
GOOD POINT.

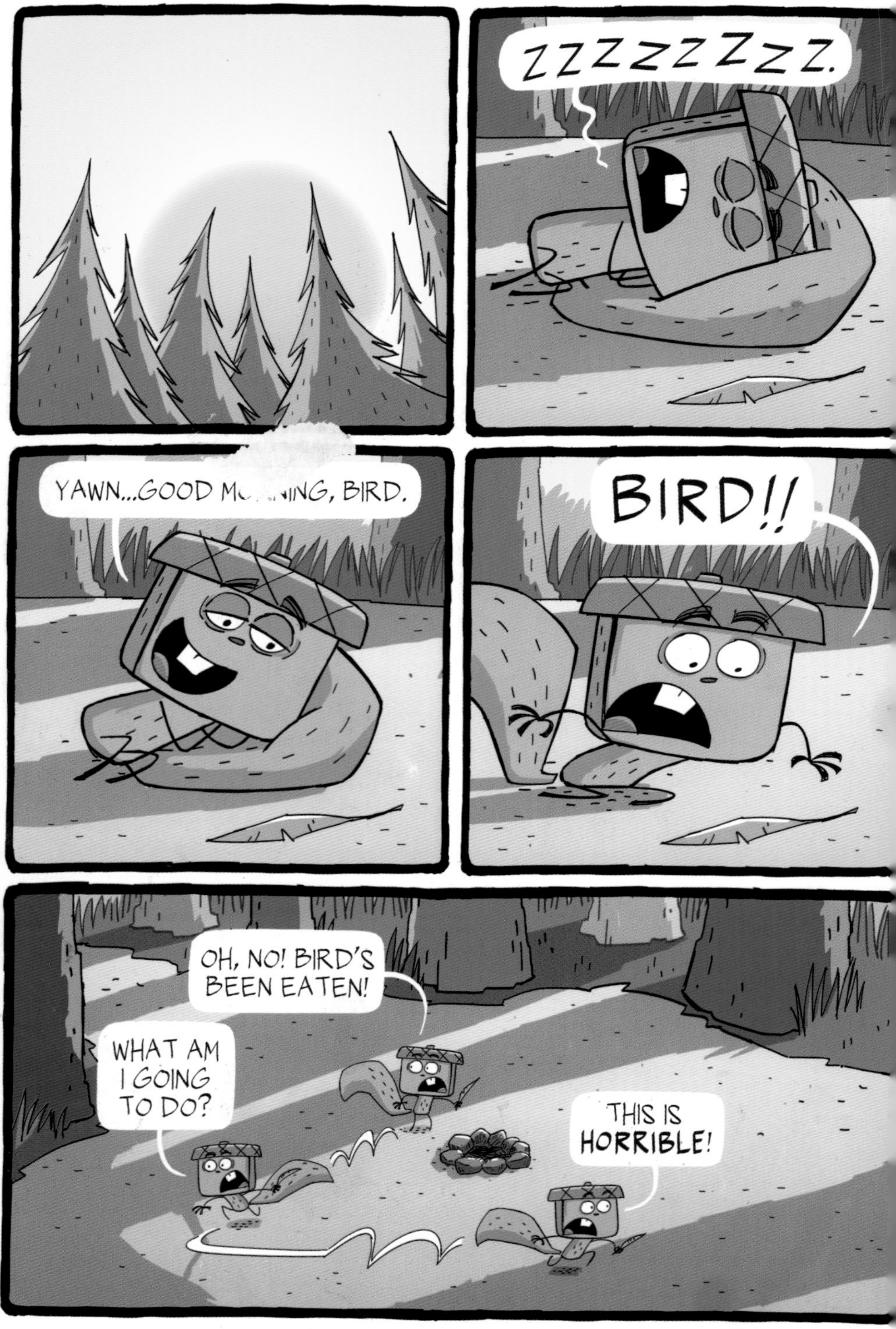
ZZZZZZZZZ.
YAWN...GOOD M NING, BIRD.
BIRD!!
OH, NO! BIRD'S BEEN EATEN!
WHAT AM I GOING TO DO?
THIS IS HORRIBLE!

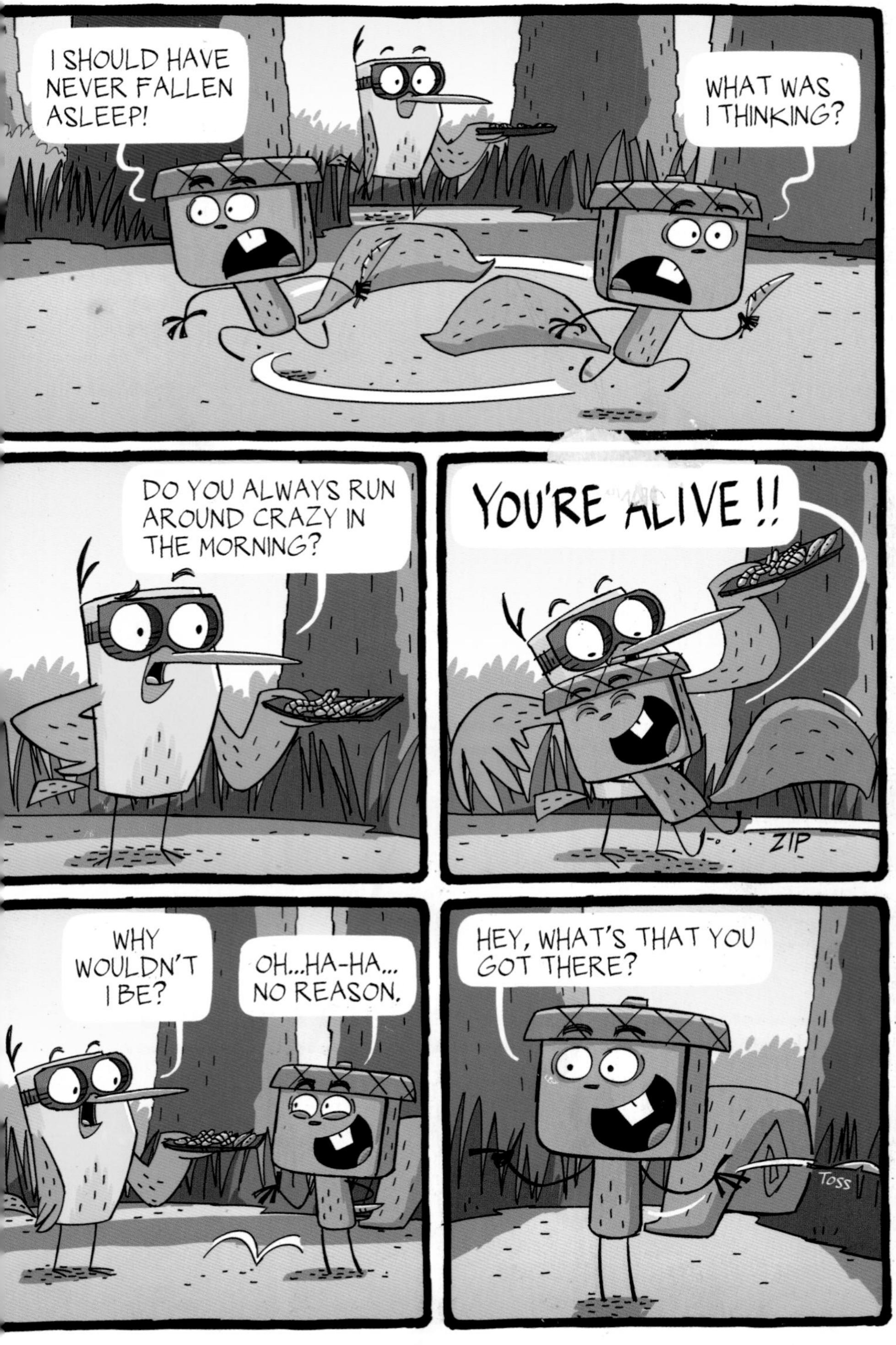
I SHOULD HAVE NEVER FALLEN ASLEEP!
WHAT WAS I THINKING?
DO YOU ALWAYS RUN AROUND CRAZY IN THE MORNING?
YOU'RE ALIVE!!
ZIP
WHY WOULDN'T I BE?
OH...HA-HA... NO REASON.
HEY, WHAT'S THAT YOU GOT THERE?
TOSS

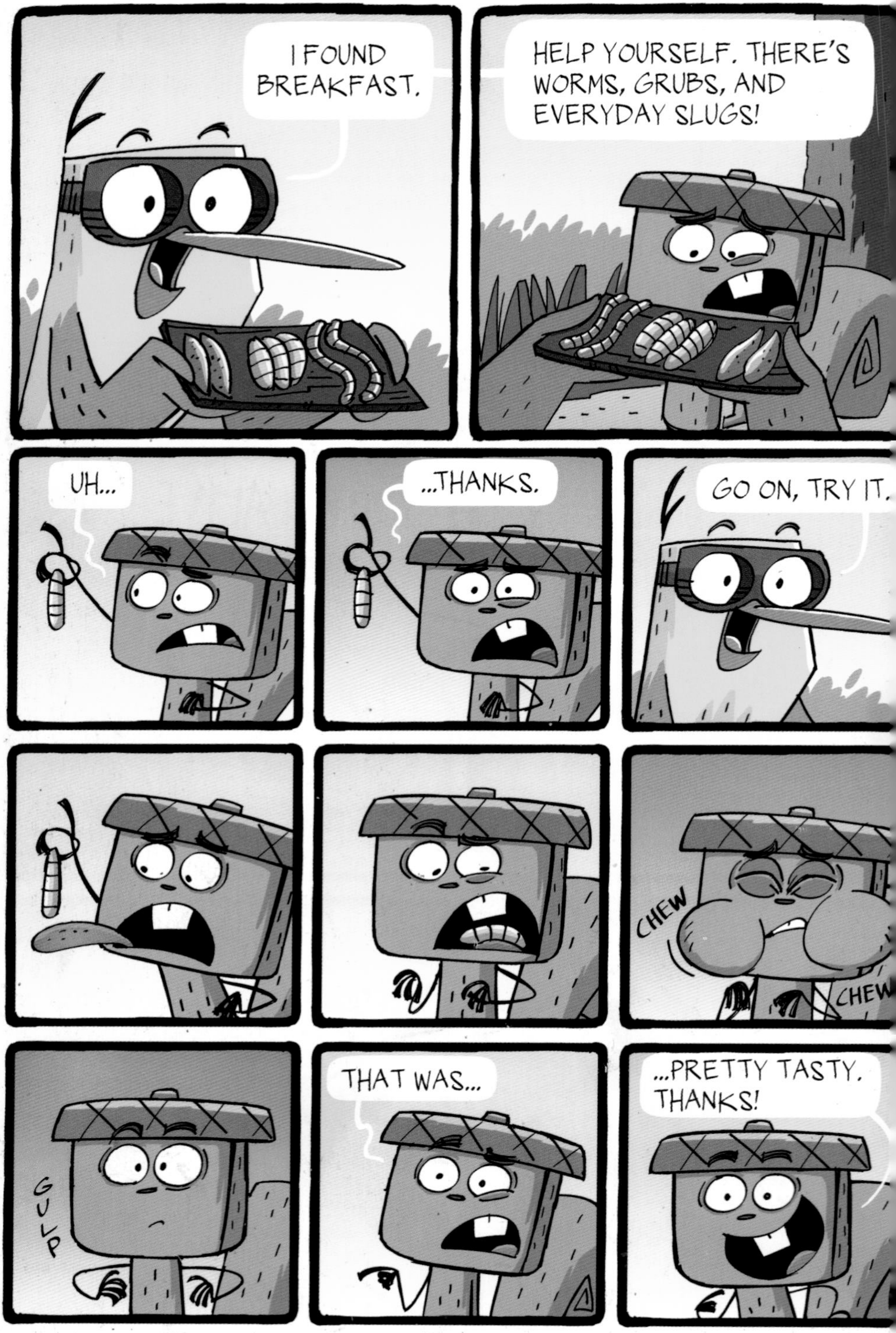

I FOUND BREAKFAST.
HELP YOURSELF. THERE'S WORMS, GRUBS, AND EVERYDAY SLUGS!
UH...
...THANKS.
GO ON, TRY IT.
CHEW
CHEW
GULP
THAT WAS...
...PRETTY TASTY. THANKS!

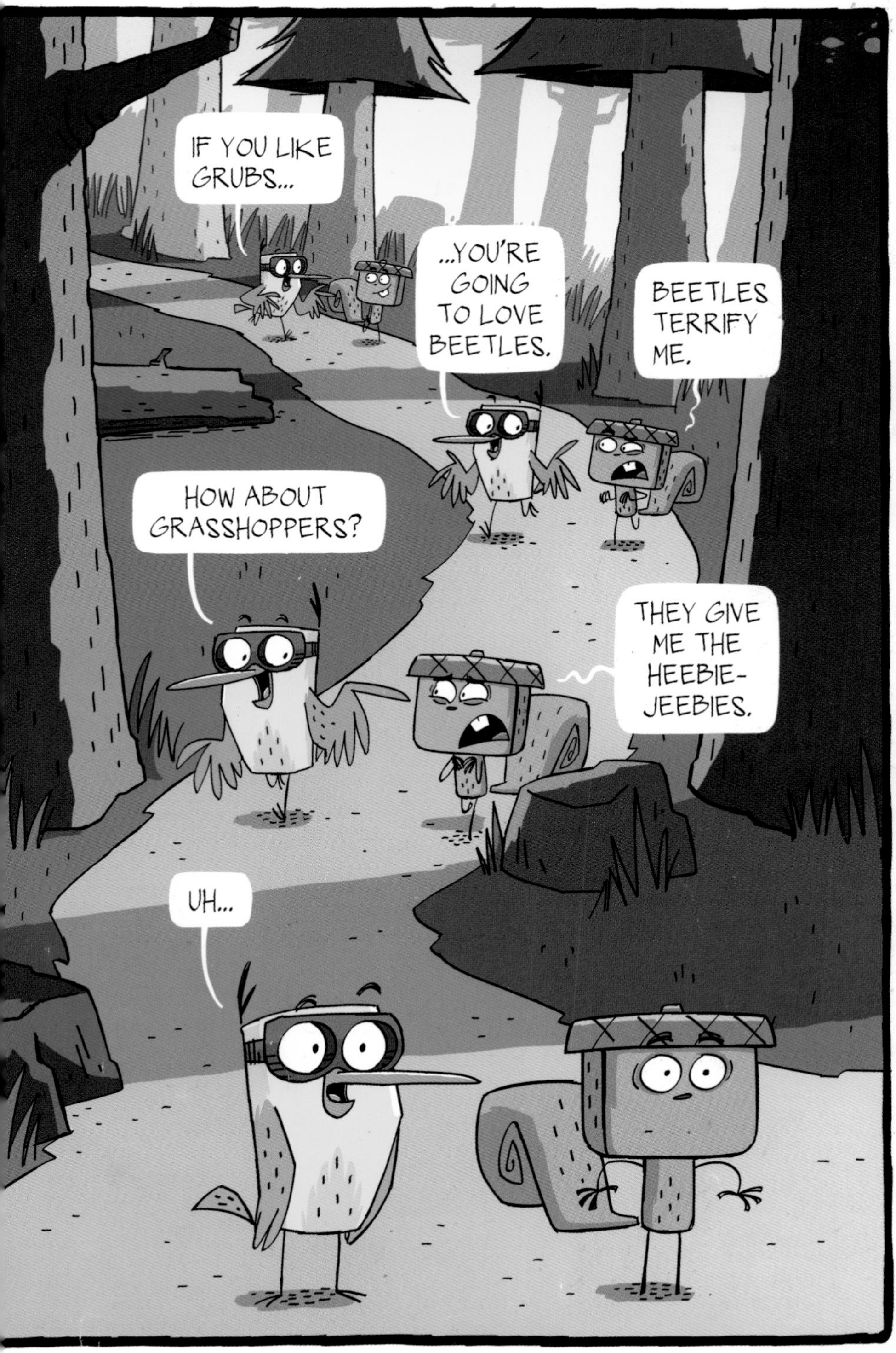
IF YOU LIKE GRUBS...
...YOU'RE GOING TO LOVE BEETLES.
BEETLES TERRIFY ME.
HOW ABOUT GRASSHOPPERS?
THEY GIVE ME THE HEEBIE-JEEBIES.
UH...

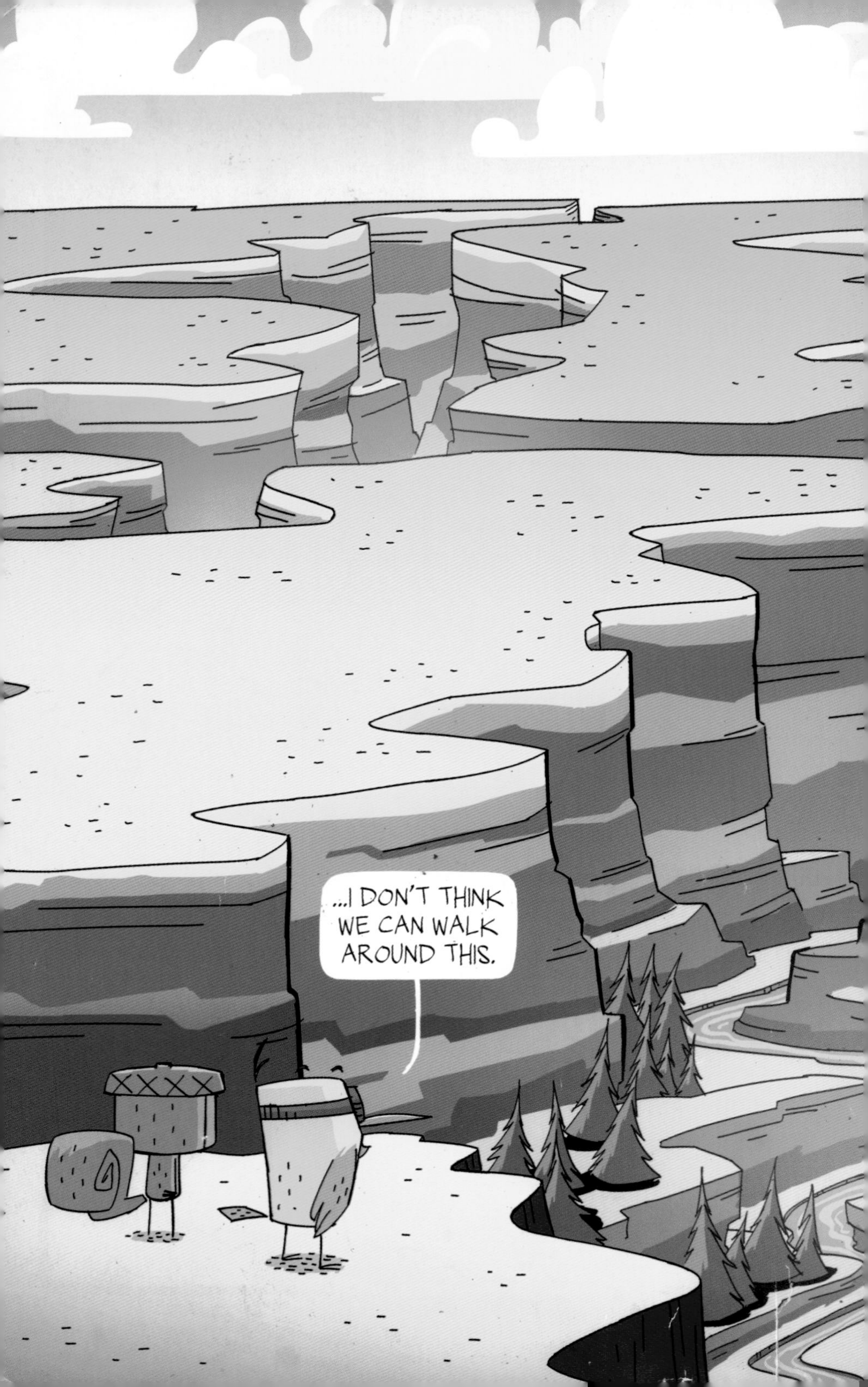
...I DON'T THINK WE CAN WALK AROUND THIS.

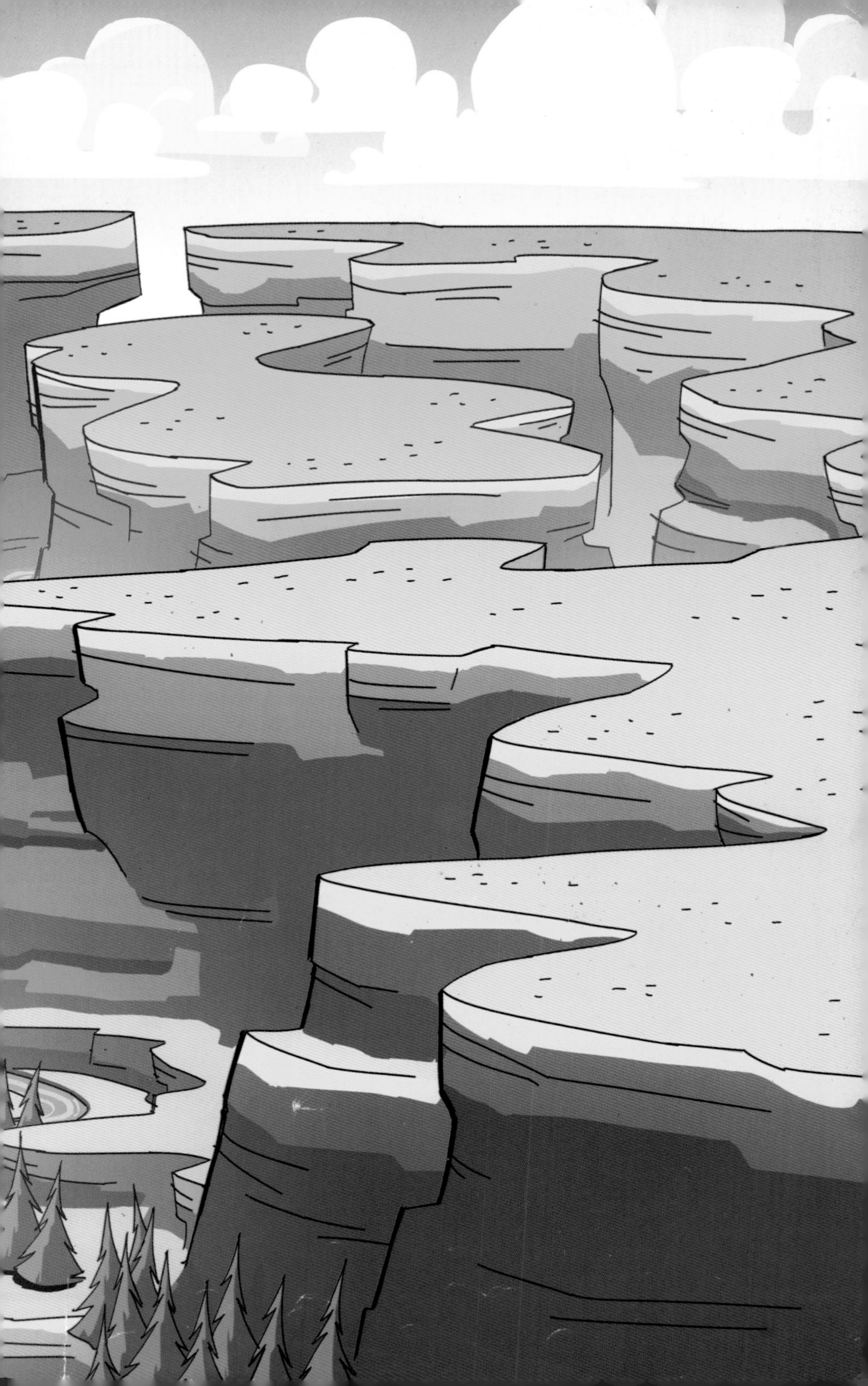

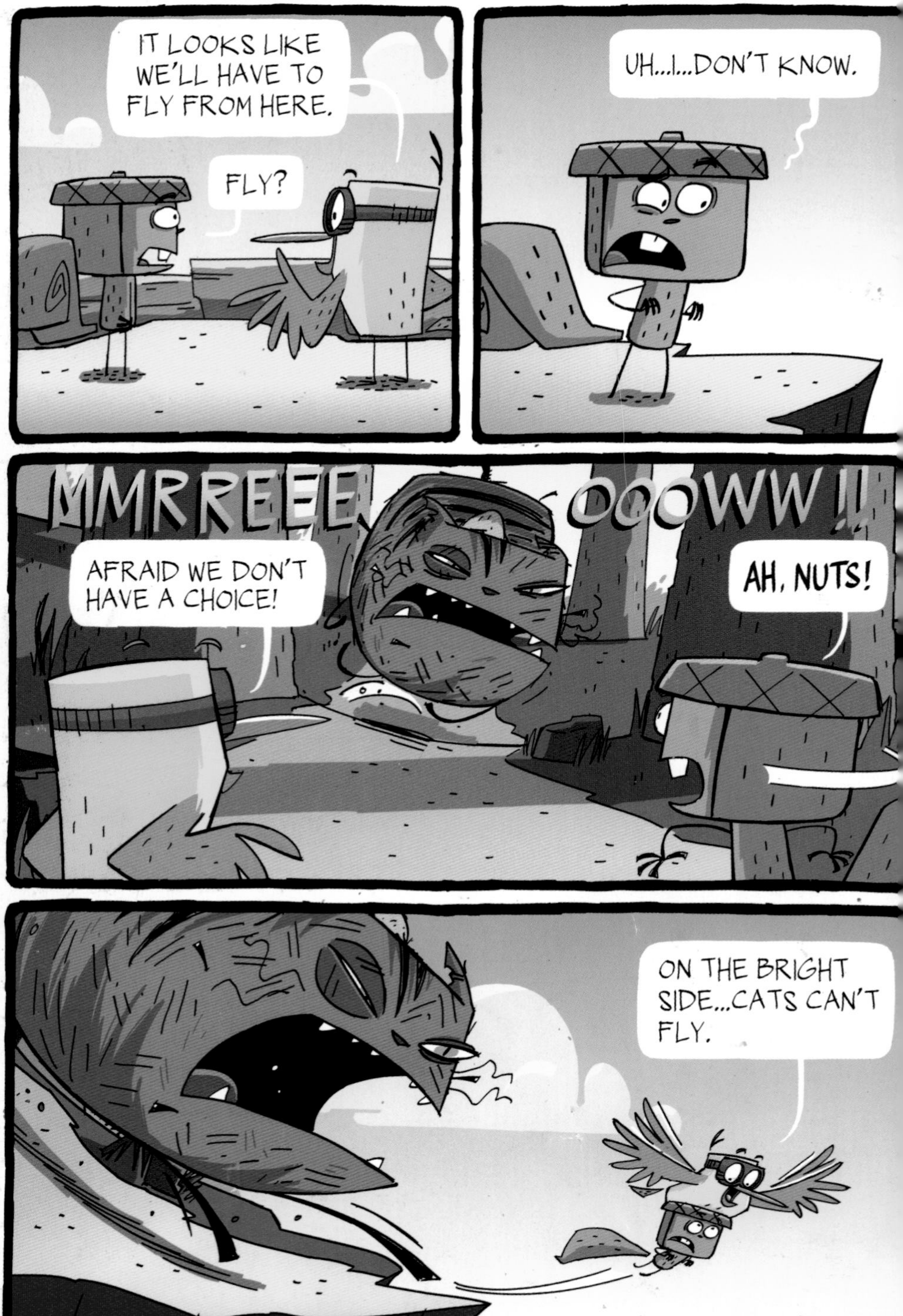
IT LOOKS LIKE WE'LL HAVE TO FLY FROM HERE.
FLY?
UH...I...DON'T KNOW.
MMRREEE
OOOWW!!
AFRAID WE DON'T HAVE A CHOICE!
AH, NUTS!
ON THE BRIGHT SIDE...CATS CAN'T FLY.

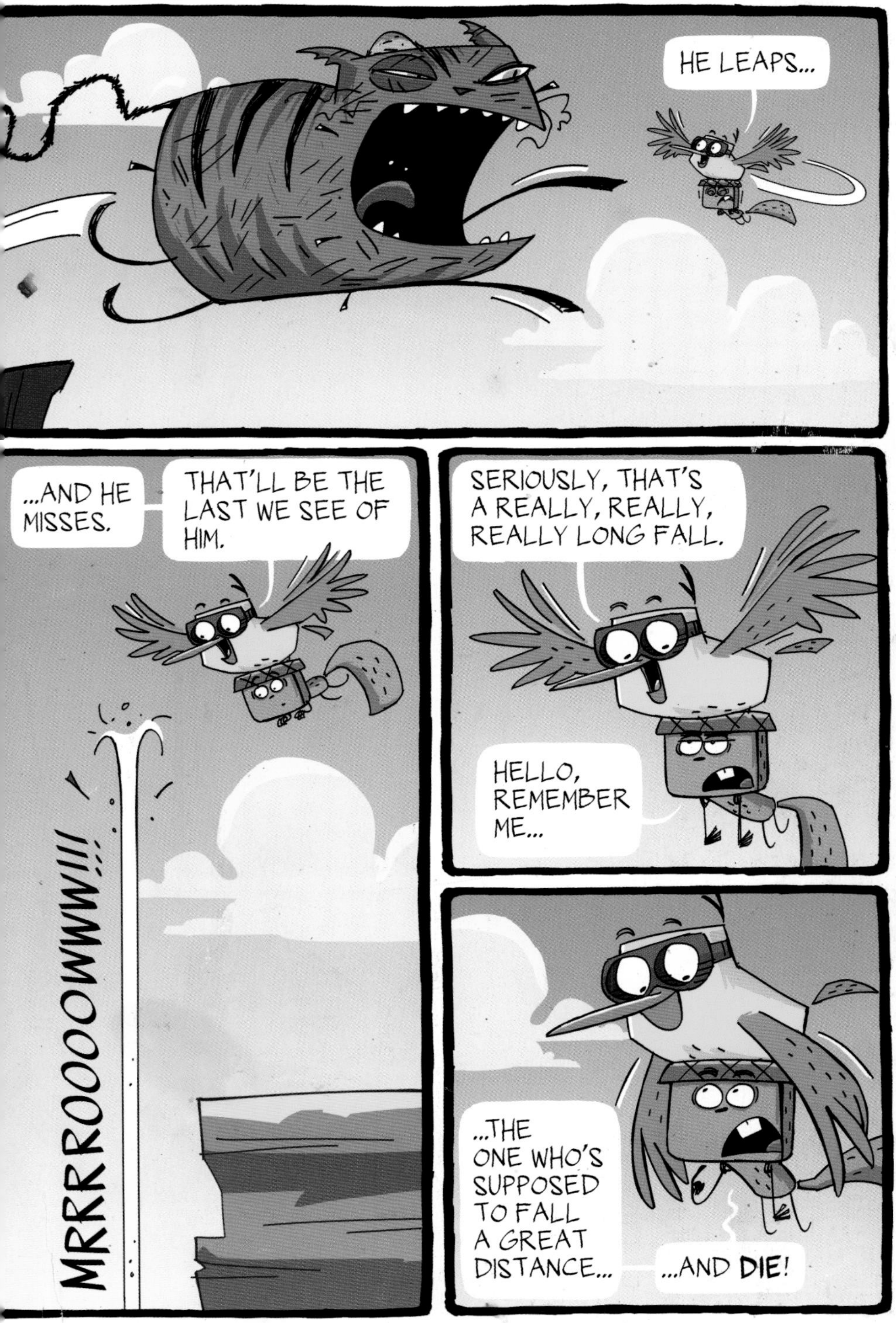
HE LEAPS...
...AND HE MISSES.
THAT'LL BE THE LAST WE SEE OF HIM.
MRRRROOOOWWWW!!!
SERIOUSLY, THAT'S A REALLY, REALLY, REALLY LONG FALL.
HELLO, REMEMBER ME...
...THE ONE WHO'S SUPPOSED TO FALL A GREAT DISTANCE...
...AND **DIE**!

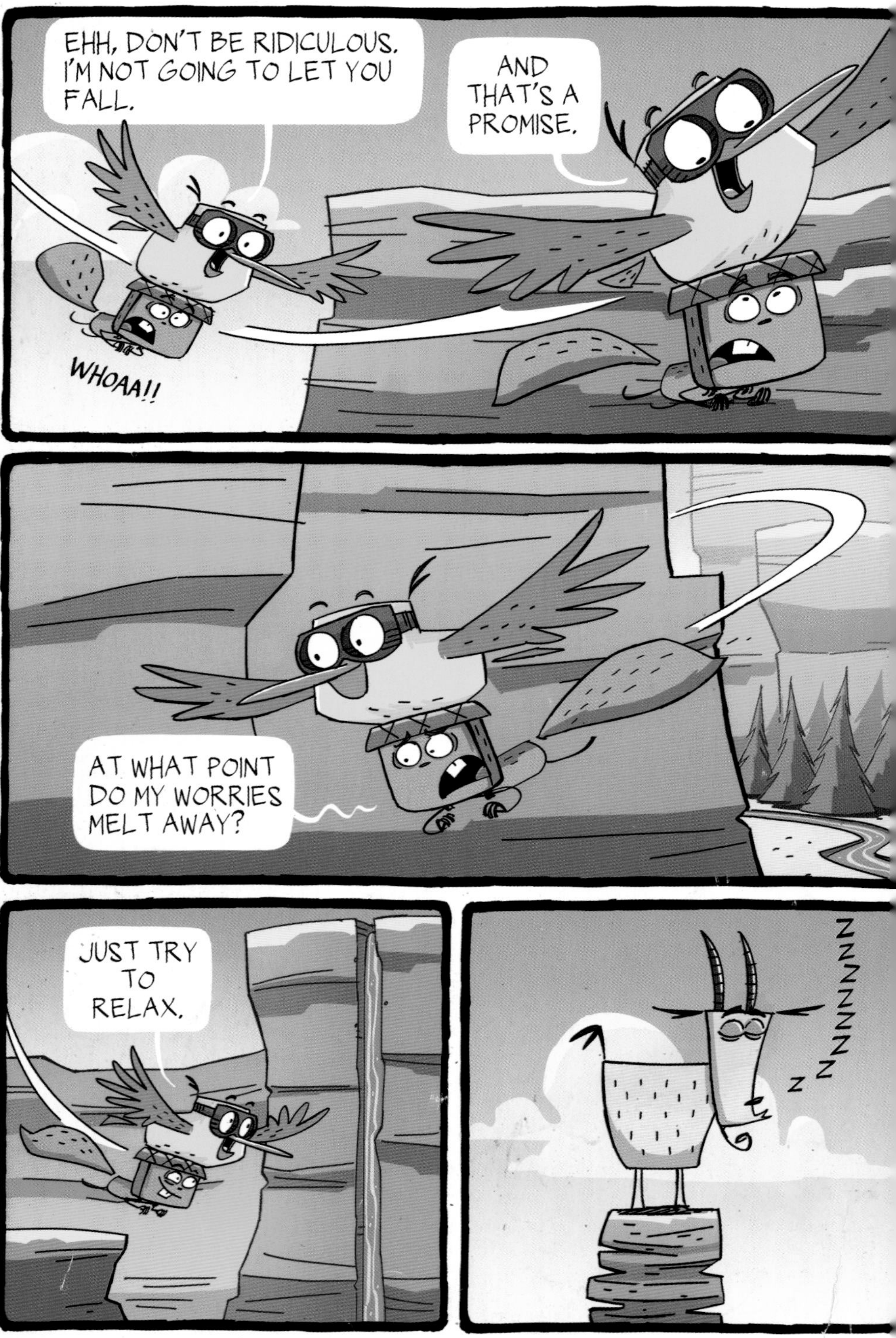
EHH, DON'T BE RIDICULOUS. I'M NOT GOING TO LET YOU FALL.
AND THAT'S A PROMISE.
WHOAA!!
AT WHAT POINT DO MY WORRIES MELT AWAY?
JUST TRY TO RELAX.
ZZZZZZZZZ

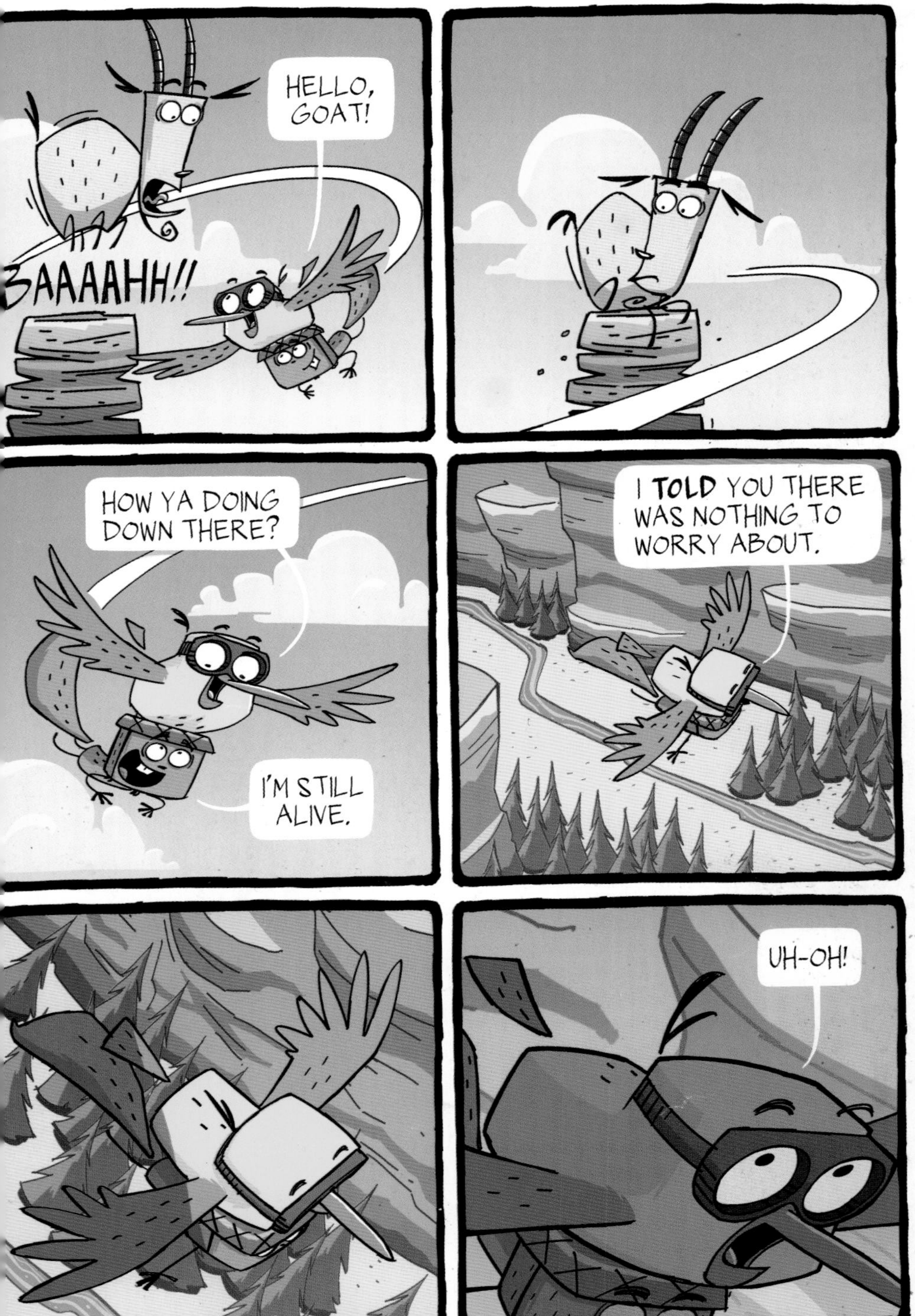
HELLO, GOAT!
BAAAAHH!!
HOW YA DOING DOWN THERE?
I'M STILL ALIVE.
I **TOLD** YOU THERE WAS NOTHING TO WORRY ABOUT.
UH-OH!

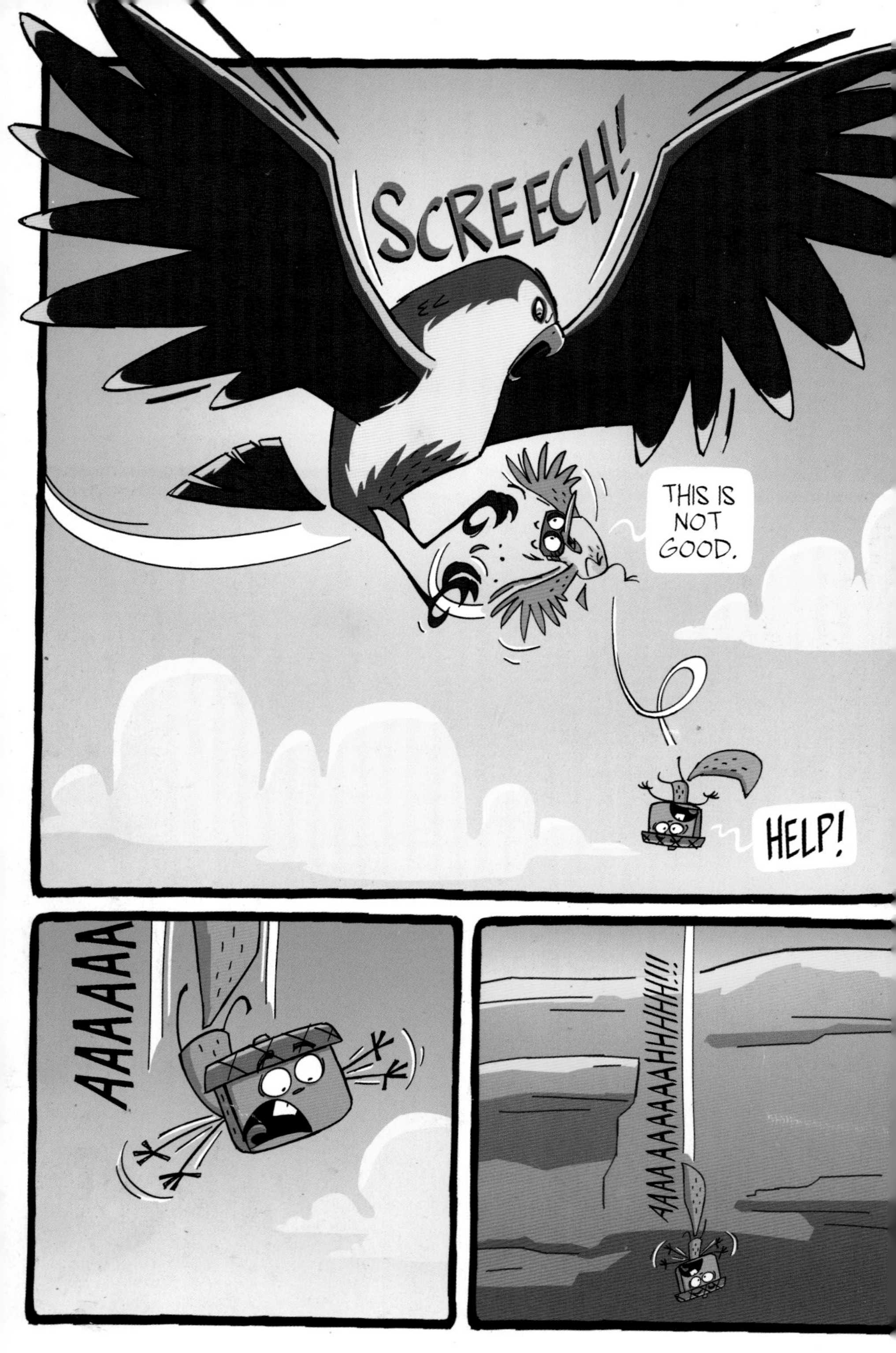
SCREECH!
THIS IS NOT GOOD.
HELP!
AAAAAA
AAAAAAAAAAAHHHHH!!!

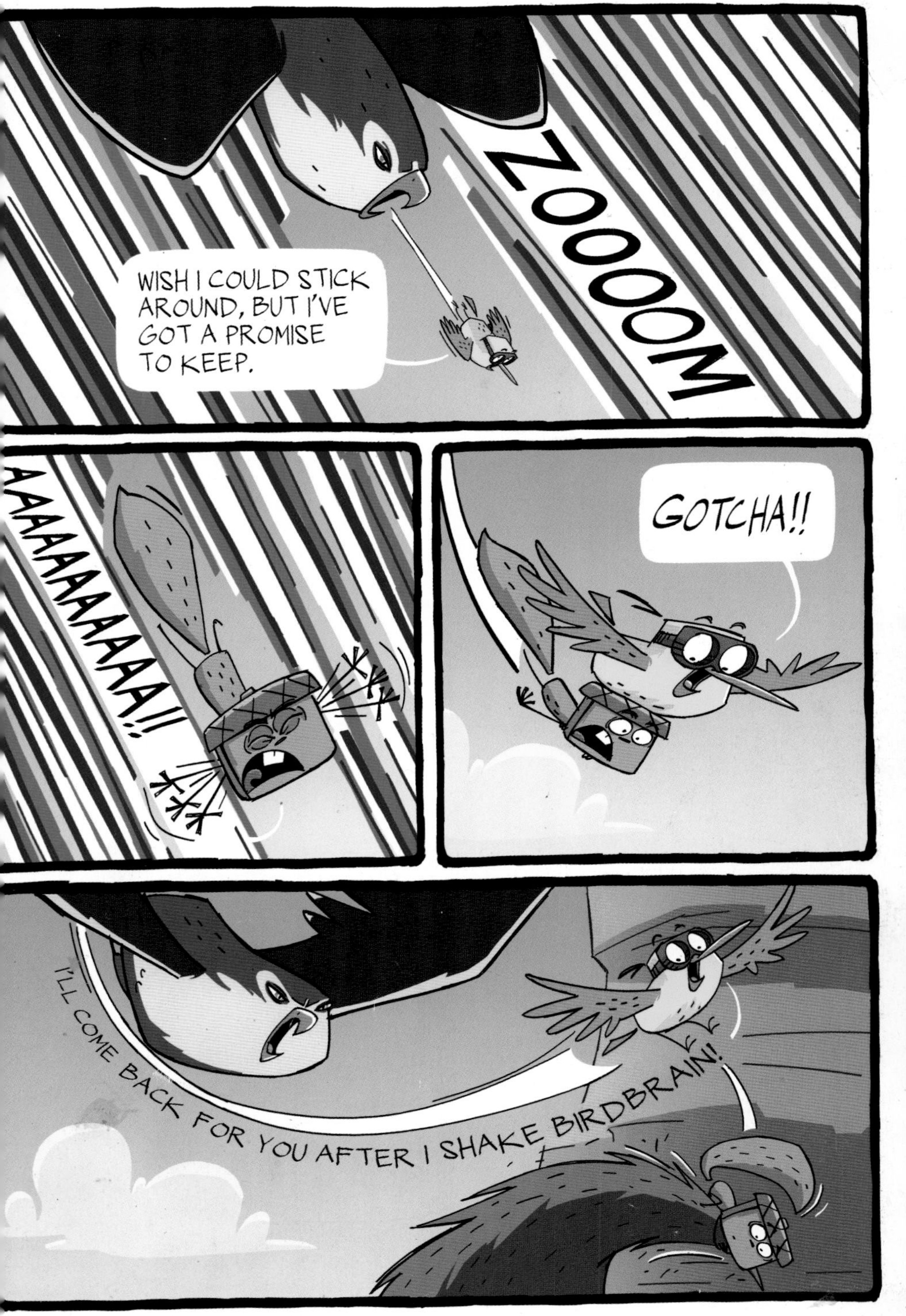
WISH I COULD STICK AROUND, BUT I'VE GOT A PROMISE TO KEEP.
ZOOOOM
AAAAAAAAAAAA!!
GOTCHA!!
I'LL COME BACK FOR YOU AFTER I SHAKE BIRDBRAIN!

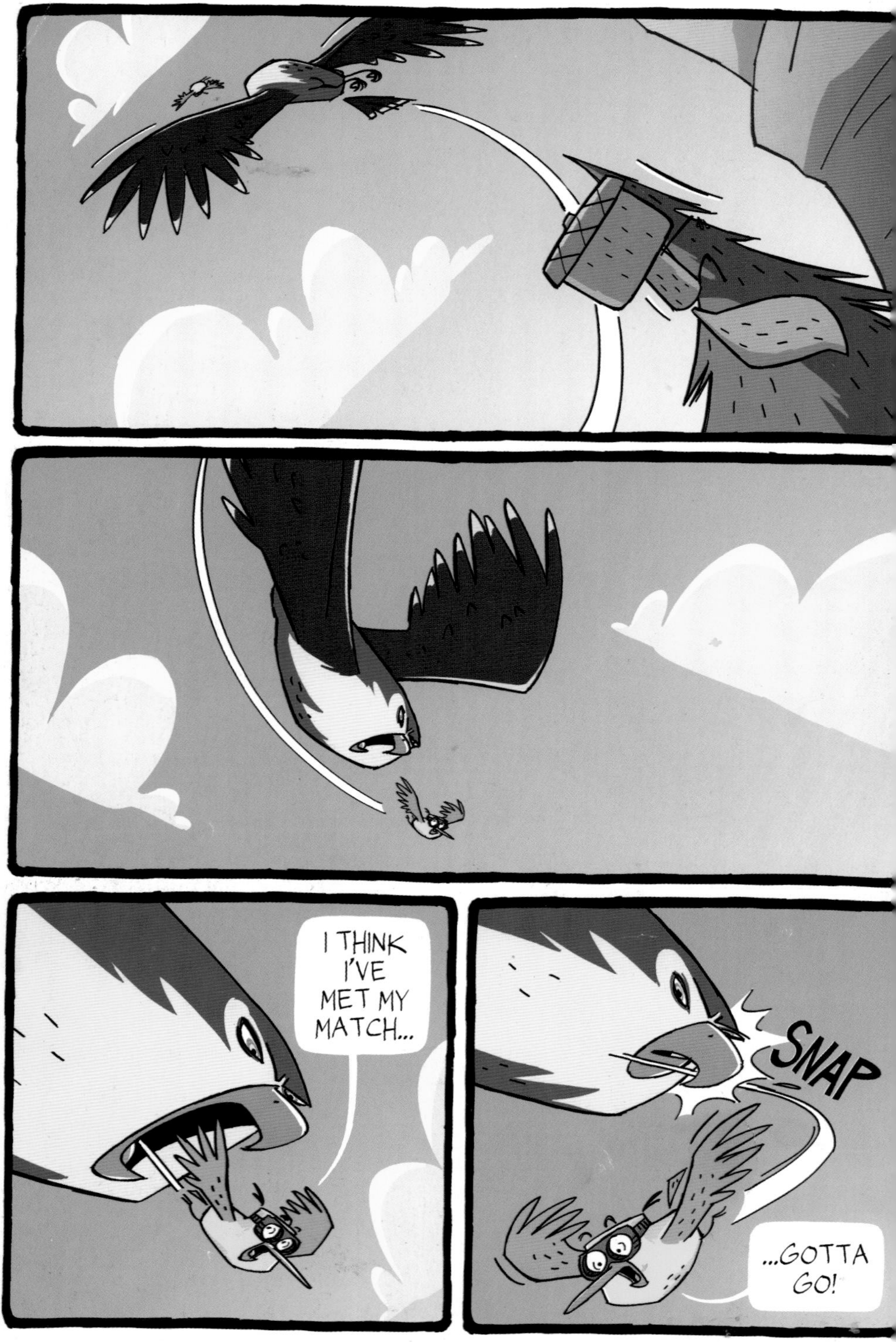
I THINK I'VE MET MY MATCH...
SNAP
...GOTTA GO!

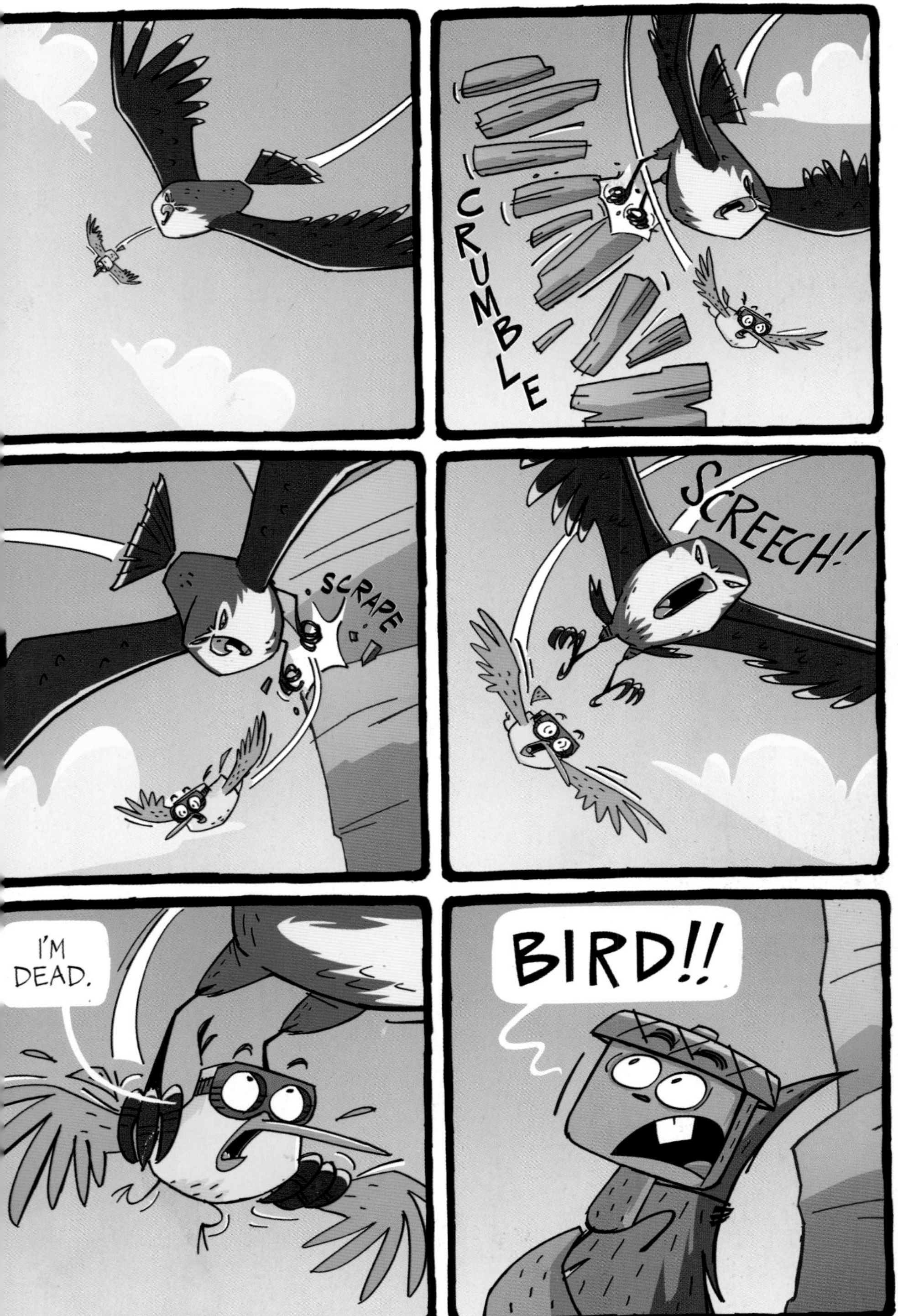
CRUMBLE
SCRAPE
SCREECH!
I'M DEAD.
BIRD!!

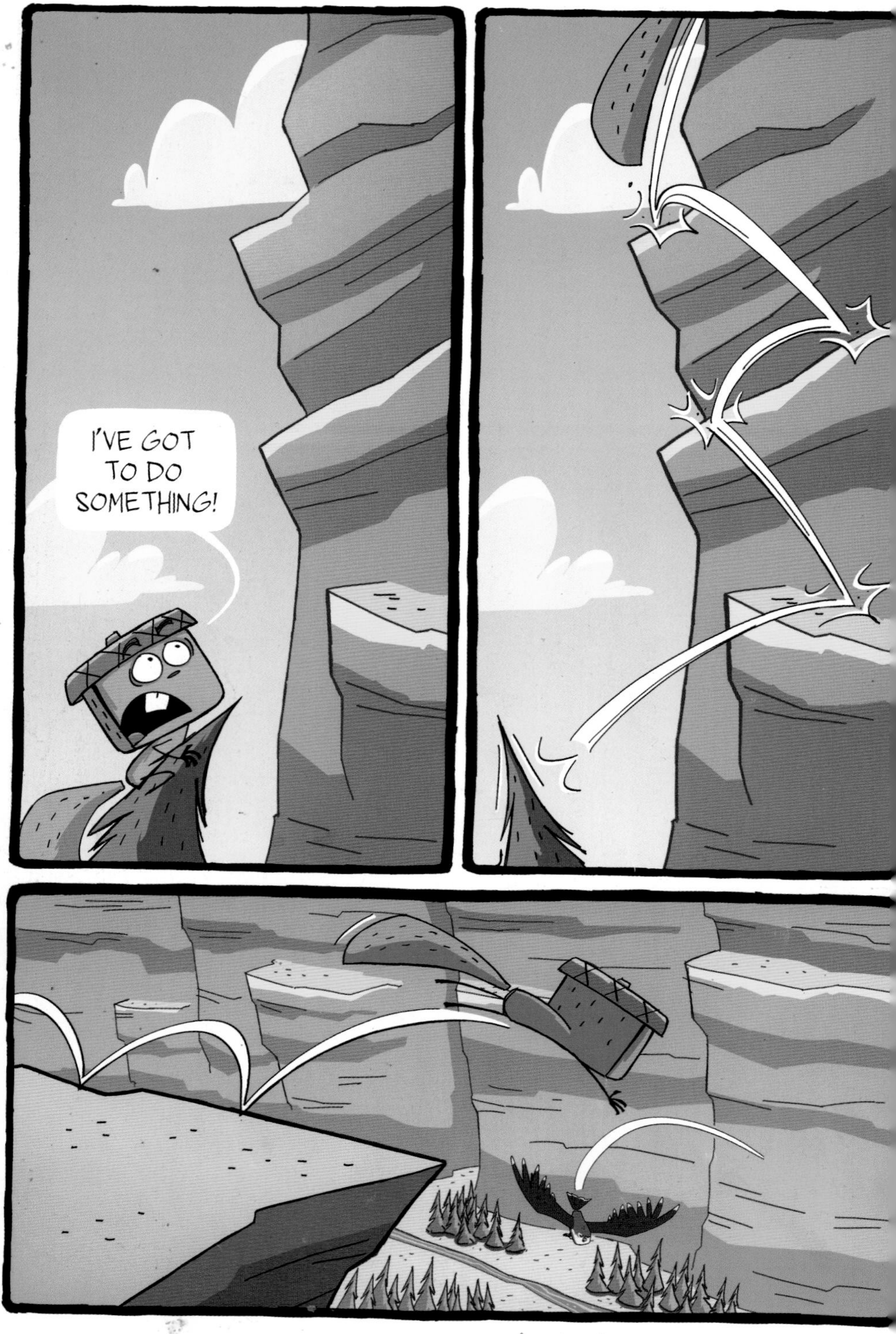
I'VE GOT TO DO SOMETHING!

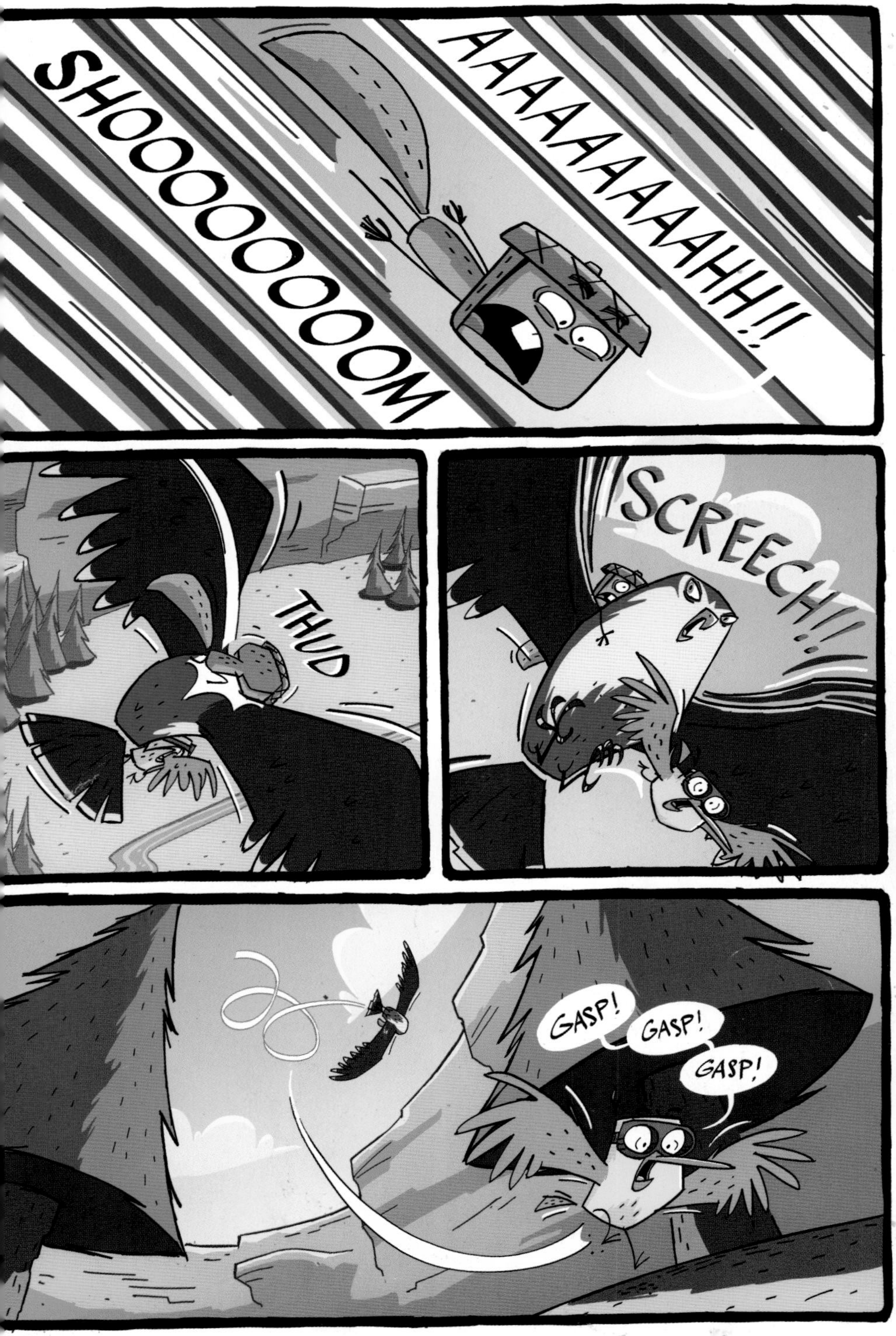
SHOOOOOOOOM
AAAAAAAAAHH!!!
THUD
SCREECH!!!
GASP!
GASP!
GASP!

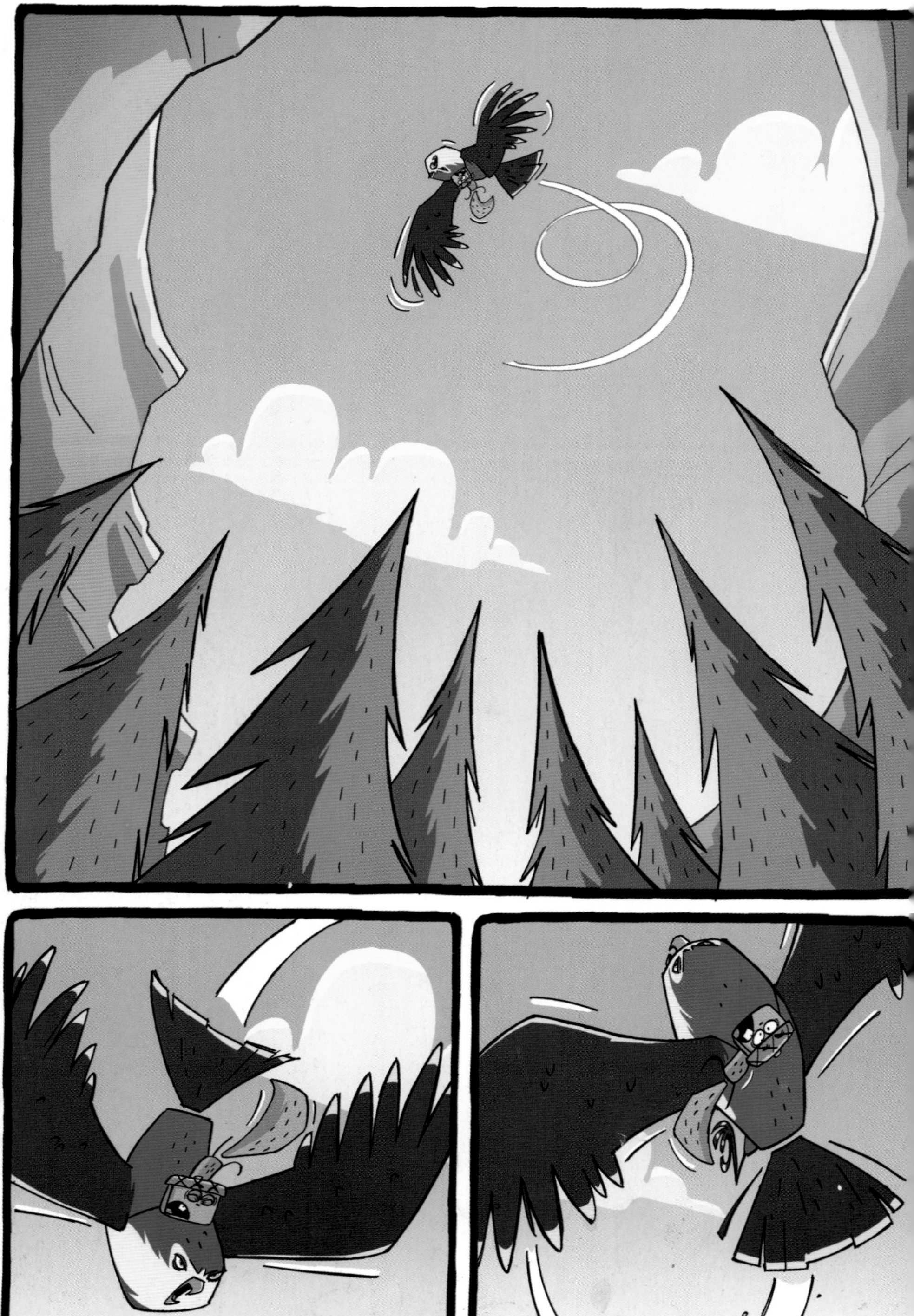

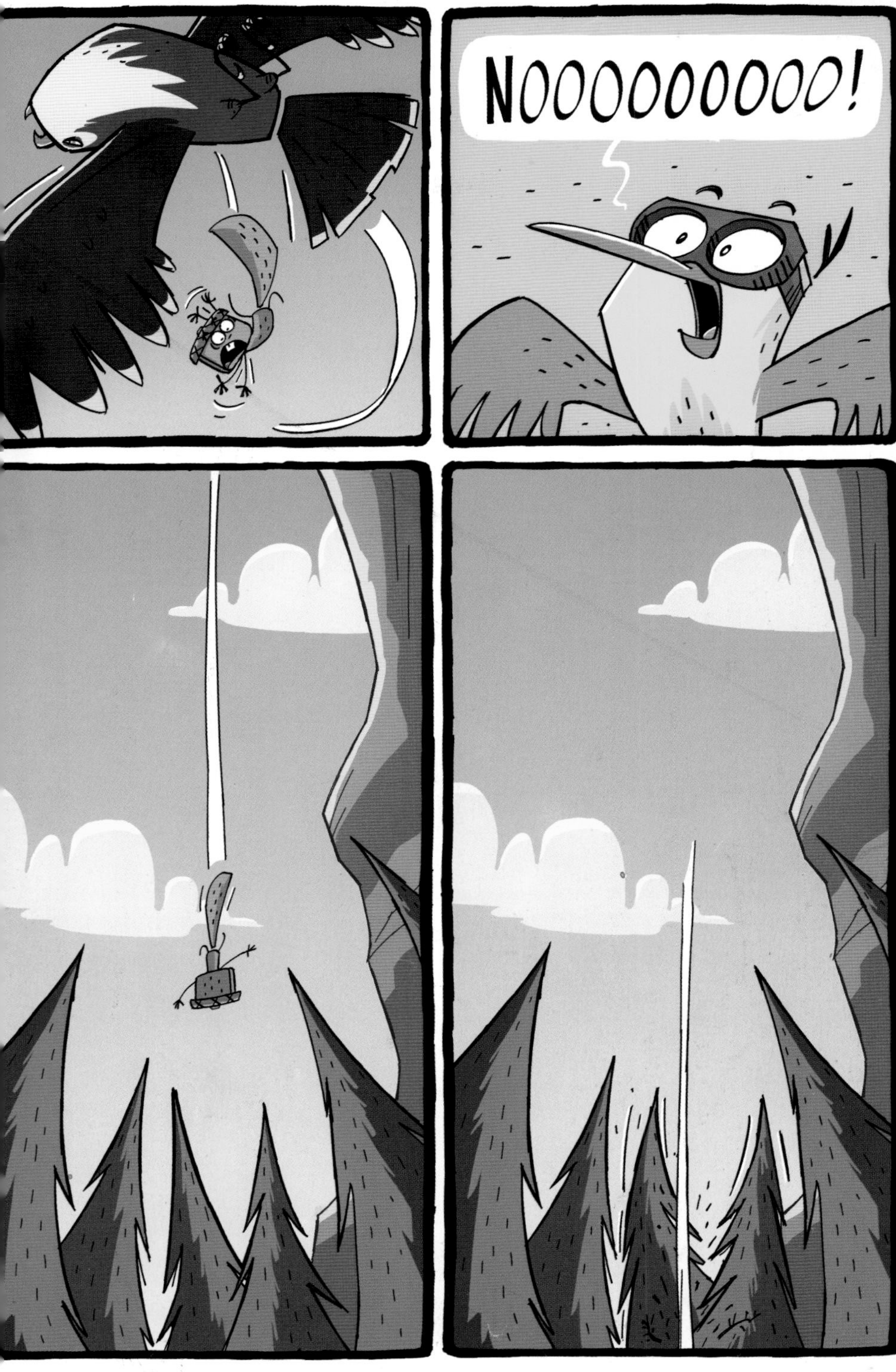
NOOOOOOOOO!

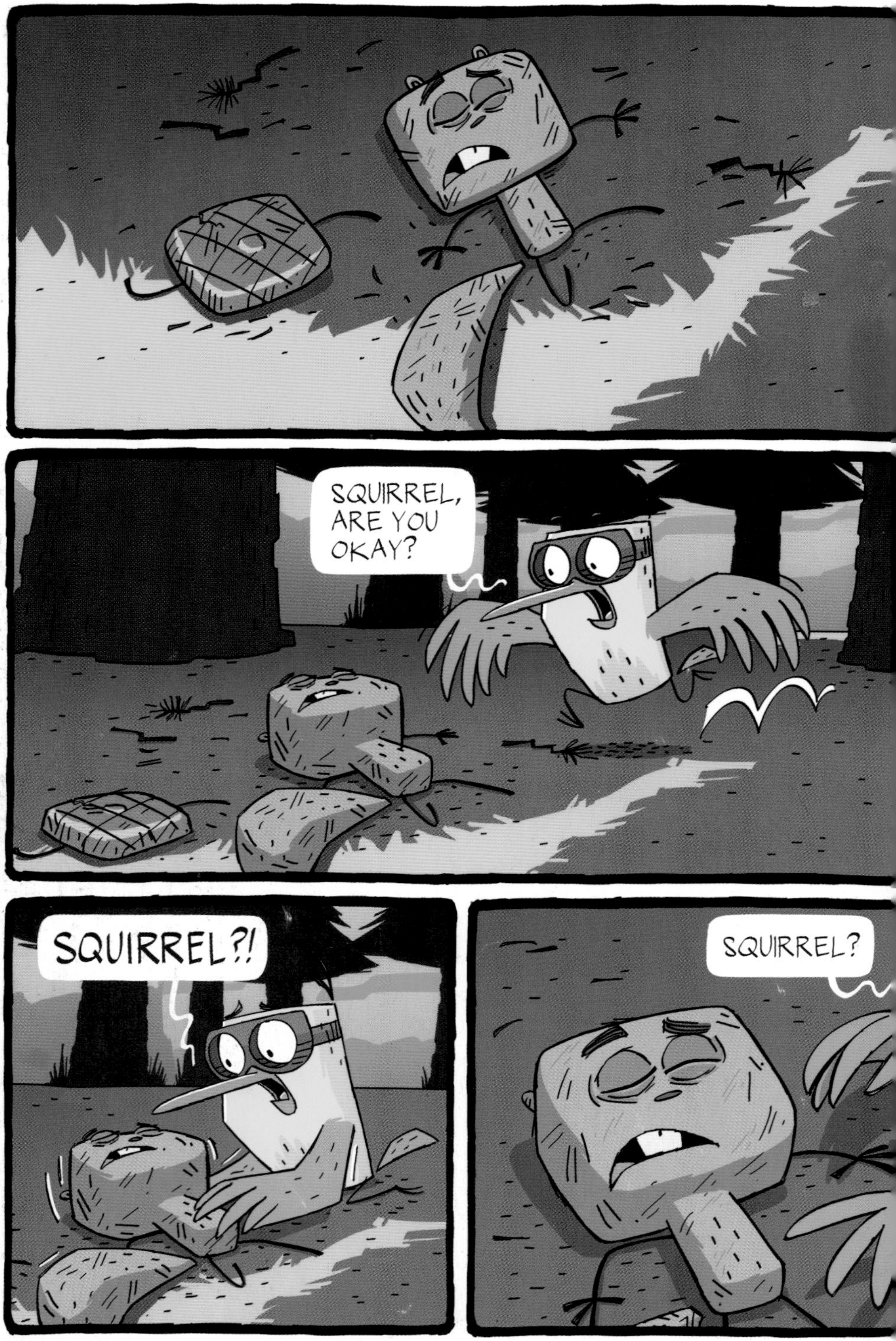

SQUIRREL, ARE YOU OKAY?
SQUIRREL?!
SQUIRREL?

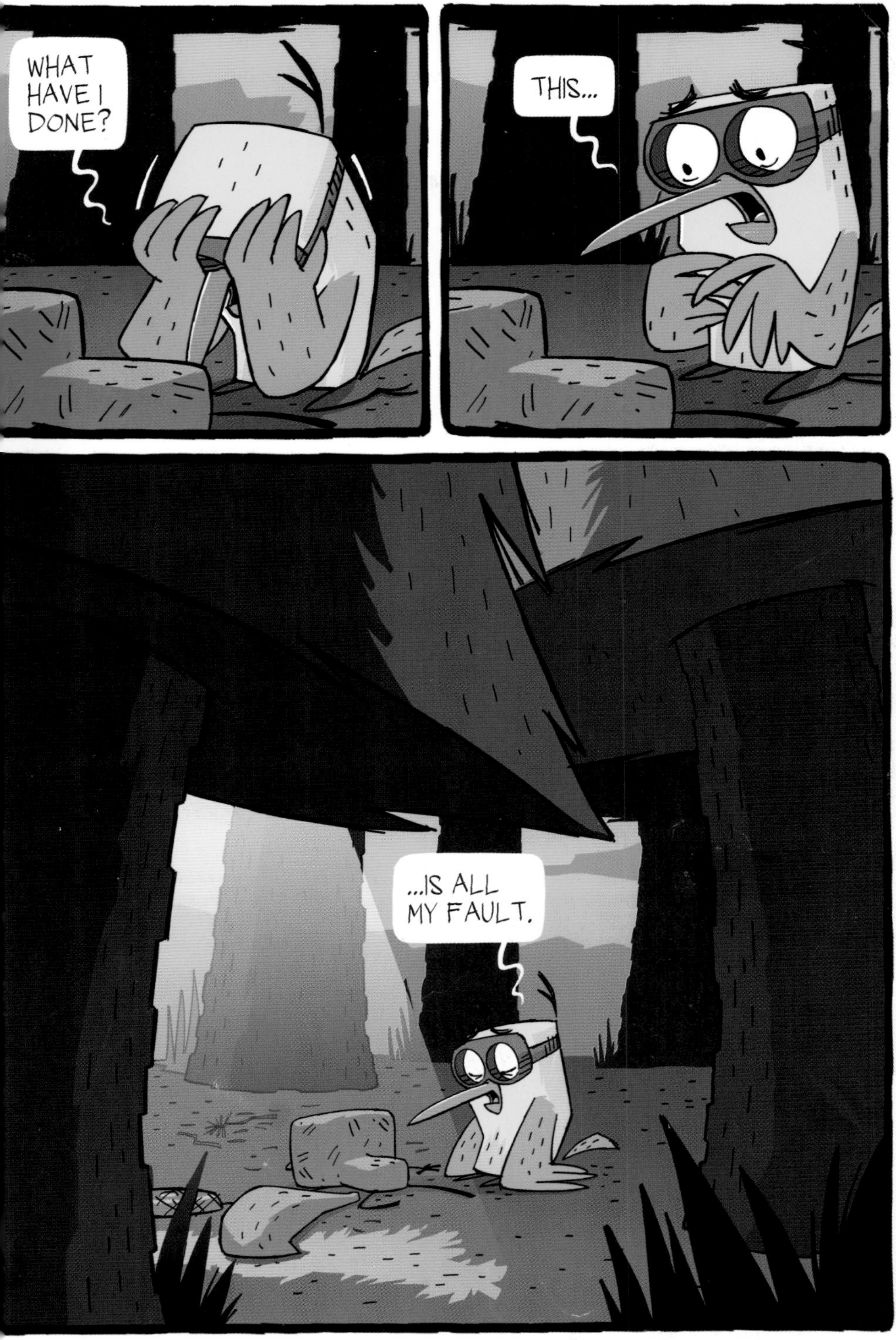
WHAT HAVE I DONE?
THIS...
...IS ALL MY FAULT.

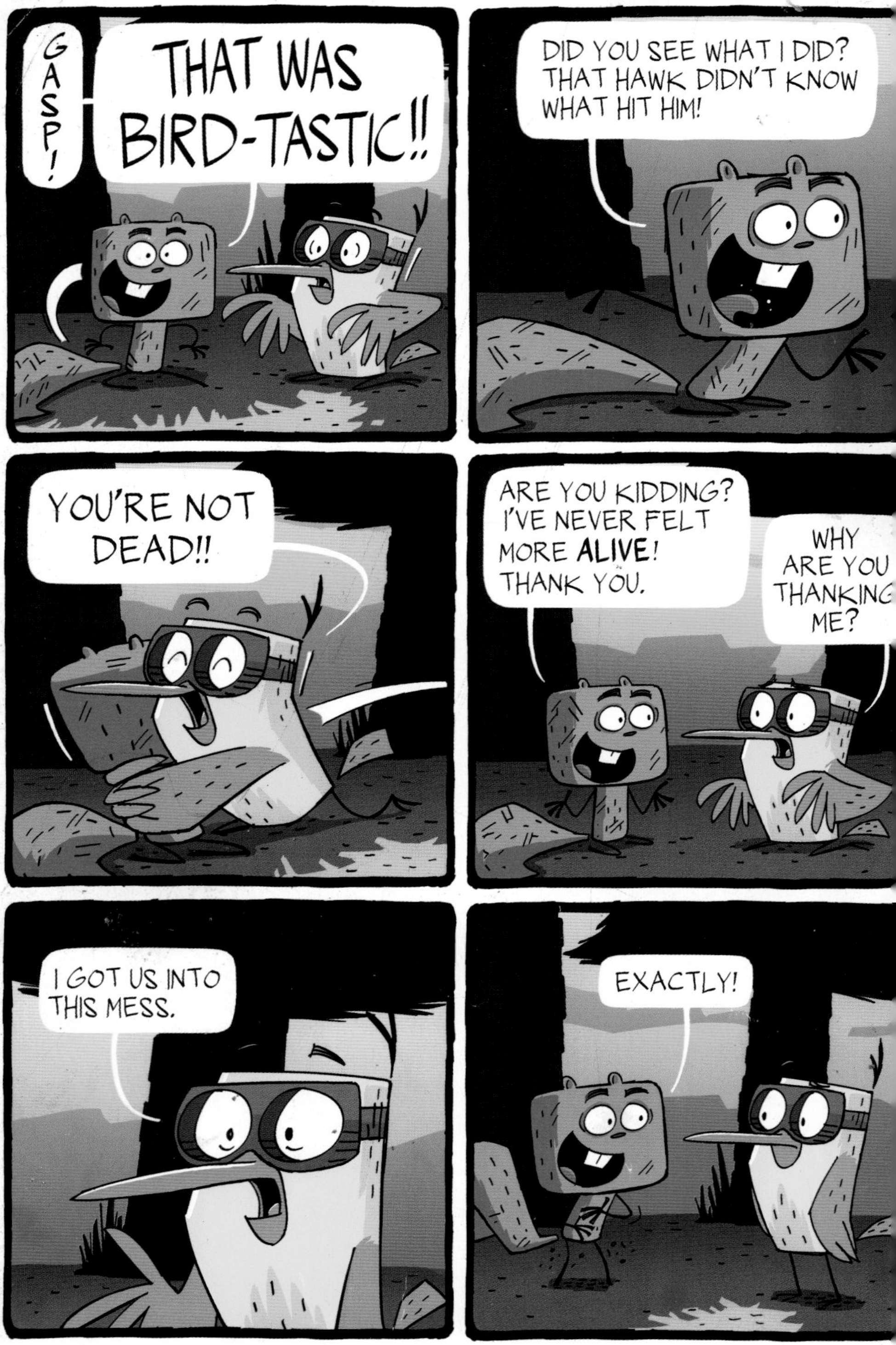
GASP!
THAT WAS BIRD-TASTIC!!
DID YOU SEE WHAT I DID? THAT HAWK DIDN'T KNOW WHAT HIT HIM!
YOU'RE NOT DEAD!!
ARE YOU KIDDING? I'VE NEVER FELT MORE ALIVE! THANK YOU.
WHY ARE YOU THANKING ME?
I GOT US INTO THIS MESS.
EXACTLY!

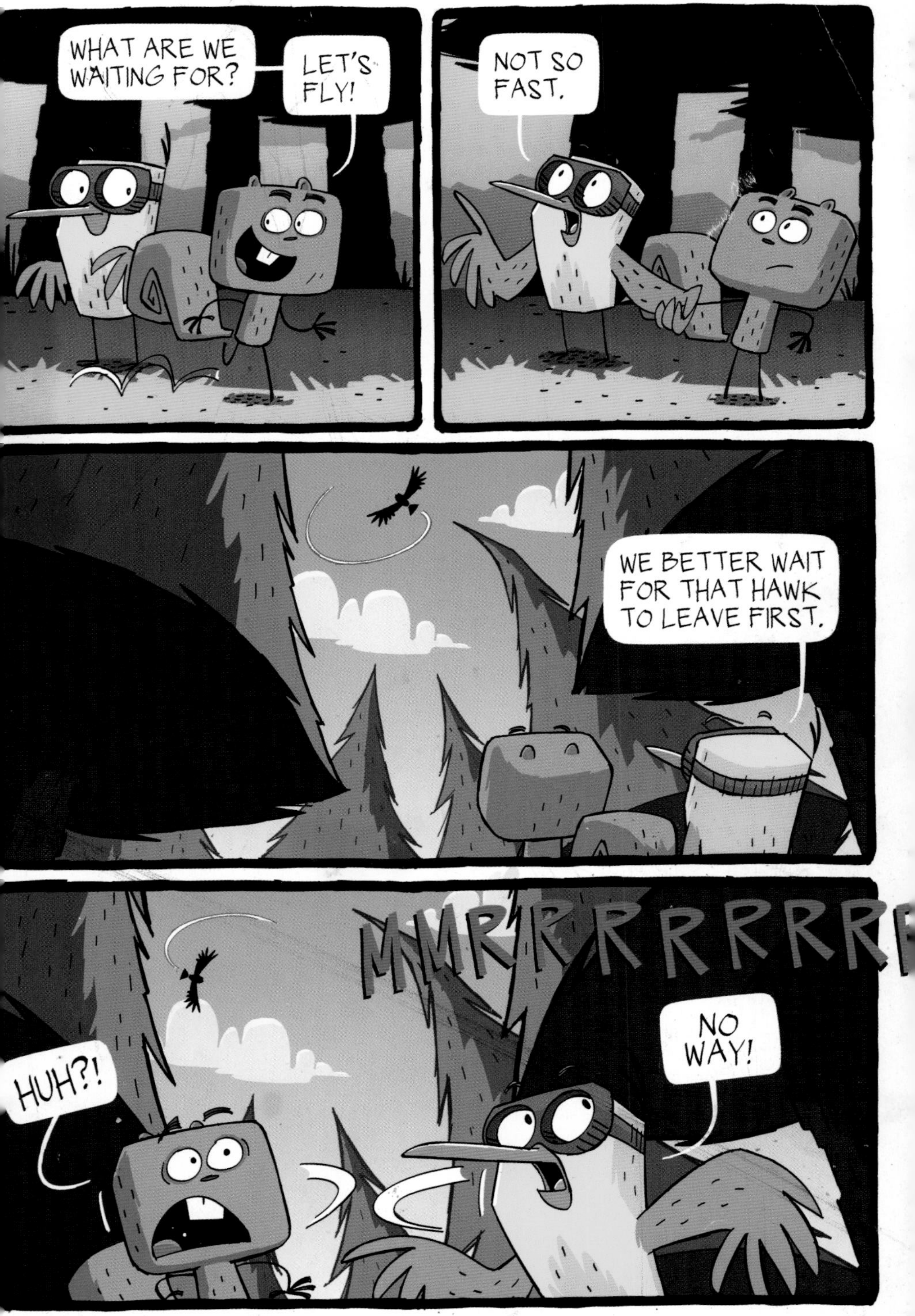
WHAT ARE WE WAITING FOR?
LET'S FLY!
NOT SO FAST.
WE BETTER WAIT FOR THAT HAWK TO LEAVE FIRST.
MMRRRRRRRR
HUH?!
NO WAY!

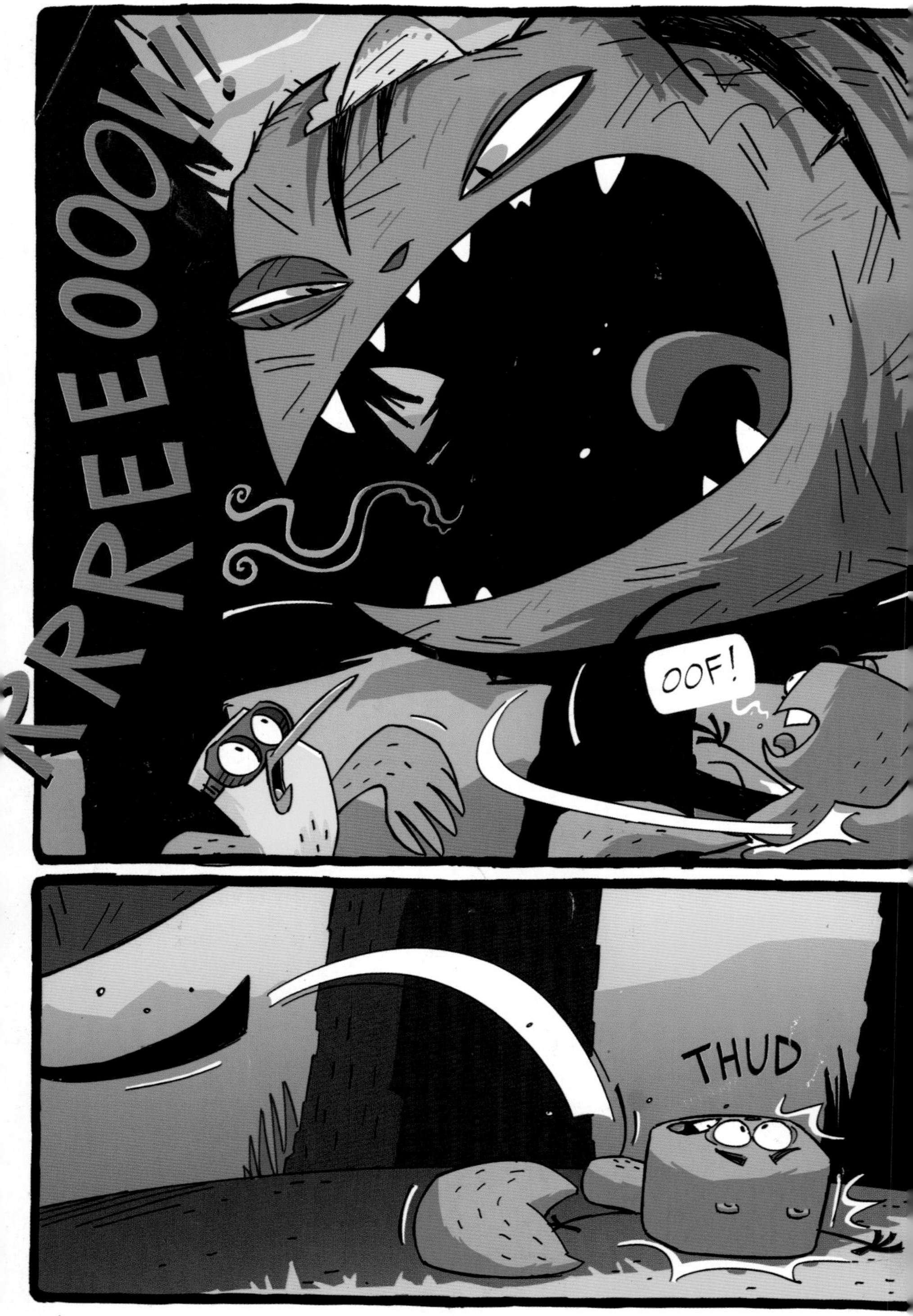
RREEOOOOW!!
OOF!
THUD

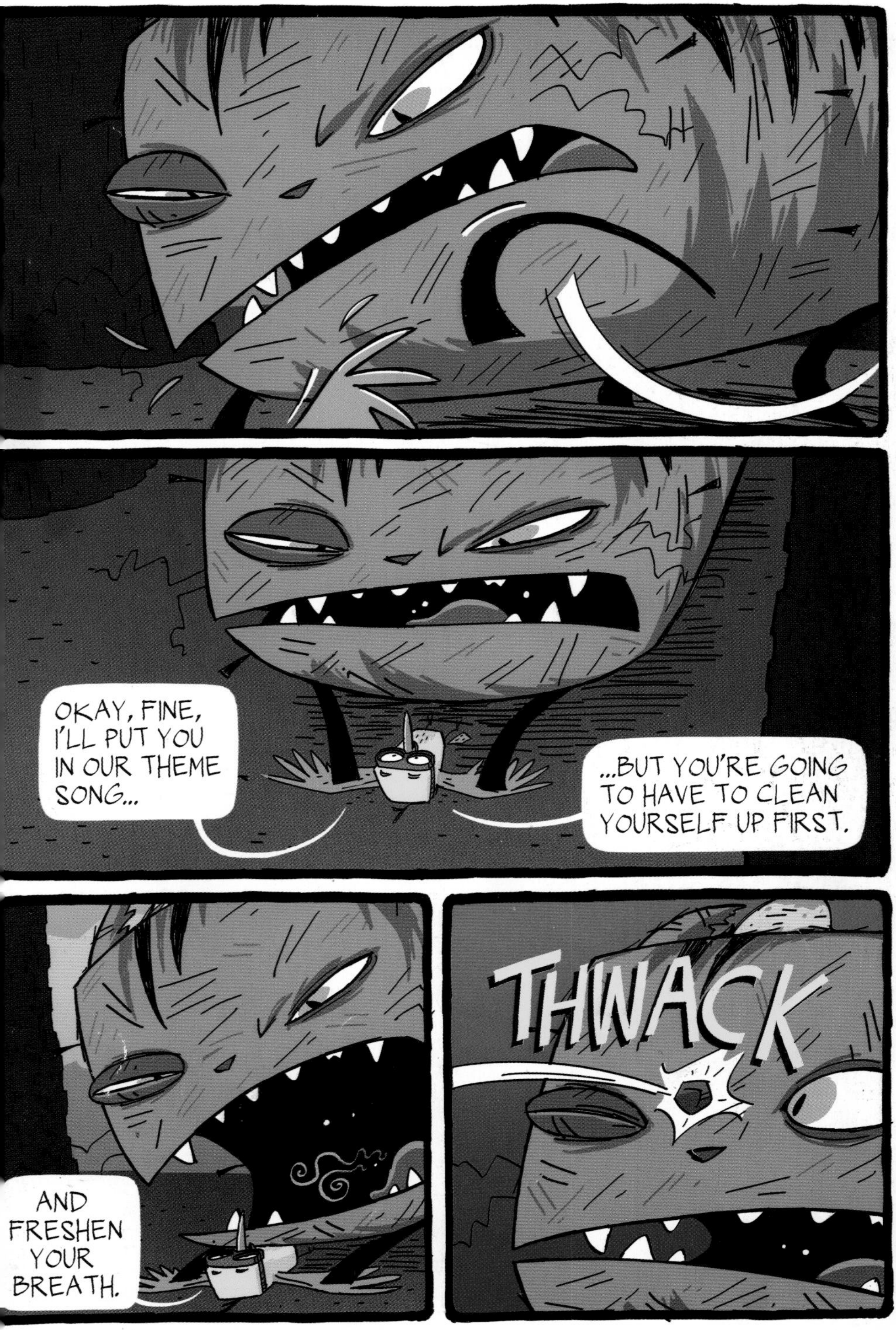
OKAY, FINE, I'LL PUT YOU IN OUR THEME SONG...
...BUT YOU'RE GOING TO HAVE TO CLEAN YOURSELF UP FIRST.
AND FRESHEN YOUR BREATH.
THWACK

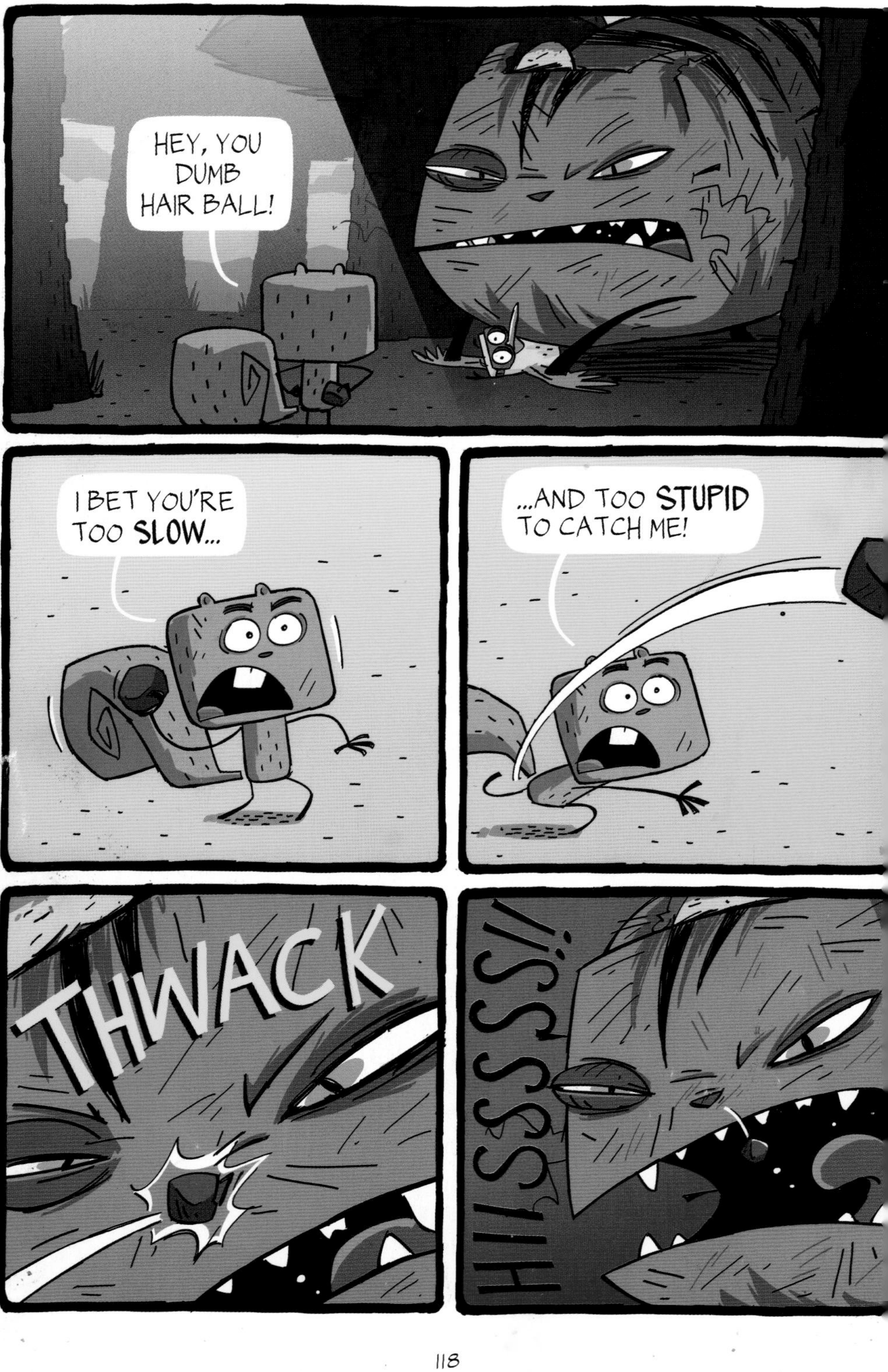
HEY, YOU DUMB HAIR BALL!
I BET YOU'RE TOO **SLOW**...
...AND TOO **STUPID** TO CATCH ME!
THWACK
HISSSSS!!

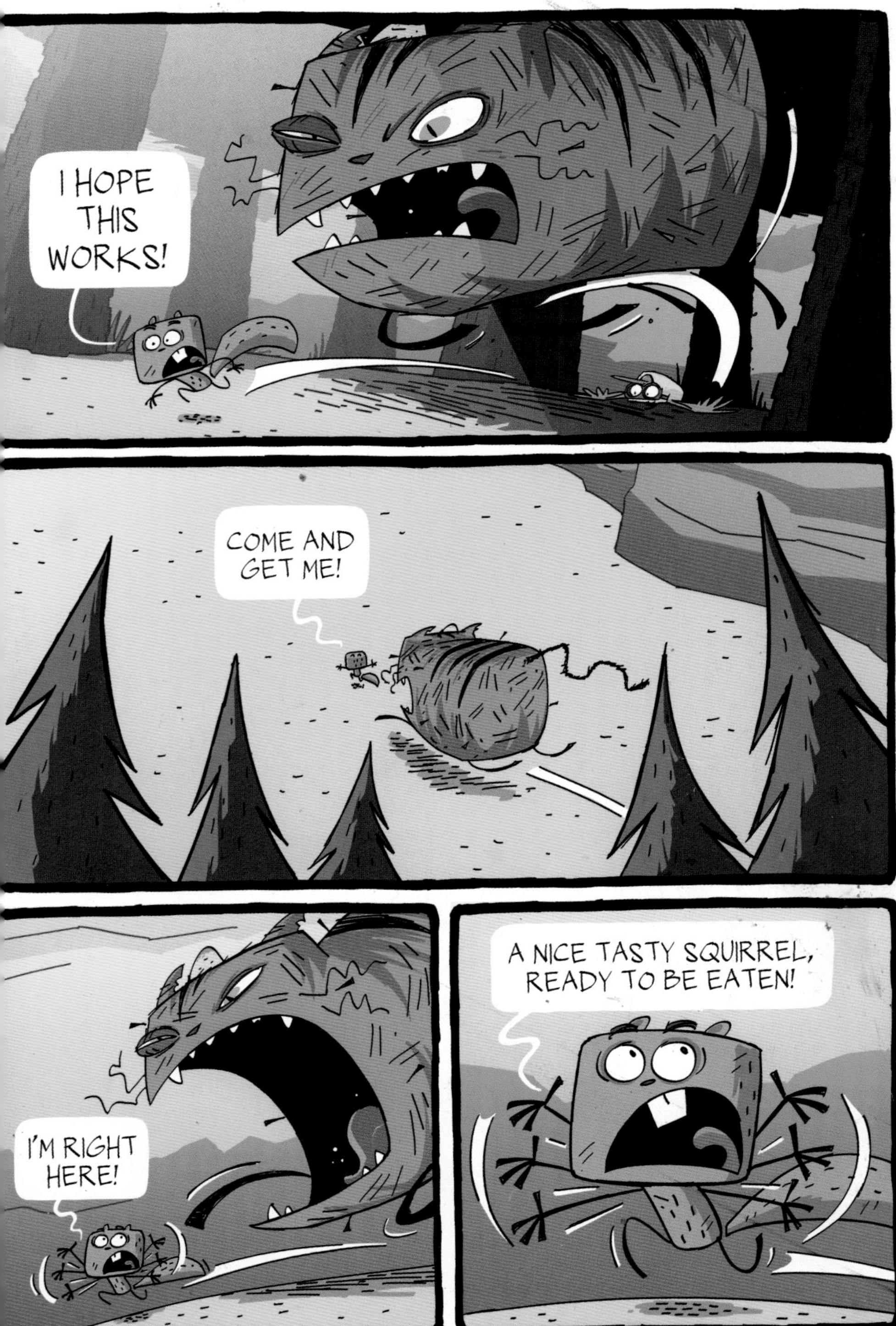
I HOPE THIS WORKS!
COME AND GET ME!
I'M RIGHT HERE!
A NICE TASTY SQUIRREL, READY TO BE EATEN!

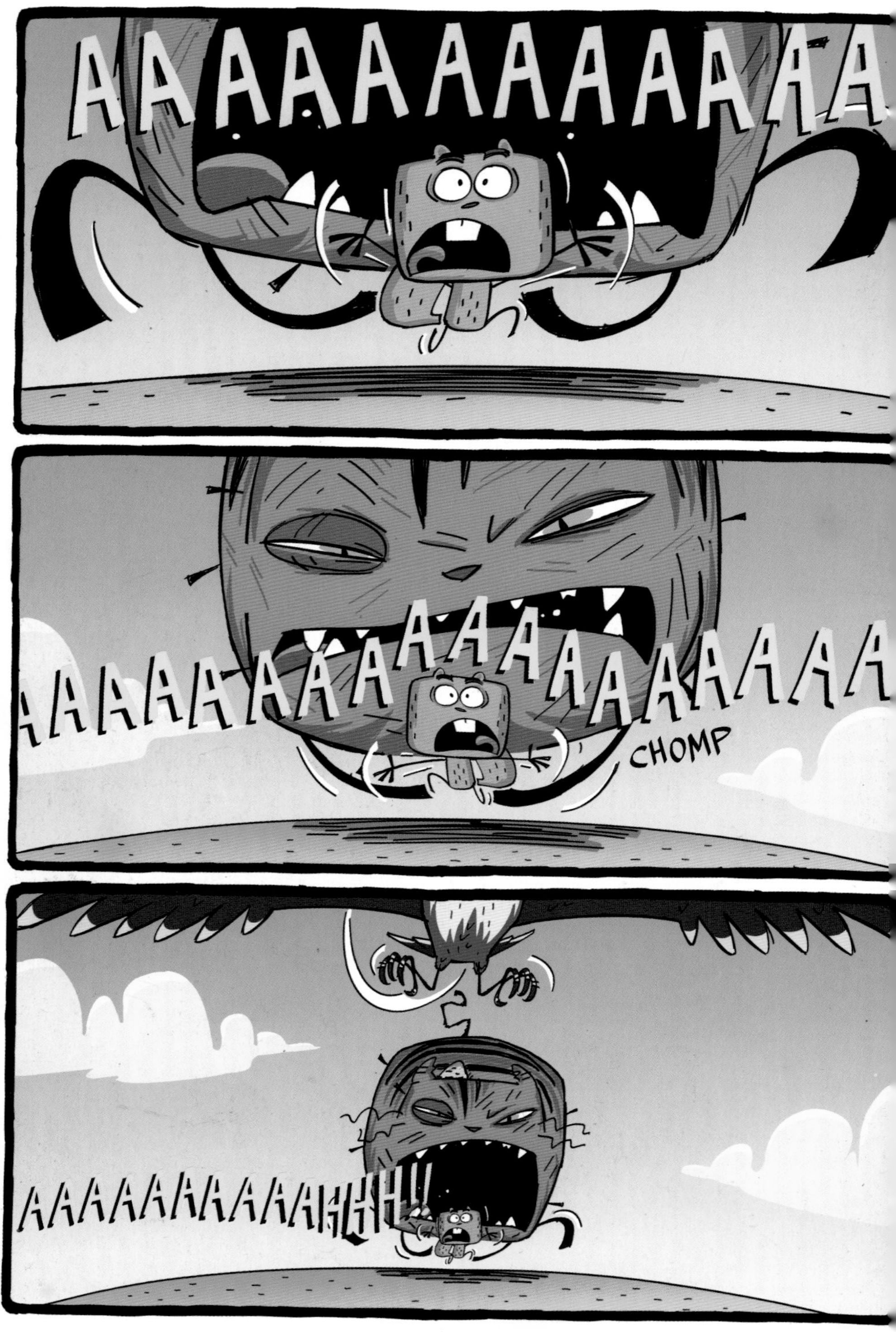
AAAAAAAAAAAA
AAAAAAAAAAAAAAAAAAAAA
CHOMP
AAAAAAAAAAAAHHH!!

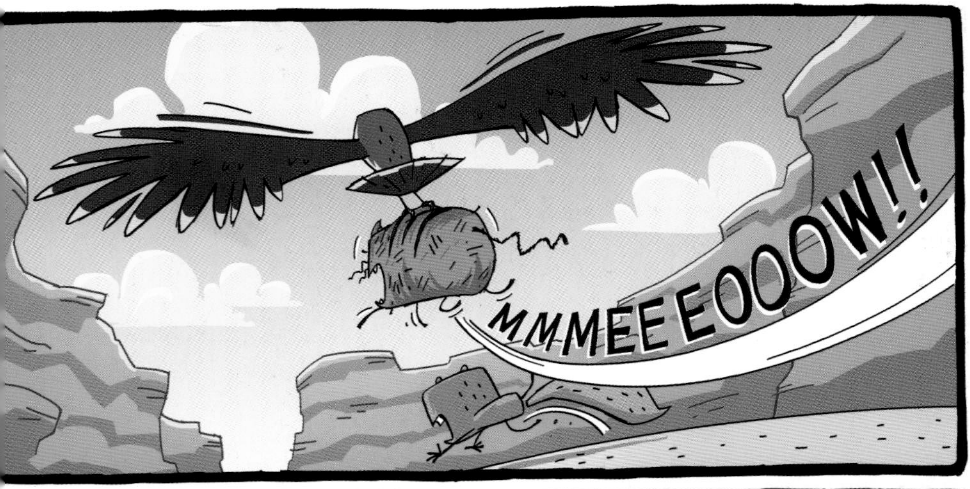
MMMEEEOOOW!!

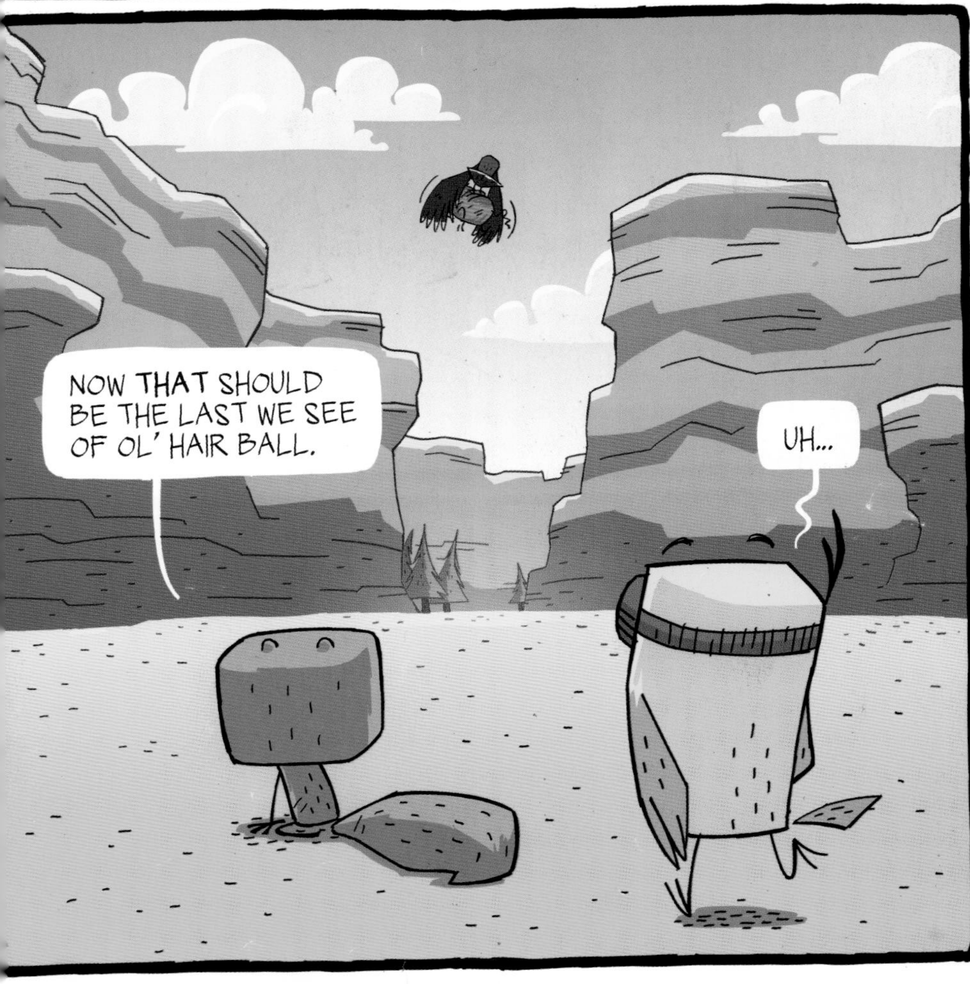
NOW THAT SHOULD BE THE LAST WE SEE OF OL' HAIR BALL.
UH...

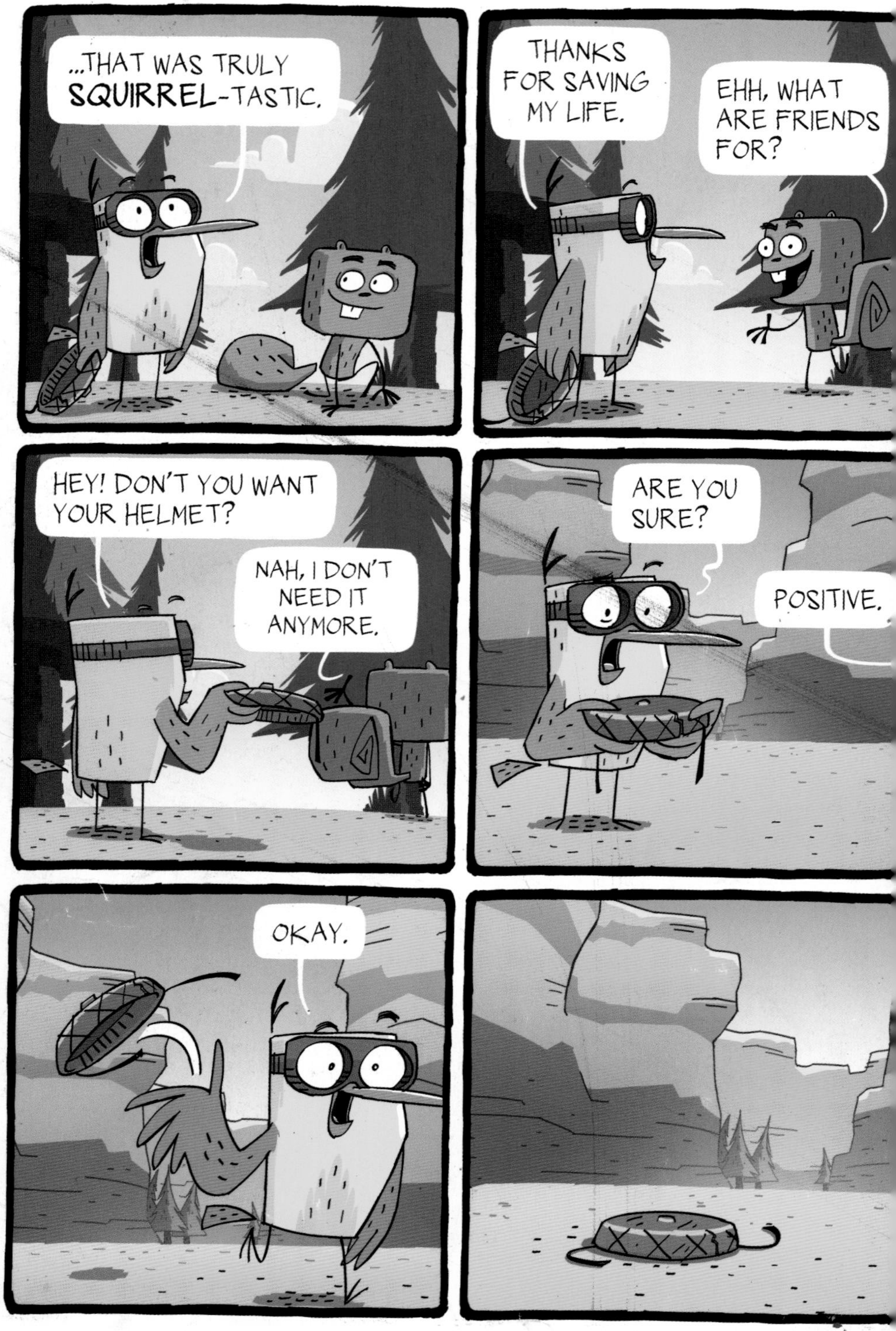
...THAT WAS TRULY SQUIRREL-TASTIC.
THANKS FOR SAVING MY LIFE.
EHH, WHAT ARE FRIENDS FOR?
HEY! DON'T YOU WANT YOUR HELMET?
NAH, I DON'T NEED IT ANYMORE.
ARE YOU SURE?
POSITIVE.
OKAY.

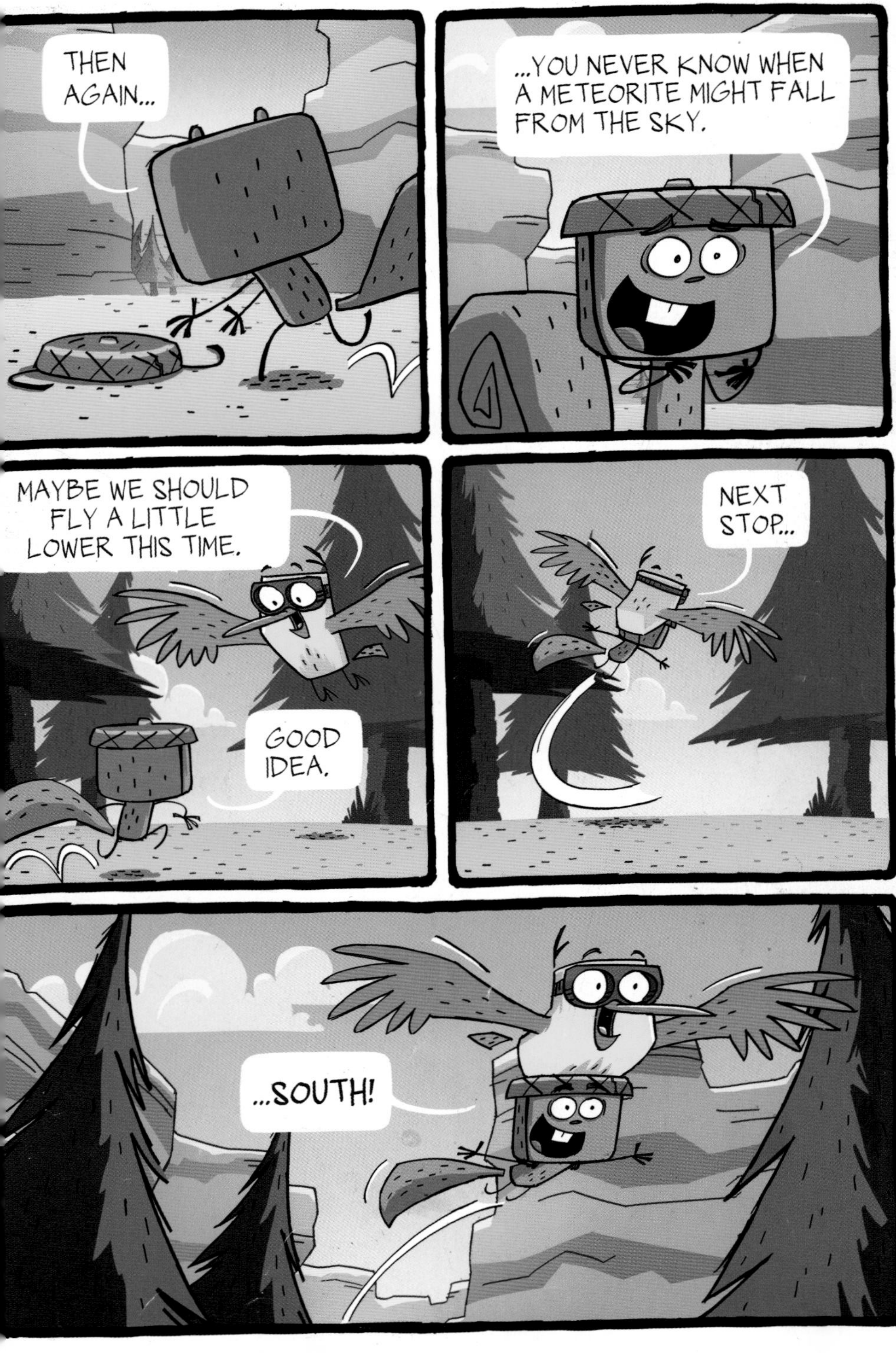
THEN AGAIN...
...YOU NEVER KNOW WHEN A METEORITE MIGHT FALL FROM THE SKY.
MAYBE WE SHOULD FLY A LITTLE LOWER THIS TIME.
GOOD IDEA.
NEXT STOP...
...SOUTH!

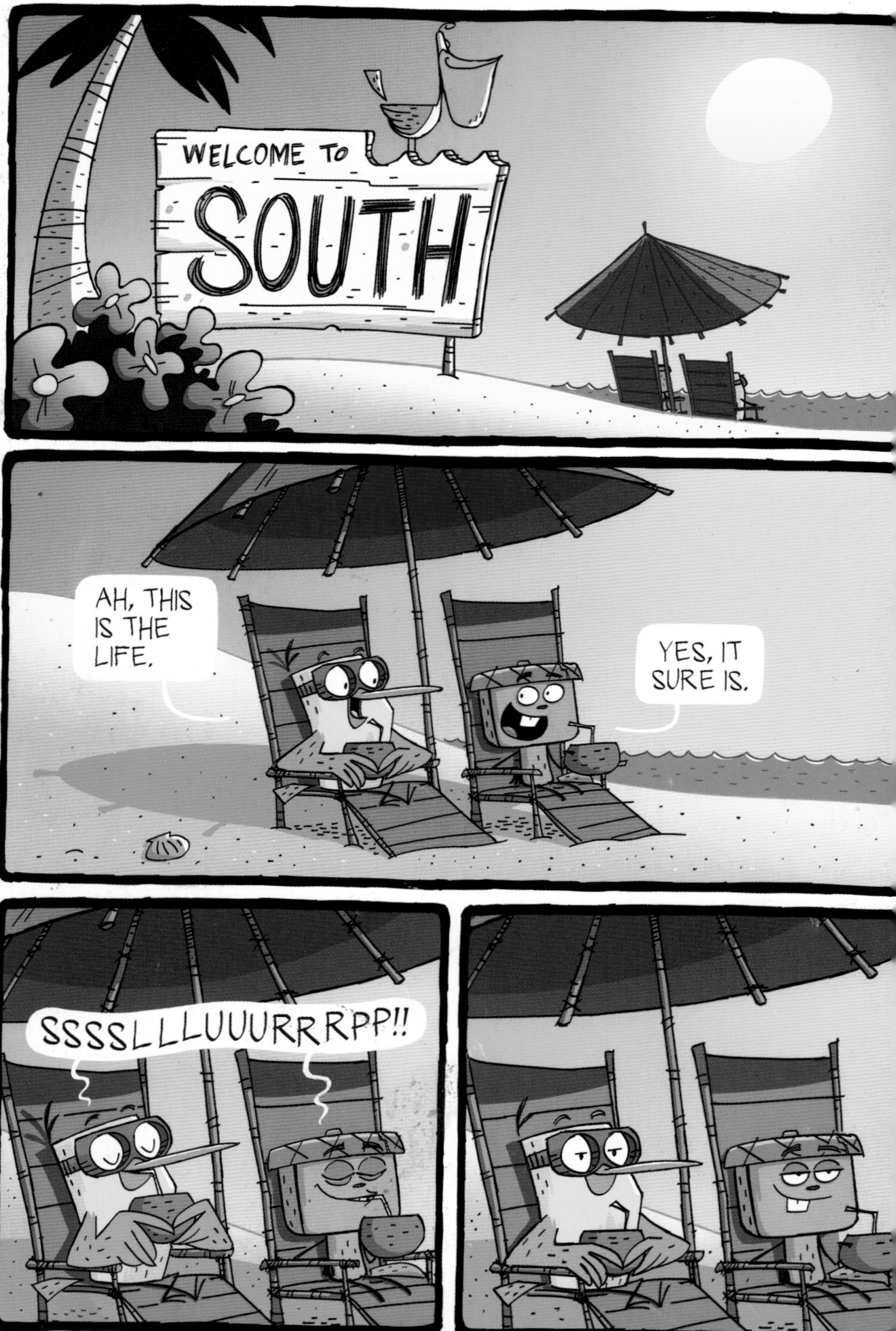
WELCOME TO
SOUTH
AH, THIS IS THE LIFE.
YES, IT SURE IS.
SSSSLLLUUURRRPP!!

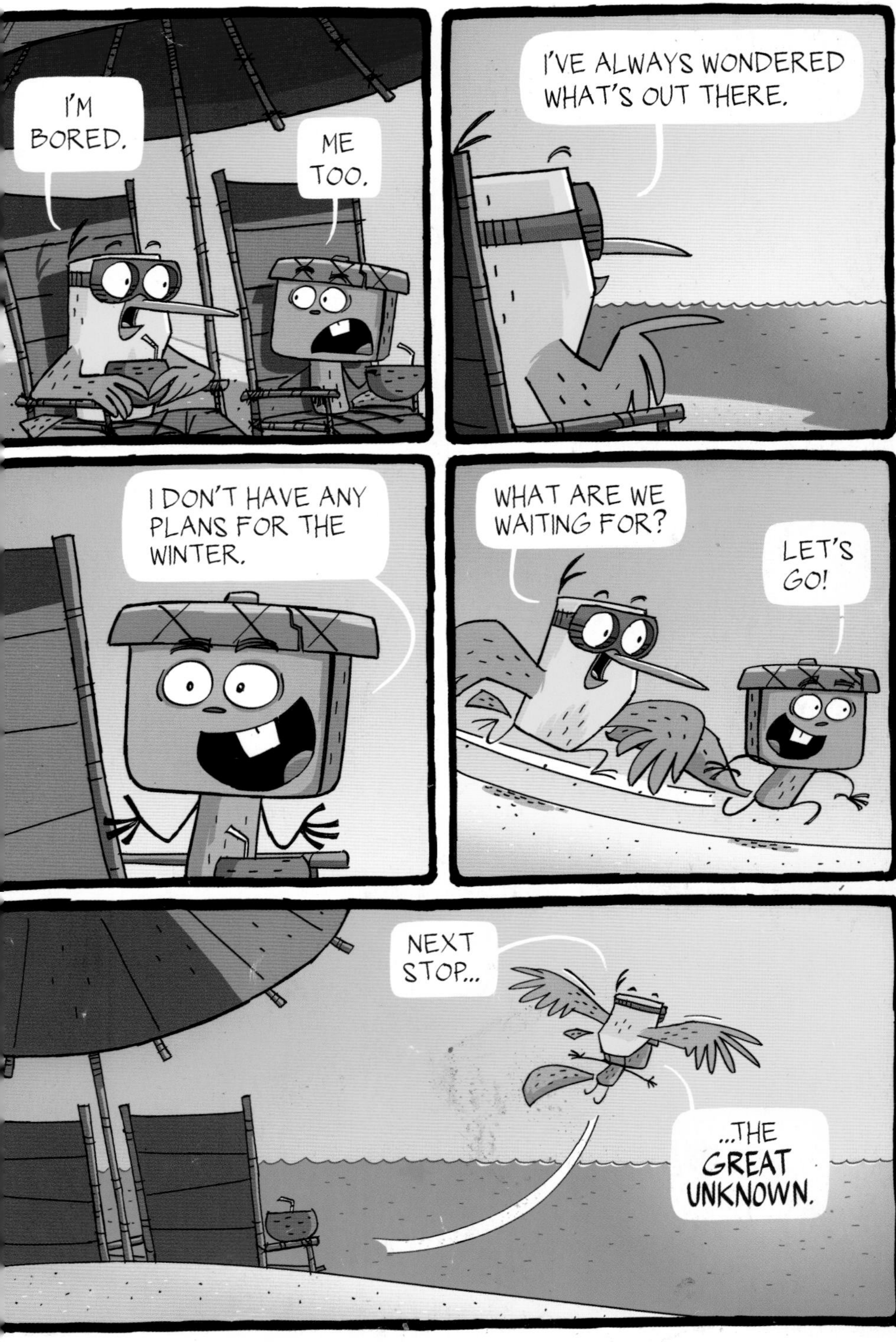
I'M BORED.
ME TOO.
I'VE ALWAYS WONDERED WHAT'S OUT THERE.
I DON'T HAVE ANY PLANS FOR THE WINTER.
WHAT ARE WE WAITING FOR?
LET'S GO!
NEXT STOP...
...THE GREAT UNKNOWN.

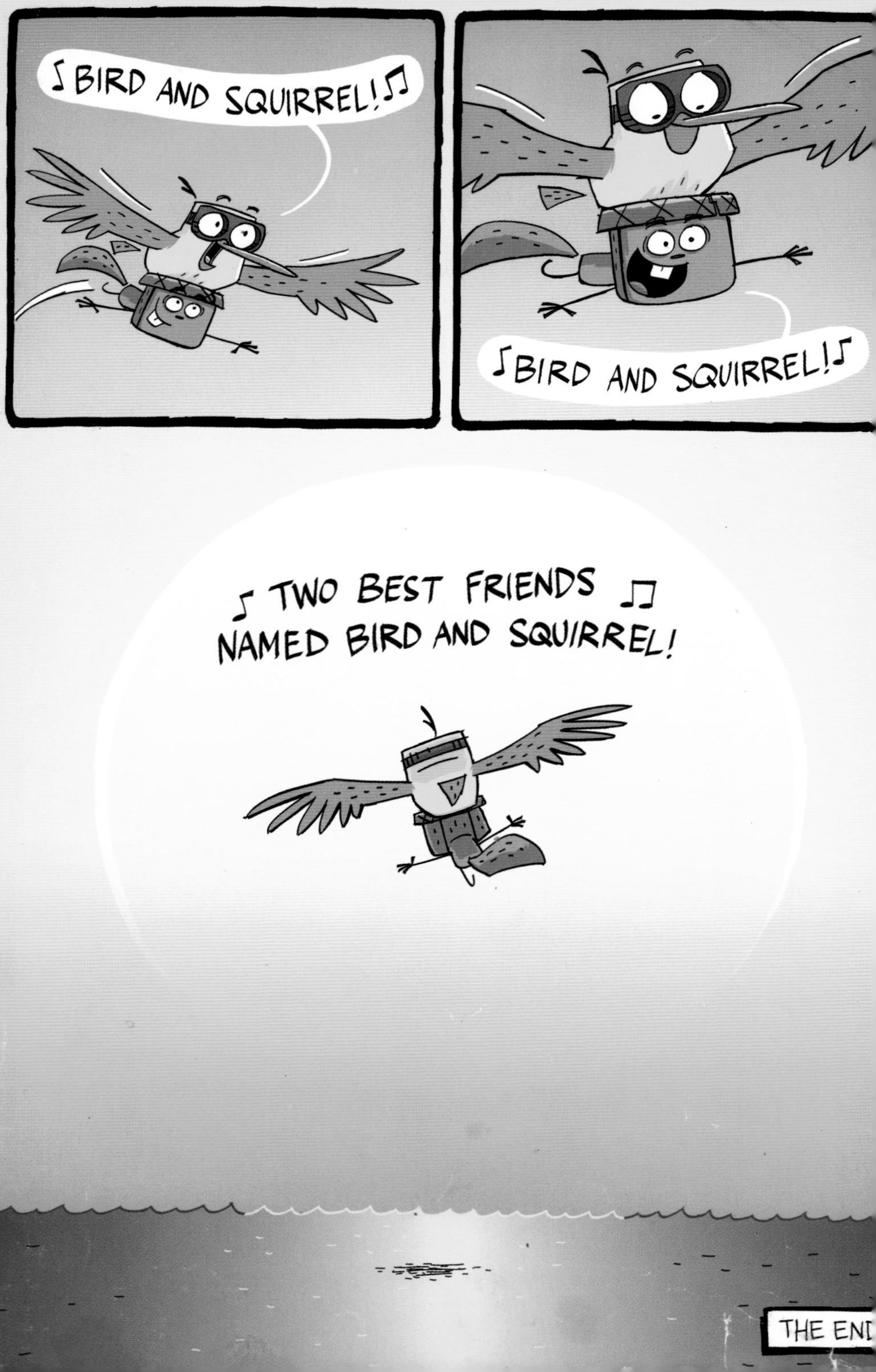
BIRD AND SQUIRREL!
BIRD AND SQUIRREL!
TWO BEST FRIENDS NAMED BIRD AND SQUIRREL!
THE EN